Our
SONG

Our SONG

KELLY HENNELLY

2025

Illustration and Book Design by Alissa DeGregorio
ISBN: 979-8-218-60591-9
Self-published by Kelly Hennelly
Printed in the United States of America

First Edition: 2025

For Mom, who loved a good cup of coffee and a good story more than anyone.

I wish you got to read this one.

Magnolia

"You have to take me with you, Charlie," I whined, sitting cross-legged on our Uncle Cole's old, musty couch, playing with the fringe of my cut-off jean shorts. It was another one of those hot and unforgiving days in downtown Savannah, and my brother Charlie had just made his first friend since we moved here.

There'd be hell to pay if he didn't let me tag along.

"You're not coming, Magnolia! You're so embarrassing. You cry all the time and look—gosh, Magnolia, stop crying!" Charlie tossed a box of tissues at me, and I blew my nose so hard my shoulders rattled. I could feel the telltale redness creeping across my eyebrows and nose. It would take all night to calm down.

I pulled out another handful of tissues and sighed dramatically. "I'm only crying because you said I cry all the time! You always have to be so mean to me. For no reason."

The truth was, though, Charlie wasn't a very mean big brother. He was actually a very gentle soul. His only fault was that he was moving on faster than I was. From the move to Savannah, from the threshold of childhood to teenager, from our parents dying and leaving us with our one and only surviving family member—a bar owner we barely knew with a smelly old couch and not a clue how to raise a couple of kids.

Charlie watched me closely, pacing back and forth on the dingy carpet of our apartment, and as he always did when I was stressing him out beyond belief, he ruffled his hand through his long, auburn hair. I watched as he let his guard down, relaxing his shoulders a bit as he remembered that he was pretty much all I had left in the world.

"Alright," he relented. "You can come."

I jumped up from the couch and wrapped my arms around his neck so tight he groaned.

"But it'll get scary and you can't cry, no matter what, alright? I don't want my only friend here to get scared away by you and your wide range of emotions."

My wide range of emotions were pubescent angst and dead parents, but I wanted a friend, too, so I nodded in agreement. That evening, Charlie and I strolled through Chippewa Square with the sun setting at our backs. "Who's this friend you're so excited about anyway? You're acting like he's the pope or something," I said, letting out a laugh so hard it led to a loud snort that echoed throughout the square.

Charlie rolled his eyes.

We were heading toward Jones Street, lined with nothing but million dollar townhomes. Not the kind of neighborhood Charlie and I lived in. Or belonged in.

"Lee Wilder," he finally answered, stopping in front of a four-story mansion that was lit up like Christmas morning. The lazy front porch looked over the cobblestoned road, and every window in the house glowed with a faint yellow ember—cozy and inviting.

"Your friend's rich, Charlie," I whispered harshly, plunking my grubby bottom on one of the lazy white rockers on their porch, leaving Charlie to knock on the Wilders' front door. I figured if I was hidden away, I wouldn't embarrass him so early on.

"I think his dad's a lawyer. His momma is an antique dealer. She's working on the Mercer House right now."

I shuddered. The Mercer house was the scariest place in Savannah. Wasn't too long ago that Jim Williams, who owned the Mercer House, had dropped dead in the very spot where he shot his young lover, Danny Hansford, after an altercation.

"I'd never step foot in that spooky old house! You'd have to be dumb as a one legged possum wandering down a dark highway to go in there." My voice was high pitched, but I stayed crouched down in my rocker, hiding out of sight.

"Well, I guess we're pretty dumb then." A boy no older than Charlie, but taller and more lean, stepped out into the light of the porch. He dangled a set of keys in Charlie's face quickly before snatching them away, letting out a yelp. His early summer tan had brought out the paleness of his blue eyes and his dark-blond hair was kissed by the sun already. He had a smile stretched wide across his face that flashed straight, white, post-braces teeth flanked by deep, swoony dimples.

The boy popped a dusty blue baseball cap on backward, letting a few wild curls escape at the sides, and my stomach twisted with that nervous energy you get when you really see a boy for the first time and start wondering what it might feel like to kiss him.

In an instant, I had my very first crush.

He extended a long, tanned arm toward me. "I'm Leland Wilder, but you can call me Lee. I'm dumb as a possum, but very pleased to meet you," he drawled, throwing a wink at me.

I was helpless to do anything but shake his hand and smile.

We locked eyes, and he studied my face as he took in my freckles and my long, wild red curls. As he moved onto my ratty Salvation Army overall shorts and pink t-shirt, he let out a sigh, accompanied by a slanted smile.

"Well, I'm Magnolia Pruitt, and it was nice to meet you, but I'll be going now. I'll be sure to send some nice flowers to your parents when y'all bite the dust tonight." I hopped off the porch in one leap, foregoing the steps all together, and started down the street as fast as my dirty Chuck Taylors could take me. I didn't need someone staring at my mangled old clothes, wondering about what kind of life I had. "See ya at home, Charlie," I called behind me.

I was halfway down the block when I heard hurried footsteps closing in on me. "You're dressed for the occasion, though," Lee said, breathless. He flashed me a big smile that sent my stomach into a tumble.

"Besides," Charlie called from behind us, "who else is going to tell the story of the two bravest guys in Savannah taking on old Jim Williams's ghost?!"

I snickered and moved on down the street, shoving my hands in my pockets. Charlie sauntered ahead of us, and Lee kept by my side. Every now and again, he would start to say something, think better of it, then shut his trap. He kept looking over at me, smiling, then back down to his feet.

Whatever he was up to, if Momma was still alive, she would have told me to stay far away from it.

As we walked, Lee told us that his momma, Eunice Wilder, had been chosen by the Daughters of Savannah Civic Society to oversee the preservation of the Jim Williams collection and historic Mercer House, which was set to become a museum—Jim's dying wish.

As we got closer to the house—and closer to our souls possibly becoming ethereal nourishment for the bevvy of ghosts within—my nerves began blazing off like fireworks. My palms were greased with sweat, and I was breathing hard like I'd been smoking my whole young life.

We stood in Monterey Square, looking up at the big old house towering over us like a monument. I kept thinking about Jim Williams's spirit knocking around those empty, echoing halls full of secrets and stories.

I didn't care how fancy a house was. If it was haunted to the gills, I'd rather sleep in a cardboard box in an alley.

Not like our living situation was anything better than a cardboard box these days, though.

"Magnolia," Lee whispered, inching closer toward me, "I promise you right now that I won't let anything happen to you. We're going to go in there and see if the spirit of Jim Williams is haunting the place, and then we'll get the hell out of there and get some pralines down at the river. Okay?"

Of course, anything sounded like butter coming out of Lee Wilder's mouth, so I just nodded in agreement.

When Jim Williams died after his sprawling trials, Eunice Wilder had taken over business at his house and, as a prominent antiquarian in Savannah, a lot of Jim's former clients. These days, she was tasked with getting the house ready to become a museum on the first floor, and the second floor was being prepped for the remaining members of the Williams family to move into.

Eunice, however, needed to be better at the business of not leaving her keys out in the open so that her idiot son didn't go finding them and using them to commit felony acts of paranormal stupidity.

We cut through the courtyard and tiptoed up the back stairs onto the big porch that hugged the back of the Mercer House.

"Did you know," Lee hissed, practically spitting in my face, "there was a family living here like a hundred years ago, and one of their maids' kids fell off the roof and impaled himself right there on that fence?"

I could feel the bile rising in my throat and my little pulse hammering in between my ears.

"You're full of shit, Lee," Charlie said, inching up from our little huddle to peek in the window. "It's pitch black in there. How are we supposed to see?"

Lee pulled a flashlight from the pocket of his navy-blue Savannah Academy hoodie and handed it to Charlie. "Always got to be prepared, brother."

I rolled my eyes.

Lee used his mother's key to crack open the tall, sturdy doors and pushed us inside. I flattened myself up against a wall, thwacking the back of my head against an oversized picture frame. "This is the stupidest thing we have ever done, Charlie Pruitt!" I was steaming and hissing through my teeth.

"Relax, Maggie," Lee said, grabbing my hand, as if my heart wasn't already racing out of control. "Good Lord, you're sweaty." He wiped my hand on his jeans, then closed his fingers around mine again.

Charlie led the way, flicking on the flashlight, turning his head back and forth dramatically, like he was in an espionage movie. He tripped over his loose shoelace and gasped for air like the ghosts were squeezing his neck like a lemon. I flung my hand over my mouth to shove down the howl trying to escape my throat.

Lee gave my hand a few squeezes, practically dragging me down the hallway. "Jim Williams was the biggest collector of antiques and fine art in all of Savannah. He threw the most wild parties around Christmas time. I heard my parents would always came home trippin' over themselves trying to get in the house after one of his galas."

I poked my head around a corner into what I assumed was once a grand dining room—and possibly my death at a very young and tragic age. There were painter's drapes covering most of the furniture and ladders lining the walls. I figured it must have been part of the restoration Eunice Wilder was part of.

We reached the front of the house and turned a corner into a formal sitting area. A low rumbling sound filled the room—a humming that buzzed in my ears and vibrated through to my bones. My whole body shook with fear. Lee gripped my hand, but I could feel him quivering, too.

"W-what's that noise?" Charlie finally said, stammering over his words like the big baby I knew he was. I moved in closer to Lee, and Charlie waved the flashlight around the room, landing on different varieties of beheaded and stuffed wild game.

"Stop, it's like a strobe light, and it's making me sick," I said, trying to let my eyes focus on the room around me.

The noise grew louder as we made our way through the sitting rooms toward the back of the house. Just as we reached what Lee said used to be Jim's smoking room—where we'd first entered—a painter's tarp suddenly rose up with a howl and flung its ghostly form straight at Charlie's head.

"It's the ghost of Jim Williams's lover! Get out!" Charlie screamed before creaming into me, arms flailing, knocking me back into a couch and running off with the flashlight. The whole room was plunged into darkness, and I froze with fear, trying to stay as quiet as possible to not upset the spirits, or to let Lee know that I was an absolute chicken on the verge of tears.

I felt movement around me and stayed very, very still, until it made contact with me. I fought back the urge to shriek and throw punches into the air, but judging by the size of the entity, I wasn't in much danger.

The mischievous ghost, now purring loudly and licking my knuckles, settled onto my lap. After turning in a few circles, she curled up into a ball, using me as her mattress.

"It's a… cat," I stammered when I was finally able to get my breathing back on some sort of normal pattern.

"Maggie, are you okay?" Lee's voice sounded like it was coming from the floor.

"I'm fine. Where are you?" The cat, annoyed by my talking, shoved its head under my hand, demanding to be petted.

"I think I'm under a table." A loud thud and a few cuss words confirmed this as he cracked his head twice off what sounded like a hard piece of mahogany. "Are you okay?" he asked again, as he crawled across the floor to the sound of my voice.

I giggled. "I'm fine. I think I've adopted a cat, though. It won't stop kissing me."

He had made his way up off the floor and onto the couch next to me. "My momma said that sometimes strays make their way into the house from time to time. She likes you." I could feel his smile in the dark, and our hands met while we took turns rubbing the top of her head. Each time it happened, my breath caught in my throat.

"What do you say we go get those pralines now?" he finally said, breaking the silence and snapping me back to reality.

"What about Charlie?"

Lee pulled me up off the couch, letting his hand rest for a minute at the small of my back. "Let's check at your place, but if I had to guess, he's off trembling in a bush somewhere."

I held the cat in my arms like a baby until we reached the door to our apartment, directly next to the bar, listening to her coo and purr as she licked my forearm, locking her big brown eyes with mine.

I let myself up the stairs and called out for Charlie. No answer. The bar below was loud enough that I knew my uncle couldn't hear me come into the front hallway and question my whereabouts this evening.

Poking through the rooms of our apartment, Charlie was nowhere to be found, so I dumped the cat off in the bathroom with a can of tuna and some water and met Lee back downstairs.

"Maybe she'll give him another scare when he gets home. He deserves it, leaving us behind like that," Lee said, as he ran a hand through his wild blond hair.

When I reached the bottom of the stairs, he grabbed my hand again, so naturally like it was something he had been doing his whole life—holding on to me.

We made our way down toward the river, breaking our grip on each other only long enough to make it safely down one of the narrow staircases that led to the cobblestoned road that winded down to the river's edge. Once we reached the bottom, he took his hoodie off, draping it over my shoulders. I was so damp from the summer heat and humidity that the soft cotton stuck to me like cellophane, but I didn't mind.

He guided me to the riverfront and sat down on a concrete paver, patting the spot next to him for me to join. We both draped our legs over the side, and I bent over to watch the water putter and flow on its journey to the Atlantic Ocean.

"I'll go grab some goodies," he said, and I noticed he had been staring at me. "Don't go running off on me now, okay?"

I nodded, quickly dropping my gaze back to the water, trying not to stare at his handsome, sun-kissed face.

In the few minutes he was gone, I imagined every possible way I could embarrass myself when he returned. I tried to stay calm and collected, but this was a teenaged boy in my general vicinity—one I wasn't related to, no less—and honestly, I felt like I was about to be knocked into the river and swept downstream. My body started to shake.

Before I could talk some sense into myself and dash back toward McDonough Street as fast as my little legs could take me, Lee reappeared, still wearing that same bright smile.

"This is my treat," he said, sitting beside me again, holding a sleeve of pralines and Coca-Cola in a glass bottle. "You were really cool tonight, Maggie. None of the other girls at school would even give it a second thought to go in there like that. And there you go, busting in there all brave and strong—and coming out with a souvenir to boot. You were a little sweaty there, though. But you handled it better than Charlie and me. You're something else, alright."

No one had really ever given me a nickname before, and when he called me Maggie, my heart skipped a beat. It felt like a secret between us. I couldn't stop smiling, my cheeks warming up. It was like he'd wrapped me in a special little moment that only belonged to us.

I sipped on the Coke with my legs dangling over the side of the river wall, too nervous to do anything else. I finally turned to look in his direction and caught him staring straight at me again. His big blue eyes were dancing with the lights shining off the river, and he was wearing a smile so wide it almost knocked me straight into the murky water.

"This has been really fun, but I should go check on the cat." I stood up, and he scrambled to his feet.

"At least let me take you to see my momma. We have some old pet stuff in the basement, and she's been dying to meet y'all since I told her you moved into town. Besides, I intend on making you my girl, so we may as well get the introductions out of the way."

"Excuse me?" I stumbled backward.

"You heard me." He grabbed my hand again, smiling sideways at me, giving me an up-close glimpse of the crooked dimple on his right cheek. "Now let's go get some litter for Pickle."

"Did you just name my cat?" I wasn't sure if I was more offended that he told me I was going to be his girl or that he named my cat. I did know, however, the entire scenario was making me want to run from him as fast as lightning before he figured out how much of an emotional train wreck I was.

Or worse, realized how much better he could do than an almost-thirteen-year-old with a bad attitude and hand-me-down clothes from the state.

"You mean our cat? Yes, I did. We're in this one together, you know?" He laughed and planted a kiss on my cheek so quickly, it wasn't until we got back to his house and I wiped the sticky praline residue off my face that I knew it was real.

Being outside the Wilder house was one thing. Standing inside was another. Every meticulous inch of their four-story home was like something out of a magazine. Dust didn't exist here. Neither did carpet that smelled like moldy keg beer and three-dollar gas station menthols.

The floors were so shiny I could see my reflection, and the chandelier overhead sparkled like a million tiny stars. I fiddled with the fringe of my shorts, suddenly aware of my scuffed shoes and how they looked against the edge of the spotless rug. And then there was her. Eunice Wilder. She was the most beautiful woman I'd ever seen—aside from my Momma—with her hair pinned back all elegant, pearl earrings that caught the light, and a cherry-red dress that made her look like she belonged on the cover of a magazine. I felt small and messy just standing there, but then she smiled—warm and real—and bent down to my level. "You must be Maggie," she said, her voice soft and sweet like honey. In that moment, I didn't just want her to like me; I wanted to be her someday. Graceful. Kind. Effortlessly beautiful.

"I'm sorry for the mess," she gestured to her pristine home. "And this should be everything. Next time y'all find a stray down by the river, you bring him here first, though. I'm not sure Cole will appreciate coming home to find a cat in his house without someone talking to him first."

Eunice Wilder's voice was gentle and soothing as she set the reusable grocery bag filled with litter and food beside me. Taking a seat across the table, she crossed her stockinged legs at the ankles and gave me a sad smile, her lips pressed together gently.

I took a bite of one of the cookies she left out. "He won't care," I started boldly. "He sleeps in the office of the bar anyway. He hasn't really been in the apartment much since we moved in."

I didn't want to look up, but I could feel Eunice and Vance Wilder's concerned eyes washing over me. Lee sat next to me, close enough for comfort, but not touching me directly. His presence was calming and kind, and I let the feeling wrap around me like a blanket.

"Oh, I see. So, what do y'all do for dinners? Or to get ready in the morning for school? Not that it's our business, you can tell us or not. Up to you," Vance Wilder said, spreading his hands in a disarming gesture.

I met Mr. Wilder's concerned stare with a tight-lipped grin. "Charlie and I are pretty good at taking care of each other, Mr. Wilder. Speaking of, I should get home to my brother. He'll likely be worried and probably have a few questions about Pickle the cat."

Eunice let out a small giggle, and they both rose to their feet when I stood. "Leland will walk you home, of course. You come back and see us any time, Magnolia Pruitt. Our door is always open."

"Your family is really nice, Lee." He hadn't tried to hold my hand again as we walked toward my apartment, and my fingers suddenly felt cold and empty. He was quieter than he had been all night.

"Everyone's got their flaws, Maggie. Besides, you haven't met my brother yet."

We stopped at a corner to let a horse and carriage pass. "Why do you keep calling me Maggie? No one ever does."

He looked both ways before guiding me across the street. "I figured as much. It's the first thing I ever gave you—a nickname. But it won't be the last."

I rolled my eyes. "What is with you, Leland Wilder?"

He stopped and turned me toward him, smiling so big I thought his stupid face might break.

"Magnolia Pruitt, you're the kind of girl they write songs about, you know that?"

That made me cackle and snort. "You're thirteen years old, Lee. And we just met! What makes you think you can go around talking to me like that? You sound like the kind of boy my momma would warn me about if she was still here."

"Well, you'll just have to wait and see then, won't you?"

CHAPTER ONE

Magnolia

I was surrounded by mounds of paperwork with the stench of stale beer and cigarettes permeating in the air from another slow night at the bar. My brother, Charlie, sat across from me, mindlessly thumbing through a stack of papers I had handed him to keep him busy—fully knowing he wouldn't understand a lick of it.

With his head bent, I noticed some silver strands poking through his once vibrant auburn hair. Small, slightly noticeable flecks of freckles still dotted his nose and cheekbones, not quite like the millions of round, brown spots that used to cover his entire face.

Having just turned thirty, he didn't look like my big brother anymore, but a stately, well-groomed gentleman. He looked up and shot me a sympathetic smile.

"I think you're kind of in deep shit, Magnolia. The bar really isn't in good shape," he murmured, as he leafed through another pile of papers.

"Do you even understand anything that's in front of you right now?" I asked.

He let out a puff of a laugh. "No, not a word. I can help you cover some of Cole's funeral costs, but the overhead from the bar is quite a lot. I just don't understand. Why did he leave this place to just you and not both of us? You shouldn't be the only one taking on this debt."

"What would you have done, though? Shut down the art studio? Your river-front rent is astronomical as it is. At least I own this building now."

He nodded, and I watched the wheels turn in his head. Charlie had moved out of our apartment shortly after graduating from Savannah College of Art and Design. He took odd jobs around the city, eventually saving enough money to open his own studio on River Street.

The owner of the building, Jordan, allowed him to rent the studio apartment just above the space for a small fee, on the condition that he would collaborate on wine tastings and art shows. Jordan had recently opened his own wine shop, Cheese, Please!, in the space next door with his partner, Doyle.

And while I missed having my brother around, I was glad to free up the space in my apartment that was filled to the brim with his pieces of junk… or art.

Charlie was a reclamation artist, or so his business card proclaimed. Charles Abner Pruitt, Reclamation Artist, it said—I wouldn't just make that up. He had gone to SCAD to study painting and fine art, but somehow, in the throes of boredom and artistic frustration, he'd begun finding discarded items from the streets and dumpsters and he turned them into works of art. He did sculptures, paintings, pretty much anything. He took ugly things and made them beautiful.

"It's mixed media art," he told me one time, and I nodded and smiled because that's what you were supposed to do when you fully supported and loved someone but had absolutely no idea what they were going on about.

After he moved out, he left me with a few of his "installations," as he called them. One time, he was hanging a map of the USA made of old license plates and mile-long CVS receipts over my mantle and I said, "I'm sitting on a cash cow if you ever get famous. Maybe move things along for me, slice an ear off or something."

He was not amused by that.

"Well, back to what I was offering," he said, snapping me out of my thoughts. "At least let me help pay for the funeral and the leftover hospital bills. You can't do everything on your own, you know."

I leaned back and looked around the bar. We were so young when we came here. I was twelve, and Charlie was thirteen—Irish twins, my mother always called us. She was an O'Malley, one of the original Irish families in Savannah that forged a union of strong Irish immigrants called the Hibernian Society that helped put on the very first St. Patrick's Day parade in Savannah back in 1824.

Over one hundred years later, an O'Malley stood in front of the very building on McDonough Street that Charlie and I sat in and scooped it up, putting in a pub and a meeting space on the first floor and a two-bedroom apartment on the second floor. My momma and Uncle Cole grew up right above the very same bar Charlie and I grew up in, but Momma never wanted it that way.

After Momma met Daddy at the University of Georgia, they moved into a small beachside condo on Tybee Island before opening their own coffee shop and bookstore. The two things they were good at. Momma loved making drinks, no matter what kind, and Daddy loved stories. They loved each other so much that they blended their dreams into something amazing, a true reflection of their bond.

Charlie and I adored spending our weekends at the bookshop. In the off season, when the tourists went back up North and left the island to the natives, we'd cozy up by the fire, sipping on Momma's famous hot chocolate and listening to one of Daddy's wild made up stories about the ghosts of Bonaventure Cemetery.

Sometimes, in the warmer months, we'd all pile in the car and head into the city to do some shopping and get some ice cream at Leopold's, waiting in line with the scores of tourists, pretending we were from somewhere else other than right down the road.

We'd sit laughing on a bench in Forsyth Park waiting for my Uncle Cole to join us, and he'd always show up with cocktails to-go for the adults and Shirley Temples for us kids to sip on while we picnicked in the perfect Savannah sun. Then, we'd head on back to our quiet, beachside town, Charlie and I dreaming about moving to the big city someday.

We just didn't know it would be so soon.

Momma and Daddy went on a dinner-date for their anniversary the summer I turned twelve, just before the start of seventh grade. They never came home. According to the police officer that scooped us up in the middle of the night, alongside a children's welfare worker, a drunk driver flew through a red light and wrecked their car. And their lives.

And ours.

Momma always said that there weren't a lot of O'Malleys left in the world. Most had moved away—moved on from Savannah and those days of big parties that spilled out into the squares at all hours of the night. And with Daddy having no family of his own, losing his own parents when he was in college, Momma held on tight to her brother Cole.

So that night, when everything changed for Charlie and me, we had to hold on tight to Uncle Cole, too.

"It doesn't have to be the worst bar in Savannah anymore, you know?" Charlie rose from his chair and slid behind the bar, pouring us a couple of bourbons. His neat, mine on the rocks. "I mean, you're a member of the Daughters of

Savannah Civic Society now, right? Can't you get them to throw a charity event here or something?"

I picked up the pile of papers in front of me and fanned myself. Lord, it was hot in that bar, but I wouldn't dare turn on the air conditioning. Nothing like the start of fall in the south, crisp autumn air a distant dream and lingering, endless heat creeping all around.

"First of all, I was lucky to even be granted access to their elusive girls' club. If I wasn't an O'Malley and I wasn't a business owner now, they wouldn't have even given me an invitation. Dane probably pulled a few strings anyway."

"Speaking of pretty boy, when does he arrive from Atlanta to whisk you off your feet again?"

I rolled my eyes. "Tonight, actually. I'm hungry. Can we go up and order a pizza? I can't look at this anymore. I'm getting cross-eyed."

We took our bourbon and padded up the staircase that led from the back of the bar, and what used to be Uncle Cole's bedroom, to my second-floor apartment. When we were kids, we were convinced the bar was haunted by the ghost of drunken Irishmen and we'd run up the winding steps as fast as we could, getting our long, gangly legs wrapped around themselves and whacking our heads and limbs off the old wooden stairs. Now, the dark hallway was a welcome reprise from the sweltering heat of the hot, sticky barroom.

While Charlie ordered, I changed into a less-sweaty tank top and flumped down on my bed to check my email and go through my usual rounds of what my best friend, Sutton, called my stalking sessions. While I didn't maintain social media for myself, I did have accounts for the bar on all platforms since Uncle Cole made me a manager right around the time social media came into full swing. And while I didn't exactly follow a lot of people, I still had access to the search bar, which sometimes was a bad, bad thing.

In the middle of scrolling, very delicately, through Instagram as to not accidentally "heart" something, Charlie hollered from the kitchen that the pizza had arrived.

"What were you doing in there?" he asked, as he settled down on a chair. My cat, Pickle, promptly jumped on his lap and swatted at his face. "Good Lord, I hate this stupid cat," he yelped, tossing a pepperoni on the floor for her to snack on so she would leave him alone.

"Everyone loves Pickle. She's possessed with the spirit of a dead antiquarian, after all."

Charlie sighed in exasperation, taking a bottle of sweaty coke from the table and pouring it over our half-drank bourbons.

"Speaking of things we don't talk about—ever—Eunice Wilder told me you were coordinating the flowers for her big birthday bash. How very charitable of you. And, might I add, unlike you."

I shoved a slice of pizza in my mouth so I didn't cuss at my own brother. Eunice Wilder, Archon of the Daughters of Savannah Civic Society, had been a huge part of mine and Charlie's life since we arrived in Savannah. She took us under her wing and filled in the gaps that Uncle Cole couldn't fill on his own, try as he might.

Through a cheese-filled grin, I turned to my brother and said, "Why wouldn't I help? She's done so much for us."

Pickle had finished her pepperoni and was now pouncing sideways at my brother like a predator, haunches up and hissing for more food.

Charlie made a disgusted face at me, swallowing his own bite. "Please chew your food. For someone who has been to more galas than I've been on dates, you're still a damned animal. Anyway, so back to this party, you're going, right? Or are you just doing the flowers?"

My sister Spidey senses went off, and I locked eyes with my brother over the table.

"Yes, I am going. Sutton is going to be working the party with her catering company. And, as previously discussed, I am bringing the flowers. Why do you ask?"

Charlie finished chewing his next bite and gave me a snicker from across the table. "Well, I'm asking because—dammit, Pickle!"

Pickle had latched herself onto his leg and was biting frantically at his shin. She jumped up onto the table, stuck her head into the pizza box, and wrangled herself out a slice. Plopping down across from Charlie, she kept one eye on him as she noshed.

"Anyway, as I was saying, do you think Lee will come?"

I thrusted my seat back from the table and spun toward the window, flinging it open in one swift movement. It startled the cat, who now had fur sticking up every which way while covered in pizza sauce. She threw paws at Charlie.

"You and this cat were made for each other. You're both unhinged as shit. Magnolia, get your damn cat!"

I crossed over to the table to give Pickle the death glare, and she jumped down on the floor and groomed herself, leg stretched in the air, purring loudly. She was proud as heck for thinking she won the fight—this time.

I moved back to the window, staring down at the alley below. The scent of warm, hot garbage crept through the open window, and I could feel a wave of nausea rising in my throat.

"Touched a nerve, did I?" Charlie smiled, mouth full of pizza.

I turned to face him, leaning back on the windowsill. "I mean, he hasn't come to one event in the last ten years, so I'm not sure what makes you think he would come home for this one."

Charlie nodded, and Pickle paced around his chair. "You're probably right. I've sent him a few messages this week, but he hasn't responded. He did buy a piece of mine from my online gallery a few months ago."

"Wow, what a great best friend," I scoffed, reaching for the bourbon and pulling a swig directly from the bottle.

"Well, it's complicated, of course," my brother offered.

"Right. I'm sorry that's yet another thing I ruined for you and Lee." My shoulders tensed up, and I let out a long, bourbon-scented sigh.

"Well, that's just about all the self-loathing I can handle for one day," Charlie said, inching his chair slowly away from the table so the cat didn't maul his leg. "Are you coming to the wine tasting tonight? I'm showing four pieces I think you might like."

My brother, ever the opportunist.

"I have to work tonight, clearly. I have one bartender left, and I can't afford to keep her on all night. Stop by for a drink when you're done. Bring Doyle and Jordan. It will be fun."

Charlie crossed the kitchen and kissed my forehead, letting his hand rest on my shoulder. "You're my baby sister, and we've been through so much. We'll get through this one, too. Don't even think about Lee. I'm sorry I brought it up. Besides, you're happy now, right?"

I kept my eyes on the floor and nodded slowly.

"Happiness isn't tangible, Magnolia. You had a vision of how your life would work out, and this isn't it, but that's okay. It's not about a relationship or your career. You're not where you thought you would be at this point in time, and with who you thought you would be with, but you're here. And you're surrounded by great things and great people who love you."

"Thanks, Charlie," I said, leaning in for a hug. "I'll see you later."

CHAPTER TWO

Lee

My phone rang for the fourth time that day. I didn't have to look at the screen to know who it was, and I knew the longer I put it off, the more agitated she would get.

I tuned my guitar and let my eyes pan around the room. My floor to ceiling windows, looking down over the heart of Nashville, were designed to keep my eyes trained on the hustle-and-bustle below and inspire me to want to be more than just a songwriter. I was supposed to be inspired to become one of the greats—or whatever my manager said when he secured this condo for me.

"Lee!" my songwriting partner, Ryan, called from the living room, sounding perturbed that his game of Call of Duty was being interrupted. "You have a call," he grumbled, as he pushed my bedroom door open and flung his cell onto my bed, rushing back out into the living room while adjusting his headset.

I crossed the room and peered down at the phone, chortling as I saw the name on the screen. Women. The FBI should be run by southern ladies, and southern ladies alone. They can find anyone, anywhere, anytime.

"Hey, Momma," I laughed, lifting the phone to my ear.

"Leland Wilder! I have called you fifteen damned times today! Why aren't you answering my calls? You're supposed to be here. Today!" Though she had only called four times, I wasn't about to correct her. From the sound of it, her party was stressing her out, and the clanking of ice against the glass—and the time of day—led me to believe she was on her second highball.

"I'm sorry, Momma. The label needed me to send over a few things before I left, so I'm just now getting back from the studio. I'm packing up now," I lied.

"Mmhmm," she said, clearly not buying any of my bullshit. "Well, I'll tell you this. If I don't see your behind tomorrow by noon, I'm canceling my party, getting on a plane to Tennessee, and personally ripping that guitar out of your hands and burning it to ash. Do you hear me?"

I gave my eyes a slight roll, but in true Eunice Wilder fashion, she could not be fooled.

"And don't roll your eyes at me. I'm serious. This means a lot to me, and I haven't seen you but one time in ten years. That's a long time for a momma to go without seeing her baby." She was laying the sugar on, and thick.

"I know it. I'm sorry, Momma. I'll be there. I told you, I wouldn't miss it for the world. After all, it's only once that you turn thirty-five. Again."

She let out a low, slow laugh. I had her back in a sweet spot where she no longer wanted to strangle me, for now. If I only had that effect on the other women in my life…

"Bring that Ryan with you. He seems sweet. And judging from the five minutes I had to wait to get through to you, he may need to step away from the video games for a bit," she added, clinking her glass again.

"Deal. I'll see you tomorrow." I put my guitar back in the corner of the room, looking out over Nashville, feeling that familiar tug in my heart again. The one that showed up when I felt like I was happy where I was, but it never truthfully felt like home.

Like I wasn't truly where I was supposed to be. Homesick for a place that no longer existed.

For *someone* that no longer existed.

"I'm glad to hear it, sweetie. We can't wait to see you. We all have so much to tell you."

After ripping Ryan's headset off, hollering at him for answering my momma's call, and de-escalating the fist fight that almost ensued, I retreated to my room to get my suitcase together.

I scanned my closet for a few things to pack—something a bit more polished than my usual t-shirts, jeans, and boots. I limited myself to three days' worth of clothes, though, to avoid the temptation of staying any longer.

Once I had everything situated, I grabbed a huge, industrial-sized garbage bag and began picking up the beer bottles strewn around the apartment, left over from the three-day party that ended sometime around six that morning.

I elbowed my way into Ryan's room, eyeing him as he packed a months-worth of clothes into a suitcase.

"We have a maid, Lee. What are you doing?"

Letting the cans and bottles clank against each other as I dragged the now almost full bag behind me, I shot him a look. "You know I hate her having to pick up after one of these stupid ass parties. We're never going to get this next album written if we keep fucking around."

"Your insane writer's block and severe addiction to finding your next 'muse' in one of the many, many gorgeous women who grace our condo is the reason why we can't write the album.

Not the parties. Those should help. Pontoon-rock is really popular right now. We should write about beer," Ryan nodded, tossing four bathing suits into his suitcase.

I finished cleaning up the mess cluttered about his room and brought the clinking bag down to the dumpster. From the alley, I could hear tourists already starting to kick their party up a notch, exploring the food and the bars of Nashville, snapping pics and writing stories only these streets, this city, could provide the backdrop for.

Unlike my snoozy, laid-back hometown of Savannah, Nashville was always ready for a good time. And if Ryan was to be believed, this city was where I'd find someone new to write songs about. Someone who could reach in, take another piece of my heart, and help me find the words again.

Because, truthfully, I hadn't been able to write a single, solitary hit since my first album.

The one I'd poured my soul into when the very first, and biggest, piece of my heart was yanked out of my chest—leaving me hollow and wordless ever since.

CHAPTER THREE

Magnolia

I was sprawled out on the floor when my phone buzzed. It was Sutton calling for the thirty-fifth time today—only this time, she wanted to FaceTime.

"What?" I growled while Pickle made biscuits on my head, purring madly.

"What the hell are you two doing? Are you day-drunk? God, is the cat drunk?"

"Pickle is pizza drunk," I hiccupped, trying to untangle her from my hair so I could sit up. "I am… Yeah, I'm kinda drunk. Do you think Lee is going to come home for the party?"

Her eyes went as big as saucers, and then her face fell into a frown. "Good Lord, Magnolia. Why on earth are you worried about that? What would it matter?"

"I'm not worried. Okay. I'm not, not worried. I'm just… Don't you think this whole thing is weird?" I grabbed both of Pickle's little paws and yanked them from my head, ripping a few chunks of hair out of my scalp as I tried to escape her death grip.

"Pickle! Leave your momma alone!" Sutton half-laughed, half-yelled at the cat before letting out a long breath in anticipation of one of her infamous, long-winded "get Magnolia off the bridge she's about to leap off" speeches.

"You're seeing someone. He's probably seeing someone because he's a singer, and he lives in Nashville. There's more cut-off denim shorts, titty shirts, and cowboy boots per capita than there are Starbucks. And let's revisit that first statement. You. Are. Seeing. Someone."

I nodded into the phone, padding across my room and sitting on the edge of my bed.

"And besides," she added, her voice growing higher by the minute, "look at your life! You're a business owner. You have a *hot* boyfriend. You might still be sleeping in the same full-sized bed you had in high school, but you've got all these renovation plans!" She paused, a grin spreading across her face. "You little Joanna Gaines, you. And, not to mention," she continued, leaning into her camera with a teasing tone, "you're vice semi-quasi secretary of the Daughters of Savannah Civic Society. You're basically Savannah royalty now."

"They let me change out the sweet tea jugs last week, and I got to pass out the agendas. Shut up. Just listen." My voice grew more animated. "Lee has a Grammy! And *he's* also super hot. And yeah, I mean, did you see that girl he brought with him to the Country Music Awards? She was like twenty-one." I rolled my eyes, feeling the frustration creep in as I kept yapping. "And then, oh Lord, have you been on his Instagram lately? He's always got that stupid ass guitar and at least four blondes around him at all times." I sighed, shaking my head. "And then the comments, oof. How pathetic do I sound right now?" I lunged myself back down on my pillows dramatically, disturbing Pickle in her spot of slumber, and she dug her claws back into my scalp and screeched like a banshee.

"Listen. You don't sound pathetic. Unhinged, maybe. A little obsessed? Yes. Girl, why are you tormenting yourself like this? He left. You're here. Time and life don't stop just because Leland Wilder went off to Nashville and never came home. This isn't a dollhouse where you can walk away and expect everything to stay just as you left it. Life doesn't work that way. When you come back, you have to be prepared for the pieces to have shifted, for nothing to be quite the same as it was before."

I rubbed my head and let my hands fall over my face, trying to fight mid-day bourbon-infused tears. I could feel the anxiety creeping through my bones, making my heart slam against my chest. "What would I even say to him? After all this time, honestly, what could I possibly say?"

"If I had to guess," Sutton sighed, "an awful lot that was left unsaid."

I thought I felt better when Sutton and I hung up after she talked me off the ledge, but I was still sitting on a hot-bed of nerves. It had been *years* since Lee came home. On one hand, he was due to show his face back in Savannah, but on the other, he was probably busy banging half of the state of Tennessee, wooing them with his guitar and his stupid, baby blue eyes.

And she was right, I was seeing someone. But it was new, despite the fact that for the last few months everyone around us marveled about how "it was time" and "it just seems right" whenever we walked into a room together.

But that was just the thing. It was something fresh. Full of all those awkward firsts every couple goes through. I wanted to trust again, but I couldn't. I wanted to wear a relationship like an old, worn-out sweatshirt—full of holes but comfortable from years spent breaking it in. I wanted to feel secure, but it wasn't happening.

Because in the end, no matter how good it felt, it all ended up in a donation pile eventually.

CHAPTER FOUR

Lee

"Brooooooo! We're going to hit up every single one of these haunted tours. This one, dude, you can go into the haunted house. Can you imagine the material we could get from this kind of shit? Unbelievable, my guy."

Ryan was sitting in a chair by the window of the airport, both of us nursing beers and scrolling through our phones. Only one of us was looking forward to the trip.

I stopped my incessant stalking—it's not like she had any personal social media of her own—to address the madness unfolding in front of me. "You want to write an album about a haunted house? Who would buy that?"

He began belting out some lyrics, "This house is haunted… with the ghost of you and the ghost of me… I'll eat some fried chicken and be happy… Man, I have to pee. Hey! That rhymed. Write that down." He hopped up and jogged toward the bathroom, humming to himself along the way.

Savannah was haunted, alright. Ghosts of the town's past floated through the squares and houses, but nothing haunted the city more than memories. And I had far too many to count.

For the most part, I'd put the memories on shelves in my head and let them collect dust, but going home was going to kick that wreck right back up, and I knew it, which is why I stayed away for so long. I couldn't imagine strolling through the squares, lazing by the river, seeing her face. It would undo ten years of work. All the girls, all the bars, all the booze and the songs.

Ryan skipped back and slipped into his chair across from me in the Diamond Lounge. We weren't celebrities by any means, but every now and again, our label treated us to some perks and flying in style was one of them.

I'd been writing music forever, but nothing compared to the stuff I

"

cranked out my first year in Nashville. My heart was shattered, and I channeled all that pain into my songs. It felt like I was just surviving from one day to the next, struggling to find a spark of hope while dealing with the loneliness of a new city and missing her.

I sent my demo tape to a bunch of studios, and *Horizon Sound Studios* ended up picking up my album, *Fading Echoes of Us*. Jesse Lynn Carter, one of country's hottest stars, heard our single "Walking Away Slow" and reached out. Meeting him was a game changer; he helped me refine the song, blending his own magic with my raw emotion, turning it into something incredible.

Even though winning a Grammy with Ryan was amazing, the loneliness never really left. All the success and accolades felt bittersweet, especially when they didn't fill the emptiness inside. It was like living a dream while still missing the reality of what I once had.

"So, are we going to see her?" Ryan asked, motioning for two more beers from the server and pulling me from my thoughts.

"My momma?" I quipped, playing dumb.

"Magnolia, you idiot. You know, the inspiration behind about seventy-five of our songs? Does she know you have a framed picture of her in your writing space?"

"That's a picture of our friend group, you asshat. And she's not the inspiration behind our music. She's just another chapter in my life." The server dropped our beers, and I gave her a sly smile to match her googly-eyed stare.

"I just don't get it, man. All the girls in Nashville fall at your feet every time you get on stage, and no one has been able to really land you. I know it's because of her."

He wasn't half-wrong there. I'd had my fair share of women, and they drew to me like flies on shit the second I picked up my guitar.

But despite all the women and all the attention, the moment I got in my car and left Savannah for Nashville, loneliness hit me like a freight train. That hollow ache never let up, and no matter what I did, nothing could fill that gaping void.

"I guess you're not going to answer that," Ryan said, pulling me back to reality again. "Do you think your dad's going to cold clock you when he sees you?"

"Hard hitting questions today, my friend. You should have been a journalist." I took a long sip of my beer and avoided his stare-down.

"All I'm saying is I need to try this Mrs. Wilkes's fried chicken," he said, shoving a website in my face and throwing his hands up. "They say it's the best."

"You haven't tried my friend Sutton's cooking. You'll fall in love," I offered, feeling a pang in my heart for my friends like I did most every day.

"Yo! Is she hot? If she can cook *and* she's hot, I call dibs."

I had to laugh. "She's gorgeous. But stay away from her, seriously. She was like a sister to me."

Was being the operative word there. I hadn't talked to her in years, which sucked, because we were once so close. I stared out onto the tarmac and let my mind wander back to a time when things weren't quite as complicated as they were now... and had been for years.

CHAPTER FIVE

Magnolia

I decided to hire one of those traveling karaoke setups for a Friday night, hoping it would pull in a crowd of SCAD students or maybe a few wandering tourists if they heard "Don't Stop Believin'" blasting out of our walk-up to-go window.

Kasey, the only staff member I hadn't let go, was having a blast behind the bar, reliving her nineties wild child days and busting out her best moves. I gave her the heads-up that I was heading out for the night.

"Go, boss lady," she cheered, her eyes twinkling with mischief. "You need to let loose. Have a great dinner with your guy, then go hang out with your weirdo brother. It's not my kind of night, but you've been burning the candle at both ends. You deserve this!"

I watched as she unwrapped a CrunchWrap Supreme from Taco Bell, her twin top knots bouncing with every move as she threw up a peace sign when the DJ switched from Journey to Whitesnake. She belted out the tune between bites, occasionally garbling the lyrics as she crunched through her food, completely unbothered by the crumbs sprinkling across the bar.

"Anyway!" I shouted over the music. "I'll be back around 11:00. You've got this?"

She waved me off with a smirk and another bite. "Seriously, do you think I can't handle the eight people who'll stroll in tonight? Go on. Have fun. Just go."

I trudged up the back staircase and into my apartment, rifling through my closet for something that didn't scream 'disaster.' This was our fifth official date, not counting the group hangouts, and I knew it was time to seal the deal. I was looking forward to it, but…

Just as I pulled out a sleek, low-cut maxi dress, my phone blared with the obnoxious siren of "Party Like a Rockstar," a throwback to high school days.

"Hi. I really need to change this ringtone. What's up?" I tossed a few more dresses onto my bed and sank into my desk chair, flipping open my laptop to check the camera feed from the bar below.

"Where are you guys heading tonight? I'm wrapping up this engagement party, and I'm itching for a drink. Are you hitting up Jordan and Doyle's?"

I scrolled through the camera view, watching the five patrons at the bar. They were just sitting there like statues, not moving, not drinking, and definitely not paying any attention to the two hundred dollars an hour karaoke DJ I'd hired.

"Oh, well, excuse me, let me check my itinerary for the evening." I said, jumping back into the conversation. "It was emailed to me around noon."

"Someone's definitely his momma's son," Sutton mused. "Speaking of, let's hit the shops tomorrow for the party! We'll start with a nice brunch at Clary's, get a little buzz going, then hit the stores on Broughton. Maybe swing by Pence's before I head over to the Wilders' place. Sound good?"

I made a rather loud sound of disgust, and I could all but hear my best friend's blood pressure boiling from the other end of the line.

"Magnolia, don't even start. What were you planning on wearing? Leggings? A t-shirt from that one time you ran that road race with me and walk-slash-cried the whole time? That was just a one mile fun run, by the way. Can we please get you a dress? Maybe something you don't wear with your beat-up Chuck Taylors?"

"First of all, I ran that whole mile! I only cried when we got to the end and they had run out of finish line beer." I smirked while digging further into my closet. "And second of all, for the record, I have a nice top and a pair of jeans ready to go. Besides, I'm just going to sit on the veranda and get drunk until you're done working. What does it matter what I'm wearing?"

"You can't run races just because there's beer at the finish line. You own a bar—you can drink for free whenever you want. And honestly? What if Lee does decide to show up? You wanna wear your same old jeans from twelfth grade? Who, by the way, can still fit in those clothes besides you? And hi! We need to be showing off our new boyfriend and our banging body. We need a dress."

"So then, go get a dress," I counter-offered.

She huffed on the other end. "I have to wear a chef's coat, you ass. And probably a hairnet." I could hear her chopping up something in the background, her telltale sous chef soundtrack of Shania Twain blaring around her. "Come on, Magnolia. This is a big deal to Eunice, and she loves you more than her own children. Besides, I'm so bored. This is my fifth party in a week. I don't want to think about flambé or gluten-free crusts. Let's shop!"

I groaned and pulled out a pair of dark-purple denim pants and my jean jacket from my closet, shoving the revealing maxi dress back in its spot. We weren't dining upstairs at The Olde Pink House tonight, so I didn't need to get too dressed up.

"Actually, Eunice and I saw some dresses when we were out getting silent-auction donations last week. I think she may have something up her sleeve, per usual. She liked me in this periwinkle dress I tried on. You know her, it's probably going to show up any minute."

I poked around the top shelf of my closet for my black cowboy boots, pushing aside bins, when a shellac-covered shoebox fell to my feet, covered in photos and clippings from magazines.

"Well, Lord, would ya look at that?" I said, mostly to myself, but I had my best friend in the world on the phone and she knew exactly what it was.

"And just like the black sheep of the family himself, the memories fall from the sky."

"I used a lot of glitter nail polish to shellac this bad boy. You can still smell it. I really can't even remember what's inside."

"Don't open it now, you boob. I don't think it's best to potentially let your mind get all occupied by your ex an hour before you meet your new boyfriend for dinner. And especially since we don't know if this man is going to come swinging back into our lives, strumming his stupid guitar, sometime in the next twenty-four hours."

"You're right. Okay, off I go. It's date five, so you know what that means," I said, jimmying off the top of the bourbon and taking a generous slug for liquid courage.

"Well, have fun. It's finally starting to feel like fall, so maybe you can crack open a window while you guys finally bone for the first time."

"Are you okay?" I asked, my heart banging against the walls of my chest. "Why do you insist on saying stupid shit?"

"Because we both know if that man doesn't get a piece of you soon, he's going to dry hump your leg like a teenager just so he can get off somehow and still have you involved. Besides, it's so fun to get you all crazy-like. It's pretty easy, too."

"I just never thought for a second that he'd be into me now or that I'd be into him. It's so awkward," I bemoaned, running my fingers across the sticky, shiny surface of the box.

"What's so awkward?" Sutton asked. "The fact that you guys have been friends for over ten years or the fact that Dane just happens to be the love of your life's older brother? For what it's worth, Dane was always into you. He pretty much never stopped. Lee just locked it down before Dane even had the chance."

I gave in to temptation and lifted the top of the box, barely stifling a gasp when I saw the first picture on the pile. It was a snapshot of Lee, Dane, and me, arms slung around each other's shoulders as we grinned for the camera. The beach at Tybee Island sparkled in the background, the sun catching the waves just right.

"Let me guess, I've lost you to memory lane?" Sutton asked, as I held the picture up to get a closer look. We all looked so young, so tan, so happy.

"Uncle Cole always said that Dane couldn't handle me since I was too feral and sassy. But Lee could—he said that he matched my energy like no one else. Wonder what he'd think of me now…"

"Cole also said that you have a bad habit of living in the past and not being able to let things go. I think that was the more accurate statement," Sutton groaned. "Put the pictures down, Magnolia. You know what your uncle would really think? That he was happy for you because you are happy. Doesn't matter which man is on your arm."

I sighed, closing my eyes and as I tried to remember what it felt like when we were young and carefree. I knew Dane had feelings for me back then. I just pretended I didn't have a clue. He was my friend and a good one. He still was.

Sutton's voice ripped me back into the present. "That man sat at the bar for almost two hours last night, hanging on your every word. And that's a huge feat, believe me. You're kind of boring."

"Speaking of boring," I said, putting the photo back in the box, "I must go now to be wined and dined by my prestigious litigator beau. I'll see you at Cheese, Please! later, yeah?"

"That's not boring, Magnolia. That's adulting. Letting a fine man take you out to dinner to yap your ear off about discovery, pleadings, and case law?

Sounds like a blast to me," she released a light, teasing sound.

After we hung up, I went to close the box of photos but couldn't resist peeking at the top few. My heart skipped a beat when I found a selfie of Dane and me from my first Fall Formal. We were grinning ear to ear, laughing with our eyes squinted from the joy. The happiness practically leaped off the picture.

Maybe what people always said was true—sometimes the strongest relationships began where the deepest friendships had already taken root.

***

"It's really good to see you, Magnolia," Dane said, as he nursed a Magner's cider, watching me closely as I tidied up behind the bar.

"It's good to see you, too. It's been a long time, and I always appreciate it when an old friend stops by."

Uncle Cole joined me behind the bar, ruffling the top of my head. "I'm heading to my appointment, honey. I'll have Charlie pick me up. I'll be a bit tired afterward, so if you don't mind opening up, I'd appreciate it."

"I can handle it. You just get some rest," I said, not meeting his eyes. That was his fourth round of chemo, and he was rapidly losing weight, his eyes sinking deeper with each treatment.

"You're my sweetheart, Magnolia Louise. Dane, why don't you take this girl to lunch? She's been working hard and could use some downtime before another night at the bar."

Cole kissed the top of my head, patted Dane on the back, and winked at me before heading out.

"He's not looking too bad. My momma made it sound like he was on death's door," Dane said, taking another sip of his cider.

"It's touch and go. It all happened so fast. One minute he was fine, the next we were at the hospital trying to figure out our next steps. They're doing everything they can, but it's spreading quickly. We're trying to stay hopeful."

Dane nodded solemnly, his eyes locked on mine. "Let's take his advice, then. Let me take you out for lunch, and you can vent all about it. We can go to Vinnie Van GoGo's, just like old times."

I turned away, pretending to clean an imaginary spot on the back bar. It wasn't a date, just two old friends catching up. No harm, no foul, and certainly no thoughts about him being my ex's older brother.

"Sure, that sounds nice. Let me just run upstairs and freshen up a bit."

As Dane and I walked through the city streets, we caught up about everything from Sutton's new career in catering for LaMonte's to Charlie's art shows and his parents' charity work. The elephant in the room, of course, was growing larger by the minute, and when we put our names down for a table, Dane pulled the trigger.

"My brother's doing well. I knew you wouldn't ask, but I also know you'd want to know. I'm sure you heard he won a Grammy for song writing. I went out to Nashville to see him a few weeks ago. He was playing in this really great beer garden that served the most wonderful hot chicken. I'm surprised y'all haven't gone to visit. You and Sutton would tear that town up."

We sat on a bench across from Vinnie's, and I was careful not to get too close to him. I didn't want to give off the wrong impression—and I didn't want him to smell the stale beer in my hair.

"Yeah, well, I actually haven't talked to him, really in a few years," I lied.

Dane nodded, pulling a sunglasses case from his interior pocket, popping on a pair of expensive-looking aviator frames. "He mentioned that. I'm sure it's hard. Y'all have gone through quite a lot. Ah, look, I think our table is ready. How lucky are we?"

Dane stood up, and I couldn't help but notice how effortlessly put-together he looked. His crisp white shirt, with the top buttons casually undone, offered a teasing glimpse of his sun-kissed skin, hinting at slight summer tan. His fitted jeans, probably some high-end brand, hugged him just right, and the navy leather sneakers he wore managed to be both stylish and functional. As I stole a glance around the hostess station, I saw that I wasn't the only one appreciating the view—three servers nearby were clearly captivated, their eyes following his every move.

He reached his hand out for me to take it. And without hesitating, I did.

After lunch, locked arm in arm, we took a stroll through Forsyth Park, talking about the old days and how much fun we would all have coming to the park together, sneaking beers and whiskey from one of his parents' many parties, and laying in the sun, laughing and talking for hours.

"I might be jumping the gun a bit here, but would you allow me to escort you to the Fall Formal this year? I know it's a while away, but Momma mentioned you're

now on the board of the Daughters of Savannah Civic Society, so you're going anyway. And she's roped me into coming home so she can show me off. I know she's looking for me to find something—or someone—to anchor me back to Savannah. Might help to have an old friend there to help me weed through her prospects."

I unlatched my arm and rubbed my sweaty palms on the front of my shorts. Lunch was one thing, but the Fall Formal was a whole different ball game. "I'll think on it. It's… it's just…" I started, my voice shaking slightly.

"Say no more. I get it. You have a lot going on, and I respect that. Let me walk you home, and if you do change your mind, you know my number. At least I think you do, but you hardly ever use it," he offered, and we both let out a chain of nervous chuckles.

A few weeks later, after taking Uncle Cole off life support, I made my way out of the hospital carrying a bag of my uncle's belongings, blurry-eyed and feeling more alone in the world than I ever had. Charlie had stayed behind to take care of the paperwork, and I stepped out into the warm Savannah sun, clutching the plastic bag to my chest and holding back a sob.

Dane stood in the courtyard of the hospital, hands in the pockets of his gray slacks. He had his suit coat draped over his arm, sleeves rolled up to the elbow, and as I got closer to him, I could see the beads of sweat gathering around his ash-blonde hairline.

"I got here as soon as I could. I left… I… Well, I probably don't have a job now," he said, running his hands through his hair, causing it to stick up on all ends. He looked worried and nervous, and his eyes glazed over with tears.

"I was in a trial. But it's not important. You are, Magnolia. You're more important." He grabbed me and pulled me into his chest, and the tidal wave of emotions I had been holding in for days came flooding out. I stood and cried into his expensive button-down for what felt like hours.

After that, Dane hardly left my side except to go pack up his townhouse in Atlanta. He helped Charlie and me with the funeral arrangements, he jumped behind the bar when I needed to rush upstairs to have a good cry, and eventually, our small friendship blossomed into something more.

We were walking down the river on a cool, pre-fall night when he laced his fingers through mine and shot me one of his mega-watt smiles. He'd become a little more laid back since returning to Savannah, and his typically clean-shaven face showed off a few days of stubble that looked sexy, yet fitting, for the buttoned-up lawyer.

"I'll go with you," I offered, stopping to lean on the ledge of the river, looking out over the deep, black water.

"You think you could be a little more specific?" He turned to me and brushed the wind-whipped hair out of my face, brushing my cheek gently.

"Anywhere," I laughed, turning myself toward him. "But, specifically, the Fall Formal. I would love to be… your date."

His eyes lit up for a moment before darkening with desire. Then, before I could even think, our lips met—soft at first, but quickly turning into something deeper, more urgent, as everything we'd been holding back for the past month finally broke free. There was longing, a raw need, and a deep appreciation, but most of all, that intense, undeniable lust we'd both tried so hard to ignore since he came back.

He ran his hands up and down my bare arms, leaving a trail of goosebumps in their wake. Warmth curled in my stomach, and my heart pounded like crazy. I pulled back slowly, meeting his deep blue eyes.

He bit his lower lip, and I could see he was fighting the urge to kiss me again. He let out a puff of air. "That, Magnolia Pruitt, was absolutely worth the wait."

CHAPTER SIX

Lee

"Welcome to Savannah Hilton Head Airport. If you're catching a connecting flight, please stop by the kiosk to check your flight information and departing times. If Savannah is your final destination, welcome home!"

Home—such a weird word. I hadn't felt at "home" for the longest time. No matter how perfectly I decorated my condo or how many people filled the space, home had slipped through my fingers. It wasn't something I could touch or feel anymore—it was a distant memory, just out of reach, no matter how hard I tried to grasp it.

Nashville didn't feel like home, neither did the studio or the live music circuit. Home wasn't a different girl in my bed every weekend or the case of beer it took to forget the one thing I couldn't get off my mind, ever. It wasn't the bars, the clubs, the social media influencers who staged dates with me, and hookups for likes and shares. I didn't feel at home when my head hit the pillow at night, and my heart called to be somewhere else.

And when the plane touched down on Georgia's red clay soil for the first time in ten years, it didn't feel like coming home as I thought it would—it felt like I was an outsider, visiting a city I no longer knew.

Because to me, home was lounging by the river, sharing pralines with my best friends. It was curling up in Magnolia's full-sized bed, hiding under the covers, pressing kisses to her freckled skin, trying to keep quiet so we didn't wake her brother. It was stealing kisses from Maggie in my momma's kitchen, arms wrapped around her curvy hips, face buried in her long, curly red hair.

And I'd long since been evicted from that home.

I nudged Ryan, deep in an all-you-can-drink first class mimosa coma, and pointed to the front of the plane where the flight attendant opened the door, letting in a cascade of humidity that enveloped the cabin. He stretched out, nodded, and stood up to grab his bags, banging his head on the plane's low ceiling.

"You good, pal?" I stifled a laugh, standing up slowly and cautiously, as I watched my friend struggling to get his luggage from the overhead compartment.

"Not off to the best start here. I think I need a heavy brunch and a good nap. What time's the party?"

"I know a good spot, and you'll have time to get some beauty sleep, and hopefully shower, before the festivities."

We wandered into the terminal, and I glanced around, searching for a sign pointing me toward the Uber pickup—or better yet, a giant neon sign telling me to get my ass back on the plane because this was a bad idea.

As we drove through the tree-lined streets, making our way toward the river, I looked out the window for any hint that this place might have changed. As if the new restaurants and storefronts would give me a clue as to the kind of person Magnolia was now.

Of course, since she didn't have social media, I had to keep tabs on her through the bar's Instagram. Charlie, on the other hand, had a very active digital life, mostly for his art, but every now and again, I got a glimpse of the gang all together, a fleeting snapshot into what life might be like for them.

When Dane visited Nashville a few months back—he hadn't been home in a while either—he'd brought me up to speed as best he could. Never asking why the cord had been severed between all of us, but likely assuming with his critical, legal trained mind that time and circumstance did the trick.

After all, he was just as much an outlier these days as I was. Last we spoke, it was as if Magnolia, Sutton, and Charlie had lost his number, too. Guilty by blood-association, I'd assumed.

I sent him a text to let him know we were about to check into the hotel, which he read but did not reply to. Momma told me he'd lost his job in Atlanta and was now working with our father, which meant he was probably sitting in that big old white building on Bull Street wasting an entire Saturday working on some brief or argument my father would ultimately take credit for.

The life that Dane, the golden child, was groomed for and the life I pushed away every chance I got. The life I walked away from, getting me cut off— not just financially from my parents, but socially, from most of my friends as well.

Ryan and I checked into the hotel and made our way on foot toward the restaurant. We took a slight detour down Jones Street and stopped in front of my parents' sprawling corner-lot home.

"Let's just run in quickly and see if Momma's home. She probably caught wind that I've been in the city for fifteen minutes and is already stewing because I haven't stopped by yet."

"This is quite the house, Wilder," Ryan mused, as we walked up the staircase and onto the porch. I reached for the doorknob to let myself in but hesitated for a moment and decided to knock.

"Leland! Oh, darlin', it's so good to see you," my parents' long-time house-assistant, Dottie, said, as she wrapped me in a warm hug.

"Hey, Ms. Dottie, it's good to see you, too. I'm glad you're still here, working with my parents." I smiled, stepping over the threshold into a home that felt foreign to me. Ryan, eyes trying to adjust to the dark foyer, bumped into me. "This my buddy Ryan, Ms. Dottie. Ryan, Ms. Dottie has been keeping the Wilder house running like clockwork since before I was born."

"Ah, the good old days when you kids were running around. You, Dane, Charlie, and Magnolia. I miss all the noise," she sighed, running her hands over her apron, extending her arm and leading us down the hallway and into my parents' grand sitting room. "I'm only here two days a week since life is a little less chaotic for your parents now that you boys are grown. Can I get you two something to drink? You look like you could use an aspirin—Ryan, is it?"

We both laughed, and I shook my head. "That won't be necessary, but we sure appreciate it. Is Momma home?"

She sighed again. "I'm afraid not, Leland. She expected you home last night, and I haven't seen her yet today. Probably left early to get ready for tonight. We'll see you at the party, won't we? I'm sure you're looking forward to seeing all your old friends."

"Absolutely, of course I am," I lied through my wide smile. "We're heading to brunch, but will you tell her I stopped by? I'm staying at the River Street Inn."

Dottie leaned in and gave me another tight squeeze. "I will, dear. And I will see you tonight, too. So much excitement, and so many great things to celebrate! I'm looking forward to it."

"What else are we celebrating?" Ryan asked, padding down the stairs and back onto the street.

I shrugged and led the way to the restaurant, my stomach growling at the thought of pancakes the size of a table and a hot, fresh coffee. "My brother probably won some big case with my father, who's retired but still breathing down his neck. Vance Wilder uses every occasion, related directly to him or not, to boast about his success in the courtroom."

"Sounds like a massive dick," Ryan blurted out.

"He can be," I broke into a grin. "Listen, I know everyone says their family is crazy, but mine is beyond nuts. They're the stereotypical southern assholes who only care about what other people think above anything else. Even the feelings of the other members of the family."

"Sounds like the plot of a shitty movie. Do you think you need therapy, Wilder? Must be hard being the black sheep."

I opened the door to the restaurant, letting the smell of bacon, coffee, and decades of grease hit me in the face. For a fleeting moment, maybe this small pocket of the world did feel like home.

CHAPTER SEVEN

Magnolia

"I can smell the booze seeping out of our pores, and it's making me sick," Sutton grumbled, choking back a gag as we sat across from each other at Clary's for brunch.

Our collective hangovers prevented us from dress shopping, and the most we could muster were satellite-dish sized pancakes and Bloody Marys from our favorite spot.

"Will they ever learn? Will they ever stop taking advantage of free cheese and wine while their friends try to run an upscale business? Stay tuned to find out!" I said dramatically, sipping slowly on my cocktail.

"Honestly, I think the best part was when you jumped on that horse Charlie made out of old bicycle parts and tried to ride it while yelling, *'Hi-ho-silver!'* at the top of your lungs. That was about the point where Dane started feeding you cheese and cutting your wine with water so you didn't embarrass him anymore." She eyed my outfit—pumpkin-covered leggings paired with an old Savannah Academy hoodie that had once belonged to Lee—and burst out laughing. "What are you wearing?" she asked.

"Listen, I woke up in my bra and underwear with Pickle trying to get romantic, licking the cheese and cracker crumbs out of my cleavage. I just found the first clean things I could and put them on." I took a sip of my coffee, letting the warm liquid pool in my empty stomach. "Any clue what happened to my boyfriend last night?"

Sutton almost spit out her drink. "Boyfriend? Oh, the strides we've made."

I shrugged, a vague recollection of saying goodbye to Dane flitting through my mind before my brother walked me home. I remembered Dane's snarky, offhand comment about how much simpler things would be if I moved into his swanky Drayton Tower apartment. Beyond that, though, everything was fuzzy. Lord knows how I responded to him.

"Well, I'm sure he's sorely disappointed you two didn't get fully acquainted with each other last night." Sutton winced, her eyes darting around the room nervously.

The blurred lines of last night started to unfurl a bit, and I recalled Dane getting handsy in the back hallway of the wine shop and my insistence that someone take me home before things went too far. Had he gotten a little rough? Or angry? I couldn't remember.

I shook my head, trying to rattle any sense of recollection to the front of my mind. "I'm going to wash my hands and dry heave a bit over the toilet before the pancakes get here. When she drops them off, will you ask her to bring a gallon of water to the table?"

In the bathroom, I took in the state of myself. Last night's mascara was smudged, and my spotty foundation was letting the freckles I always tried to hide peek through. At least my new short haircut was still on point. Eunice had treated me to a keratin blowout the last time we hit the day spa, and now my once-wild curls fell effortlessly into a sleek, long bob. I gave myself a nod of encouragement and headed out of the restroom, ready to face the day.

Shaking my hands to air dry them in the small, stuffy hallway of Clary's, I sauntered back to the table, taking my seat across from Sutton, whose back was against the wall of framed photos from the movie *Midnight in the Garden of Good and Evil*. I couldn't really be sure, but it looked like John Cusack was slightly judging my hangover.

"Hey, serious question," Sutton started, bringing her cup of coffee to her face. I surveyed the table and our various beverages and let out a chuckle.

"Is it why two girls who drank so much last night are so thirsty today? Good question." I chose the glass of Diet Coke from the assortment of drinks, taking a long, eager sip. Sutton's eyes grew as big as the pancakes in front of us, and she moved the coffee cup closer to her face, covering her mouth.

"Nope. Not that. But yes, this is ridiculous. I was just wondering, um… remember that time you said that if you ever saw Lee again, you'd strangle him with the strings of his stupid guitar and shove his Grammy up his ass?"

Still keeping my eyes on my best friend, who was now visibly sweating out the wine, I nodded. "That sounds an awful lot like something I would say, yes."

"Well, now's your chance." Cringing behind her coffee cup, she let out a series of long, panicked laughs.

"Good morning, ladies. Sutton, seriously, I would know you two in Times Square. Hiding behind a coffee cup isn't going to help."

Lee Wilder himself was standing over our table, and I was caught with my mouth open like a grouper fish, unblinkingly staring at him with a huge bite of pancake dangling off my fork. Sutton howled.

"I know a massive hangover when I see one," he said, turning to the table behind us. "Mind if I borrow this chair?" The couple, some locals, were instantly starstruck and nodded, murmuring about how much they liked the latest single he'd written for Rhett Dawson.

Sutton finally lowered her coffee while my mind emptied of all coherent thought. Lee watched me with amusement.

"Um, hi," he offered. A fourth chair made its way to our small table for two, and a tall, raven-haired gentleman took a seat next to Sutton, watching the awkward reunion unfold.

"Which one's Magnolia?" he asked, grabbing my fork and taking a bite of our breakfast. "Has to be the one that looks like a deer in headlights. That makes you Sutton, the chef. I'm Ryan, Lee's writing partner."

Sutton watched Ryan with disgust, and I finally closed my mouth, swallowing my bite without chewing.

"Magnolia, I…" Lee started, nervously biting his bottom lip, an uncharacteristic tick for someone known for his brazen confidence, especially around folks with vaginas and pulses.

"You know what," I practically screamed, shoving my chair away from the table and colliding with the table behind me, knocking over their plates and drinks, sending everyone into a shouting frenzy. "I just remembered I need to go get those flowers! The flowers, yes."

"Magnolia, you got the flowers yesterday," Sutton, ever so subtle and not picking up on social cues due to her borderline still-drunken state, stared at me blankly.

"Yes. Ha! But the flowery flower ones are not just the regular flowers.

They're… flowers." I fumbled with my wallet and threw a twenty-dollar bill at my best friend, gritting my teeth at her to shut her mouth.

"Yes! Oh right, the flowery flowers. Okay, girl," she winked. "I'll call you later."

She turned her attention to the random gentleman sitting to her right, helping himself to her bacon. "Excuse me, who are you? Stop eating my breakfast." She slapped Ryan's hand away from her food and shot me a wide-eyed, crazy grin.

I dashed out of the restaurant, pushing through the dozens of patrons gathered by the register waiting for a table. A light rain had started outside, and people had been moving from the front of the popular dining spot into the counter-seating only area. If I had a bulldozer, I would have run them all over.

As I marched through the drizzle, my heart raced. I thought I'd braced myself for this moment, but nothing could have prepared me for the whirlwind of emotions I felt when I saw him. The raw pain, the undeniable pull, and the sudden urge to strangle him…

I was halfway down Abercorn Street when he caught up with me.

"It's been ten goddamn years, and the first time I see you, you run away! Magnolia, please, talk to me!"

I spun around, my hangover making everything wobble along with me. A wave of nausea crept up my throat, and I shot Lee a hard look, trying to get my bearings. Over the past ten years, he'd somehow grown taller and filled out. His t-shirt stretched tight over a muscular build, showing off the results of whatever workouts he'd been doing. He clearly had been taking excellent care of himself. The lanky kid I remembered had turned into a confident, well-built man, and it threw me for a loop.

His dark-blond hair, once cropped short, was now slightly longer and darker, letting his natural curls peek through. His big, sky-blue eyes locked onto mine as he gave me a quick, half-hearted smile. My eyes settled on his full, soft lips, and as if on cue, he ran his tongue across the bottom one, making my stomach drop.

"Hi," he offered, bringing me back to reality. I said nothing in return.

I'd known Lee for most of my life, and I could tell when he was wrestling with whether or not to reach out and touch me. I took a step back.

"What are you doing here?" I finally spat out.

CHAPTER EIGHT

Lee

A rush of bittersweet nostalgia swept over me, blending with a pang of sadness and something else I couldn't quite put my finger on. Was it longing? Regret?

Her hair was different—those bouncy, iconic curls now straightened to perfection, skimming her jawline. I nearly gasped when I saw the freckles still dotting her face, though they were half-hidden beneath layers of makeup trying to conceal them.

Her eyes were clouded with a deep, almost below-the-surface sadness, but she met my gaze with her typical, defiant edge—a flicker of the fiery spirit I remembered shining through.

Even hungover to the heavens, she was still a knockout.

The girl I used to love was still in there, even if she was buried way down inside the stranger in front of me.

When I noticed her and Sutton cowering in a corner, I was transported back to the old days. Sutton and Maggie sitting at a small table together, working off a hangover and talking about boys, huge stacks of pancakes piled so high in front of them you could barely see their faces.

I felt a twinge of guilt that she didn't get to eat her meal.

The real giveaway that my Maggie was still in there? She flipped me off before stomping down the street in her dirty Chuck Taylors and my old hoodie—an outfit I'm pretty sure my momma didn't approve of and definitely didn't pick out.

For the first time in ten years, I felt my heartstrings tug, and the warmth of being near her wrapped around me like a blanket.

Even if she probably still wanted to murder me in my sleep.

"Charming, that one," Ryan said, as I sulked back to the table, sliding into Maggie's empty seat.

Sutton, still white as a sheet, offered up a small, knowing smile, probably working out exactly what had just unfolded in the middle of the street in her head.

I finished off Magnolia's Bloody Mary and signaled for the server to bring another round. "How is she?" I finally asked Sutton.

"She's fine, Lee. Losing Cole was hard for her, but she got through it. We all were there for her." Sutton twisted her napkin nervously before looking up at me. "You could have called, you know? It didn't have to be to her, but you could have reached out to me or Charlie—especially Charlie. We were your best friends, and we needed you."

Ryan, trying to hide his discomfort, shoveled some more of Sutton's pancakes in his face, reaching over her to grab her cup of coffee.

"I see you've brought home a stray," she said, eyeing him suspiciously.

"He's a good friend. Be kind." The server dropped our drinks off, and judging by Sutton's body language, I'd said the wrong thing.

"Kindness to good friends, right? Can you imagine how we would feel if you'd offered us that type of kindness instead of walking away? Or not reaching out to us when we needed you the most?" Slamming her napkin onto her plate, she shot me a weary, tired look. "You've known him for five minutes, but you've known us your whole life. How pathetic. But I can't say I'm surprised. We've never been good enough for you. You can cover the rest since you've swooped in yet again and ruined everything." She rose from the table and threw the twenty-dollar bill from Magnolia at me. "You and your damn brother always have to screw everything up. See you tonight."

Sutton made her dramatic exit, just like Maggie had. But I didn't chase after her. I'd already been shot down by one of my best friends. I didn't need to go two for two.

"Yeah, your friends seem great." Ryan inhaled the rest of Sutton's plate, only stopping to wash his breakfast down with one of the thirty-five beverages in front of him. I had to laugh—the girls hadn't changed a bit. Big hangover, lots of options for rehydrating.

Although, the more I thought about it, they had changed. Sutton looked leaner, and I knew from Momma that, aside from being a chef for LaMonte's, the biggest catering company in Savannah, she'd become a serious runner—even finishing the Boston Marathon two years in a row.

Magnolia had changed the most, though. Not just physically, either. I expected to find a hollowed-out shell of a woman who had lost yet another important person in her life. Instead, I saw someone confident, strong, and put together—even if she was wildly hungover and sporting leggings covered in Jack-O-Lanterns.

I watched her walk out of the bathroom, that smile of hers highlighting the tiny dimple on her right cheek. It pulled me in, just like it used to, reminding me of all those times I kissed that exact spot.

She was, and always would be, perfect. No matter what.

"I don't think they're my friends anymore," I finally offered.

"Well, as Nashville's resident bad boy, I think you know how to do damage control better than anyone else," Ryan said, turning his attention away from the carnage in front of him and onto his cell phone.

I wasn't exactly the resident bad boy, but when I'd arrived in Nashville and was scooped up by the label, they'd treated me to a bit of a makeover. They wanted me to stand out from the crowd of crooners who flocked to the city to get their big break in country music, which apparently meant being a playboy.

Maggie wasn't the only one whose arm was twisted to change.

The label had linked me up with Ryan, who had come to Nashville a few years before I did and had made quite the name for himself in the song-writing circuit. They'd hired me a personal trainer, a stylist, and had someone come in and chop off my darkening curls, giving me a sharper, clean look.

And the cherry on top? They'd brought in social media influencer, Janelle Hunter, as my arm candy. Long, blonde hair and even longer legs coupled with her huge online following made us Nashville's hottest romance.

Not like there was any actual romance there at all.

My phone buzzed right as Ryan and I exited Clary's. I stopped to sign an autograph and take a picture with the restaurant staff before checking the message.

JANELLE: I miss you! Did you see my latest post? 150k views in 15 minutes. I did a dance in my new bikini to that song you wrote for Wyatt Jameson and everyone loved it. LELAND: Wow, that's great.

JANELLE: You could at least try, Leland. You miss me too, right, babe?
LELAND: Right, sure do miss you lots, darlin'.

I clicked the phone off and scrubbed my hand over my face. Lying didn't sit well with me, even when it was a mutual charade. Running into Maggie had stirred up a storm of feelings I wasn't ready to handle, and now, with Janelle in the mix, things were about to get even messier.

CHAPTER NINE

Magnolia

Back in my apartment, I paced for a while, glaring at my phone, fingers hovering above Charlie's number, then Dane's. I bit my lip, then flicked my thumb across the screen, unsure which one would make this better or worse. Either way, they'd find out Lee was home soon enough, and I could already picture the looks—the pity in their eyes like a weight on my chest. I didn't need more of that—my own self-pity was already a loud, unwelcome guest.

Pickle paced back and forth, too, before finally dropping herself on top of the glittery box that held what felt like a lifetime of memories. As I stared down at it, I knew opening it would unleash a flood of emotions—memories of a first love with someone who, just by seeing them for a few moments, made my heart skip a beat.

Could have been the hangover, too, of course.

"Scat, Pickle," I said, nudging the cat aside. As I lifted the lid and sifted through the stack of photos, I found a CD in a clear case, Lee's scratchy handwriting scrawled across the cover. I pulled it out, and beneath it were two tickets to my first Fall Formal and my dried corsage. I set them aside and smiled as I came across a photo of Sutton and me in our formal dresses, arms draped around each other's necks, grinning at each other.

Buried below some movie ticket stubs and a disposable camera I never bothered to drop off to be developed was a small, leather-bound book with a gold rose embossed on the front.

My journal. I flipped through the first few entries, giggling at my juvenile doodles and loopy, dreamy cursive decorating the pages. Putting it to the side, I picked up the CD again and cracked open the old, plastic case.

Crossing over to the stereo, I unplugged my scent warmer and plugged in the old music machine, praying it would still work. I pushed the eject button, lifted out the ancient, dusty Backstreet Boys CD, cringing a little, and replaced it with the CD from the memory box.

After hitting *play* on the stereo, I sank to the floor, sorting through the rest of the pictures in the box. The music wrapped around me like a warm hug as I sifted through memories, trying to separate the good from the bad.

I missed the days before everything got tangled up. Before kisses and dances, before booze and messy intentions turned us all upside down. I missed just laughing and hanging out with my friends. I missed being part of something irreplaceable, no matter how hard I tried to recreate it.

I ran my finger over the edge of a small photo album, my gaze lingering on a picture of the group of us, laughing in some summer haze. It felt like a lifetime ago—the days when everything was simple. When we were all just friends, no complications, no broken promises. The sound of us all laughing, our voices overlapping, felt like it belonged in a different life.

The floodgates opened, and I found myself in tears—and they just kept coming for what felt like hours, soaking my hair and face. Eventually I felt arms lift my shoulders off the ground. A set of lips pressed themselves to my sweaty forehead, but I kept my eyes screwed tight, almost afraid to open them to see who was on the other end of this mess on my floor.

"It's okay, baby girl. I'm here," he said, voice low and deep, sending an arrow straight through my heart.

Pickle hissed, and I opened my eyes to find her glaring at Dane suspiciously from my bed, fur bristling on the back of her neck.

"I'm sorry," I stuttered, sitting myself up. All around me, the contents of the box were scattered, fat tears streaking across some of the photos. "I just miss us all being together," I murmured, my voice thick with emotion. The words slipped out before I could stop them, like something long buried. I tugged at the hem of Lee's old hoodie, tracing the worn fabric between my fingers, my voice cracking with every syllable. "I just miss... us. All of us. The way things used to be." The room felt smaller, the air heavy with things left unsaid.

"You know, this is Lee's most well-written album, but the third one really shows his maturity." Dane leaned back on my dresser, pulling his legs up to his chest.

I peeked through one barely open eye, trying to gauge his mood as he stood there, taking in the sight of me like this.

"It's okay, Magnolia. I'm not ignorant of the fact that you used to date my brother." His voice was even, but there was a slight hesitation in his tone, as if he was trying to keep his true feelings in check. He managed a small, tight smile, though it didn't quite reach his eyes. "I just hope that if he does come home, y'all can patch things up. He's been your friend for most of your life." Dane rubbed my back, and I took in the irony of it all. Here I was, in shambles yet again, and Dane was comforting me.

"I don't deserve you," I muttered, burrowing myself deeper into his embrace.

He ran his hands through my hair and sighed. "You do deserve me. What you don't deserve is to feel this way. You've come so far. You've really been making great strides with the bar, you're the vice-archon of the Daughters of Savannah Civic Society, you've joined the Chamber, and, let's not forget, you have a pretty great boyfriend."

I let out a laugh. It was the first time he called himself my boyfriend out loud. "I know. I'm just having a moment."

"Moments are allowed. You've had a hard time the last few months. But let's not get so wrapped up in the past that we forget our future. And I know we have a great one together."

I tried not to think too hard about that. While we were taking things slow, I knew that Dane had high expectations for me and for our relationship. He was like his mother in that they had good intentions, but sometimes I felt like a project to them.

Like a broken doll that they were convinced, once fixed, would be the best and prettiest doll in all of Savannah, ready and waiting to do whatever they wanted me to do.

Eunice had no girls of her own, just her two boys who couldn't have been more different. When Charlie and I came along, she was helpful and kind, working hard to get us on our feet and working to make sure her old friend, Cole, had everything he needed to raise the two of us properly.

Having overseen the restoration efforts for SCAD when the school scooped up several historical buildings in downtown, she had the in when it was time to enroll Charlie and get him on track to a budding art career. But for me, the more stubborn of the two, she was never quite sure what to do other than dress me up like a Barbie and take me to tea and the spa.

The Wilders had offered to send me to business school. They'd offered to send me anywhere if I wanted it. Eunice once honed-in on my small, juvenile hobby of watching old, classic films and tried to create the narrative of me being an actress or a director one day. I just liked going to the old theater in town. Not because of the black-and-white films, but because they had better air conditioning than my apartment.

"You can be anything you want," she'd always told me, *"and you're not stuck following in the footsteps of the rest of the O'Malley clan, running that old bar. You were never tethered to it. Your momma made sure of that when she left the city and let your uncle run things."*

But she was wrong. I was as anchored as they came. The bar was in my soul and my heart, pulsing through my veins just like it was through Uncle Cole's. Living in the home my mother grew up in, hearing the sounds of the bar below was like a lullaby, something that connected us now that she was no longer here. Even if it wasn't my momma's dream, it was mine.

And when Lee left for Nashville, I couldn't be bothered to finish my application to the University of Georgia or even think about college at all. I wanted to do the same thing I'd always wanted to do.

Stay home.

"Let's skip heading to Pence for drinks. I'll text Sutton. She'll understand," Dane said flatly.

I nodded and used the sleeve of Lee's old hoodie to wipe away my tears.

"He's home by the way," I finally blurted out, not making eye contact. "Sutton and I ran into him at Clary's this morning."

Dane flinched as he pulled his phone out of his pocket and began typing furiously. "I'm heading back to Momma's. Why don't you get yourself dressed?" He still wouldn't look at me when he said, "I hate seeing you like this, Magnolia. You have so much potential."

Dane took his leave, and I sat alone on the floor, letting the last track on Lee's album fade into the air as if it were giving me one final lyrical embrace.

"I saw you standing there, with that look in your eye,
Like a summer storm was brewing, right beneath the sky.
You said forever was a promise, that we both believed,
But forever's just a whisper when the heart's got to leave.
So I'm walking away slow, trying to let it go,
Every step I take, I'm letting the memories show."

CHAPTER TEN

Magnolia

I slammed the stereo off, the abrupt silence slicing through the room. My journal fell from my hands, clattering to the floor, as I snatched up my buzzing phone, my heart racing with the sudden interruption.

"So, I'm at the Wilders getting set up, and the long-lost brothers just had one hell of a reunion," Sutton whisper-yelled, letting the water in the big, farm-style sink in the Wilders' kitchen run at full speed so that no one would hear her.

"Ugh." I sniffled as I pulled myself off the ground and surveyed myself in the mirror. I had about two hours to get ready, and things were looking rough. "Did Dane tell him? He left here about ten minutes ago."

"Not that I could hear," Sutton sighed. "Now Dane's locked in the office with Vance, and it's all hushed tones, and Eunice is running around like a cat in heat… oh shit… hang on. Hey, Eunice! Why, yes, it is Magnolia on the line. Sure, hang on. She wants to talk to you, sorry!"

Sutton handed the phone to Eunice, and I sank onto the edge of the bed to brace myself.

"Hey, darlin'," she drawled. "Thank you so much for getting the flowers all situated. They're so lovely. As I told you, you've always had impeccable taste."

"Of course, Eunice. I was just about to get ready to head on over. Y'all need me to stop for anything?"

"No, no. I did want to tell you, though, that Lee is home. What a nice surprise it was walking in my front door today and seeing his face. I hope this won't make you uncomfortable."

"Not at all, Eunice," I lied. "I am so looking forward to seeing an old friend." If Lee wasn't going to tell his momma I practically spat at him earlier, I wasn't, either. Saved me the lecture on all the money she spent on refinery classes for me.

"Well, I'm looking forward to seeing you. I know Dane is, too. Did you get the package with the dress I sent?"

"Let me check."

I padded out into the front hallway and scooped up a few packages waiting by the door. With my music up so loud, I must not have heard the delivery driver.

"Got it. Thank you, Eunice," I said, dropping the packages on my kitchen counter. Pickle jumped up and swatted at them, trying to knock them down.

"I can't wait to see how beautiful you look. It's a special night, you know."

I hung up the phone and tore open the box from Fancie's Boutique, pulling out the knee-length, periwinkle cocktail dress and accompanying shawl.

I let out a frustrated sigh and opened the second package, the heat from the box seeping through the cardboard. Inside was a to-go container from Clary's, the familiar comfort of buttery pancakes and sweet syrup wafting up as I pulled it free. A folded note sat beneath the box, the handwriting unmistakable:

I'm sorry I ruined your breakfast. No one should miss out on the best pancakes in the city, especially after running into their ex. Looking forward to seeing you later. - Lee.

Whelp. Lee was officially back. I set the note aside, staring at the pancakes, the memory of his thoughtful surprises rushing back. Birthdays, random Tuesdays, afternoons when I'd find something waiting for me—always perfectly timed, always exactly what I needed, even if I didn't know I needed it. His gifts had always felt like a promise, but I'd learned the hard way that promises were fragile things.

I stabbed a fork into the pancakes, taking two quick bites before tossing the box in the trash. This time, I wasn't falling for his shit. Not again, and definitely not now.

Back in my room, I ran a straightening brush through my hair, the hot bristles smoothing out any lingering waves. I locked the whole style in place with enough hairspray to keep the humidity at bay and knock a satellite out of orbit, all the while wishing for the wild curls that used to tumble down my back—before

Eunice convinced me to chop them off for a more "sophisticated" look.

I took my time with my makeup, carefully blending away the dark circles from another sleepless night and artfully concealing the freckles I never quite embraced. A spritz of perfume, a dab of pink lip gloss, and I took a long look in the mirror, barely recognizing the woman staring back at me.

I had no idea who the hell I was anymore.

I slipped into the dress, its fabric cool against my skin, and stepped into a pair of nude wedges that added just the right amount of height. In the living room, I grabbed my purse and Eunice's gift, placing them carefully on the table. A quick glance at the clock told me I had a few minutes to spare, just enough time to pour myself a glass of wine. I took a slow sip, hoping it would calm my nerves.

But could anything truly take the edge off walking into a party where the man you were supposed to build a future with was waiting while your past, with all its muddled memories and unfinished business, kept pulling you back?

***

I sauntered into the party a little early, nerves buzzing in my chest. I perched on the kitchen counter, trying to steady myself as I poured a glass of wine for me and Sutton, who was busy bustling around the kitchen, putting the finishing touches on everything. I took a sip, hoping it would calm me down, but the jitters remained. I reached over to grab a bacon-wrapped scallop, and she swatted at me.

"Where is everyone?" I steadied my voice before sipping my wine slowly.

"The boys, you mean?" she asked, raising an eyebrow and flipping on a blow torch to flame up the tops of her lobster mac and cheese. "I have no idea. Dane's still locked in the office with Vance. Eunice is in there now, too. I haven't seen Lee since I got here."

I nodded. "Has my brother graced you with his presence yet?"

"No," she said, busily decorating small cups of something with chives that was unidentifiable yet smelled delicious. "He's on his way, though. He stopped by earlier to help Jordan and Doyle drop off the cases of wine and the charcuterie platters."

"Do you need help?" I offered, my mouth salivating.

"You could help me tremendously by going away," she giggled. "Stop eating that chopped bacon, Magnolia. LaMonte will kill me if this party isn't perfect. The only reason he even let me come today is because Eunice threatened him." She pushed out an exasperated sigh and wiped her hands on her apron. "Why don't you go hide in the upstairs bathroom for a while? No one will look for you there, and you can finish your glass of wine without snacking on my creations, which will cause me to lose my job and thus force me to punch you in the back of the head."

I rolled my eyes and slid off the countertop, stomping down the hallway and up the wide staircase to the second floor of the Wilder property. I'd spent half my childhood between these walls, but knowing both Wilder boys—Wilder men—were somewhere in this house made the air feel thick and foreign.

I shut the bathroom door behind me and crawled into the wide garden tub, letting the cool porcelain chill the backs of my arms and legs. I was sweating profusely already, and nothing exciting had even happened yet.

My eyes closed, and I let the quiet fall over me. The soft hum of the activity in the kitchen and the band doing soundcheck downstairs were soothing and distant. My heart picked up again at the thought of running into Lee at the party and attempting to avoid him at all costs so as to not have to fake my way through another hair pulling conversation in which I fight the urge to kick him.

After Lee left for Nashville, the Wilder family drew me in closer than ever. I always suspected they knew letting him go was a significant sacrifice, though I never voiced it or let it show. For years, I felt a heavy guilt for pushing him away and effectively taking their son from them. But as time passed and Lee's success grew, so did Eunice's pride. It became clear that letting him go had been the right decision.

No matter how hard it had hurt. And no matter how that hurt never seemed to completely fade.

The bathroom door flung open, startling me so much that I jumped up and whacked my head off the side of the tub.

"My Lord, you are still so graceful, aren't you? Are you okay?" Lee shut and locked the door behind him—something I should have done myself—and rushed to my side, trying to push down a laugh.

"I'm fine. Please go away, and let me be concussed. Maybe I'll slip into a coma and not have to go to this party." I rubbed at the tender spot on my temple, avoiding his eyes. He was so close I could feel him breathing on my arm, sending a shooting pain of familiarity through my entire body.

"I see you haven't lost your high sense of drama. It makes me happy to know at least that hasn't changed." He finally let out that laugh, a low and chesty rumble, like he always did when something was really funny.

I was not finding the humor in this. "Go away, Lee. I'd love nothing more than to punch you right now, and that never ends well for either of us." I finally looked up and met his eyes. Quiet pools of ocean blue, twinkling back the reflection of a girl I knew once before.

A slow grin tugged at his lips. "You're right, that usually leads to a whole different kind of tussle for us."

I groaned, covering my face with my hands as I sank deeper into the tub.

"I am sorry. Truly. Are you really okay?" His eyes searched my face. "I know you hate these types of things, and it looks like Momma's got you in a dress and everything. Are those high heels?"

"They are wedges, thank you. I don't trust myself not to take down this entire party in anything higher than an inch."

"You look great, by the way. I meant to tell you that this morning, but you were too busy causing a scene and flipping me off for me to get a word in edgewise. Did you have trouble picking up the flowery flowers?"

I rolled my eyes. *Here we go.* "Please do not start with me. You have to realize how thrown off I was running into you this morning. I didn't expect that you'd actually show up."

He looked hurt by that. He should have been. While I was the one who told him to go, I never once asked him to stop coming home to see his family. Or to not keep in touch.

"I get that you're a great success, but Eunice and Vance miss you terribly. Dane, too." I tripped over Dane's name, hoping it didn't betray what I had hoped he already knew, so I didn't have to be the one to tell him.

He snickered. "Great success, that's pretty humorous. Maybe at one time. I guess you haven't heard that my third album was a total flop."

I hadn't discounted his talent—he was still great. Winning a Grammy for best breakthrough songwriter with his first album was proof of that. It took him almost eight years to put out the follow-up, and while the critics had been harsh about this latest one, I wouldn't have written him off just yet. It wasn't half bad. But then, what did I know?

Maybe I just couldn't separate the music from what was woven into those lyrics—maybe because deep down, I knew they were about me, even if I didn't want to admit it.

Of course, I couldn't let him know I knew these types of things.

"What's humorous is you thinking I actually listen to any of your music," I lied, very poorly.

"Right. Well, I can't say I blame you, really." He was quiet for a moment, looking around the bathroom as if searching for something to say. "I saw Charlie at his studio this morning," he muttered softly. "I had bought a few pieces off him a couple of years ago when we met up in Atlanta, but some of his new stuff is really neat. Did you see the one he created out of the old dining room table and the washing machine parts? He's a genius."

"He never told me that. I just thought you ordered something from him off his website?" I could feel my face growing redder by the second.

"What? About the dining room table piece? It really is something… I actually might buy it."

"No," I laughed angrily. "That you guys met up in Atlanta. He should have told me that!" I was yelling at Lee when I should have been yelling at Charlie, but he wasn't the one hovering over the Wilder guest bathtub.

He let out a wild guffaw. "Well, you react so rationally all the time, Magnolia. It's no wonder he didn't mention it."

I had been feeling sorry for Charlie all these years. He lost his best friend, and a huge part of that was my fault. And all this time, I thought they hadn't kept in touch. Turns out, my brother is just a rat-faced liar.

"I need to go home," I announced rather theatrically.

"Oh stop, Momma would kill you." He stood up and crossed the room toward the door, turning back but not meeting my eye. "Besides, your new *boyfriend* might be wondering where you've run off to."

I slid further into the tub as fast as I could, careful not to hit my already bruised head—or ego—on the way down.

Once the door was shut, and I was sure Lee had made his way back downstairs, I crawled out of the tub and leaned against the bathroom counter, face flushed with embarrassment as I stared at my reflection. Seeing him twice in one day after all these years was more than I'd bargained for. The memories I thought I'd buried down deep were creeping up on me, tightening in my chest. The nostalgia was making it hard to breathe, the weight of it all was overwhelming.

And I had to go downstairs, hook myself through Dane's arm, and pretend like everything was just fine.

About a half hour later, I ambled through the party, now on its way to full swing. Guests were still pouring in, and people were lining up at the bar for libations, grabbing the appetizers Sutton had prepared, and huddling up in small groups to pass on the gossip of the day.

I weaved my way through a small cluster of Eunice's friends, catching snippets of their conversation about Lee's return. The mere mention of his name sent a shiver down my spine, and I couldn't ignore the sideways glances and whispers that trailed after me as I passed. It felt like every eye in the room was watching me, waiting for a reaction I wasn't ready to give. I needed to get away from the buzz, so I slipped out of the grand foyer and toward the back of the house, craving a quiet corner to gather my thoughts. Or to drink said thoughts away.

I passed by Sutton in the kitchen, giving her a quick look and nod before snagging a bottle of wine off the counter. Without a word, I retreated to the back veranda. I didn't bother with a glass—I didn't need it.

I made it to a plush chair tucked toward the back of the oversized porch where a large potted azalea bush offered just enough cover to give me a bit of privacy. The veranda stretched out, overlooking the lush backyard, but from where I sat, I was mostly out of sight—just a hint of the party visible through the gaps in the blooms. I sank into the cushion, pulling back on the bottle, grateful for the small slice of solitude.

"There you are!" Charlie shouted, rounding the corner and instantly drawing attention to me. Heads turned, and suddenly, all eyes were on the woman in the corner, drinking wine straight from the bottle. I shrank into myself, shooting my brother a dirty look.

"I am not speaking to you right now, Charles Abner Pruitt. In fact, I may never speak to you again," I hissed.

He squished himself next to me on the chair, yanking the bottle out of my hands and taking a swig. "Ah, you've run into Lee, apparently. I'm sorry, it felt like a betrayal that we were still friends."

We both aggressively wiggled around in the chair, trying to get comfortable. "I was mad at him because he had given up on your friendship, Charlie. I was pissed at him for not calling you, yet he's your best customer! And you've just been casually hanging out with him from time-to-time. You probably knew he was coming this weekend, and you acted like you had no idea!" I grumbled, pushing against his shoulder to make room for myself on the chair he was trying to hijack. "Hey, by the way, are you calling a piece of furniture you painted metallic orange 'art' now? What am I missing?"

He rolled his eyes, handing the bottle back to me. "That's not the reason you've been mad at him, Magnolia. You've been stewing all these years because you told him to leave, and you didn't believe he actually would." My brother stood up, watching over me sadly. "And honestly? It's burnt sienna with a copper overlay and reclaimed copper piping from discarded washer and dryer parts. It reflects the state of the industrial society we're living in. Don't you ever listen to me?"

Sutton found me about an hour later when I had, over the course of that short time, become borderline drunk and irrationally sad.

"I have a concussion and a broken heart," I proclaimed, as she handed me a small plate of all of the things the caterers had carried past me, but that I had rejected, hesitant to lose my buzz.

"Eat something before Eunice sees you like this. What are you doing, Magnolia? This is pathetic." She was right.

I shoveled the food into my face quickly and shot her a spinach-toothed smile. "Why am I like this?" I laughed with a mouth full of quiche.

She laughed right along with me. "I don't know, but Lord, have I spent the better part of my life trying to figure it out."

I put my head on her shoulder and let her rub my arm.

"Dane's been looking for you. I told him you've been mingling and that pleased him, of course. Once you let that food sop up all that sav blanc you've been guzzling, you might want to get up and do just that."

She scurried back to the kitchen, and I took a few minutes to gather myself, trying to shake off the weight of the day's emotions. The wine had hit me harder than I'd realized, and I burped twice, the taste of grapes and spinach quiche rolling over my tongue. Feeling a bit wobbly, I gave myself a quick pep talk, determined to embrace the role of Dane Wilder's social and definitely not super drunk girlfriend. With a deep breath and a final glance down at myself, I squared my shoulders and set off to rejoin the party, hoping to blend in despite the swirl of emotions and booze still tugging at me.

"There you are!" Dane crossed the room, politely pushing through the crowd to meet me as I pretended to listen, attentively of course, to a very numbing Daughters of Savannah Civic Society conversation about lemon meringue.

"Yes, here I am." I leaned into the kiss he planted on my cheek. "Ms. Hattie Beckett has been telling us all about her secret for the perfect whipped topping."

"Cream of tartar," Hattie Beckett leaned in and whispered conspiratorially.

"Gross," I mumbled under my breath, letting out another small belch.

"How delightful, ladies," Dane said a little too enthusiastically, guiding me away from the gaggle of women with a gentle hand on the small of my back. "It's so lovely to see you all here. My momma is so happy to have all your smiling faces celebrating her today." He beamed his perfectly straight teeth at the crowd, and they ate it up like pie.

"She sure does know how to throw a party, that's a fact. We're all hoping the next one will be in honor of you and Magnolia!" Hattie Beckett was beaming, and Dane went white as a sheet. "Eunice tells us we should have the happy news any day now!"

I politely excused myself before rushing toward the back door in search of freedom, fresh air, and a quiet place to vomit.

I darted down the back stairs, only to realize I was now marooned in the backyard with no clear escape route. I scrambled behind a wall of bushes that lined the fence, trying to camouflage myself in the greenery. There I was, blending in like a desperate, sad chameleon, hoping the plants would somehow take pity on me and shield me from the chaos I was trying to avoid.

"Hattie's completely off her rocker, Magnolia. Don't listen to her! Are you dry heaving in there?" Dane's voice whined from just outside the bushes, confirming that my brilliant hiding spot was anything but. I could practically feel the frustration rolling off him. The shuffle of footsteps on the stairs and the soft murmurs of Charlie and Sutton told me the search party had officially been expanded. Great. Just what I needed—reinforcements to block my dramatic exit.

I had my back up against the cold iron of the fence, trying not to toss my cookies. I tried to steady my breathing and wipe the last ten minutes of memory from my mind. The thought of Dane proposing after what, four and a half dates—considering I'd practically ghosted him after the last one—was absurd. I mean, what was he thinking? Did he lose a bet or something? Was I being *Punked*?

"Charlie, clean this up before Eunice sees or hears her," Sutton whispered angrily.

"This is Dane's mess. It's his fault, wanting to propose to her after, like, four dates," my brother growled.

Wracking, violent sobs overtook me.

"Damnit, Charlie! Come on, baby, come out of the bush. I promise I won't propose to you."

"Wait, you were going to do it in front of all these people?" Sutton asked, letting out a sarcastic laugh. "That's bold. Just what Magnolia loves more than anything, to be the center of attention."

"I thought she would appreciate the grand gesture. It's my grandmother's ring and on my momma's birthday…"

"Oh heaven have mercy, Dane," Charlie was cackling now. Through the leaves, I could see him bending over onto his knees, holding himself up as his body shook.

"Charlie, please go ask around to the busboys and see if anyone has a valium," Sutton commanded. "They're all suspiciously mellow today, so they might have some good shit."

Charlie sauntered back toward the house on a mission, trying to catch his breath from laughing.

"You're in deep shit, Dane. Deep. Shit. Are you pulling this stunt because your brother's here? Or is it because you've been acting like a real shithead lately?" Sutton meant business. I could hear it in her voice.

He shook his head. "No. My *father* and I have been discussing it all afternoon, and Momma thought it was such a good idea, she brought down my mimi's ring." There was a hint of smugness to his voice. "My parents thought it might be a nice way to let everyone know that Magnolia had moved on. I mean, I guess because my brother's home…"

I could practically smell Sutton's irritation brewing through the twigs and leaves.

"Jesus," she let out a long, heavy breath. "Anything, Charlie?" Charlie was back and handed something over to Sutton.

"I'm not developing a pill problem over this! I might feel better if you all went away!" I cried.

"The bush speaks," Sutton mused. "Come on out of there, sweetie. Charlie found you a joint and a bottle of tequila."

"Only if Dane goes away." I sounded—and felt—like a child.

"Alright, I'm going. Give me that. She's not going to smoke it." Dane grabbed the joint out of Sutton's hand and stomped off.

"Is he gone?" I waited a few beats before I crawled on all fours out of the bush, my periwinkle tea dress now covered in dirt and regret.

Sutton bent down to pick pieces of brush out of my hair. "This is, hands down, the most extra dramatic bullshit I have ever seen. Honest to God, next time just go home. It's not like it's a very far walk."

Charlie crossed his arms and glared at me like he was upset, but the way the corner of his lip tipped up, I could tell how amused he was.

"He was chasing me. I didn't have a choice. I felt like a giant ring was charging down the hallway at me, and I panicked. And y'all know I can't move fast after all that booze and food in these shoes." I grabbed the bottle of tequila from Sutton, took a hefty swig, and handed it back to her. "We could all use a drink right now," I said.

***

With the party winding down, I took refuge behind the azalea plant again, trying to stay out of sight. A wave of guilt washed over me. I hadn't even managed to catch Eunice all day, and here I was, once again, making everything about me.

"So, I hear you've had an eventful day. I'm not at all surprised." Lee was standing just below the veranda, looking up at me from the yard where, not too long ago, I'd been squatting among the bushes like a spy who'd bungled her mission. He had his hands in his pockets, and when I turned to meet his stare, I saw him grinning like he'd just caught me in a particularly ridiculous moment of a sitcom.

Which was exactly what that doomed afternoon felt like.

"Please don't." I shook my head. "This day has been traumatizing enough as it is."

His smile quickly changed to a slight frown, and he rocked a little bit on his heels. "Come on down here and talk to me, Maggie. I won't bite."

I looked around to make sure I wouldn't bump into anyone, especially his brother, as I made my way down the stairs.

A small, gliding porch swing hung under the veranda, in one of the few shaded areas in the Wilder backyard. When we were kids, we would practically live under there, hiding from the sun and his parents. I'd read a book, and Lee would strum at his guitar, furiously scribbling lyrics in his notebook, every now and again stealing a glance at me.

"Sit down, Maggie. I told you I won't bite." He patted the seat next to him, and I settled in, kicking my legs out. The chair swung back and forth, creaking with the sound of rust and years gone by.

"I can't believe him," I confessed.

Lee gave a resigned sigh. "I can. He's loved you a real long time. Can't say I blame the guy for being overly enthusiastic." I could feel him smiling next to me, but I couldn't look his way.

"We've only been going out for a few months. I never even—" I stopped myself and sighed, putting my face in my hands. Lee always had a way of stealing the truth from me. He didn't need to hear about my lack of intimacy with his brother, though.

He was quiet for a minute and then tapped my leg softly, sending a shiver down my spine. "I told Momma you were having such a great time, but you got into the pecan pie and gave yourself a wicked stomachache like you do, so you had gone home to rest it off. She's sorry to have missed you, but she's glad you had a good time."

I tucked a strand of hair behind my ear and finally turned to face him. "Thanks, Lee. I mean it."

"Don't mention it." We pumped our legs together in unison, letting the chair swing back and forth, our eyes having a conversation we were both too anxious to have ourselves.

"Let me walk you home," he finally said, breaking the silence but not our eye contact. "You have someone up in that apartment of yours I am just dying to see."

When we got to my place, Pickle greeted Lee with a full symphony of howls, screeches, and hisses, showing him more affection in twenty minutes than she'd ever shown anyone before. Then, she plopped down by the window for a nap, clearly exhausted from her marathon of love.

"Look at her all cuddled up cozy. She's still the cutest thing I've ever seen." He was trying to make me believe he was talking about the cat, but he was staring straight at me.

I had kept a good distance between us in the kitchen. When we had climbed up the back staircase up to my apartment, the air felt charged, buzzing with the echoes of old memories. I could almost feel the ghosts of our younger selves, sneaking up those stairs together, whispering secrets in the dark, cool hallway, trying not to wake up Charlie or Uncle Cole or hint at what we were planning to do behind my bedroom door.

"This place hasn't changed a bit." Keeping his eyes trained on me, he took a sip of the tall, cold Jack and Coke I had poured for him. It pained me how much I liked to see him smiling at my kitchen table, eyes locked on mine and talking to me so effortlessly.

A small smile escaped my lips. "I'd like to paint it someday and brighten it up. The walls are all yellow from folks smoking in the bar—it comes up through the vents. Everything needs to be replaced, but since you and Charlie are best friends forever still, I'm sure you've heard the bar is in the red."

He nodded knowingly, taking another sip. His mind was racing, I could tell.

"How long will you be in town?" I didn't want to know. I didn't want to ask. But I had to.

"Few days, maybe a week. I don't have much worth running back to Nashville for, at least. Charlie and I are making some plans, and I think Momma wants me to sing for her bridge club. Better than any gig I'm getting back there." He sounded sad and defeated, like he was giving up on something. I wanted to cross the room and pull him into my arms, kiss his forehead, and let his blond wisps tickle the top of my nose.

I let out an annoyed sigh instead.

"You are clearly done with me, so I should go. Thanks for the drink. And the reunion with my two favorite girls."

I rolled my eyes. "Leland Wilder, don't you dare start putting on the charm. I've had enough Wilder man drama today to last me a damn lifetime."

"You have no idea how much I regret that we're standing so far apart in this kitchen. That you had a day like today that would lead you to say something like that. Every single move you and I have made these past few years has led us to this moment, and it's nothing like I thought it would be." He crossed the room in three quick steps and grabbed both of my hands in his, lacing our fingers together. I hadn't felt an electric charge like that in a long, long time, and my body reacted the way it always did when Lee Wilder touched me. "Standing here with you, feeling this distance between us, it just feels… sad. Like everything's left unfinished and there's a million things still hanging in the air."

My heart was pounding in my chest. I was staring at his lips knowing, remembering, how sweet and salty they tasted. How soft they felt. How they fit mine so, so perfectly. Unlike anyone else.

An image of his brother popped into my head. One of my best friends. My fiancé, if things had gone his way this afternoon. I broke our linked hands and turned away from Lee's sad, knowing eyes. "I'm sure I'll see you around sometime, Lee."

"I sure hope so, Maggie. I really do."

CHAPTER ELEVEN

Lee

I left Maggie's and took a walk down by the river, not ready to go back to the hotel. Not ready to face whatever I was avoiding. Ryan, who'd given my mother's party the slip in favor of a historical trolley ride through the city, texted to say he was stopping by a bar before heading back. Typical.

I paused at one of the old picnic benches by the water, the kind Maggie and I would hang out on as kids, and sank into it like it could somehow offer me answers. The sun had just dipped below the horizon, casting the city in shadows that stretched long over the river. I stared out at the dark water, watching as the city flicked on its lights, like Savannah was starting to wake up as the night crept in.

My phone buzzed again, snapping me out of my thoughts.

"Hey, baby," Janelle's voice was smooth, cool, but there was something else underneath it. Something familiar I wasn't sure I was ready to deal with. "How was your momma's party? I was waiting to hear from you."

I let the words hang there, like a reminder of everything I was trying not to think about. There was an ache in my chest, something I couldn't ignore anymore, even though I was pretty damn good at it.

I pressed the phone to my ear, but all I could hear was the city, the rush of the river, and the whisper of my own thoughts.

Thoughts of *her.*

In all the excitement that came with the day, I had forgotten to call Janelle before the party started. Instead, I was creeping around my parents' house, stalking my ex-girlfriend until I found her in a bathtub, then watching with amusement when my idiot brother tried to pull a fast one on her and she wasn't having it.

My whole day had been centered around Magnolia, but that was nothing new when I was on my home turf.

"I'm sorry, doll. Today just got the best of me, I guess. How's Nash?"

Janelle yammered on about her trip to the gym, brunch with the girls, and the four hours she spent shooting some outfits for an upcoming Instagram promotion. The more she talked, the more my mind drifted back to Maggie.

"Are you listening, sugar?" she cooed. I'd caught the tail end of her saying something about the paparazzi.

My phone buzzed again with a text from Ryan.

RYAN: Turns out, this bar I'm at is owned by a gorgeous redhead. She looks crazy familiar. You should stop by.

I glanced down at the message, and a knot tightened in my stomach. He was at O'Malley's. And Lord only knew what was going to come out of his mouth.

"Janelle, I have to run. My momma needs some help cleaning up after the party. I'll call you later," I said, hopping off the picnic bench and moving as fast as my feet would take me toward Magnolia's bar.

"Love you," she said, for the first time in our quick courtship.

"Same, bye." I didn't know what possessed me to say it, but I did.

And it was obvious that I didn't feel it, so saying it was stupid. I'd probably just opened a door I wouldn't be able to shut without a major fight. It felt uncomfortable. Guilty. A flicker of regret passed through me as I imagined the hope on her face just before I hung up on her.

But that feeling was short-lived because I moved briskly through the darkened streets of Savannah toward that old bar on McDonough Street. I stopped by Sixpence Pub quickly for a bourbon in a to-go cup, trying to appear like I had been out on the town instead of sulking down by the river.

I'd been up in the apartment earlier, but pushing open the door to the bar felt surreal. Back in high school, the bar was like our unofficial hangout spot—a common room for the five of us. Cole let Charlie, Dane, and me hook up a video game system to the big TV while the girls did homework—or secretly plotted our demise. We'd all munch on pizza from Vinnie Van GoGo's and sip cold sodas from the fountain behind the bar, the place buzzing with the kind of energy only teenagers can bring.

I stepped into the dark barroom, surveying the empty pub before me. Ryan sat at the long wooden bar to my right, and the tables that peppered the length of the room were empty. As was the stage.

When Cole was running things and the bar was in its prime, local acts from all over Georgia would come to sing at O'Malley's. I remember begging Cole to let me grace the stage.

"Welcome to O'Malley's," a short, voluptuous bartender called as I let myself in. Her hair was tied up in space-knots on the top of her head, and she had her O'Malley's t-shirt cut to reveal her ample cleavage and tied tightly in the back to show off her abs. At first glance, she looked somewhat familiar, but I couldn't place her.

I scanned the bar for Maggie and found her doing busy work on the other side of the room.

"What's up, my man!" Ryan hollered, and Maggie, who was busily washing dishes, finally looked up. Her face fell.

I took a seat next to Ryan, and Maggie quietly fixed me a Jack and Coke, setting it in front of me after finishing what she was doing.

"Thought I got rid of you today." Her tone was aggressive, but I saw the small trace of a smile playing at the corners of her lips.

"Well, we can't let this clown out on the loose unattended, can we?" I patted Ryan's back, and then leaned into my drink and took a generous sip.

"It's nice to see you in here again," Maggie said. She looked a little more relaxed, as she normally did when she was behind the bar, and it was as if the moment that passed between us less than an hour ago hadn't even happened. She leaned over the bar and shot a quick, sideways glance at Ryan. "Your friend is very, very drunk."

As if on cue, Ryan shot his head up. "Hey, where's the chef? She's smoking hot."

Maggie and I both scoffed and rolled our eyes.

"Well, she should be gracing us with her presence momentarily. She's just finishing things up at the Wilder house." Maggie vigorously wiped at nothing on the bar, shooting glances at the door every now and again.

"Is my brother stopping by? Maybe we should go," I offered when I caught on.

"I don't think so. I haven't heard from him since, well, the incident." She let out a long sigh and topped off her own glass with some Diet Coke.

"Oh snap, did I miss some drama today?" Ryan perked up, and the familiar-looking bartender slowly made her way down to our end of the bar so she didn't miss any of the good gossip.

"Nope. No drama, just a good ole fashioned Savannah shindig." Magnolia shot daggers at her employee, who scooted back toward the opposite end of the bar to continue her side work.

"I'm sorry," was all I could offer, and Magnolia shrugged, locking eyes with me while sipping her drink.

"Stop apologizing," she said quietly. For the first time, I noticed how tired she looked. It had to be a lot, juggling the bar, a boyfriend, her social life, and the contributions to Savannah society that my mother had roped her into.

I shot her a sly smile. "I just can't think of anything better to say, I guess."

"Kasey here has it bad for your brother. Let's not give her any more ammunition." Magnolia turned to busy herself by the register, and I studied Kasey a bit.

It took me a moment to place her, but then it all came back. She went to high school with us and had the biggest crush on my brother. Of course, time and circumstance made her look somewhat older and a little worse for wear. I remembered a few early mornings when Dane was home for his holiday breaks, and she would creep down the staircase of my parents' house, slowly and quietly so she didn't wake Momma and have to face her wrath.

Deciding not to let Magnolia in on that little tidbit, I changed the subject. "So, how long have y'all been seeing each other?"

Magnolia let out a long, dramatic groan. She knew this was coming at some point. If I wanted her friendship back—and I absolutely did, more than anything—I was going to have to accept the world she was living in now.

A world in which I no longer existed.

She finally looked up at me, a hint of weariness washing over her. "A few months. Things got a little murky after my uncle passed away, so I wouldn't exactly call that period romantic, but he was by my side the entire time. Never left it. I don't know if that was because of the friendship we'd had all our lives or our new dating relationship; it's hard to tell. He helped get everything together for the memorial, helped out with the bar when I had a few nervous breakdowns here and there. He's a great person. I just…"

"I should have called. I'm really sorry about that," I interrupted, partly because I don't think she really heard me when I told her so outside of Clary's and partly because I didn't want to hear her go on about her relationship with my brother anymore. Even though I was the idiot who asked in the first place.

"Saying sorry again, huh? But you should have, you're right." She leaned over the bar again, resting her chin on her hands. "But that's in the past, and there's nothing either of us can do about it now. What's done is done."

Our eyes met again, and we held each other's gaze for a few beats, silently sharing a conversation only we could hear. Regret and sorrow hung heavily between us.

And a tinge of forgiveness.

She may not have wanted me to say that I was sorry a thousand times over, but I was. And she knew it. When you'd been friends with the same group of people your whole life, sometimes you didn't have to say the big things over and over because you'd been there through everything. Through braces and puberty, through first kisses and fights. First loves, first breakups, and first heartbreaks. We'd done that all together. So, when you told someone you'd known your whole life that you were sorry, they knew when you meant it. And if they loved you, like they'd always loved you, they'd forgive you.

The door to O'Malley's burst open, pulling us both out of our trance, and Sutton strolled through with her arms full of my momma's signature takeout containers.

"Who's hungry, bitches?"

"Me. I am starving," Ryan hiccupped, eyeing Sutton up and down as she placed the containers on the counter and dropped into the seat next to him, giving him a quick one-over.

She leaned back in her chair and reached across Ryan to rub my back a bit. "It's good to see you here."

Magnolia had gone to work fixing Sutton a drink, and we all dug into the leftovers.

"Save some for me," Charlie called out, coming from the back hallway that led to the apartment. He took the seat to my left and patted my shoulder.

"Magnolia, I put an extra case of wine in the back hallway. It's leftover from the party, and Jordan said you can just sell it off."

"Thanks," she offered, but her voice held a soft, somber note.

Between bites and refills on our drinks, the four of us fell into an easy rhythm, the kind that only came from years of shared stories and memories. Charlie leaned back in his chair, shaking his head as Sutton launched into a tale that had Magnolia laughing so hard she had to wipe a tear from her cheek. I couldn't help but smile at the sight of her like that—completely at ease, her laughter spilling out like she didn't have a single care in the world.

The bar hummed with an energy I hadn't felt in a long time, the kind that only came with being surrounded by people who knew every version of you and loved you anyway. The sound of their voices, the overlapping chatter, felt like stepping into a song I hadn't heard in years but still knew all the words to.

Ryan, on the other hand, was trying his best to follow along, nodding too much and laughing a beat too late. It was clear he was out of his depth, and maybe a little too drunk to keep pace, but no one seemed to mind.

"Lee, why don't we take him into Cole's old room to lie down for a bit," Maggie offered, coming around the front of the bar. "There's a TV in there, and I just changed the sheets."

She pulled a key ring from her back pocket and padded down the hall as I helped Ryan off his barstool and across the room. Cole had added an extra bedroom for himself when Maggie and Charlie got a little too old for their bunk beds. Charlie took Cole's old room, and Maggie had her own space as a teenager, something I took advantage of as much as I could.

I set Ryan down on the full-sized bed. "Bathroom's over there," I pointed, dragging a waste bucket across the room and placing it by the bed. "Just in case."

Ryan's eyes had shut quickly, and Maggie and I both felt the electric charge of being together, somewhat alone, in a small, confined space.

"Remember when you were going to turn this space into a green room?" I said, looking around. My eyes fell on a picture frame housing a snap of Magnolia and Charlie the year they moved to Savannah. Knobby knees, freckles, and wild curls covered both siblings.

"I had big plans for this place. Turns out, I'm probably going to have to sell it." She opened the door that led into Cole's office, now belonging to her, and crossed the room to sit behind the big steel desk. She opened up the bottom drawer and took out a capped bottle of Maker's Mark and two rocks glasses and poured us both a finger of the warm, amber liquid.

"Sell it? Why would you do that?" I took the seat across from her and sipped slowly on my drink, keeping one eye on her. This was the first time all day that she looked relaxed around me.

"Well, as you can see, it's 10:30 on a Saturday night in Savannah, and there's not a soul in sight that doesn't belong to me personally. I mean, except for you and your friend." She shrugged, pulling back on her own glass.

I cracked a small, sideways smile. "I don't belong to you, huh?"

Magnolia snorted and leaned back, looking up at the ceiling. "Sometimes I wonder if you ever really did."

The words stung, but she was being honest, and it had been a long time since the veil lifted between us and she could speak freely. The fall when we got together changed our communication style. She was no longer my best friend who could say anything. She'd turned into a girlfriend, for the first time ever, and had begun to choose her words wisely. It was one of the greatest downfalls of our relationship. It was what ended everything.

I went to open my mouth to tell her that I did belong to her when the office door flew open.

"What are y'all doing back here?" My brother, drunk as a skunk, teetered in the doorframe, casting both of us a suspicious look through slitted, half-open eyes.

"Talking, clearly. With a desk between us. Not quite sure that warrants the dirty look you've got plastered on your face right now." Maggie's tone was calm, yet firm, and I knew she was trying to shut down an argument before it began. A situation I was very familiar with.

"You really couldn't help yourself, could you?" my brother slurred, shooting daggers at me. He went to take a step forward and tumbled to the side, knocking over some photos Maggie had lined up on a bookshelf.

"Dane, get out of my office. Now. Get in an ride share, go home, and you can talk to us tomorrow when you've slept it off." Still in her chair, Maggie spun around to face the back wall, effectively turning away from her drunk boyfriend looming in the doorway.

"It doesn't surprise me in the least that you'd go slumming the second you had the chance," Dane spat before slamming the door and stomping off. I heard him crash into a table, and Sutton's gentle voice as she led him away from

Maggie's office.

"Maggie, please tell me you do not allow that man to talk to you like that ever?" She'd swiveled back around and topped off both of our drinks.

Her eyes were glazed over with a thin film of tears. "Every single one of us has been acting a little out of character since your plane landed in Georgia, Lee Wilder. I know we're all glad you're here, believe me, but I think you need to remember that when you left, you left different versions of the people you've seen today."

"That's not true. Dane's still an asshole," I laughed, but that laughter didn't reach across the desk whatsoever.

"I like your brother, Lee. I've been having a great time getting to know him on a relationship level. He treats me kindly, he supports me, believes in me, and he gives me the space and freedom to be myself."

She said the words, alright, but I knew Magnolia Pruitt better than anyone.

She didn't believe a damn word of what came out of her mouth.

CHAPTER TWELVE

Magnolia

I scooted everyone out of the bar and locked up behind them, closing earlier than I normally would on a Saturday night. But with no patrons aside from my friends, and coming off of one of the longest days I'd had in a long time, I was pretty much toast by midnight.

I had Lee shoot Ryan a text, so when he woke up in the morning with a raging hangover and no clue where he was, he wouldn't think he'd been kidnapped and stashed in the back room of a bar. Which, technically, he kind of was, but no need for him to panic about it.

After trudging up the back staircase, washing the day off my face, and slipping into some sweats, I laid on the couch and mindlessly scrolled through my phone while watching some bogus reality show on Netflix.

Pickle jumped up and curled herself into a ball in the crook of my legs, making mashed potatoes on my calves and purring loudly. I scratched her little calico head. "I missed you, too, my little Pickle Pie. Did you have an exciting day, too?" She yawned and dramatically plunked her head on my legs, letting her little beady, green eyes close—probably drifting off to a dreamland starring Lee Wilder himself.

I had seventeen text messages from Dane, and none of them were kind. Most of them accused me of cheating on him with his brother, and one went so far as to call me a washed up bartender who was using him to further my status in Savannah society.

I might have been washed up, but being a part of the Savannah elite was never on my radar. It was on everyone else's but mine.

The last text message, before he passed out I had to guess, was a garbled hodgepodge of letters and numbers, but peppered in there was an ultimatum. I took a screenshot of the messages and sent them to Sutton.

SUTTON: So, he called you trash, accused you of cheating on him with his brother, and then said if you don't move in with him, he's breaking up with you? Am I deciphering this right?
MAGNOLIA: All translations of these drunken hieroglyphics seem to point to that conclusion, correct.
SUTTON: He was shit-faced. I know that's not an excuse, but his behavior when he's drinking has been really off the wall lately.
MAGNOLIA: Right. I'm off to watch shitty reality TV and forget about this day. Love you.
SUTTON: Love you more.

***

I was ripped from a deep sleep by the sound of my phone ringing obnoxiously, and a loud banging coming from downstairs in the bar.

"Hello?" I answered groggily, trying to see the clock through a mass of Pickle's fur as she slept soundly on my head.

"Maggie, I'm on my way over," Lee said, sounding rushed. "Ryan's still drunk, I think, and he's convinced he's been kidnapped. Did you lock him in Cole's room?"

I jumped up, knocking Pickle to the ground. She let out a wild shriek and shook her body sleepily, then shot me a dirty look and stretched herself out.

Throwing on a hoodie and sliding myself into some slippers, I flew down the back staircase and opened the door to the bar. "Yes, of course I did," I said breathlessly into the phone. "Imagine waking up drunk and finding out you're unattended in a bar. And let's be real. I don't know this kid from Adam. What if he crept up into my apartment last night and threw up in my hair?"

Lee's laugh came softly through the phone. "That's what you're worried about? Throw up in your hair?" I heard him getting into a car, shutting the door, and telling a driver where to go.

"I mean, yeah, I just had a keratin treatment." I slowly opened the door to Cole's bedroom. Ryan was crouched in the corner, and the smell of urine smacked me in the face. I shuddered. "Did you pee in the bed?" I bellowed, flipping on the light switch.

Ryan shrank back and threw his hands up over his face. "Don't murder me!"

"Ryan, it's Magnolia!" I put my phone down and flung back the sheets, checking for wet spots.

"I peed in the bucket. I'm sorry. How did I get here?"

"There's a toilet over there in the bathroom, you idiot!" I put my hand over my nose to cover up the smell and to hide the fact that I was about to burst out laughing in this poor man's face. I marched past Ryan and opened the curtains and the window to let in some fresh air. "You were drunk last night. Very, very drunk. We let you sleep in the bedroom down here. This used to be my uncle's room."

Ryan nodded and looked around. "Why did you lock me in here like a captive?"

"Because I don't know you, aside from the fact that you like to drink in excess, and there's a lot of booze out there." I motioned to the barroom and saw a figure standing in the doorway, peering through the windows. "Your knight in shining armor is here. I'll go let him in," I called behind me.

I opened the door, and Lee, holding three delicious-smelling coffees, seemed taken aback. I was sure I looked like a swamp monster, but let's be real, I was ripped from sleep by chaos. I still had no idea what time it was.

Lee studied me for a second, and his eyes lit up. "Nice hoodie."

I grabbed the coffee from him and closed the door to the bar, locking it shut. I peeked down at my sleep shorts, fuzzy slippers, and my Savannah Academy hoodie.

Or, rather, Lee's Savannah Academy hoodie.

"This old thing? No clue where it came from." I placed the coffees down on a table in the middle of the bar and made my way to Cole's bedroom to retrieve Ryan and my cell phone.

I shot Charlie a text and dialed Sutton, watching Ryan slump down in an old mahogany chair. He let his cheek rest on the cool, sticky table.

"We need pancakes," I said when Sutton answered, hopping behind the bar to whip up a pitcher of Bloody Marys and some ice water. "And we need Advil.

And Jesus. Charlie's on the way—he's grabbing candied bacon and some biscuits from Collins Quarter."

"I'm on it," Sutton said before clicking off the phone.

"Y'all are like the Avengers," Ryan said, his face still smooshed into the table.

"These guys are professionals," Lee offered, watching me move quickly behind the bar. "There's not a hangover in town this squad can't handle."

I pried the lid off the coffee cup with my name on it and laughed. Light cream, no foam, sprinkle of cinnamon.

He remembered.

I dropped the waters and the pitcher of Bloodys onto the table, the sound of glass clinking against wood cutting through the low hum of conversation. As I unlocked the door, it barely had time to swing open before Sutton came barreling through, Charlie close on her heels. She threw a quick nod in our direction, her no-nonsense energy rippling through the room, and made a beeline for the bar.

In one fluid motion, she unpacked her portable griddle and plugged it in, her hands moving with the kind of precision that came from years of practice in the kitchen. The scent of warm oil and sizzling batter wasn't far behind.

Meanwhile, Charlie eyed the layout of tables like a general plotting strategy. With a low grunt, he dragged one closer, then another, until he'd transformed the mismatched arrangement into a long, sprawling table that demanded attention. And a tablecloth. Ryan shot him a bemused look, but Lee just leaned back in his chair, smirking like he'd seen this routine a hundred times before.

"Do we need all that room?" I asked, plating the finished pancakes for Sutton.

"Jordan and Doyle are coming by. They had a long night, too. Doyle's sister, the one that lives in New York, just found out she's pregnant. I guess she doesn't even know the guy." Charlie passed the Advil bottle down the table, then scooted into the back office and, as if having read my thoughts, reappeared with a long tablecloth.

"Did they just seriously pull off a brunch in five minutes?" Ryan finally sat up and started in on the beverage buffet before him.

"This is Savannah, we've been trained to throw impromptu parties since we were in the womb," Lee answered, smiling at me from across the room.

Jordan and Doyle opened the door to the bar carrying plates of cheese, a few bottles of champagne, and two bouquets of flowers. I pulled two pitchers down from a shelf and filled them a quarter of the way up with water. Doyle reached over the bar and handed me the bouquets to put in the makeshift vases.

"Which one's Lee?" he leaned in and whispered, eyeing the table suspiciously.

"The cute one," Sutton laughed, flipping the pancakes.

I rolled my eyes. "The one in the backwards baseball cap. Who keeps staring at me."

Jordan joined Doyle at the bar, and they both turned slowly, but not at all discreetly, toward Lee.

"He's way cuter than Dane," Doyle offered, and Jordan whacked his arm. "But not cuter than my husband," he added with a wince. Jordan giggled and took the pitcher of mimosas I'd made, bringing them to the table. "But seriously, he's super hot," Doyle added when Jordan was out of earshot.

I ignored him, turned on the overhead speakers, and cued up a light acoustic playlist, cradling my phone in the docking station. Sutton and I carried plates of food to the table and joined our friends. By the time we sat down, Doyle was now in full swing telling the tale of his sister, Tally, and her New York City antics.

"So, how do y'all know each other?" Lee asked, pointing between the lot of us.

"Jordan and Doyle own the wine shop next to my studio. They own the entire building, actually, and I rent from them," my brother shared, passing his plate of biscuits down the table.

"And we adopted them," Sutton added. "Jordan's from New York, and Doyle's from Newnan, a few hours north of here."

"Jordan supplies the bar with wine, and we work together on the Historical Holiday Tour every year," I noted, smiling at Jordan across the table.

Lee watched us all with a faint, melancholic smile, and I couldn't help but wonder how tough it must be for him to return to our lives and feel like an outsider. I sent him a sympathetic glance from my end of the table, and he responded with a casual shrug. It was another one of those unspoken exchanges we often shared.

Jordan, catching the silent interaction, broke the quiet. "So, where's Dane Wilder, Esquire, this morning?"

Everyone shifted uncomfortably in their seats.

"Probably sleeping it off," Sutton huffed, giving me the side eye.

"Everyone had a rough night last night, huh?" Doyle said, jutting his chin at Ryan, whose eyes began closing slowly now that he was in a food coma.

"You gonna tell them? Or am I?" Sutton grumbled, nudging me under the table. I shook my head and fired her a warning-shot look. "Dane sent Magnolia a bunch of nasty texts last night and told her if she didn't move in and marry him, he would break up with her."

I whacked Sutton on the arm and glanced around the table. Everyone had turned to stare at me, their mouths hanging open, Lee's face burning with rage.

"He was drunk. He didn't mean it." I looked at my brother for some help, but he shook his head and turned his attention to the bacon in front of him.

"What is it?" Lee said through gritted teeth, staring Charlie down.

"Charlie, don't," I warned, but Charlie had an audience now.

"That's not the first time he's said something shitty to her."

I scooted my chair away from the table, and Sutton grabbed it, pushing me back in.

"Is this an intervention?" I laughed nervously.

"No, but..." my brother started, leaning across the table. "I think we can all agree that you don't deserve to be talked to like you're garbage. It gets worse when he's drunk." Charlie sat back in his chair, and Lee looked like he was going to pounce.

"That's not true," I whispered. But it was true, and almost everyone at the table knew it.

The beginning of our relationship was wonderful, and Dane was always so doting, showering me with attention, affection, and praise. As time went on, though, he became hot and cold. I never knew what to expect.

Right on cue, my phone buzzed from the charging dock where it rested.

"We're all here, so that has to be him," Sutton mused, as I pushed back from the table and reached over the bar for my phone. I rushed toward my office and shut the door behind me before answering.

"Hey," I said, slightly out of breath.

"Magnolia, I am so sorry—why do you sound like you've been jogging?"

I plopped down in my office chair and ran my hands through my bed-head. "I'm downstairs. We sort of all assembled for an impromptu brunch, and I ran into my office to talk to you."

"I suppose I'm not welcome after what I said last night, am I?" He sounded almost upset with himself, but I could tell he was more upset with me. Or maybe I just felt that way after the conversation at the brunch table.

"It's not that, Dane. I'm not that petty," I lied.

"Is my brother there?"

I paused, covering the phone to muffle the deep sigh that escaped. "He's here. Ryan had to crash in Cole's room last night—he was too drunk to function. Lee showed up to take him home."

"Aha, and then the rest of our friends just happened to show up? And no one called me?" His voice grew slightly louder, tinged with agitation.

"Well, frankly, Dane, I didn't expect you to be awake so early after last night. We should have sent a message, so I apologize."

"That's a good girl," he cooed like I was a Goldendoodle who had learned how to sit pretty. "I'd like to take you to lunch this afternoon. Can you be ready by 1:00? I'll send a car. I want to talk to you about what happened last night."

"Which part?" I laughed.

"All of it. If you don't want to get engaged now, that's fine, Magnolia, but I do think we should move in together. Living above that dirty old bar has got to be getting old, and besides, if you decide to sell it, you'll need a place to live when it's all said and done."

I leaned back and ran a hand over my face. "I can't do lunch today, but I'll call you later. I'll think about it, alright?"

Dane cleared his throat, the sound sharp with agitation. "Fine. I'll talk to you later."

I slipped back into the bar, the buzz of conversation and clinking glasses filling the air around me. I set my phone down with a soft click, the sound sharp in the quiet of the moment. As I sank back into my seat, my gaze drifted over the room—Lee was gone. Ryan's head had fallen onto the table, his slow, steady breathing the only sign of life.

"Where did he go?" I turned to Sutton, whispering.

"He didn't say, but I bet we can both guess."

After finishing up our brunch and throwing Ryan in a cab with Sutton so he could go nap it off in his hotel room, Charlie and I took the leftover pitchers of mimosas into my office to look over some more paperwork.

It was coming up on crunch time, and I had a decision to make, and soon. Dane and Vance had me all but convinced I should sell the bar and the property, and it was probably the best decision, but my heart wouldn't—couldn't—put a for sale sign on something that had been in my family for so long.

"I think we talked about this before, but what about knocking down the back half of the bar and putting a kitchen in? You could open it up to a lunch crowd, or even brunch. Our little shindig went just fine today." Charlie was absent-mindedly scrolling through social media, not paying attention at all to the stack of papers in front of him. "You should be posting more on the bar's Instagram. I told you, use hashtags."

I whirled around in a circle in my chair and then sunk my forehead into my palms. Still in my brunch outfit, sans bra, I looked and smelled like a dumpster.

"Where am I going to get the money for that kind of renovation? My trust fund from when Cole sold Mom and Dad's store went to part of your tuition, and I've had to drain the rest to keep this place open. You used your share for the part of the studio. I don't know…"

"The Wilders will loan you the money, but it would be more like a dowry for marrying Dane, I suppose."

I growled at my brother. "I brought it up to Eunice and Vance over dinner a few weeks ago. Just to put out some feelers. Dane brought up that the building itself would give me enough money to sit pretty for a while until I figured out my next move. Eunice and Vance agreed. They don't want to help me, Charlie. They want me to cash in what I have, move into that high-rise of Dane's, and plan my wedding over tea with the rest of Savannah society. Eunice invited me to bridge. *Me. To bridge.*"

Charlie let out a small chuckle and leaned over my desk, locking eyes with me. "Don't do anything you don't want to do, Magnolia. You're not shackled to this place or to the Wilder family. You don't owe anyone anything."

My brother meant well, but he was flat out wrong. I owed *everything* to the Wilders. When I tossed my application for UGA in favor of going to community college and letting Charlie have part of my trust fund, they offered to pay my tuition, no questions asked.

When I left community college and started working at the bar full time, Eunice filled up my social calendar quickly so that I could network and make connections with other local business owners to help me bring the bar to the next level, instead of remaining a divey, hole in the wall. And when Uncle Cole died, and I was short on funds for the funeral, they hopped right in and helped me and Charlie pay for everything. Not to mention the fact that, over the last eighteen years, they'd made us feel like family.

I owed a lot to them. I owed them everything.

"I just wish things weren't so damn complicated," I finally blurted out.

"Like with the bar or the fact that your ex-boyfriend just waltzed back into our lives and it's throwing quite the wrench into everything."

"Both," I admitted.

"For what it's worth, baby sister, I'm glad he's home. I can see the chains that lead to that big old house on Jones Street starting to strip. It's a good thing."

"Oh, shut up. I like being with Dane. Lee showing up now after all this time changes absolutely nothing."

"Right, let's all keep telling ourselves that." My brother stood and walked behind my desk, planting a kiss on the top of my head. "Don't make any rash decisions just yet, love. We will figure it out. We always do."

***

After showering the remnants of last night's chaos off my skin and making a half-hearted attempt to look human again, I straightened up my apartment, tossing clothes into the laundry basket and pushing scattered papers aside. Once I'd gotten things in order, I trudged downstairs, the quiet of the early afternoon wrapping around me. I was sorting through the beer bottles when a knock at the bar door pulled me out of my rhythm.

"Peace offering. It's tacos from Lizzie's. I remembered that you used to eat about forty-five of these in one sitting. My hotel is right down the street from there, so I figured I'd just, well. Okay, I'm sorry. I wanted to talk to you. But also, tacos." Lee was standing in front of me, holding out a takeout container of delicious-smelling tacos with a stupid, panty-dropping grin strapped on his face.

"Come on in. I figured I would be bailing you out of jail today for beating up your brother, the way you stormed out of here." I walked back behind the bar, and Lee took a high top seat across from me.

"I had to talk myself out of that. I went for a run and hit the gym at the hotel instead."

My eyes shot down to his white t-shirt, clinging to his chest and showing off his seriously impressive muscles. I scanned over a tattoo that sprawled across his arm and peeked out from under his shirt, winding across his pecs. I caught myself staring and went back to counting beer bottles. "Well, I'm proud of you, then. That's more of an effort than I put in today. So what brings you by?"

He leaned over the bar, snagging one of the bottles I'd been counting. With a swift motion, he popped the cap off against his forearm, his muscles flexing as he did, giving me a brief but undeniable reminder of how much time he'd put into working on his body. "Well, I've been thinking it over since I got back. Honestly, I was already considering it before I came home. But now? I'm leaning toward sticking around."

I snapped my head up, catching myself on the ice chest in front of me before I toppled over. "What? Why? Wait, what?"

Lee laughed and knocked back his beer. "Not exactly the reaction I was hoping for, but I'll take that shocked bewilderment as a compliment. Anyway, I'll be honest, there's not much for me in Nashville anymore. I can write music anywhere, and I always wrote the best music here."

"What about your label? What about Ryan?" I tried not to sound like I was in the middle of a massive panic attack, but I could feel my heart trying to escape from my chest and run down the street as if it had been set on fire.

"It will all work out. I talked to my manager about it some this morning after I left. This is my home, Magnolia. I belong in this city, with you… you guys. My friends." He leaned over a bit on his elbows and locked eyes with me. "This morning was exactly what I needed—being with you and your brother, with Sutton. And Jordan and Doyle are a great fit in your friend group. *Our* friend group."

"And Ryan?" I finally asked again, bile rising in my throat.

"I think Ryan wants to stick around, too. We could get a condo together and rent a small studio space. I really think it will work out. I'm even thinking about coming in as a partner for a local business."

"Oh, well, that all sounds nice, I suppose. Which business?" I took in a deep breath and held it.

He leaned back in his chair and looked around the bar. His broad, glistening smile reached his eyes, and I knew that mischievous look from a mile away. "This one."

CHAPTER THIRTEEN

Lee

The look on her face when I mentioned wanting to become a partner in the bar was priceless. Her emotions flickered from shock to wariness to genuine happiness in seconds. But eventually, her expression softened into concern.

My phone buzzed repeatedly in my pocket. I hopped off the stool and walked around the bar, wrapping my arms around her in a long, tight hug. Something I had wanted to do from the second I saw her in Clary's.

"Just think about it," I said gently, as I prowled backwards out of the bar, keeping my eyes on her the entire time. She stood, frozen in her spot, watching me exit with her mouth wide open and her eyes locked on mine. "I'll call you later," I shouted before closing the door to the bar and skipping down the street.

Strutting back toward my hotel on the river, I grabbed my phone out of my pocket. Six missed calls and twelve text messages—all from Janelle.

Fuck. I totally forgot about Janelle in all of my scheming and plotting. A pang of guilt gnawed at me. Maybe I should have let this "situationship" run its course and call it quits. Was I ever really interested in her anyway? That wasn't fair to her. Being back in Maggie's orbit had my head spinning. I dialed her number.

"Hey, I am so sorry. This has been the craziest weekend," I said gently when she answered the phone.

"That's alright, baby," she said slowly, but I could hear the anger in her high-pitched tone. I'd heard it multiple times when she was trying to not lash out at her staff or her handlers in public—or at me when I didn't pose for the perfect Instagram photo. "I was just about to call your momma and put out a search party, darlin'. You scared me, that's all. How's Savannah?"

I wanted to tell her about my plans to save Maggie's bar, and about hanging out with my friends and how *real* everything felt for the first time in a long time, but I decided to wait on that and give Maggie time to make up her mind.

"Savannah is great. I've seen some old friends, and I've gotten a work-out in here and there." That would appease her. "And Momma has me set up to sing some background music for her bridge club tomorrow. It will be nice to see some old faces."

"Aren't you flying home tonight?"

I stopped in front of Charlie's studio, watching him in the backroom, door open, working on a piece. Sutton sat, legs crossed, on a stool, plugged in to something on her iPad, but chatting away while Charlie nodded and laughed at whatever was coming out of her mouth. My heart swelled. This was more than just Maggie. I missed my people. My tribe.

"I'm actually hoping to stay for a little while. There's some great material here. Not too much longer, though. Hey, I have to run. I'll call you tonight."

I clicked off the phone before she could fight with me on that and slipped it back into my pocket. It immediately began buzzing with text messages.

The door to Charlie's studio jingled as I pushed it open, and Charlie and Sutton both looked up and smiled—like a warm, across the room hug that I had been missing for so long.

"So, let me get this straight," Sutton said, carrying in takeout bags of charcuterie from next door. "You have a girlfriend, she's not going to want you to stay—like, at all—but you're going to invest in Magnolia's bar because…"

"Because he still loves her," Charlie mused, standing over the sink to wash his hands.

"No, not because I still love her. Not like that anyway," I lied.

"I think it's a good idea." Charlie dried off his hands and stood back to admire his work so far. "She really needs the help—financially, of course. Your brother is going to blow a gasket, though."

"Don't tell me that feral creature you dragged into Savannah is staying with you, too," Sutton said, plating the cheese platters and turning her nose up at the thought of Ryan.

I watched Sutton closely as she arranged the cheeses and meat cuts on a plate with such care. Still so classically beautiful with her sharp features, cool-blue eyes, and flowing blonde curls. Of the lot of us, she had aged the least. It was no wonder Ryan couldn't shut up about her. She still had no clue how beautiful she was, after all these years.

"Ryan will probably be down to stay." I poured us all a round of white wine from Sutton's next-door haul and passed out the glasses. "He's my writing partner. If the label lets me stay, he'll stay."

Sutton popped an olive into her mouth and chewed slowly. I could hear the wheels in her head churning away. "I'm just worried about you staying home and Dane losing his mind over it. You know they're already struggling to keep their shit together as it is. Her giving up the bar was his ammunition to finally gain control over her wild ass."

The way she said it was comical, but all of our faces fell. Maggie sounded like a captive with Stockholm syndrome rather than a woman in love. Charlie's shoulders slumped as he picked at his plate.

I needed honesty from my friends—our friends—if I was going through with this.

"Dane is leaving for a two-week trial in Atlanta tomorrow. I'll head to Momma's and break the news tonight over Sunday dinner. If he has an issue with it, he can tell me rather than her. He doesn't—how do I say this without sounding like an ass…"

"He doesn't beat her. He's not abusive toward her if that's what you're worried about…" Sutton's voice was quiet, contemplative. She rattled her head as if she was shaking off the thought of saying more but stopped herself. My blood was already boiling. "I mean, physically anyway. He's just… Dane. He's a lot like your father in the way that they want what they want and they'll do anything to get it. Even if that means buttering you up real good before dropping you on your head and asking you why you're so slippery, if you catch my drift."

I chewed on that for a second, thinking of my parents' relationship. The way my dad would love and dote on Momma, then in the next moment, blame her for a trial gone wrong because the sheets weren't crisp enough and he slept like shit. My momma was as strong-willed as they came, but Daddy had always been, and always would be, in charge. "I'll take care of it. Momma has a way of making sure that what she wants is pushed through. And she loves Maggie. She would want what's best for her, I hope."

Charlie nodded and finally looked up, meeting my eyes. "I hope you know what you're doing here, Lee. This is my sister we're talking about."

His sister, who, after all these years, I would still do anything for.

CHAPTER FOURTEEN

Magnolia

Dane sat across from me, sipping a Manhattan with the kind of practiced ease that came from a lifetime of Sunday dinners and formal gatherings. His fingers tapped lightly against the glass, a subtle giveaway that he wasn't as relaxed as he wanted to appear. "It's one dinner, Magnolia. My parents will be so disappointed. And I'm leaving for a few weeks."

I stared at the condensation dripping down my water glass, pooling across the bar top, willing it to buy me a moment to think. Kasey's last-minute text asking me to find someone to cover her shift couldn't have come at a better time—a perfectly wrapped excuse to sidestep the storm brewing inside me, and the one I was certain was about to erupt at the Wilder family dining room table.

"I can't tonight," I said, keeping my voice even. "Kasey called in sick, and I need to cover." I gestured around the empty bar. "There's no one else who can do it."

Dane's mouth pressed into a thin line, his frustration barely hidden. He didn't push back, but the weight of his disappointment settled between us, thick and heavy.

The truth was, I wasn't sure I could handle sitting at a dinner table and pretending everything was fine—not after seeing Lee that afternoon, and especially not after the bombshell he dropped about wanting to invest in the bar. My thoughts spun wildly, crashing into each other, too loud and overwhelming to ignore.

I took a sip of water, the coolness doing little to calm the heat rising in my chest. Dane was still watching me, his gaze softening, but I couldn't meet it. Not when the excuses I'd offered, no matter how true, weren't the whole story.

"This trial is expected to last for two weeks, so that should put me home just in time to help you start planning for the Historical Holiday Tour. We should get a jumpstart by Halloween so that we can have everything ordered and ready for Thanksgiving. Or you could just sell the bar, forget the tour, and we could head to Vale for the holiday. Unless you *really* want to go through with this charade."

Since he flung open the bar door earlier, he had been yammering about my options with the bar and how much I could get for the building if I sold it. He painted a pretty picture of bridge club, charitable work, and of course, he was up-selling his condo and the view of the city any chance he could get.

"I'm going to wait until after the first of the year to make a decision," I stated. On all matters at hand, including the bar. "I usually have a pretty good holiday crowd, even though the city is quiet. I booked a Christmas party for Levy's Jewelers, so I want to see that through. It should be good money, open bar and all that."

Dane nodded thoughtfully and finished his drink. "Well, I should head out. I'll call you when my plane lands in Atlanta. I'm staying at the Glenn if you need to get a hold of me."

I smiled, taking a good long look at him before he jetted off. He looked weary, almost tired, which was rare for Dane. "Are you feeling okay?" I asked, rubbing my hands up and down my arms, feeling a sudden chill.

He barked out a cough, clearing his throat. "Something's been going around the office. A couple of the paralegals have been out this week, which has made prepping for this trial hell. I'll be fine. I'll nap on the plane."

He hopped off of his stool, and I met him around the front of the bar and let him kiss me long and slow. For the first time since we had been together, something felt off. Something felt different. But I pushed it down and kissed him back like I meant it.

Because I did, after all. Didn't I?

The second the door shut behind him, I texted Sutton.

MAGNOLIA: Can you stop by? I need to talk to you.
SUTTON: About Lee investing in the bar? Or about Dane bouncing for two weeks and your ex-boyfriend sticking around?

Man, news sure did travel fast.

MAGNOLIA: Can you just come over here, please?

I put my phone down, poured myself a glass of wine, and waited to hash this out with my best friend.

"Tell me it's a bad idea, Sutton. Tell me it's a bad, bad idea." Sutton and I had moved to a table in the corner of the bar, and I watched the door like a hawk, waiting for a patron… or for the Wilder brothers to come bashing through the door, fists flying at one another. Either would be more exciting than just sitting here, waiting with my thoughts.

"I think it's a great idea, honestly. You can turn the bar into the place you always wanted it to be. You can finally get that kitchen addition and put me on staff, and I can go down to part time at LaMonte's. I'm drowning there anyway. Fried chicken, pies, booze, and local talent. You could, conceivably, have it all."

My head was spinning, a light sheen of cold sweat trickled across my brow. Since Lee had waltzed back into Savannah, it felt as though everything was suddenly changing. Rather than selling the bar, I found myself presented with the chance to rescue it. I wasn't sure why my body was reacting to this as negatively as it was.

"Are you having a panic attack?" Sutton asked. She reached over and felt my head. "Dude, you're burning up. Didn't you say Kasey has the flu?"

I felt my cheeks. They were on fire. "I haven't seen her in a few days. I don't know what's wrong with me. Might be the stress."

Sutton studied me for a minute. "Nope, not the stress. Glassed over eyes, sweating profusely. I think you're getting sick, hun."

I growled and sulked into my seat. "I cannot be sick right now. There's too much going on."

Sutton picked up her phone, eyeing me warily. "Your sister isn't feeling well. If you can't come cover the bar, can you send Doyle or Jordan, please? I can't catch the plague. I have to cater Eunice's bridge club tomorrow, and I need to do prep. Bring Lysol." She laid down her phone. "Go lay down," Sutton said to me, scooting her chair back and heading behind the bar. She began wiping it down with disinfectant, shooting me a stern look. "I'm serious, Magnolia, go. Now. I had my flu shot. I'll be okay."

I stomped up my back staircase, hit my bedroom, flopped on the bed, and didn't wake up for a long, long time. When I stirred, I was covered in sweat and cat fur. Pickle had, as she often did, wrapped herself around my head and was licking beads of sweat from my hairline. I let out a groan.

"There are some flu meds and Advil on your nightstand. If you can, try to take it." Lee was looming over me, and I noticed the still darkness outside my open window. He changed out a damp face cloth and replaced it with a cooler one. Pickle hissed at him.

"Your momma doesn't feel good, Pickle, but that's no reason to be ornery. How are you feeling, Maggie?"

My body felt like it was on fire, and my muscles were stiff and achy. I sneezed twice. "I should have got that flu shot," I mumbled.

"Probably. Little late for that now, though. Can I get you anything else?"

I suddenly realized that my ex-boyfriend was playing nurse, and my heart picked up speed. "Where's Dane?"

"Atlanta. His flight left this morning, remember?"

I tried to sit up. My body wasn't a fan of the sudden movement, and the room began to spin. "What day is it?"

"Monday night. You've been out for over twenty-four hours. You wake up every now and again, make a bunch of incoherent noises, and then fall back to sleep. I have to say, you're still super cute when you're out of it."

"Shut up," I groaned. I'd been asleep for more than a day. That meant Lee had told everyone he was staying and that he was investing in the bar, and Dane had left, probably pissed off at me, and I was knocked out for hours on end. I needed to talk to Dane. "Where's my phone?"

"Your boyfriend is fine, albeit a little under the weather himself. He even offered to draw up the contracts for us so I could become a partner in the bar. Sutton told him she would stay with you while you were sick, and Charlie would check in on you from time to time. Of course, I had to beat them both back with a stick to take care of you. They told him you would call when you were feeling better."

I noticed my phone on the nightstand. I had one solo text message from Kasey telling me she felt better but was heading out of town.

"Who's watching the bar?" I croaked out.

"Doyle's down there now. Last I checked, he was acting out his Tom Cruise in *Cocktail* fantasies and flinging around vodka like a baton twirler. I don't think he's broken too many bottles."

I moaned again and flipped on my side, moving my body away from Lee. How had Dane gone twenty-four hours without checking on me?

"Think you can eat yet? Sutton has some soup in the crockpot and…"

I fell back into a deep, dreary slumber as Lee yapped about lemon drop soup and my fever.

CHAPTER FIFTEEN

Magnolia

On the third morning, I woke up perkier than I had before, my body resisting any more sleep. I didn't quite feel strong, but I felt enough like myself to sit up on my elbows.

I was glad to be awake and free from the dreams that had whisked me back into the past. Dreams, or memories, of me and Lee in this room together. The first time, the millionth time, the last time…

Lee was snoring at the foot of my bed, sleeping upright with his back against the wall. Pickle was curled in a ball on his lap, twitching with a case of her own happy dreams. They probably involved Lee, too.

I couldn't look away from his face. Even asleep, he had that same familiar look, the one that hadn't changed since he was eighteen, save for a few more lines etched in from time and life. His chest rose and fell in a slow, steady rhythm, and a warmth started to spread in my chest as I watched him, a familiar pull in my stomach.

No. I shook my head, trying to shake off the feeling. This was not happening—not in my bed, not like this.

I snapped myself back to reality and kicked his leg, my foot connecting harder than I'd planned. His eyes flew open, a confused grunt escaping him as he jerked awake. "Lee, there's another bedroom and a whole couch. Get out of my room."

Pickle flew off his lap with her fur standing up straight on her back, and she pounced around my bedroom floor in her sideways fighting stance.

"Hush now, Pickle," Lee said, stretching his arms out in front of him. She happily obeyed by plopping down and throwing a straight leg into the air, licking her rear end.

Lee turned his attention to me. "If I slept in the other room, I would have missed an awfully nice fever dream of yours, which, if I understood the dialogue correctly, you and I were getting along quite well again."

I let out a yelp and buried my head into my pillow.

"I can't believe you still talk in your sleep. It's so charming."

After a while, I dragged myself out of bed and into the kitchen. Sunlight streamed through the open windows, mingling with the faint smell of paint and bleach hanging in the air. Lee was perched at the kitchen table, cradling a cup of coffee. Next to him, a steaming mug of tea waited patiently. I shot him a glance, my curiosity piqued.

"Did you paint? What happened here?" I asked, taking in the transformation. My once-beige walls were now gleaming white, and the musty cigar-smoke smell had vanished. It looked and smelled amazing.

"Was I in a coma? How long was I out?" My head spun from dehydration, the lingering paint fumes, and sheer bewilderment. I slid into the seat next to Lee, making sure to keep my distance.

"Three days, on and off. I had some free time, so I touched some things up and wiped some things down." He was seriously undermining his hard work. The more I looked around, the more I noticed things he had patched up and deep-cleaned.

"You didn't have to do any of this," I mumbled quietly, staring down into my mug.

He scooted his chair closer to mine and put his hands on either side of my face so fast my head started spinning. "You're right. I didn't. But I wanted to, so I did."

Our faces were practically touching, but I kept my eyes on my lap.

"I'm dating your brother, Lee. We can't be playing house like this," I finally said, the sound coming out muffled since he was still squishing my cheeks.

He let out a long sigh and sat back in his chair with a soft smile. "If all you can offer me is your friendship, then I will gladly take it. But that doesn't mean I won't spend the rest of my days trying to make you happy, even if you think you don't deserve it."

Lee busied himself wiping down all the surfaces with Lysol and collecting a mountain of used tissues before standing in the doorway of the kitchen, leaning against the doorframe and giving me a look that was full of tenderness and quiet longing.

"I'm going to head downstairs for a bit to check on things. Will you text me if you need anything?" he finally asked after watching me for a few minutes.

"Sure," I started, feeling myself overheating from the fever… or from the nerves. "I'm just not sure what to say, Lee…"

He laughed, pushing himself off the doorframe. "Let's wait until you're feeling better, then we'll come up with some creative way for you to thank me."

I rolled my eyes, but my stomach turned around in a million circles. Lee Wilder was flirting with me—again—and my body, sick as a dog, was responding to the call like an old friend. Traitor.

"Oh! There's one more thing. Hang on." He dashed toward the living room, rifling through some bags before rushing back down the hallway. He set an envelope down in front of me.

"Is this the paperwork for the bar sale?" I asked, my fingers nervously tugging at the tab. "I haven't really had a chance to think…" I couldn't finish my sentence, struck silent by the awe I felt. Inside the envelope was something I hadn't seen in years—actual printed photos.

"I found a disposable camera in a shoebox in your room," he said, hovering over my shoulder as I began flipping through the pictures. "Don't worry, I didn't read your diary."

I spun around to face him, a playful, nostalgic grin spreading across both our faces. "This is incredible—look at these! We were so young. This one's from your gig at Lizzie's." I handed him a photo, and he examined it closely. It wasn't just his first gig; it was our first night together.

"Wow," he murmured, studying the next few pictures I showed him. "Look at us. We were so happy back then."

"Young and clueless, more like it," I teased, meeting his eyes again.

A shadow crossed his face, and the mood shifted. "I should get going. I'm glad you're starting to feel better." He dropped his stack of photos on the table where they fanned out like a rainbow of memories and time gone by and shut the door heavily behind him.

I was still sorting through the photos when Sutton came crashing through the door with a key lime pie and two forks. "Ya hungry? Feeling better? Ready to tell me every single detail concerning Lee Wilder locking himself up here for three days and barely letting anyone else in to see you?"

"He was busy, probably didn't want anyone to intervene." I motioned to the bright white walls and polished chrome appliances.

"Holy shit." She sank down next to me, snapped the top off the pie, and dug in. "So, he's staying, right? Please tell me you begged him to stay. I have some work I need done in my condo. Wait, what are these?" She picked up the pile of pictures, her eyes glistening at the memories.

"He had those printed during one of his many trips to the pharmacy. Can you believe it? And we actually didn't really get a chance to talk about him staying much. He did, however, tell me that he would spend the rest of his life trying to make me happy. In a friendly capacity, of course."

"A friendly capacity… right. That sounds legit. Speaking of the Wilder clan, have you talked to your boyfriend?"

My eyes flew wide open, and I darted into my room to check my phone. He still hadn't called or texted to check on me. I shot him a quick text.

MAGNOLIA: Feeling much better. Heard you weren't feeling so hot yourself. How's the trial?

Little conversation dots popped up, then disappeared. "He's probably busy," I shrugged, putting the phone down and spooning up a tiny bite of pie.

"Charlie tried to get the scoop from Lee, but it didn't work. You know who *does* have the intel, though? Ryan."

The way she said his name piqued my interest. I swallowed a cool, tangy bite, but everything still felt like shards of glass going down my throat. "Um, so, are you talking to Ryan? And what exactly did he say?"

She did a little shimmy in her seat. "We're not like *talking*-talking, but when I put him in the Uber after brunch last weekend, he asked for my number so he could refund me the ride bill, and we've been texting here and there ever since. I was on bar duty last night, and he stopped by."

"Thank you for doing that, by the way. So, what did he say?" I leaned my head on my hands, my body fighting the urge to crawl back into bed.

"Well, for starters, he said that there was quite the kerfuffle with Dane and Lee over Lee staying and buying into the bar. I guess Vance got involved, but Eunice actually stepped in and stood up for you, saying that this bar was your home and if Lee wanted to stay and help you out, no one was going to stop him."

The notion of Eunice Wilder standing up to Vance and Dane shocked me. Eunice was a strong woman, but usually, when Vance wanted something done his way, she let him have it gracefully. She called it a Southern woman's charm. I let out a dramatic gasp, then sputtered into a coughing fit.

"Ew, you sound gross. Charlie and I were shocked, too. Anyway, Eunice had Dane fax *her* the agreement, and she's going to call you so you can sign your end of it. I guess she's a notary or something, so she can do some stuff for Vance if there's not a paralegal or an assistant at his beck and call at all hours."

I tried a bit more of the pie but stuck mostly to my tea, listening to Sutton catch me up on three days' worth of gossip, which in our world was akin to a century.

We moved into the living room, and Sutton covered me with a blanket and bounced into my room to get my box of tissues. She came running out with Pickle on her heels, hissing wildly.

"This damned cat. Isn't it like a hundred years old now? Shouldn't she be dead?"

Pickle and I both glared at her.

She sank down on the couch next to me and stuck her feet under the quilt. "So, are you going to do it? Are you going to let Lee buy into the bar?"

I hadn't had much time to process it, but spending three days in close quarters with him, having him care for me—it was a lot for my heart to handle. Especially since I couldn't even get a text back from my boyfriend.

"Well, it would mean Lee and I would be up each other's asses more than I'm comfortable with. I really need to think it through some more. And I should probably talk to Dane about it."

"I thought you two were just friends. What would it matter?" Sutton reached for the remote and started flipping through the channels. "He does look awfully good, though. Those Wilder boys sure do age well. Are you catching feelings?"

"We *are* just friends. And that's all we're going to be from here on out. So no, no feelings have been caught here."

Catching feelings? Caught them eighteen years ago, and they never went away, apparently. What was the difference?

I let out a sigh that turned into a wheeze. "It was awfully nice of him to take care of me, though. And it's pretty obvious he's quite handy with tools and a bucket of paint." I finally noticed that my ceiling fan was working for the first time since I was in high school and the baseboards had a fresh coat of paint as well.

Sutton checked her phone and groaned. "Shit, I have to go. I'm sending Charlie over to cover the bar, though. Jordan and Doyle have me catering—solo, I might add—for a huge fundraiser tonight at their shop. Charlie dropped off some pieces to show, and Lee and Ryan are going to play. I wish you could make it."

For some reason, that set me off real good.

"Why is everyone more successful than me? Charlie's drowning in custom orders. Dane's buried so deep in that trial in Atlanta, he's probably forgotten what daylight looks like. Lee and Ryan? Already snagged a damn Grammy. Jordan and Doyle are running the most profitable business in Savannah. And you? You're over here freelancing appetizers for their fancy fundraising parties. Like, 'Would you like a canapé with a side of crushing existential dread?' Ugh."

I was fully committed to the whining now, and honestly, I didn't care. I felt like I was getting left behind. Again. And on top of it all, I wasn't feeling great. Everyone's allowed a temper tantrum when they were under the weather, right?

Sutton looked at me with soft, sad eyes. "We are not more successful than you, Magnolia. We're just all moving forward instead of hanging on to the past. Every single one of us has faced some sort of hurdle, and we've overcome it. Maybe you should try it?"

"Ouch."

"I know, that was mean. I'm sorry. I love you, but someone had to say it. Let Lee invest in the bar and let go of whatever weird thing you're holding on to. He wants to do it—for reasons that are probably beyond human comprehension—and you need him to do it for reasons that everyone understands, and those reasons are called 'foreclosure' and 'bankruptcy.' So either figure it out on your own, or cut the string that's been tying you two together since the dawn of time and see if you can survive as business partners."

"And what if it doesn't work?"

She kissed the top of my head and shot me a wide-eyed smile. "Then, we'll find you a new dream."

CHAPTER SIXTEEN

Lee

I was sitting across from Momma and Daddy at their ridiculously long dining room table, feeling less than thrilled about the whole situation. They'd summoned me for an official "discussion" about my interest in buying into O'Malley's, but I knew it was more like an interrogation. They were trying to figure out what I was really up to.

Daddy had propped up his laptop in front of Dane's empty chair, where Dane was joining us via video call, scarfing down his room service like he wasn't casually trying to multitask a major family decision that could alter the fate of Magnolia's entire life between bites of filet mignon.

We were all munching, working our way through the mountain of Trust paperwork, and it was clear from the way Momma kept topping off her wine with very generous pours that she was about done with our shit.

"I'm just saying, Leland, if you're serious about running the bar, there may not be room to indulge in your little extracurricular singing activities." Daddy was teetering on the edge of belligerent, his tone somewhere between "concerned father" and "unnecessary life coach."

I stared at him, my mouth hanging open, the words stuck somewhere between my teeth and my throat. Instead of saying something I'd regret—like I usually did—I shoved a huge bite of pasta into my mouth. I chewed, focusing on the texture, the flavors of the meal, anything to keep me from opening my damn mouth.

Dane laughed from the monitor, his head propped against the headboard of his hotel bed like he was settling in for a good show. He briefly glanced at something—or someone?—next to him, the corners of his mouth twitching in a way that made me wonder just how much of this conversation he was actually paying attention to.

"Shut up, Dane," I said childishly. "Laughing away while you haven't even called your girlfriend, who's been sick for days."

"Probably another one of her wicked hangovers, if I had to guess. And where's your girlfriend while you're busy shacking up with mine?" He glared at me through the computer camera. If he had been in the room, in real life, I would have punched him in the jaw.

"What are you talking about?" I spat. "You were sick yourself when you left. Was that a hangover? You know what? I've heard you can be awfully critical—"

"Now, now, boys. Please behave so we can get through this. Leland, you didn't tell me you were seeing someone?" Momma took a gulp of her wine, and I noticed she had barely touched her meal.

"Sorry, Momma," I offered.

"She's one of those social media influencers. The label set them up," Dane piped in, rocking a shit-eating grin. I wanted to jump through the computer. "He still can't get a real date," he added smugly.

My father took his glasses off and rubbed his face with exaggerated frustration. "Enough, you two. I've reviewed the paperwork the accountant from the Trust sent over, and it seems you have more than enough to buy some shares. But money isn't the problem, Lee. Magnolia is the real sticking point here."

Dane rolled his eyes. "If I didn't believe Magnolia was secure in her relationship with *me*, sure, it might be an issue. But she is, so it's not." His smug tone only made my blood boil more.

"That's not what your father means, Dane," my mother said, voice laced with agitation. "He means that she might have trouble handing over more than half of her share to our family. As it stands, she can barely afford to own a quarter of the business. I'm thinking ten percent, and that's generous."

I arched an eyebrow. "I'm going in as a silent partner. She's not handing the bar over to me or to our family."

"That's not what we drew up." My brother forked a bite of steak into his mouth and then washed it down with a sip of red wine. "If you go in as a partner on this, it's not just you that owns the bar, it's the Wilder Family Trust. We will have control over the building and the bar as a unit."

"Are you *freaking* kidding me?" I snapped.

"What, Leland? If you're going to continue to write music and have your career here in Savannah, you're still going to need to travel and head into the studio. The Trust needs to be put into place to make sure the bar stays afloat. It's obvious Magnolia can't be trusted to handle it. She's already run it into the ground." My father didn't meet my eyes when he said it. He just kept thumbing through the paperwork before him like he was casually reading off a lunch menu.

"Because the reality is," my brother interjected, "if you didn't offer buy into the bar—the building and the business—I was going to. This was almost a done deal before you decided to catapult your ass back into our lives."

A sudden shadow flickered in the corner of Dane's screen, and before anyone had the chance to react, he quickly shut off the video.

A moment later, Momma casually glanced down at her phone. "Dane lost connection," she announced, her tone just a touch too innocent. "Said he'll call back later. Anyway, why don't I talk to Magnolia tomorrow? She and I can go over this together."

I raised an eyebrow, biting back a grin. *Lost connection, huh? More like "his connection decided to join him in bed."*

I hadn't heard a single word about Dane investing in the bar—neither from him nor Maggie. If he was so ready to swoop in and save it, why wait on me to invest through the family Trust? Why not just pull the trigger himself?

And who the hell had been lurking in the corner of his screen? I had no idea what Dane, or the rest of my family, was up to, but I was hellbent on figuring it out—and stopping it. I wasn't about to let them sink their claws so deep into Maggie and the bar she loved that both ended up lost forever.

CHAPTER SEVENTEEN

Magnolia

I met Eunice at Rocks On the Roof, perched right above the river. We sprawled across one of those plush, oversized couches, a couple of small plates and a bottle of wine between us, the paperwork sitting in the middle like an unwelcome third wheel.

I stole glances at her from beneath the brim of her massive sunhat, trying to decode her expression. But with her oversized sunglasses and an air of practiced calm, she might as well have been a poker pro holding the world's best bluff.

"You look like you're feeling much better. Leland tells me he did some work on the apartment while you were ill. How very kind of him. It's good he's getting in the swing of fixing up that old building before he becomes partial owner," Eunice rambled.

Something was up with the Wilder matriarch, and I didn't think it had anything to do with her son buying the bar. She handed me another stack of papers, and I'd finally had enough. "Are you going to tell me what's really going on here, or are you going to make me figure it out on my own? Because you haven't touched your food, or your merlot, and you haven't hugged me. All of these things are bizarrely out of character for you."

She removed her sunglasses and shifted in her seat, taking a slow, deliberate sip from her wineglass. For the first time, I noticed how exhausted she looked. Her hair, barely visible beneath the oversized hat, was tousled and unkempt, and she wore barely a trace of makeup. It was clear that the weight of everything had been taking its toll on her.

A far cry from the always-perfect, well put together woman I'd known my whole life.

"You know, I might be dating your son, and, you know, dated your other son, but you've been a part of my life for so long… You can tell me anything, Eunice." I reached over and grabbed her hand, and small tears pooled in the corner of her eyes.

"I need to… talk to you about something," she finally said, sniffling slightly and dabbing at her tired eyes with a cocktail napkin.

"Anything," I said confidently, but my heart was racing. Whatever was on her mind was big—bigger than Lee investing in O'Malley's.

"This is going to sound… Magnolia, this is really hard to say, and what I say today needs to stay between us. Do you understand?"

I nodded and picked up our glasses from the table, handing one to her and holding on to mine for dear life.

"Did you know your momma and I were the very best of friends once? You are so like her sometimes, you know? She was headstrong and smart as a whip. She had the biggest heart in the world."

My stomach dropped. I had no clue that my momma and Eunice were friends. No one had ever mentioned it—not even Uncle Cole. It was like discovering a hidden chapter in our family's history, a bond that had been quietly coursing through our veins all this time—a connection forged long ago by our mothers. "I had no idea. I figured y'all knew each other from around town, but…"

"We more than knew each other. Our relationship was quite like yours and Sutton's. We spent almost every second together until I went away to college. But we had the best times together. Summers on Tybee Island, stealing whiskey from O'Malley's and drinking it after dark in Forsyth Park, exploring the tunnels beneath with nothing but a flashlight and a prayer."

I nodded, not wanting her to stop talking for one second about my momma. She paused for a moment and looked out over the river, letting the memories wash over her. "So, did something happen?" I asked softly, wanting Eunice to come back to me and tell me more. But judging by the look on her face, whatever had gone down between them… it wasn't good.

"Well, there's a lot to the story, but her and I had a falling out when I broke your Uncle Cole's heart."

That was definitely not the best moment to take a sip of wine. The second her words landed, I sputtered, sending a fine mist of merlot across the table—and straight onto Eunice. "Oh, Lord, Eunice, I'm so sorry!" I gasped, half-choking, half-apologizing as the wine burned its way through my nose.

I grabbed at my sleeve in a panic, dabbing at her with all the finesse of a toddler cleaning up a juice spill. My thin sweater soaked through almost instantly, leaving both of us dripping and me flushing with a fresh wave of mortification. Eunice blinked at me, her face caught between horror and amusement, as a single red droplet traced a deliberate path down her cheek.

Eunice motioned for the server, who came running over. "Napkins, please. And two shots of tequila. We may need it."

In all my life, I'd never seen Eunice Wilder take a shot of anything that wasn't meticulously prepared, garnished, and served in the finest glassware. We sat quietly for a moment, and when the shots were dropped off at the table, I'd somewhat regained my composure and had expelled the remaining wine from my nostrils. She lifted her shot glass to cheers with mine, and we locked eyes for a moment before shooting them down.

"I guess I'll just start at the most important part. I loved your uncle. I loved him very, very much."

I watched her in complete bewilderment. Fancy-pants, immaculate, Daughter of Savannah Civic Society herself, Eunice Wilder was once in love with my scruffy, no-frills bartender Uncle Cole. I just couldn't wrap my head around it.

"We fell in love when we were kids. Not unlike you and Lee. I realized that almost too late. He even escorted me to the Fall Formal once. My daddy had an absolute fit over that one." She paused, staring out over the river as if the memories were flickering in front of her like an old film. "It's strange, really. Almost like history's trying to play out the same old scenes, even if the players have changed. Just like how you and Lee are finding your way back to a friend-ship, it feels like we're all destined to relive these moments, no matter how much we try to rewrite them."

She laughed and looked down into her lap, playing with a napkin she used to clean up the wine that I had nose-hosed onto her blouse.

She went on. "We had a few beautiful years together until I went to Bos-ton. That's where I met Vance, you know. Well, not met him, but re-met him, I guess. Our parents had been friends. I was at Wellesley, and Vance was at Har-vard. We ran into each other at a party in Boston and sort of formed this weird, southern alliance amongst all those Yankees."

I imagined a young, vibrant Eunice, traipsing through the snowy streets of Boston, and of all people in the city, she ran into Vance Wilder.

"Anyway," she continued, "Vance and I went home for Christmas break, together but not dating, of course. I still loved your uncle. We wrote every day, and he would send me sketches of things that he drew on the back of O'Malley's napkins. He was so romantic. But when we got back to Savannah that winter, my daddy and Vance's daddy had caught wind of the two of us spending time together, and well, my father gave me an ultimatum."

I was hesitant to say anything, so I nodded for her to continue. Given the kind of outdated, sometimes absurd expectations I'd faced being drawn into their world, I could only imagine what she'd been through.

"Politely as ever, of course, my father told me if I wanted to continue my education in Boston, I should let Vance court me. His father had struck some sort of deal with Daddy, and, well, my father was named a partner at the Wilder firm by spring. Vance and I were engaged by fall."

My eyes went as wide as saucers. "I don't know what to say. So, what did you do about Uncle Cole?"

Eunice released a weary breath. "Your uncle came to see me in Boston right after my engagement to Vance hit the pages of the Savannah Local. He begged me to change my mind, but I knew how important it was for my family that I marry Vance, so I broke things off with Cole. For good."

I wanted to tell her I could only imagine how difficult it must have been, but she always seemed unfazed by her relationship with Vance. As the pounding in my ears grew louder and my blood pressure spiked, I clamped my lips together, swallowing my thoughts before they could escape.

"Anyway, your momma called me once she found out and said she would never speak to me again, and that was that. She kept to her word and never did. It broke my heart. I'd run into her occasionally, but once she moved to Tybee Island with your daddy, that was pretty much the end. He'd always give a polite hello, but your momma… well, she was as stubborn as ever." Her laugh came out as a breathy, shaky sound, and she quickly caught it with a sniffle. Her words shattered my heart into a million pieces.

I nodded and put my hand on her shoulder, offering her what little comfort I could.

Eunice turned to me and gave me a sad, tired look. "I need you to under-stand that I don't regret one second of my life. I have never wanted for anything. Vance and I have a wonderful home, great friends, and we work well together. I was able to continue my education and fulfill my dream of becoming an antiquar-ian. And, most importantly, I have two beautiful, albeit insane, sons. And both of them are just crazy about you."

I took our bottle of wine out of the chiller and refilled our glasses, letting her continue. She looked away from me, and I could see her shoulders rattling as she fought back tears.

"I learned to move on from the love I had for Cole. It took some time, and my obligations to Vance were a great distraction. But not having your momma, or her love and friendship in my life, was the worst heartbreak of it all. The void she left behind when she walked out of my life echoed louder than any other loss I'd ever experienced."

Her words hit me like a truck, and I leaned back in my seat, feeling the weight of the conversation. "I miss her, too. But I know my momma. She prob-ably loved you until her last breath."

"Like I said, our friendship reminded me so much of yours and Sutton's. I often wonder what our lives would have been like if I'd had the courage to listen to her when she asked me to instead of doing what I thought was right," she said, her voice tinged with regret.

We let the quiet settle between us for a moment. The traffic-heavy river bustled below, full of bellowing cargo ships and troves of tourists milling up and down the cobblestone streets. The sounds of laughter, of normalcy, wafted up toward us as we both struggled to figure out what to say next.

Eunice turned and met my eyes, tears streaming down her face. "Do you love Dane, Magnolia?"

"Of course I do. I always have. In a different way, of course. It's all very complicated," I offered nervously, bouncing my leg up and down and fighting the urge not to chew on my bottom lip.

She let out a small laugh. "Is it, though?"

"It is. If we're being honest with each other, having Lee home—and now wanting to stay home—is complicating things. I'm appreciative of him, truly, that he would want to step in and help me with the bar, but I can't help but wonder if this is some weird, sick thing to get back at Dane for something? I don't know."

Eunice shook her head. "No, it's not that. I think Dane is confident enough in your relationship not to let Lee's homecoming get in the way. And I know my Leland; he will put up a fight if he wants something. I saw it last night when we were going over the paperwork. And I know he'll do it. He'll fight like hell if he wants you back."

I couldn't tell from her tone if she thought that was a good or a bad thing, but I decided to change the subject.

"Do you mind if I take a look at the Trust paperwork?" I asked, nodding to the folder beside me.

She shook her head, a slight frown playing on her lips. "Before we go over this, I need to tell you that if Leland buys in, the Wilder Family Trust will be the majority member of your business. Even though it's Leland's money, when he moved to Nashville, our accountants, and the Trust, have had control over his finances."

I opened up the package and glanced over it. "What does that mean?"

"Being blunt," she said, waving her hand for the server, "if Dane wants to sell your property, which I now believe he's wanted to do this entire time, he has the right to do it. Basically, the Trust would have majority control over everything. Leland has a right to vote, of course, but does not have as large a share as Dane or Vance, who could both override any of his decisions."

"Why are you telling me this, then? Wouldn't it ruin whatever plans they have if I don't agree to these terms?"

"I've been going back and forth about this for days, but if I didn't tell you, I run the risk of watching someone I love as much as I love my own children lose her career, her passion. I'll never tell you what to do with your life or your business, Magnolia Louise, but I will tell you, sometimes we make choices for ourselves based on what we think others want for us. Sometimes, we make decisions for the people we love, thinking it will make them love us more. And sometimes, we do things for people because we think it's the right thing to do." Her eyes narrowed in on me, and a deep seriousness settled over her features. "I'm here to tell you that the only person you should be doing anything for, whether it comes down to love, finances, the business, anything… is you."

I gulped down the rest of my wine and burst into tears.

CHAPTER EIGHTEEN

Magnolia

I wiped the bar top in slow, deliberate circles, though the surface was already clean. My gaze flicked between Charlie and Sutton, searching for some kind of reassurance in their faces.

"It not a good idea," I muttered, more to myself than them. My voice wavered, but I kept scrubbing. "Is Dane only dating me so he can sell off this building? I know it takes up a city block, but it's been in our family since they came to Savannah like a million years ago."

The rag slipped from my fingers, landing with a dull thud on the counter. I didn't pick it up. After leaving Eunice, my thoughts had been spinning so fast I barely remembered the walk back to O'Malley's. Outside Rocks on the River, I had hugged her, murmuring a distracted, "Thank you," before heading straight to the bar, where Charlie and Sutton were waiting to watch me unravel.

My relationship with Dane felt insincere, and since I had barely heard from him since he left for Atlanta, I was even more confused. Why wasn't he calling me? Why didn't he want to talk about anything? Was he only pushing me to move in with him to get me out of this building before he sold it to the highest bidder? The idea clawed at the edges of my mind, and I couldn't stop it from digging deeper.

"I just can't picture Eunice and Cole together. Like, can we focus on that for a second? This is the most mind-blowing revelation of all the revelations," Sutton said.

Charlie and I both rolled our eyes in unison.

"Sutton, my sister has potentially been in a fake relationship with someone who wants to sell her livelihood off. My entire family's livelihood. Focus," my brother groaned.

"I'm focused. Believe me. But I still can't get over it."

"Anyway," I continued, passing them both refills, "I don't know if I can go through with it."

My brother leaned over the bar and grabbed my hand. "You cannot, in any capacity, keep this bar running on your own. You can't. I hate telling you this, but it's the truth."

"But can she marry someone who wants to get rid of this place? Who's to say that when she marries Dane, he isn't just going to use that influence to sell the bar anyway?" Sutton swirled her straw in her drink contemplatively, her voice high pitched and nervous. "These faux marriages go south all the time. Don't you guys listen to true crime podcasts?"

The door to the bar opened, and we all turned to watch a sullen-looking Lee Wilder rush in. He bypassed Charlie and Sutton, crossed behind the bar, and wrapped me in a hug.

"We're not going to let anything happen to this bar. Or to you. I promise you, I won't ever let it happen."

I hadn't realized how much I missed being held by him until that moment. That just the simple act of him being close to me made every fear and every ounce of anxiety float away. Whether it was the years of friendship or the love we once shared, I needed him now, more than ever.

I needed him back in my life.

"Let's talk about it, the four of us. We'll come up with something," he said, pulling back and running his thumb gently over my cheek, wiping away the tears.

"Actually, Charlie and I have to run. Right, Charlie?" Sutton elbowed my brother, who nodded in agreement.

Charlie came behind the bar to drop off their empty glasses and poured their fresh drinks into to-go cups. He handed one to Sutton over the bar, and she mimed "call me" as they walked out the door.

Lee leaned on the beer cooler behind me, watching me closely while I busied myself hand washing long-stemmed wine glasses, scrubbing off the tiny, barely noticeable imperfections with such a brute force I almost broke one in half.

The relentless hum of the air conditioning filled the empty bar, amplifying the tension between us. It felt like the room was conspiring against me, turning our close proximity into a pressure cooker. I wanted to scream.

"I found an apartment," he finally said, breaking the silence. "It won't be ready until the first of the month, though. And my label said I could stay, so long as I churn out my next album on schedule. So, I'm staying. For good. Or for now. I guess it will come down to whatever happens."

I tucked my hair behind my ears and looked down at my feet. I didn't know what he meant by that, but I felt a wave of relief wash over me. "That's great news."

"And I'm going to try to invest as much as I can into the Trust so that I'm the majority shareholder instead of Dane."

I gasped and steadied myself on the bar. "That's an awful lot of money to spend on a dive bar, Lee."

"I'm not spending the money on the bar, Maggie. I'm spending it on you."

CHAPTER NINETEEN

Lee

I wanted to kiss her. It wasn't the first time since I had arrived back in Savannah that I wanted to take her gorgeous, freckle-peppered face into my hands and feel the softness of her lush lips again. Just the thought of it lit a fire inside my soul that burned brighter the longer we stood there, glaring at each other.

I took a step away from her.

I willed myself to change the subject before I lifted her up onto the bar, ran my hands through her hair and grabbed the back of her head, kissing down her neck until I got… "We should start talking about knocking down the back rooms and building out. I had the blueprints ordered and the city ordinances pulled. You own quite a bit of space back there in the alley, so you won't need to build inward."

She was staring at me with a mix of shock and bewilderment, her bottom lip caught between her teeth. I took a few more steps back, trying to rein in my frustration. She was driving me crazy, but she was my brother's girlfriend. As much as I wanted to growl in frustration, I knew I had to respect that. Even though, deep down, I was painfully aware that Dane wasn't giving her the respect she deserved.

I had to find out who was in the corner of that video call. I *had* to get to the bottom of what Dane was really up to. Did he genuinely want Maggie to move in and take the next steps in their relationship because he was a man in love? Or was there something darker lurking beneath the surface?

Was he going to take everything away from her for his own selfish gain?

A strong sense of urgency gnawed at me. I had to prove to Maggie that Dane wasn't who he seemed, that moving in with him and giving him that kind of control over her life—over her business—if they got married was a colossal mistake. But how could I do that without exposing my secret?

The hug we had shared was enough to fill my cup, even though I already felt it emptying again. For a brief moment, the comfort of her closeness made everything else fade, but as soon as she pulled back, the weight of reality came rushing back. It wasn't the kind of emptiness I could fix with a hug. It was a quiet reminder that even when we came close, the distance between us still lingered.

But I could feel myself slipping back into that place with Maggie, where things felt easy, where everything felt right. Where small, innocent touches sparked something deep inside me, stirring a longing that I could barely contain, my body calling out to her, craving more.

It was a spiral, and if I wasn't careful, it would whip itself into a full-blown tornado

"I was thinking of starting slow. Lee, renovations will cost a lot of money. I don't want to go overboard," she stated flatly, turning away from me to tidy up the bottles stacked neatly, and clearly untouched, behind the bar.

If she had any idea just how overboard I wanted to go, she would throw me out.

"Well, I have a little bit of cash on hand at the moment that's not tied into the Trust. What were you thinking?"

"Actually, this wouldn't cost much money at all." I caught the twinkle in her eye as she worked out what was going on in her head. "I'm thinking you could sing. Saturday night. Here."

Maggie and I spent the rest of the night hashing out ideas for the bar. I agreed to play a gig on Saturday night, and she immediately started spreading the word on social media. *"Grammy Award-winning songwriter, Leland Wilder, for one night only!"* She kept checking her phone, and every time she got a ping, she'd light up, talking about all the likes and comments rolling in. Her shoulders squared up, and for the first time in a while, her smile reached her eyes again.

"Charlie told me I need to use hashtags, so I think that's helping it gain some traction," she quipped, her voice growing higher by the minute as her excitement escalated.

I knew all too well how to make her happy, and just being there, doing it again, stirred up a whirlwind of emotions I'd long buried. My ego swelled with every burst of pep in her voice, the same energy that used to ignite everything between us. The way she lit up when talking about her plans—it was a reminder of all the things we had once dreamed of. We ordered in some takeout, and she hopped up every now and again to tend to the to-go cup window, moving with the same easy grace I'd never quite gotten over. Every moment felt like a pull, a whisper of what could've been.

"It will be nice to have people in the bar again instead of just stopping by on their way to somewhere better," she grumbled, sitting back down next to me. Our knees brushed briefly, and a jolt of electricity shot through me, like a spark igniting something that had never fully gone out.

In the few days I'd been back in Savannah, everything about Magnolia crept back into my heart and my soul. All those years of shared moments—those little things we used to do without thinking—came rushing back, the kind of memories that never really faded, only lay dormant, waiting for the right moment to resurface. The laughter, the love, the intimacy—the way her touch felt like home. It had taken miles and distance, years of burying myself in albums and lyrics, to convince myself I could let her go.

But it took one look across a crowded breakfast restaurant a little over a week ago for it to all come screaming back.

My phone buzzed in my pocket. I didn't need to check it to know who was trying to get my attention. On the Uber ride over, I'd scrolled through Janelle's Instagram feed, filled with meticulously staged "girl power" selfies and those well-timed inspirational quotes about moving on from heartbreak.

Her followers had been all over it, and now they were swarming my social media, too, hunting for answers and demanding to know what was going on.

"I'm just going to use the restroom. I'll be right back."

Maggie nodded as I pushed away from the table where we had been enjoying some cold beers and good company. The second I walked away, I felt the emptiness crawling into my soul again.

"Janelle, what the hell are you doing? Your fan club is all over my Instagram, looking for answers. Someone just commented 'Fess up, douchebag.' Girl, what are you up to?"

Janelle let out a frustrated breath on the other end, and I heard her step out of her loud studio where she self-shot all of her digital content and into her quieter living room.

"Lee, you've been gone for over a week. I have barely heard from you, and when I do, you're rushed. Then, I see this post from some dive bar in Savannah that you're playing there on Saturday. News to me, you were supposed to be back by then."

I ripped off my baseball cap and tossed it on the sink in front of me, running my hands through my hair. "I'm sorry, you're right. I should have called."

"You should have done more than called Lee. You made me look like a fool." She paused, letting the words linger like a storm cloud hanging over us. "Which isn't shocking since I'm certainly not the first person you've done this to. After all, this was a setup, wasn't it? Besides, I can spin this. I have a new athleisure line coming out that will coincide well with the breakup weight loss."

Everything was a business opportunity for her. But standing in the bathroom of a bar I was about to invest in, with the woman I still wanted more than anything in the world just outside the door, I guess I was guilty of the same shit. Except, for me, it was just *one* "like," *one* "heart," I was trying to gain.

"I'm sorry, Janelle," I offered again.

"It's whatever, Lee. I'll send my breakup NDA over to your label."

She hung up quickly, leaving me alone in the bathroom with my thoughts swirling like a blender on high. Here I was, taking a risk on someone who had long closed the book on our relationship—hell, the entire series—ten years ago. Someone who was dating my brother. Someone who was moving forward with her life while I was still all caught up in the past, whether I wanted to admit it or not.

Someone I was, indubitably, insanely, still in love with. And always, always would be.

CHAPTER TWENTY

Magnolia

After Lee had locked himself in the bathroom, he left almost abruptly. Ever the gentleman, though, he tipped his hat to me as he backed out the door, keeping his eyes fixed on me the whole time.

I tried calling Dane, but, yet again, he didn't answer. I sat on the edge of the bar, watching the door for someone, anyone, to walk in. For someone to buy a drink, have a seat, bring their friends in. To bring me some answers.

I knew that, out of all my friends, I was the one on the sinking ship. But it was my sinking ship, and I would go down with the band at the end if it meant that I gave it everything I had, even when there was nothing left to give.

Because at the end of the day, this was the last connection I had to my mother. To Uncle Cole and the family that came before Charlie and me. To the generations of O'Malleys that crossed this threshold and called 21 McDonough Street home. Who raised their babies in the upstairs apartment and came down at night to run the bar when it was in its prime.

A bar that was once a true staple in the community, a place that was a common area for Savannah's Irish. A place that cost blood, sweat, tears, and most of all, pride to keep open.

O'Malley's was in my blood, and I couldn't let it go. Not without a fight.

Dane, on the other hand, I was happy to watch march out of my life if that was what he wanted. Something about it, though, felt uneasy to me. Almost as if I wouldn't have the confidence to let him go if Lee wasn't making this huge financial sacrifice to help keep the bar open and my tether to the Wilder family wouldn't be truly severed.

Because even being surrounded by the memories and ghosts of my own family, the Wilders had done so much for me, and I couldn't, and didn't, want to let them go.

I wondered what it was about the family that tied me to them. Was it the warmth and kindness that Eunice had extended to me for all of these years? The stability and firmness of Vance? The decades of friendship and, eventually, the dramatic up-and-down romance with Dane? Was it me holding on to what I felt for Lee?

I thought about the way he'd been looking at me since he got back—like I was some sort of puzzle he'd been dying to solve but had lost the instruction manual for. That time when he brushed past me in my kitchen, and I swear, the air between us got hotter than the oven. Every moment we spent together, I'd watch his eyes flickering like he was trying to memorize everything new about me—trying to convince himself that maybe I hadn't changed, that I was still the same girl he left behind. But we both knew I wasn't.

Grief had done its work on me. It had wrapped itself around my heart, making it heavier, quieter, until it turned me into a stranger, even to myself. I wasn't the girl he'd walked away from.

But even still, it was like he was testing the waters, waiting to see if I'd jump back in. And God, part of me wanted to—if only to see where that look in his eyes was going to lead this time.

But I had to stay focused. I was distracted enough as it was with Dane's hot and cold attitude, trying to keep the lights on in the bar, and making sure nothing happened to the legacy that my family left behind. I didn't have room for distractions. Or, at least, that's what I kept telling myself.

One thing was for sure. I wasn't going to let anything happen to O'Malley's. To my home. To my livelihood. No matter who got hurt in the process.

Even if it was me.

CHAPTER TWENTY-ONE

Lee

The night before my gig at O'Malley's, Charlie and I were sitting in his studio drinking some cans of Scattered Sun beer and talking about his latest work—a floor to ceiling portrait of Maggie made from candid shots he had taken of her, and black and white photos of the generations of O'Malley's that had owned the bar. Aside from gathering some local beer bottle labels, he'd asked me if he could use some of the song lyrics from my first album, the one I wrote almost exclusively in their apartment the summer before I left.

It was a piece that he and I talked through when I had decided to stay, and it was something we wanted to give her when the deal went through and the renovations were finished. I was more than happy to assist, and looking over the lyrics of the songs that our friends and Magnolia inspired me to write gave me a sense of purpose I hadn't felt in a long time.

My muse was coming back to me. I could feel it.

Charlie stopped his strategic placing of some song lyrics around Maggie's eye when he took a break and sat on the stool next to me.

"Did you hear Kasey's back? She just walked into the bar for her Friday afternoon shift as if nothing had ever happened."

I shrugged. I hadn't been to the bar since I picked up Maggie's marked-up paperwork the day before. She hadn't said much, aside from letting me know that she had made a few edits to the documents. When she handed over the envelope, I had the feeling that there was some sort of trepidation on her end. Almost as if there would soon be an invisible anchor between her and I that she didn't want to be there.

"Anyway, she fed Magnolia this whole story about how she gave the flu to her mother and had to take care of her and how since she hadn't been working, her cell phone got shut off. I think it's bullshit, though."

I was half listening to Charlie when Sutton bashed through the door, handling a couple boxes of pizzas. She rested them on the counter between us and picked up my open beer, taking a swig from it, shooting me a sidelong glance. "I'm still not used to you being home." She smiled when she said it, but I knew my presence, now quasi-permanent, was making everyone uneasy.

Just when everyone had gotten over Maggie and me being in the same room together after all these years, we were joining forces like never before. I didn't blame them for being overly-cautious.

Charlie had my back, though. "I like it. Dane and I never really had much in common. And when you and my sister get together, it's like trying to break the cone of silence on a couple of twins. You know, the weird-ass ones that only communicate with each other with their minds?"

Sutton opened her mouth and showed Charlie her chewed-up slice of pizza, almost choking from laughing at herself. Tears pooled in her eyes. "Feel closer to me now that you've had my see-food?"

Sutton was still an absolute idiot. And it was refreshing as shit.

Being home with my friends was indescribable. Ryan and I had already stayed up until 1:00 in the morning working on some new tracks for the Saturday gig and for the new album. I was full of material already, and we both agreed they were solid tunes. Being home, even for a short time, had already reset my soul.

Of course, being in close proximity to Magnolia was helping the cause quite a bit.

I thought of her the day we talked about what her vision for the bar was. Her short hair, a look I was finally warming up to, falling like a slick curtain at her shoulders. Though she had it professionally lightened, the vibrant orange still shot through when the sun hit it just right. Her sea-gray eyes lit up every time she talked about something new or where she wanted something to go, or even how she wanted me to play at the bar.

A dream we had held so long ago now coming true. Our youthful vision for the future, in some ways, was finally right before us, and I was feeling the excitement of old promises being kept coursing through my veins, igniting my heart with a vibrant exuberance I hadn't felt in over a decade.

Not all the promises we made to each other were coming to fruition, but

I would take what I could get when it came to Maggie.

"Is that Magnolia's giant-ass, judgy eyeball?" Sutton said, waltzing up to the larger-than-life portrait with a slice of pizza dangling in her hands.

"That's my baby sister's eyeball, yes." Charlie met her in front of the mammoth canvas, and they both stared up at it, talking about Charlie's inspiration for the installation and how he thought it would look great on the new wall separating the bar and what would become the kitchen.

"So, just like her giant face. Glaring at all of us," Sutton offered.

They continued chatting, and my thoughts drifted to what the new normal would be like for all of us when Dane came back next week, and I was still here. It wouldn't be the same, that's for sure. They'd either pick up where they left off, or there would be a blowout between the two of them, and our foundation would be rattled once again.

At least this time it wouldn't be my fault. Or would it?

"Do you think they'll stay together?" I interrupted Charlie explaining the theory behind this piece to Sutton, something about all of the O'Malleys before Magnolia becoming one with her and the building.

They both turned toward me, and Sutton groaned.

Charlie finally snickered. "Brother, I love you, but let's let this ship decide, on its own, where it's going to dock."

"Besides," Sutton added, "we've all been through this before, and we're not kids anymore, so the drama isn't as fun as it used to be."

"Let's be honest, it's still kind of fun." Charlie shrugged and slinked back into the chair across from me again.

Sutton threw her hands up in surrender. "Fine, it's kind of fun. But it's not *as* fun. We all have jobs now. I can't be up all night listening to her whine about you or your idiot brother or her idiot brother or me, the biggest idiot, if shit hits the fan again. Her life is kind of normal now." She walked across the room and put her hand on my shoulder before continuing. "I love you, Leland, like a brother. For real. But I can't go through it again with you two. None of us can."

I decided to plead innocence and just offer her a shrug. "I didn't mean it like that, Sutton. Not like I want to get back together with her. You guys know I have a girlfriend, right?"

Both Charlie's and Sutton's heads snapped back, and Sutton let out a wild howl, cackling like a maniac. "Bullshit, Lee," she said. Charlie nodded in agreement, chugging his beer to stifle his laughter.

"Hand to God," I said, grabbing my phone off of the table. I pulled up Janelle's Instagram, strategically scrolling through her "poor me" posts and showing off the ones of us together, from just a week and a half ago, when life was normal in Nashville.

"Holy shit, she's hot," Sutton declared right before Charlie yanked the phone out of her hand.

"Wow," he offered, eyeing me suspiciously. He handed me back my phone. "It's sort of odd, though, you know, that we're just hearing about this mystery woman now. Does my sister know about her?"

"Why does it matter? She's with my brother anyway. Our deal is strictly a business deal. My personal life doesn't matter."

Sutton let out a sarcastic laugh. "But her personal life does?"

"Only where it concerns my brother. Come on, Sutton, her life might be 'normal' now, but this is Dane we're talking about. Cocky, full of shit, up to no good Dane Wilder."

My oldest friends in the world had been apart from me for so long they couldn't see through my bullshit. Or maybe I had been away from them for so long I couldn't tell if they just didn't care what I was feeding them. Shit or not.

"Besides," I continued, "Janelle's coming tomorrow night to watch me play at O'Malley's. If Maggie doesn't know about her yet, she will then. Speaking of, I have to make sure she's all packed. I'm going to go give her a call."

I could feel Sutton and Charlie both burning a hole in the back of my head as I strolled out of Charlie's studio, trying to play off that I was feeling confident and cool. Though, in reality, by the time I hit the sidewalk, my armpits were soaked and I was teetering on the edge of a panic attack.

How the hell was I going to get someone I just broke up with two days ago to come to Savannah and see me? It wasn't like I could just text her and say, *"Hey, I know we're done, but can you drop everything and fly down here?"* It was a long shot—an insane one at that—but I was desperate, and desperation makes you do crazy things.

CHAPTER TWENTY-TWO

Magnolia

Jordan and I were setting up some quaint, Southern-inspired floral displays around the bar, chatting idly about what kind of refreshments we'd be serving and what drinks would pair best. The scent of freshly cut flowers mingled with the rich aroma of wood polish, filling the air with a comforting warmth.

The night before, Charlie and I were up until 3:00 a.m. touching up the bar and scrubbing every inch until it gleamed, and Sutton even stopped by to help me restock the shelves.

I was as nervous as a long-tailed cat in a room full of rocking chairs, but the excitement bubbling inside me, along with the butterflies dancing in my stomach, had me zipping around the bar, barely able to stay still.

According to the Facebook event, over 200 people had RSVP'd to come watch Lee perform, and I wanted to be as prepared as possible.

"I think it looks great in here," Jordan said, looking around the room and nodding. I could tell by the tone of his voice that he was being genuine. Jordan was from Brooklyn, and he never bullshitted any of us, ever.

"Thanks, I know you mean it. I appreciate all of your help, Jordy." I slid a glass of sauvignon blanc down the bar toward him, perfectly chilled, just the way he liked it.

"This is nice. What vineyard is this from?" He swirled the wine around in his glass and sniffed it slightly before taking another sip.

"Would you shit yourself if I told you it came from a box?" I winced as I pulled it from the ice chest, showing it off like Vana White. He faked a dramatic gasp.

"Of all the cases of impeccable wine I have sent over here, you choose to do me dirty like this. I am offended, Magnolia Pruitt."

I smirked in amusement. "I'm trying to cut costs as much as possible since Lee is hell bent on tearing this place apart. I know he's funding most of it, but I don't want to owe him anymore than I already will. Or do, I guess."

Jordan nodded. He swirled the wine around his glass a bit more, looking thoughtful for a moment. "I get it, sweetheart. It's a tough spot. Prince Charming comes back on his white steed, ready to take you away from Lord Voldemort and the Evil Empire to save the shire, and you don't wanna look like the damsel."

"I think you have your classics mixed up," I giggled, leaning over the bar. "And I think I'm kind of sick of being a liability to the Wilder family. It's always something with them. The dresses, the makeovers, the romances. Now my bar. It's like they always want me to be a different version of myself. But I just feel like I owe them so much."

Jordan took a long, out of character sip of his wine. "Tell me, Magnolia, would you be truly happy with a life without the Wilders in it? Could you visualize that?"

I stepped back and leaned against the beer cooler, running my hands through my hair. Since Charlie and I landed in Savannah, the Wilders had been woven into the fabric of our daily lives. Lee and Charlie? Always thick as thieves. Me and Lee? We went from best friends to young lovers. Dane and I had been close for years before we began dating. And Eunice and Vance? They'd always felt like a second set of parents. The love I had for them was different, but no less real.

The void I would feel if they weren't a part of my life was something I couldn't ever imagine.

When my life crumbled, and our friend group formed, I didn't just feel like I had people to lean on—I felt like I was part of something bigger than myself, like I'd stumbled into a family I didn't even know I was searching for. The kind of love that ran deeper than blood, the kind that held you up when you couldn't stand on your own. It was a bond I never imagined possible, stronger and more unconditional than anything I'd ever known.

For the first time since losing my parents, I felt like I truly belonged.

"I couldn't. I really couldn't," I admitted. "There's something about..."

"Lee?" Jordan smiled and leaned back in his chair, folding his arms across his chest.

I gave a weary shake of my head. "Yes, there's something absolutely undeniable about Lee. There always has been. But it's more than that. As a whole, they're reliable, consistent, you know?" I shrugged. "I haven't felt that kind of security since before my parents died."

"Well, I think you have your answer," he said, hopping off the stool and gathering his boxes and bags. "But just because you have your answer doesn't mean you have to make a decision right away. Let it play out and see what happens. Speaking of reliability, has Dane even called you once since he's been at trial?"

I shook my head. "He's been busy, I know. He's sent me a few emails, though."

"Magnolia, we make time for the things and people that are important to us. If he wanted to, he would. Don't forget that."

Just then, the door to the bar swung open and in walked Lee, guitar slung over his back like he'd just strolled out of a music video. He had on a white button-down, sleeves rolled up like he was about to fix someone's car, and a pair of fitted jeans that didn't need any fixing at all. His baseball cap was turned backward, wild curls spilling out like they had a mind of their own. For the first time since he'd come back to Savannah, my stomach did a full somersault at the sight of him.

And for once, seeing him didn't fill me with that familiar rush of nerves or send my mind spiraling. Instead, it felt like a small but vital piece of me was quietly sliding back where it belonged, like the first sigh of relief after holding your breath for far too long. The chaos that had followed me around for years seemed to ease, and for the first time in forever, I felt a sense of normalcy creeping back in, like maybe, just maybe, everything was starting to fall into place.

"I just wanted to stop by and drop my guitar off. I have my amp and some other things in the car. And to see if you needed any help for tonight," he said, his tone flat and almost bored.

"See what I mean?" Jordan picked up his boxes and made his way to the door, shooting Lee a smile and a nod as they crossed paths. "See you tonight, y'all. Can't wait!"

Lee made his way to the bar and swung his guitar off his back, watching me closely. The atmosphere shifted, tense and charged, and I could tell something was off before he even spoke. Maybe things weren't sliding back into place after all.

"What's wrong, Lee?" I asked before he could begin. I'd known him almost my whole life, and I knew, beyond anything, when something was eating at him. And something surely was.

"I need talk to you about something, and I have a feeling it won't go over well with you, and so I'm just going to say sorry upfront. Okay?" He wrung his hands together and locked his eyes down on his lap so they wouldn't meet mine.

"What did he do?" I asked, point blank, crossing my arms over my chest and bracing for the worst.

"Who? What?" Lee finally looked up, and his shoulders relaxed for a second. "Oh, Dane? No, nothing. At least as far as I can tell. Wait, he still hasn't called you?"

"We've emailed a few times. It's fine. What did he do, though?"

Something washed over Lee's face. Was it fear? Remorse? I couldn't tell. He was hiding something, though. I knew that much.

"Nothing. It's nothing. It's just… I'm seeing someone, Maggie. She's coming tonight. Ryan's picking her up from the airport now."

My heart dropped into my stomach, and I had to lock my knees to keep myself upright. There was no way I could let him see how shocked I was by this—no chance in hell. But the bile creeping up my throat and the sudden urge to start swinging at him were both dangerously close to bubbling to the surface.

"That's wonderful!" I shrieked, scaring myself and making Lee jump. "I *cannot* wait to meet her!"

"Why are you yelling?" He wrinkled his face at me while my blood pressure rose to critical heights.

"I'm probably just nervous about… tonight," I lied through my teeth.

All I could envision was this gorgeous, golden-haired set of legs in cowboy boots—like the dozens of women I had seen when I stalked his Instagram—showing up and knocking out the entire bar with her million-watt smile, mouth full of carefully placed veneers lubed up with Vaseline. And then frumpy old me, skulking behind the bar in an O'Malley's tank top and cut-off shorts, reeking of stale beer, cheap whiskey, and bankruptcy.

"Oh." His shoulders dropped, and he looked a little more calm now that me screaming at him wasn't a direct result of the bomb he just dropped on me. "Don't be nervous. It's going to be awesome. Ryan and I have some great covers, some new stuff to toss in, and the chart toppers from my albums. We'll make some serious money tonight. That's the most important part."

And, right on cue, my wide range of emotions came flying to the front, and I did what I always do when I'm nervous to the gills.

I immediately started crying and snotting.

Lee jumped up on his chair and dove over the bar, putting a hand on my shoulder. "What the hell is wrong?"

I lied again, sweeping my arm across the bar, gesturing to the decorations and setup. "I just wish your brother was here to see all of this."

"Me too, Maggie. He'd be really proud of you." He took a step back, and the second he took his hand off my shoulder, it felt like someone ripping a blanket off me in the middle of the night, leaving me cold and vulnerable.

I observed him for a minute. Something felt off about the whole thing; the air between us was different. I didn't spend every waking minute in his orbit like I used to, but something wasn't right. He wasn't telling me the whole story. "Do you need any help getting your stuff out of the car?" I finally asked after blowing my nose into a cocktail napkin loudly, breaking the silence.

"No, I'm good. Thank you, though."

"Fair enough. I'm going to go up and get ready." I made my way past him and around the bar toward the back hallway. "Please lock the door. I left you a key on top of the register."

"See ya, Maggie," he called behind me, as I rushed up the back staircase as fast as my legs would take me.

I dialed Sutton as I flung open the door to my apartment. A startled Pickle jumped down from on top of my cabinets and latched onto my leg, screeching like a banshee. I let out a blood-curdling scream.

"What in the hell is happening? I have an engagement party tomorrow, and I'm working on a new bananas Foster in a cup, and so help me God, if Lee just kissed you, I do not have time for that right now. I mean, I have some time, but not, like, a lot. What's going on?"

"He didn't." *Why did I sound so disappointed?* "Pickle attack. Did you know Lee has a girlfriend?"

The sound of a deep, tired breath slipped through the receiver, carrying a hint of irritation. "I did know that, yes. I didn't want to say anything because, honestly, it didn't sound legit. So, I was waiting to see if she really showed up." There was a brief pause before she added, "Have you been crying?"

I let out a horrified gasp. "I might never speak to you again. For at least an hour. Are you freaking kidding me?"

"Magnolia, seriously? What do you even care for? *You* have a boyfriend. Right? Did we forget about Dane?"

I ripped my pants off and stomped down my hallway to the bathroom to doctor my new wound courtesy of my demon-infested cat. Guess I wasn't shoving myself into those cut-off jean shorts tonight after all.

"I didn't forget about Dane." I rested the phone on the bathroom counter and cleaned up the blood. Foolish cat. "Dane, however, seems to have forgotten about me. He's only emailed me twice since he's been gone, and he reads my text messages but doesn't respond. Do you think he's having an affair? That new paralegal is super cute."

"No, he's not having an affair. You're hyper-paranoid because Lee is in town. Probably because you know you're not doing the right thing every time you give Lee that googly-eyed stare down, so you assume Dane is up to something, too." Sutton was aiming to sound light and playful, but she sounded weary and flat.

Either way, I was going to punch her when I saw her. "You've known me practically my entire life. You're really going to sit on the other end of the phone and try to act like I am someone who would do something like that?" I stood up and could see the redness creeping up my chest and on to my cheeks. I was pissed, and she wasn't exactly wrong, so I was embarrassed, too.

"I've known you practically your whole life is exactly right, girl, and I know that the second Lee decided to bust up into Clary's, nothing has been right since. This little song and dance you two are doing is insane. You're going to risk everything for what? A trip down memory lane? You have a boyfriend, he has a girlfriend. You're both adults now. If you want to change that, you will, but you won't. Because you're both frickin' weird as shit. I don't have time for this. Bye."

Sutton hung up on me, and I stood in the mirror staring at a woman I hardly knew anymore. Someone who was thinking about kissing her ex-boyfriend semi-regularly. Someone whose heart stopped when she found out he had a girlfriend. Someone who couldn't tell the truth to anyone, not even herself.

I shoved myself into a pair of body-hugging jeans and a skintight black tank top with "O'Malley's" across the front, the O fashioned out of a shamrock. I went with a little bit more makeup than usual since there would be a lot of new people and faces in the bar tonight, including this supposed girlfriend of Lee's.

I straightened out my asymmetrical bob and slipped into a pair of black cowboy boots. I went with a pair of glittery hoop earrings and a shimmery stack of bangle bracelets. Dabbing on a bit of Momma's Chanel Number 5, I surveyed myself in the full-length mirror.

I was curvy, I was gorgeous, and I had a great personality. So, why in the world couldn't my own boyfriend text me back?

I snapped a pic and shot it off to Dane. *"Miss you,"* I typed and waltzed out into my living room. Pickle hissed at the sound of my shoes clomping on the hardwood floor.

"What is it, girl, the shoes? Should I change?"

Lee turned the corner from my kitchen, sizing me up from head to toe. When his eyes landed on my face, they lit up, a grin spreading wide and making his dimples pop. He always used to look at me like that—like I was the only person in the room. I mean, I was the only person in the room. But still.

"I think she's just jealous because you look stunning."

"Why are you in my house?" I snapped, taking a few steps back as my pulse raced wildly. The way he was looking at me made me want to cross the living room and throw myself into his arms. I craved that feeling of being appreciated, loved, adored. Just the thought of his hands on me in these jeans that hugged every curve sent a thrill through me. For the first time in a long time, I wanted to feel sexy, desired—like I could forget everything else for just a little while.

Pickle growled, throwing me back into reality.

"I came up to let you know that I'm ready to start tuning up. Sutton just got here, and she's in quite the mood. Oh, and Charlie's on his way with Jordan and Doyle." He bit his bottom lip, eyes darkening. "God, Maggie, you really do look gorgeous."

I could hear the breathlessness in his voice, a low grumble that sent shivers down my spine. The air in the room shifted, thickening into something sultry and electrifying. My breathing grew erratic, each shallow burst a struggle as my heart raced to keep up with the whirlwind of emotions swirling between us.

From where I stood, I could almost feel his lips on mine. I remembered all the brief hugs and the small, soft touches we had shared since he had come back to Savannah. My thoughts raced to a time when I would have grabbed him by the hand and brought him into my room, shutting the door and leaving the world behind us, letting him into my bed.

He could feel it, too. I knew it. The fire in his eyes burned bright, and he licked his lips, sending a shudder down my spine. He shoved his hands in his pockets, his gaze locked onto mine, and slowly crossed the room toward me, each step heavy with unspoken possibilities.

Through the opening in his white, slightly unbuttoned shirt, I could see his chest heaving. I pressed my back against the doorframe, trying to flatten out my whole body, but he had me trapped. I had nowhere to go. Lee, with one hand tucked in his back pocket and his eyes locked on mine, lifted his other arm above my head and rested his hand just above me.

Slowly, Lee pulled his other hand from his pocket and slid his finger under my chin, raising it gently so that my eyes met his. I sucked in a deep breath, letting the smell of sweat, sandalwood, and salty air wash over me. My knees buckled.

From the back pocket of my jeans, my phone buzzed. We both startled, thrust out of the moment. I glanced down at the screen, my eyes just about bulging out of my head.

"It's Dane," I coughed out, trying not to let the regret, or the relief—I couldn't tell—sound too obvious. "I should take this."

"Yeah, you should. I'll see you downstairs." His voice was low and husky, a tempo I hadn't heard in years, and it made my heart jackhammer.

He backed away from me slowly, spun on his heel, and let out a sharp, bitter laugh before I heard him storm down the back staircase, cowboy boots clanking angrily with every step.

"Hey, baby," Dane said, the sound of the city bustling behind him. "I got your picture. You look beautiful. What's the occasion?"

"Lee's playing at the bar tonight with Ryan. We have about 200 people coming, I'm guessing, so I thought I would get a little dolled up." I was talking a mile a minute, but after that moment with Lee and not hearing his voice for over a week, I was on edge. "What's going on, Dane? Why haven't you called?"

"You didn't tell me that," he groaned. I heard him get into a car and shut the door aggressively.

"Of course I haven't. I haven't even talked to you. Is everything okay? I heard you were sick, too."

"Everything's fine. I've just been busy. Did you sign the agreement yet? My father said he hadn't seen it."

"Not yet. I gave my edits back to your brother the other day. So, what is—"

"Have y'all been spending every waking minute together or what? Jesus Christ, he cannot help himself." His voice bristled with agitation.

"He's buying part of the bar, Dane. Or the Wilder Trust is. Whatever. Of course he's been around."

"Wait, who told you that?"

I remembered my conversation with Eunice and shut my trap. "It was in the paperwork. I can read, you know." I exhaled slowly, trying to steady my nerves. I had this sneaking, overwhelming feeling I was being played for a fool. "Or was I not supposed to know? Because the way you're interrogating me makes me feel like you're trying to leave me in the dark."

Dane let out a sarcastic laugh. "I just didn't expect you to read over the whole boring thing. Alright then, I'll see you next week."

He hung up, and I sat down on the edge of my bed, wondering why he didn't bother to ask me how I was or, more importantly, tell me why he hadn't called once since he'd been gone.

The door to my apartment opened again, and I heard a small scuffle involving Pickle, and then a shriek.

"I'm in my room, Sutton," I called out.

She walked into my room holding out a container of food. "Peace offering—leftovers from the bridal shower prep. Please eat something." She eyed me up and down. "Wow, you look great. Damn, I look like a potato."

I laughed as she immediately began rifling through my clothes for something to change into, ripping my closet apart.

"Dane just called," I said, digging into my food.

She whipped around, holding a floral blouse, letting the long bell sleeves slap her in the face. "Shit! Ouch. Oh my God, what did he say?"

I shrugged. "I sent him a pic of my outfit because I'm feeling myself something fierce tonight, and he had a hissy fit about Lee playing at the bar and then didn't answer me when I asked why he hadn't called."

"Can we break up with him? Seriously?"

I shoved a huge bite of lobster mac and cheese into my face, chewing aggressively. With a mouth full of food, I spat out, "I'm not freaking breaking up with him! Besides, you're the one who's always going 'Oh, he's so great for you, Magnolia.' 'He's so kind, Magnolia.' 'Just let him hump your leg a little bit, Magnolia.'"

Sutton's face fell. "Whoa, Jesus. Okay, fine. But if the guy can't answer a simple question, what's the point?"

"I'm going to see this through. And when he comes back, I'm going to move in with him."

Her face went white as a sheet, and she crossed the room slowly, sitting down next to me on the bed. She pulled the container I was devouring out of my hands and put it on my nightstand, taking my hands in hers.

I kept my eyes on the floor and drew in a long, calming breath. What almost happened between Lee and me earlier would stay between the two of us, and I needed to keep him as just a friend in order for my business to survive. In order for my heart to survive.

If keeping Lee at arm's length and getting serious about Dane was what it took to keep my heart—and the bar—intact, that was what I was going to do. It was what I needed to do.

After all, if Eunice Wilder could thrive in the arms of a Wilder man, couldn't I?

"What's going on, girlfriend?" Sutton started, a soft, somber tone coloring her voice. "I'm your best friend. You can tell me anything, you know that. Ever since Lee's been back, I feel like there's some weird wall up between us. I hate it."

"Me too. I can feel it myself. I'm sorry, Sutton. I just… I think I need to be with Dane. I think I need to do what I should have done a long time ago."

"What's that?"

I let out a long exhale. "Just be friends with Lee. Enjoy my life as Dane's wife, go to tea with Eunice, and keep the bar. And that's all."

CHAPTER TWENTY-THREE

Lee

Sutton came crashing through the back entrance of the bar and into Cole's old bedroom. Charlie and I had turned it into a temporary green room, but we weren't quite done, and she struggled as she tripped over boxes and empty kegs. Her face was flushed as she slammed the door and locked it behind her.

"What the heck happened with you and Magnolia?" she asked, throwing her arms up in the air.

I put my guitar down and stared at her. Did Maggie tell her I had almost run across the room and ripped that sexy, body-hugging outfit off her with my teeth, and we both knew it? That I had her pinned against the wall and was two seconds away from lifting her leg and wrapping it around my waist before I…

I decided to do what I did best. Play dumb.

"Nothing, Sutton." I shrugged innocently but noticed the crazed look in my friend's eyes. "Seriously. Why?"

"She's up there talking about moving in with Dane. And this girl, she's my best friend, but she's so bull-headed sometimes there's no telling her left from right when she has her wires crossed. She can't move in with Dane. I'm telling you, Lee. She can't."

Tears formed in the corners of Sutton's eyes, and she sank down onto the couch, nervously rubbing her palms on her legs. It was only when I looked at her hard that I realized she was in just a pair of jeans and a bra.

"Where's your shirt?"

"Oh shit, I left it upstairs. I was so shocked… Lee, Magnolia can*not* do this. I know I've been playing the part of the dutiful best friend and reminding her that, you know, she has a boyfriend, and it doesn't matter that her ex is back in town, and we all know she wants to jump his bones every time they're in the same room. I've done my job, but I think I've done it a little too well. And I had to, because, you know, your dad can be awfully scary sometimes…"

Something was wrong, and I had to bypass what she just said and the stirring in my jeans at the mention of Maggie and my bones. "Tell me what happened. Now, Sutton."

She hopped up off the couch and crossed the room, grabbing the bottle of bourbon from the small bar, wiping the tears off her face as she swallowed the warm, honey-colored liquid. "Dane… tried something. Once. One time," she hiccuped and came back over to the couch, handing me the bottle and resting her head on my shoulder. "We were at a wine tasting at Jordan and Doyle's, and, well, Magnolia got super drunk, and Charlie brought her home. Dane, the gentleman, suggested he should walk me back to my place, so I didn't have to walk home alone." She took a break to sniffle back some tears. "He asked if he could come upstairs to go to the bathroom, and I didn't think anything of it, of course. We got to chatting and poured a drink. He was asking about Magnolia, and, I don't know, the next thing I knew, he was trying to shove his hand up my shirt and kiss me."

I could feel the heat rising in my chest, my hands almost trembling with the rush of anger. Sutton shifted beside me, turning to face me fully, her eyes searching mine as she took my hands gently in hers. I reached up, brushing away a tear from her cheek with my thumb, and she smiled—a soft, reassuring curve that made the tension in my shoulders ease just a little.

She took a deep, calming breath and continued. "I pushed him off me, and Dane just… freaked out. He was swearing and pacing back and forth, mumbling about how this was going to ruin everything and how he was so stupid. I had to agree with him on that, but then he said your daddy was going to kill him."

Pausing for a minute, she looked toward the window, rolling her lips together as if trying to stifle a sob. "An hour after we both decided he should leave and it would be smart of us to tell Magnolia, to tell her the truth, Vance showed up banging on my door."

I knew by the way Sutton flinched next to me I had anger graffitied all over my face.

"Magnolia's my best friend. I don't ever want to hurt her. But when your dad and I sat at my kitchen table that night and I told him everything, he didn't even seem surprised. He didn't show me any empathy. He just nodded. And… I don't know. He said some things that didn't make sense at the time, but I guess now they do. Did you know the Wilder Trust partially owns LaMonte's? That I could lose my job, or worse, get black balled from the catering community?"

I took a hard swig of the bottle between us and handed it back to her, burying down the urge not to snap at her. Did she cover this up to protect herself and her job? "My mother would never let that happen, Sutton."

Sutton chewed on a piece of skin on her lip, looking off into a corner. "I can't be involved. I need this job. I need Eunice's connections. Vance told me not to say anything to anyone, especially Maggie, but I don't know if I can let her go through with this because…"

I watched Sutton try to make sense of everything going on, the wheels turning in her head. Trying to save the career that she worked so hard for and her best friend all at the same time. Didn't make any of this right, though.

"It's more than just the Trust, and her getting enveloped into a life we both know—hell, we all know—she doesn't want," she sighed.

My patience was thinning. "What, Sutton? Just fucking say it."

"I overheard at work that the Wilder Trust wants to sell the property for ten million dollars to an investor from Atlanta. The investor wants to build a high-rise on this property, some mixed-use type of thing. Shopping at the bottom and condos on top. This building takes up an entire city block, and it's not registered on the national landmark protection. It's one of the few buildings in the city that has this much space and that's not protected. And Vance is hell-bent on pushing the deal through, so I've heard."

She thought about saying more and locked eyes with me for a minute, then exhaled deeply, the weight of it evident.

"If I'm the one that spills all of this, I lose everything. My career, my best friend, everything, Lee. But if I don't speak up… she'll lose this place forever."

"Is that why my brother is with her? Holy shit." I jumped up and paced around the room. I was going to murder my brother first, then my father. I would spare my mother, only because I had a feeling she had been strong-armed into this.

"I've known Dane forever, much like you obviously, and does this really all seem so out of pocket for him? I mean, come on now." Sutton paused and bit her bottom lip, debating what to say next. "Before this whole grabby-ass incident, when they were together, it was kind of nice… I don't know, like the nostalgia of having most of our group back together or something. But that's why he's pushing the move in and the engagement. If he has that control over her and she sees what kind of life she can have, she won't care about losing all of this."

I sat back down next to Sutton. I couldn't believe what I was hearing. I couldn't believe that, in almost twenty years, the trust between Sutton and Magnolia was about to be broken because of my greedy family. I couldn't let it happen.

"We'll think of something, don't worry. I'm going to fix this, but for now, let's keep it between us until I can figure out a plan. And Sutton, she's your best friend. She'll understand you needed to do this to protect yourself, but I can't promise you won't hear an earful from her." I grabbed her hands again, and as soon as I did, Ryan flung open the door, with Janelle right behind him.

"Holy! Shit!" Janelle screamed, throwing her hands up to her face. Ryan let out a weird, bellowed growl at seeing Sutton half-dressed.

"Oh, God. This is in no way how it looks, Janelle…" I started, but Sutton had gotten up and crossed the room, extending her hand for Janelle to take and shake it.

"Shake my hand, Janelle. I'm not the enemy. This guy, right here, is one of my oldest friends in the world, and I am going *through* it right now. Like more than you could know. Your boyfriend is the nicest person on the planet. He's my family." She looked down at herself and sniffled. "It looks bizarre because I'm not wearing a shirt, but if you stick around long enough, this will be the least weird thing you see in Savannah."

Janelle and Ryan stared at Sutton with their mouths hanging open.

She wiped the streaky mascara off of her cheeks and turned to me. "I'm going to go get clothed. I'll keep our conversation between us, and so help me God, let's go save this bar."

She shut the door to the green room, and I heard gasps as she walked through the bar and, presumably, up the backstairs to Maggie's apartment to make herself decent.

"So, that wasn't her? That wasn't Magnolia?" Janelle crossed the room and stood next to me, grabbing my hand as a way to tell me that she believed Sutton and that she was somewhat fine with what she walked in on.

"No. I'm Magnolia," the tall, intimidating redhead said from the doorway. She walked over to Janelle, and instead of shaking her hand, she opened her arms for a hug. "And it's really wonderful to finally meet you. We've all heard so many wonderful things about you."

I watched Maggie and Janelle embrace, and my heart skipped. One was here out of contractual duty, and the other was here out of loyalty. The difference between them was not lost on me.

"Let's go get this party started," Maggie said, offering me a small, sympathetic smile over Janelle's shoulder. "I'm sure y'all could use a drink anyway. I know I sure could."

Janelle and Ryan walked into the bar, and Maggie lingered behind, opening the door to her office and pretending to busy herself at her desk. I leaned on the doorframe and watched her for a minute.

When she finally looked up, she gave me a half grin. "Don't suppose you want to tell me what that was about?"

"It's not my story to tell, Maggie. She'll talk to you when she's ready."

I knew she hated this. I knew how sad she was that something could have potentially come between her and Sutton. Since the day they'd met, as different as they were, they'd been joined at the hip. They were sisters.

As much as it hurt me to keep my mouth shut, I had to protect what Sutton had told me until I could figure out how to wreck the plans my brother and father had and gather up some concrete evidence. More importantly, I didn't want to break Sutton's trust when I was finally getting back into the fold.

But what about Magnolia's trust?

"Are you sure you're okay?" she asked. "I feel like the second you landed in Savannah, everything's been kind of off for us. We used to be able to tell each other anything. And if we couldn't say it, the other just… knew. I can't put my finger on it, but it's like there's been a glitch in the Matrix or something."

I knew what it was, but I wasn't going to tell her. She couldn't see that the spark between us was growing into a flame, but she would soon enough.

"We're all just getting used to each other again, that's all. Now let's go do this show and make us some money. What do you say?"

CHAPTER TWENTY-FOUR

Magnolia

The bar was alive with the murmur of voices, the clinking of glasses, and the soft thrum of the music from the stage. Lee and Ryan were deep in sound check, adjusting the mic levels as the first wave of people trickled in, slowly filling the room. Each footstep, each laugh, seemed to raise the anticipation, a slow tide inching closer. My fingers tightened around the edge of the counter as I watched the room fill, trying to keep my breathing steady.

Charlie and Doyle had slipped behind the bar, their presence a welcome relief as they helped Kasey and me keep up with the constant flow of orders. But the weight of the crowd still pressed in, each new face adding another layer of pressure.

Sutton eventually made her way back down the stairs, looking a little less sullen and a little more clothed. Whatever was happening inside her, I knew she wasn't ready to share. I glanced at her, a knot tightening in my chest. The thought of her carrying something heavy without being able to open up made my heart ache, but I swallowed it down, knowing that would be her choice, not mine.

I made her one of her favorite cocktails and had Charlie deliver it. She was sitting in a corner with Jordan and when she took a sip, she lifted her glass and mouthed "I love you," tears pooling in the corners of her eyes.

Since Lee came home, everything had shifted for our friend group. His return really shook things up, but not all of it was negative. For the first time since I was a kid, the bar was almost at max capacity. Every time the cash register opened, my heart soared.

This might actually work. If Lee did a gig once a month, and people came in and spent money like this, that would more than cover the outstanding bills and overhead. Maybe people would want to keep stopping by on nights he wasn't singing just to hang out or to see what was happening. Visions of dollar signs danced in my head.

Happiness was coursing through my veins, and I turned up the music on the stereo, dancing and singing along with Doyle as we made drinks, skipping and yelling along to the music together. I glanced up, and Lee was watching me from across the room, completely still, guitar in his lap, eyes lit up like midnight stars.

"Y'all are really as close as they say, huh?" Janelle was sitting at the end of the bar, and I leaned over her to hand a couple of whiskey sours to the group behind her.

I finally looked her over for the first time. She was, without a doubt, absolutely stunning. Her long, sheet-straight hair fell over her tan shoulders, exposed in the peep-shoulder peasant blouse she wore. She looked, truly, like someone who worked out hard and took care of herself. She took a small sip of her Tito's and soda and turned to shoot a smile at Lee.

"We are, yes. And, as I said earlier, it really is nice to meet you." I offered her a warm smile, one that didn't quite reach my eyes if I had to guess. "I hope that you'll hang around for a while so you can see what it's like to be a part of this weird, decades-long shitshow that's become our family."

It sounded so odd coming out of my mouth, and I hardly believed a word I said myself, but now that I had my mind made up about where I was going in my relationship with Dane, I just wanted peace. If that meant embracing Janelle, then I supposed I would.

Doyle came up behind me with the rest of the drinks for the group flanking Janelle. "You absolutely want in on this. I've Googled you, by the way. Security protocol. You should think about doing some PR for the bar now that Lee's going to be part owner."

Janelle furrowed her brow and went to respond just as Kasey turned down the stereo. Lee began strumming his guitar, starting the set with "Forever Young," the song he used to sing to me when he was first learning to play.

I rushed Doyle to the back end of the bar, away from Janelle.

"I don't think she knew that, my friend," I hissed.

He opened up a Costco-sized bucket of bar snacks to refill the bowls on the tables, then took a sniff and gagged. "This shit is garbage. Anyway, who cares? She's here amongst you gaggle of gossipers. She was bound to find out at some point."

We turned toward the stage, and there was a wall of people, backs toward me and cameras up, hollering at the stage. I stopped and listened for a moment, crossing my arms over my chest, and for the first time in a long time, I let Lee's voice wash over me. It was instant serenity for me. A calmness like I hadn't felt in forever took root in my soul.

Charlie came over and leaned on the back bar with me, putting his arm around my shoulders. He kissed the top of my head with a gentle murmur. "I'm really proud of you, baby sister."

"I'm proud of all of us. Look at this team!" Sutton was now up and clearing empty glasses and plates from the tables with a practiced efficiency while Jordan trailed behind her, adjusting the floral arrangements and snapping candid photos of everyone for our social media, his camera capturing the buzz of the evening.

"We love you. We would do anything for you, just like you'd do anything for us." My brother's eyes sparkled as he took in the room. "Damn, it is so good to have people in this bar and everyone together again!"

I laughed, leaning into him and putting my head on his shoulder. "We're not *all* here, though."

"Well, the ones that matter," my brother said, smiling as he looked over the crowd again.

"I'm going to move in with him," I muttered, pulling my head away to watch his reaction. The smile that was strapped on his face immediately fell. Lee, who had been doing a good job of playing to the crowd, had slipped up on a few notes, watching our interaction.

He couldn't hear what we were saying, but probably the look on my brother's face gave it away.

Charlie sighed, shaking his head a little. "Whatever makes you happy, Magnolia. That's all I've ever wanted." He left my side to tend to a couple who signaled for help, passing by Kasey, who was leaning on the other end of the bar typing furiously on her cell phone.

"She's working hard, huh?" Sutton said, dropping empty beer bottles in the bin next to me and setting the empty glasses in the wash bucket.

"You know, she's been acting so strange since she got back. I kind of feel like she's spying on me. Does that sound weird?"

"She's probably reporting you to the health department. Look at this place," she laughed, pulling the sleeves up on my floral top she had assaulted herself with earlier to tend to the washing.

I walked over to the next crowd of people looking for another round while Lee struck up a new song, the laid back, rustic melody filling the air and drawing even more patrons toward the stage.

Lee and Ryan played another eight tracks before taking a break. Just as I turned on the stereo to fill in the gap, Eunice sauntered in. She scanned the room for a familiar face and landed on mine behind the bar.

I scooted past my make-shift staff and went out to greet her. "Thank you for coming," I cooed, wrapping her in a hug.

She had herself all dolled up, and she glanced around the room with a wide smile. "Lord, I haven't been inside this bar in so long."

I led her to the table to the side of the stage where Jordan and Sutton were guarding the chairs with their lives so if any one of us needed a break, they'd have a place to sit. A framed picture of Uncle Cole hung above the table, and she paused to smile sadly at my uncle.

"If he could see what you've done here today…" she started, trailing off as she lost herself to the memories.

"He would murder me. He'd never let Lee play here, no matter how many times he begged. He's probably rolling over in his grave as we speak."

Eunice turned her attention back to the present as she let out a small giggle and sat down, purse in her lap, and crossed her legs at the ankle like the lady she was.

"Hey, Mrs. Wilder," Sutton said, twitching in her seat. Sutton never looked shook to the core, but for some reason, she was anxious, and I could feel it radiating off her from across the table.

"Let me get y'all a round," I said, shooting Sutton a gentle, pleading smile that I hoped let her know I was there if she needed anything. She looked up and offered me a quick, fake grin in return.

Lee crossed my path and went over to his momma, kissing her on the cheek. I busied myself behind the bar and watched the two of them interact. I wished she would tell Lee, of all people, about her history and connection to this place—and more importantly, my family.

I dropped a round of drinks off at the table and caught the tail end of a conversation between Lee and Eunice.

"It's just been really nice having you home," she told her son.

He smiled and grabbed her hand on top of the table. "It's been really nice to be home, Momma. There's someone I want you to meet."

Lee got up and gently coaxed Janelle from her seat, and I moved behind the bar, trying to stay out of the way. Sutton joined me, her eyes twinkling with curiosity, while Charlie took his spot on the other side. We all watched like a bunch of nosy neighbors as Eunice leaned in to hug Janelle, both women exchanging Southern pleasantries that were as sweet as molasses.

The room felt charged, like everyone was waiting for something to snap. One by one, my friends' eyes flicked to me, like they were anticipating a reaction. Charlie's attempt to hold back a grin didn't quite work, and Sutton's smirk was barely concealed. It was as if they were all silently bracing themselves, expecting some dramatic shift from me—as if I might throw my hands up, or maybe just say something that would turn the moment on its head. You know, like I had a tendency to do.

"I'm fine, y'all!" I threw my hands up and hollered a tad too loudly, making Sutton jump out of her skin and a few of the nearby guests' heads turn my way.

"You sure you're okay?" my brother asked, reaching behind me to grab a bottle of vermouth for a very stressed-out looking Doyle. "You're screeching and getting crazy eyes."

"Yes, Charlie, I'm fine. Look at him! He's happy. I'm happy. This is how it's all supposed to be," I said.

I couldn't help but smile as I looked around the room. This was exactly how it was supposed to be—just what I had always imagined for myself when I was younger. All those big dreams were finally coming true for all of us—including me this time.

Except, were any of us *truly* happy?

***

Lee finished his last set, and the crowd began to thin out. As Sutton, Charlie, Lee, and I cleaned up, I looked around at the now-empty bar, a wave of sadness washing over me as last call came and went. I wasn't ready for the night to be over.

We scrubbed, polished, and cleaned up shards of glass all around. Once O'Malley's started looking like her old self again, I was suddenly anxious to shoo everyone out of the bar to do the one thing I had been dying to do all night.

Count the money.

"I'm heading out. Sutton, can I walk you home?" My brother's eyes were bloodshot, and it reminded me of just how exhausted I was myself.

"I'll come by and help you finish cleaning in the morning, Magnolia." Sutton yawned, scooting behind the bar. She'd spent most of the night acting weird, and her bum-rushing out the door didn't help my anxiety over her mental state.

"Thanks, guys," I called out, locking up behind them.

And then it was just me and Lee, alone yet again.

I ambled tiredly behind the bar, my arms heavy with exhaustion, plunging my hands into the soapy water. The warmth bit at my skin, but I kept scrubbing, focusing on the swirl of bubbles instead of the man moving around the tables. Across the room, Lee stacked empties with a practiced ease that spoke of muscle memory from years of playing barback for Uncle Cole. When he stepped behind the bar to shelve the glasses, the space between us felt impossibly small, and I couldn't help the way my shoulders tensed, waiting for him to say something. Anything.

"Tonight was a success, if I had to guess. Financially, I mean," he said, coming up behind me to grab some more beer mugs.

I was hyper-aware of how close in proximity we were doing this simple, tedious task, but it didn't stop my hands from shaking. I was very thankful they were submerged. "And personally, too. It looked like your girlfriend and your momma were getting along pretty famously."

Out of the corner of my eye, I saw him nod as he rearranged the mess of bottles onto their appropriate shelves. "I think so. I mean, they're both so worried about their image, neither one of them would really say if they had an opinion otherwise."

I chuckled softly. "Well, even still, it was a great night. I'll never be able to thank you enough for doing this."

Without warning, he grabbed me and spun me toward him, catching me completely off guard. I gasped, my soap-soaked hands slapping against my jeans, leaving wet handprints. My brain short-circuited for a second. *What even just happened?* I froze, my eyes locked on his, my heart deciding now was a great time to throw in some extra beats for dramatic effect. He just stood there, holding me close, like this was the most natural thing in the world, while I was still trying to remember how to breathe—or function like a normal human being.

I didn't want to move. I didn't want to make a sound. But, more than anything, I didn't want him to let me go. The thought of why I was feeling this way gnawed at me—like if I admitted how much I needed him, I'd be opening a door I'd sworn to keep shut. It terrified me. What if this was more than just a moment? What if it was the beginning of something I wasn't ready for... or worse, something I couldn't survive losing again?

"Say the word, Maggie, and all of this ends. Just tell me, straight out, that you want me. That you want to be with *me.* That everything we ever wanted when we were kids, all the dreams we had, that we can have them together. I'll send Janelle away. Hell, I'll call off the buyout, and we can have a million nights like this and get you on your feet again."

Lee's eyes were a vivid, electric blue, locked on mine with an intensity that left me breathless. There was a longing in his gaze, as if he was about to ask something that would turn our worlds inside out.

I felt the weight of his desperate need as his hands rested on my shoulders, his gentle touch sending a jolt straight through me. His eyes had this pleading look, as if the short distance between us was killing him. It was killing me, too.

I knew that any sudden move or word from me could break down the walls we'd put up and change everything right then and there.

Reaching up, I turned his hat backwards and pushed a wayward curl that had escaped out of his eye. I let my hand rest on his cheek for a moment, taking in his handsome, rugged features. He turned his face into my palm, inhaling deeply, a pained look spreading across his brow line.

A low, desperate rumble escaped him. "I won't be the one to do it, Maggie. The way I want you right here, right now... you gotta be the one to kiss me first because if I start, we're not stopping until I have you bent over this bar."

I moaned, stretching my neck to the side and letting him run his nose softly down my cheek and into the nook behind my ear. He peppered tiny, gentle kisses down my throat and landed on the sensitive spot just above my collarbone. My hips thrust toward him in response.

"I remember how much you like that," his words tumbled out in throaty breaths against my skin.

Our hips melted together, and he dipped his forehead to mine, running a thumb along the waistband of my jeans. "Kiss me, Magnolia. Remember how good I make you feel? Remember what it's like when it's just you and me and no one else, like we're the only two people in the world?"

I couldn't take it anymore. My body, the traitor that it was, was writhing and screaming for just one touch, one taste. To remember, once again, what it felt like to be wrapped up in Lee Wilder so tight, nothing else mattered.

He lifted me up and sat me on the ice chest, wrapping my legs around his back and pressing me against the liquor shelf. One push from him was all it took. I was already seeing stars and my pants were still on.

What were we doing?

I broke contact, releasing my fingers from where they were unfastening the buttons on his jeans. "We can't do this."

He released his tight grip on me and took a step back. "Are you serious?"

"I'm deadly serious. What if your brother found out you practically had my legs wrapped around your neck on top of the beer cooler? What would happen to my bar then?"

Part of me imagined a future where I'd marry Dane, partner with the Wilder family, and Lee would pop in for his gigs, turning our lives into some twisted version of "ever after." The "happily" part? I figured I'd have to sort that out on my own.

But the other part of me was writhing in pain, red flags flashing everywhere, yanking me from the fantasy that was nothing more than make-believe. How long before Dane started wandering off in a miserable marriage? How long before I lost myself, desperately clinging to my still-sinking ship? It felt like I was standing at a crossroads, where every turn seemed to come with a side of regret.

Would it be worth it in the end? I had no clue, but if nothing else, I had to at least give it a shot.

He hastily buttoned himself back up and brushed past me, avoiding eye contact as he rushed toward the front of the bar. He stopped with his hand on the door's lock, shoulders tense, like he was still debating whether to bolt down the street or say something. The anger and embarrassment hung thick in the air, and I could practically feel it radiating off him.

"I know you're smart, Magnolia Pruitt. I know you can smell a good business deal a mile away. But this thing with Dane? It's bullshit." He whipped off his hat and angrily ran his hands through his hair, mussing up his curls. He exhaled before looking back up at me again, a deep scowl lining his face. "There's so much you don't understand about my brother. Hell, about my whole family. Maybe even me."

I chewed on my bottom lip, willing myself not to move. As much as he was handing me my ass on a platter, I wanted nothing more than to reach out and wrap my arms around his neck again. "What do you mean?" I whispered.

Lee groaned and rolled his eyes, his hand landing on the door again. "I mean, if you look around, beyond the dollar signs you're trying to manifest into existence, that not everything is what it seems. Sure, we're all pretending to be happy, cheering you on and hoping you don't lose the bar, but that also means we're watching you make the biggest mistake of your life." His eyes met mine, and a sad, sullen smile played across his lips.

My heart dropped. "But that's just it, Lee, it's my mistake to make," I declared, sounding far more confident than I felt.

"I just hope you know what you're doing, Maggie. I hope you know that in the end, the only person who's going to get hurt is you."

CHAPTER TWENTY-FIVE

Lee

I woke up the next morning and treated Janelle to a brunch at Clary's. Her plane was leaving in the afternoon, and I wanted some alone time with her before she jetted off.

Mostly, I wanted her to dish on what she thought of last night and my friends. Plus, I needed a distraction from the constant replay of what almost went down with Maggie.

I couldn't stop thinking about it—the sound of her soft moans, those needy gasps as I ran my hands over her voluptuous body. How every bend, every curve still felt like a road only I was meant to travel, with my hands, lips, teeth.

I coughed and adjusted myself as we waited outside for a table, shoving my hands in my pockets to stop the nervous twitching—and to keep myself from reaching out and touching Janelle. After nearly tearing Magnolia's clothes off in the middle of the bar and getting promptly shut down, it just didn't feel right to cozy up to someone I wasn't even sure I wanted to be with in the first place—even if it was all for show.

Despite the phony circumstances, Janelle and I did have some sort of connection. Whether it was just a connection to Nashville or something more, I wasn't sure if it was worth exploring further. My heart just wasn't in it.

Instead, someone else had my heart, and they wanted absolutely nothing to do with it.

"This place is *so* Instagramable," she said, handing me her phone with the camera app open. "Here, get a shot of me by the front sign."

I obliged, handing the phone back over to her after shooting several angles. She thanked me by placing a kiss on my cheek. "I really like Savannah, Lee, but I heard something a little funny last night… Are you buying Magnolia's bar?"

My head snapped up. "Who told you that?"

"Overheard it from one of your friends. I'm just kinda tired of the secrets, Leland. I know we're together under false pretenses, but I thought we had something, a friendship at the very least. I thought you could tell me things." She didn't look up when she said it. Instead, she scrolled through her phone, chewing her bottom lip contemplatively—probably thinking up the perfect hashtags and filters for her photo.

"My writing career is so important to me, Janelle. I've always been a better writer here in Savannah than I ever was in Nash. And Maggie's my oldest and dearest friend. I want to help her out. I'm sorry I didn't tell you. It's just all really, really complicated."

She shrugged, still not looking up from her phone. "I mean, like, that's fine, but I'm your girlfriend for all intents and purposes. And if our story continues, I'm moving here, too. I think moving in together would be really good content and would shake up the algorithm, don't you think?"

I rolled my eyes, and thankfully, because she was so self-involved, she didn't see it.

"You can move here, but we're not moving in together, at least not yet. It's only been a few months."

"Weird, your brother and Magnolia are moving in together, and they've been dating just about the same amount of time as we have. You don't seem to have any issues with that, do you?" The hostess called my name, and we moved toward the inside of Clary's. As usual, the place was packed. "Whatever, I'm emailing my manager to talk about apartments. Anyway, Magnolia might need, or I guess, y'all might need a social media manager."

I cringed, thinking about Magnolia and Dane living together, sharing a bed, sharing moments like we almost did last night.

She shoved her phone back into her Birkan. "I think this will be good for *all* of us."

After a breakfast spent mindlessly scrolling through social media, I dropped Janelle at her hotel and headed down to the river, hoping to clear my head. I popped in my headphones, queued up a playlist of rising country artists, and pulled out my notebook, jotting down a few scattered thoughts and lyrics.

Since coming home, I'd felt a spark of inspiration I hadn't in years. Maybe it was being near my friends or being back where I first started writing music, but I knew being close to my muse had everything to do with it. A gorgeous, funny redhead who'd always kept me on my toes—how could she not inspire me?

I scribbled down a few verses, my eyes wandering over the crowds gathering for Sunday morning pop-up booths along the river. Tourists shuffled around with to-go cups of booze, day drinking their way through Savannah's charm, trying to squeeze out the last bits of their weekend.

That was when I saw her—perched on a picnic bench, staring out at the river. After everything that went down last night, of course she'd be here, lost in thought.

I debated walking over, sitting down next to her, being the one she could lean on, listen to whatever was swirling through her mind. But before I could decide, she must've felt my eyes on her. She turned, shook her head like she couldn't believe I was there, and then hopped off the bench, heading straight toward me.

"Hey, stranger," she drawled. She looked incredible, and not at all like she had probably been up until the wee hours of the morning putting the bar back together and calculating her earnings over and over, calling it a win.

Which I knew, for the first time in a long time, it was.

She handed me her cup, and I took a swig. Her signature coffee with a little bit of Bailey's mixed in. "Thanks again for doing the gig last night. It was such a hit. And, you know, for everything else. I'm sorry you left so abruptly before I could really tell you that."

The moment she got close, the scent of stale beer and the bar hit me. She hadn't slept. I took a long look at her face—last night's makeup still smudged around her eyes and the exhaustion written in every line.

"It was my pleasure. Hopefully, we can make this something semi-regular, and with all the changes we're planning on, make you some money."

"Mmhmm. That sounds nice." She kept her eyes on the river, and I handed her back her cup, watching her take a generous sip.

"She didn't know you were moving here," she said after we sat in a quiet stillness for a few moments. "In fact, she looked downright shocked."

"We talked a bit about it today. She's going to move here, too."

She looked at me, her eyes searching mine. "I know you, Lee Wilder.

I know you don't want this slow, unmoving life again. You can't just walk away from your dreams."

I took a deep breath, my gaze drifting for a moment. "Sometimes dreams can change when you figure out what it is that you really want. Sometimes it's not the things you thought you wanted, but the things you already had."

She let out a soft laugh, but there was a hint of tension behind it as she handed me back her drink. Her forehead crinkled slightly, worry flickering across her face. "Did you mean what you said last night? About us?"

I looked down at my feet resting on the bench. I meant what I said, and so much more. But I had to know where her heart was. I felt it last night, how she wanted me—just like I still wanted her. Like I always would. "Did you mean what you said about moving in with my brother? And marrying him?"

She shrugged. "I don't know, Lee. Yes. And sometimes, no. I was up all night thinking on it, and I'm exhausted. So much has changed since you came home. Some of it good, some of it not. And hearing you call it the biggest mistake of my life kind of struck a nerve. Is there something you're not telling me?"

Really wanting to avoid a fight, or watch her heart shatter into a million pieces, I plastered on a fake smile and said, "What about it isn't so good? Frankly, I've been having a good time since I came home, Maggie."

She sighed, took her drink from my hand, and then turned to face me. Her stare was intense as she licked her lips and looked straight into my eyes, as if she could see into my very soul. Putting the cup down, she grabbed my face, watching for a reaction. I didn't move. I'd stay in this spot my whole life if it meant she kept looking at me like she was. Finally, she leaned in and pressed her lips against mine, gently pushing my lips open with her tongue as her warmth spilled into my mouth and through my whole body.

The kiss lasted for all of fifteen seconds, but when she pulled away, her touch was still humming through my veins. It was the kind of kiss that leaves a mark, one I knew I'd feel for the rest of my life.

I fought back the carnal urge to pick her up, throw her over my shoulder, and carry her down the street to my hotel. I imagined throwing her on the bed, ripping off her clothes, and running my tongue up and down her body, listening to that perfect, sexy moan of hers as I made her mine once again.

Instead, she gently cupped my face and caught my gaze once again.

"That's the last time we ever share a kiss, Leland Wilder. From here on out, we're business partners. We're just friends. We both needed to get that out of our system, and now we can move on."

She climbed off the picnic bench and wiped the crumbs from the table off of her behind, squinting in the warm, bright Savannah sun. "I'll see you around, Lee." She smiled playfully before darting off up the cobblestone ramp and away from all the dirty, filthy things I wanted to do to her.

CHAPTER TWENTY-SIX

Magnolia

"You can't just go around kissing your ex-boyfriend to get it 'out of your system,' you idiot," Sutton said, a platter of fried chicken between us.

As usual, we were nursing some hangovers and watching shitty TV. Pickle jumped up on the coffee table and swatted at Sutton as she grabbed a piece of cornbread.

"Get this cat away from me. Seriously. I dry-heaved over this meal all afternoon, and here she is, trying to muck shit up, per usual."

"Down, Satan," I laughed, and the cat hissed and leaped off the table, perching herself on the back of my loveseat to glare at the two of us. I grabbed a drumstick and contemplated for a moment as I chewed. "No, it had to be done. Now, I can accept Dane's proposal, become an actual Wilder, and we can move on from this drama. All of us can move on from it. And I'll have full reign over my bar. Easy peasy."

Sutton looked uneasy. "Magnolia, what kind of wild, twisted logic is that? Come on now. You can't marry someone just for a business deal."

I snorted. "If Eunice can do it, I can do it, too."

Sutton spit pieces of chicken across the room, and Pickle went diving down like a seagull to hunt them. She caught one midair and hissed at Sutton. "What did you just say?"

I slapped my hand over my mouth and mumbled, "Nothing. I said nothing."

That was what I got for shutting down the bar at 5:00 a.m., chasing the night with a spiked coffee, kissing my ex, feeling invincible, and then skipping sleep. What the hell was wrong with me?

"Holy frickin' shit." Sutton scrambled to her feet, scaring Pickle to the point where she started howling like a wolf. "I *knew* it!"

"You knew nothing, Sutton. Sit down. I didn't mean it. I don't know what I'm talking about."

"Yes, you do! The day you told us about Cole and Eunice, you conveniently left out the part about Vance and Eunice having some sort of deal between them. But I knew it! There's no way she would have willingly married that snake. She's kind, loving, and smart. And Vance is…" Sutton shuddered. "Ugh, what the hell, Magnolia?"

She was hovering over me, waving a fried chicken breast around in her hand like a baton, letting the shreds of chicken fry fly all over my apartment that I had vacuumed at about 5:30 in the morning during a whiskey-induced sugar fit.

I put my hands up in a defensive stance. "Hi, Captain Crumbs, can you calm down?"

"I will *not* calm down. I don't feel good. I'm stressed out! I got up early to make you stupid chicken, and now you're kissing Lee and dropping bombs. Do you know how *hard* it is to be your friend sometimes?" She chucked her chicken at me, and Pickle wasted no time jumping up and snacking on it. Sutton took a seat across from me and glared.

"I'm sorry. I should have told you. I just… it wasn't my story to tell."

"Right, but it's your story to live?"

We stared each other down for a moment before she kneeled in front of me, putting her hands on my knees. "We've been friends for a long, long time. I have been with you through everything. Through puberty, through Lee round one, all the bad dates, your uncle dying, the Wilders basically taking control of your life. I love you, Magnolia. More than a sister. But I can't watch you throw away your life for a fucking bar."

I kept my steely gaze trained on Sutton. I wanted to hug her and tell her that I love her, too. Instead, I spit out, "The bar *is* my life, Sutton, and I'll do anything and everything to keep it in my family."

She rose, shook her head, grabbed her purse, and slammed the door behind her.

***

156

I took a long, hot shower, followed by an even longer nap. It was a restless sleep, though. I had a feeling the decisions I was making were affecting everyone and everything, including my relationship with Sutton, who, aside from Charlie, was all I had left for family these days. When I finally felt myself falling into a deep slumber, my phone buzzed. I picked it up, not even looking at the name on the screen.

"What," I growled.

"It's me. Can you let me in? The master lock is on." My brother sounded breathless and a little wary. I had a feeling I knew why he was on my doorstep.

"If you're here to lecture me, save it. I'm tired, and the bar opens up in two hours. Let me sleep."

He chortled. "What if I promised you half lecture and half brotherly advice? Would you take it?"

I groaned and crawled out of bed, padding through my apartment to unlock the hardly used front door, kicking aside boxes Lee had stored out of the way.

"Yikes, you look rough," he said when I flung open the door. Pickle stood in front of me, sitting on her haunches. She let out a long, vibrating hiss.

"Oh, shut up, Pickle!' We both hollered in unison, and Charlie pushed his way through the door and into my bedroom.

"Come on, lay back down. We can talk while you snuggle."

I nestled back in my bed, the blanket curled up around me, and Charlie sat at the foot, resting his head up against the wall. We sat quietly for a few minutes, and just before I felt the comfort of my brother wrap me up like an old quilt and drift off to sleep, he started running his mouth.

"You and Sutton need to work this out, Magnolia. We all know you're strong minded, but forcing yourself into an engagement and then ripping your best friend's head off when she's just trying to protect you is so unlike you. I mean, it's kind of like you, but come on now."

I rolled away from him and wrapped myself up like a burrito in my blankets.

Charlie jumped up off of the bed, and I could hear him pacing the room. "And Sutton is up to something. I don't know if she's squirrelly because you and Lee are freaking everyone out with your stupid will-they-won't-they drama, or if something else is bothering her. And you're way too self-involved to even see that she's hurting."

"You know what would be great?" I mumbled into my pillows. "If you would go away. Don't you have your own life to deal with?"

"Okay, so you want me to take you seriously, but then you want to hide when I talk to you about something super heavy? Come on now."

"Charlie, what I do with my time and my life is none of your business. *You* didn't inherit the bar. I did," I said, still not facing my brother. "You moved on, and you started a life elsewhere. The bar is mine, and however I can protect it, I will."

"It's funny that you say that because, honestly, I've been working over-time to help bail you out. But then Lee came back, and of course, he's going to save the day yet again. The bar might be yours, but our momma's name is on the front and her heart is buried somewhere in the walls. So, of course I care what happens. Stop being so goddamn stubborn."

I ripped the blankets off and sprang upright in bed. "*You* stop being stub-born. You and Sutton and Lee and everyone else! It's almost like *no one* wants to see me happy or to see me do something—finally—on my own!"

Charlie scrubbed his fingers through his hair wildly. I thought he was going to start ripping chunks out, he was so frustrated with me. "Marrying some-one who texts you shitty things in the middle of the night so that you can keep pouring beers for the rest of your life isn't doing it on your *own*, Magnolia."

If I hadn't been so tired, I would have jumped up and whacked him so hard across his giant, stupid head he would have seen stars. "It's a chess move, *Charles,*" I spat. "Maybe you just want me miserable, so it gives you an excuse not to get your own life together."

My brother threw his hands up in frustration. "Don't you get it? We all want to see you happy! That's why we all walk on eggshells. It's why we all cod-dle you, why we all *enable* you." He crossed the room and towered over me, his face turning red. "It's why we all stood outside the Wilder house and told Dane to leave you alone because we *know* he's a snake in the damned grass! Why, when Lee left, I sat up here every single night and held you while you fucking cried! Because you're my sister, and I love you. I'm doing my best here, but I won't stand by you if you marry him."

I let out a harsh, derisive laugh, pulling my knees up to my chest. Charlie had only gotten truly mad at me a handful of times in my life, and this was one of them. "What do you mean?" My voice cracked, betraying the fear I was trying to hide. The thought of him walking out, leaving me behind, twisted my gut. He was all I had left, the only family I had, and the idea of losing him too was more than I could bear.

"What I mean, Magnolia, is maybe I'm tired of cleaning up your messes, and I don't want to have to say 'I told you so' when shit hits the fan with Dane." He stomped out of my room, making him the third person in twenty-four long hours to slam the door in my face and walk out fuming at me.

I spent the rest of the afternoon tossing and turning, my pillow damp from tears I hadn't meant to cry. The silence of my room felt oppressive, each passing minute a reminder of the fights I couldn't take back. Lee's words still echoed in my ears, raw and jagged, and I couldn't shake the way Sutton's and Charlie's disappointment had settled into my chest like a weight I couldn't lift.

Eventually, I sat up, staring at the phone on my nightstand as if it might somehow make the decision for me. My stomach churned as I reached for it, my hands trembling slightly. This was the call I'd been avoiding for weeks—the one I knew could unravel everything, or set it all in motion.

Taking a deep breath, I dialed the number, the sound of each ring amplifying the pounding in my head.

"What's up, baby?" Dane sounded just as tired as I did, but I didn't care. I had some things to say.

"When you come home, I'm moving in, and I hope you didn't give your momma back that ring because I want it."

CHAPTER TWENTY-SEVEN

Lee

Stretching, I surveyed my apartment, my eyes drifting over the half-unpacked chaos that still cluttered every corner. It had been a few months since I moved back to Savannah, and the city was finally starting to feel like home again. Ryan was in his own apartment down the street, and across town at a safe distance, Janelle had made herself quite comfortable not only as Savannah's newest Instagram Queen, but as the social media manager for O'Malley's and Jordan and Doyle's wine and artisanal cheese shop, Cheese, Please!

Since my brother came back from Atlanta a few months ago, he and Magnolia had been absorbed in talks about moving in together. It felt like their plans dominated everything, including whatever plans we had made for the bar. With a sparkling new ring on her finger, wedding preparations had consumed every spare moment she had. So, for the most part, the small renovations we could afford with the little cash I had were left entirely up to me.

Everything had shifted the moment Dane came back. Magnolia wasn't the fiery, wild spirit she used to be. When I'd drop by Momma's, I'd find them all lost in deep, drawn-out conversations about floral arrangements and color schemes. She'd even started dressing in a way that reminded me of Momma—swapping her raggedy sweats and jeans for tailored blazers and cigarette pants in perfectly coordinated colors.

They planned a lavish wedding in Forsyth Park where they had taken their first stroll for Valentine's Day. At first, I felt my blood boil over it, remembering all of the moments Magnolia and I shared in that very same park, in front of that very same fountain, but I had to let it go.

If this was what she wanted, I couldn't stop her. No one could.

But I couldn't, for the life of me, stop thinking about that kiss by the river. Or any of the five million that came before that one.

We'd spend what little time she offered me going over paperwork and figures, and when she was done with me, she flitted off to Dane or Momma, and I stayed behind to compare paint swatches or look over the renovation plans. She decided to stay in her apartment until after the wedding, citing Pickle as an excuse, and that was the only small comfort I had, catching glimpses of her now and then.

I stopped by Cheese, Please! to pay off a balance, then dropped in to see Charlie next door. He was still working on the piece for Maggie but had slowed down a bit to focus on some custom holiday gifts.

"Hey, man," I called out.

He stuck his head around the corner of his studio and waved me back. "What's up, brother," he said, pulling a couple of beers out of his fridge. He twisted one open and handed it to me. "I haven't seen you in a few days. How's Janelle?"

"She's great," I fibbed. "We're going to dinner in a bit."

"She's really awesome, Lee. I'm glad she's here," he said halfheartedly.

I let out a puff of a laugh. "Bullshit. She's a pain in the ass, and we both know it."

He shook his head, chuckling. "She's not so bad. Sutton can't stand her as far as she can throw her, but she's a tough one. She only likes her boys and Magnolia."

My heart skipped at the sound of her name. There was a void, and I couldn't, no matter how hard I tried, fill it with anything. Even seeing her while we worked wasn't enough.

"Are you ready for the big engagement party tomorrow?" I wanted to change the subject to an even worse subject, apparently.

"Are any of us ready for this fake shitshow? At least we know the food will be good. Sutton's been driving me nuts with the menu plans. I'm like, cook the chicken, bake the pie, we're all going to be drunk anyway."

I grinned and took a seat on one of the paint-speckled stools, admiring the installation he was working on. He'd been fussing over it for months—the famous Bird Girl statue, only it was fashioned out of hubcaps and old wine bottles from next door.

"She's really going through with it, huh?" I finally blurted out.

Charlie sighed, sitting across from me. "I mean, at this point, I think it's to spite us all. But the worst part is the wardrobe—those stiff skirt suits and buttoned-up jackets. She looks like she's auditioning for the role of 'Corporate Overlord Barbie.'"

I practically spit my beer out. "She actually had on a brooch today. She stopped by Momma's before she went to drop off some bottles of gin off at the bridge club building. At least she's not actually playing bridge. Yet."

"That's my sister. When she's hellbent on doing something, she will do it no matter what anyone else thinks."

I shrugged. "I mean, I guess I feel like I'm doing all of this for nothing. What's going to happen after they get married? I have this sinking feeling that Dane's going to dig his claws into her and sell off the bar right from underneath her. Or worse, convince her it's the right thing to do. Where does that leave me?"

Charlie thought on it for a minute, then slowly rose from his stool to adjust a bottle dangling off his piece slightly to the right. It didn't make a difference to me, but I wasn't the artist. "My guess is she's just happier that you're here than if you weren't," he offered.

I hadn't told anyone about our kiss. I knew that Sutton had been privy to the information because she got hammered one night and pulled me aside to try to get me to talk Maggie out of marrying my brother, citing the kiss as one of the many reasons why Maggie didn't, in fact, want to go through with it.

I'd shot her down, walked her home, and we didn't talk about it again.

"She's been around a little bit more these days, between the holiday parties and the historic trolley tour. I don't know, it's just not the same."

"By the same, do you mean she's not shooting heart eyes across the room to you, especially when you play your gigs?" Charlie ribbed.

"Very funny. But yes," I smirked, but it really wasn't funny at all. My mind flickered back to the way she barely looked at me anymore, her eyes colder than I remembered them ever being. There used to be warmth there—a spark that felt like home. Now, it was like she was building walls with every glance, and I couldn't tell if I was supposed to climb them or leave them be.

"Dane's leaving the day after tomorrow anyway," Charlie said before finishing off his beer and meticulously saving it for some later project. "Magnolia said he'd be gone throughout the holidays, so perhaps she'll be around the bar more often and you two can resume your tortured ex-lovers routine".

"Seriously? That's shitty. Magnolia loves Christmas."

Charlie nodded. "I know, but he's got a trial that runs until January third or something. We had lunch the other day, but I couldn't hear her over the size of her Meghan Markle fascinator."

We both bent over laughing just as Sutton barreled through the front door carrying a couple of pints from Leopold's.

"What are you doing here?" She sat next to me and handed Charlie a tub of ice cream, eyeing me suspiciously. Ever since the night she tried to talk me into convincing Magnolia she was still in love with me, she'd been avoiding me. And, of course, I was the only one who knew her secret. I figured she was keeping her distance, so she didn't have to remember that she told the truth.

A few weeks after my first gig at O'Malley's, right after Dane got down on one knee on the second floor of the Olde Pink House and asked Magnolia to be his bride for real this time, Sutton and I had a heated argument about when to tell Maggie the truth about what happened between Sutton and Dane. She kept wavering, not wanting to hurt her friend but still worried about jeopardizing her own career.

So, I tried to come up with ways to tell Magnolia that I was sure he was cheating on her and that I felt like someone was in the background of that damn video call, but with what evidence? A shadow?

I just didn't have enough solid proof yet. I was relying on rumors and a gut feeling that I wasn't sure I could trust. And if I went to Maggie with just some half-baked speculation, she'd see right through me and think I was trying to break her and Dane apart because of my lingering feelings for her.

Honestly, with the scant proof I had, the one thing I was absolutely certain of was that no one wanted to unravel the delicate bond we'd finally managed to rebuild. So, I was doing my best with what I had—desperately trying to untangle the storm of feelings that refused to die, no matter how much time had passed. They weren't just lingering—they were clawing their way back to the surface, demanding to be felt, to be reckoned with.

"I was just leaving. I'll see y'all at my momma's tomorrow." I hugged Charlie and kissed Sutton on the top of her head, listening to her exhale sadly as I did so.

I thought about heading back to my apartment, but my feet led me straight to the bar . Every chance I got, I found myself drawn to the old, weathered building. There was something comforting about being there, a sense of coming home that took me back to my teenage years. I loved taking in the little improvements and the renovations I'd been working on, feeling a kind of connection with the place that made it feel like my own.

But mostly, I just liked looking at the girl behind the bar.

She was busy doing inventory when I opened the door. Boxes lined the bar and the tables, and my heart sank.

"Moving out already?"

She turned around, almost letting a bottle of tequila slip through her hands. She had her hair, now slightly longer, in a messy top knot. Black leggings hugged her curves, and she had on my old hoodie again. Black-framed glasses perched on her nose, and she pushed them up a bit before finishing the task of wiping down the bottle.

This was Magnolia in all her unfiltered glory. If I weren't here, in her space, I'd miss these fleeting glimpses of her everyday life.

"Christmas decorations," she said, jutting her chin out toward the boxes. "I wanted to get them up before we opened tonight because we won't be around tomorrow." She spun back toward the bar, and her massive emerald-cut ring caught the light, flashing so brightly it nearly blinded me.

I crossed the room and opened up a box, letting clouds of dust float across the space. It had been years since these decorations had made their way out of the attic. After delicately unwrapping the tissue from the antique ornaments and carefully placing them on the table, I made my way to a large box in the corner of the room. Inside was a decrepit, old silver tree that was missing half of its limbs. "I don't remember this mangled thing. Was this your tree?"

She beamed, coming from behind the bar to stand next to me, handing me a cold beer from the ice chest. "No, actually, it was my momma's. Or her momma's. She hated this old thing. She always made my daddy go and get a real one every year. Actually, this will be the first year I don't get a real tree myself."

She poked her head into the box and then shut it, reaching for the roll of packing tape on the bar. "We don't have to put this up. Something might jump out of the remaining branches and latch onto a customer's neck," she declared before walking away.

"Why aren't you getting a tree this year?" I called after her. I knew the reason, but I still asked at any rate.

"Dane hates all the Christmas shit." She shrugged. "If the trolley wasn't stopping by, I probably wouldn't even put any of this up."

Her cool tone didn't catch me off guard. I had grown used to it over the past few months. Yet, Christmas had always been her favorite time of year, a season she cherished deeply, so it surprised me that, especially with Dane out of town, she wasn't acting more excited.

When we were kids, Charlie would drag her down to the old lot outside the church, and the two of them would pick out the raggediest tree they could afford with what little money Cole could scrounge up. They'd sit up every Christmas Eve, keeping a years-old tradition alive to see who could stay awake the longest and catch Santa, even though neither of them believed.

Even when they were in their twenties, Cole would sneak up the back staircase after he'd hear them snoring from down in the bar and sneak presents under the tree.

She loved everything about Christmas—the baking, the cookies, the music, the lights. Lord, she'd drag me up and down every square in Savannah just to see all the big houses lit up like they were signaling aliens from space. And every year, when we got to my momma's house, she'd stop, smile, and say, "I'll have lights like this one day."

What she loved most, though, was the way Christmas reminded her of her momma, who cherished the holiday more than anything. Every year, she'd place a star made of seashells on top of the tree—a star that had once adorned the tree in the house where she was born on Tybee Island.

We quietly put up the decorations, and when we were done, she paused, taking in the room with a deep breath, her lips curling into a bittersweet smile. "Jordan will come by tomorrow to bring some holiday-inspired floral displays, and we'll be done." The half-smile still lingered on her lips, but her voice betrayed a deep weariness. "I'm going to get ready for tonight. Thanks for all your help."

She didn't look back at me as she made her way to the door that led to the staircase leading up to her apartment. I stood frozen in the middle of the room, holding on to a star made of seashells, a single, quiet tear falling down my face.

I opened Momma's front door, Janelle following close behind me. The house was buzzing with wait staff, florists, and a gaggle of other workers scrambling about as they finished the last minute touches on the engagement party.

Making our way through the sea of chaos, I pushed open the double doors leading to the kitchen, where we found Sutton sweating and swearing at herself as she popped a few pans into the oven.

Turning to Janelle, I kissed her cheek. "Why don't you go find the bride-to-be and see if she needs anything?"

Janelle rolled her eyes but marched down the marble foyer and up the winding staircase in search of Maggie. She'd find her in the guest bathroom, undoubtedly rolling around in the bathtub, letting her nerves get the best of her. If Maggie was smart, though, she would have locked the door this time.

"Here, let me help." I rolled up the sleeves of my light-gray button down and started placing bacon-wrapped scallops on a serving dish.

Charlie walked in, saw me working alongside Sutton, and rolled up his sleeves as well. Sutton pulled a pan off the stovetop, forgetting her oven mitt, and howled.

"Fuck, y'all, I can*not* do this!"

Charlie went to her and wrapped his arms around her shoulders, and I grabbed the two of them, scooting them as a unit over to the sink so she could run her hand under the water.

"It's just another party, Sutton. It's just food. Stop freaking out." I removed her from Charlie's grasp and picked her up, putting her on the counter like a child. She pouted.

"Besides," Charlie added, grabbing a dish towel for her to wrap her hand in, "when the kitchen at O'Malley's is done, you won't have to work at LaMonte's anymore."

"We should tell her," she whispered, looking down at the burn on her hand.

"You want to tell her now"—I gestured wildly toward the food strewn about the kitchen—"while you're in the middle of cooking for her engagement party?"

Sutton huffed. "Well, Lee, we should have told her earlier, but you said you'd come up with some grand plan to tell her and never did. And when I suggested you bring up the kiss with Magnolia…"

"Wait, what are you guys talking about?" Charlie said, head volleying between us like he was watching a tennis match. "When did you kiss my sister?"

"I mean, we dated for a while, Charlie…"

"Don't be stupid, Lee," Sutton interjected. "Maggie kissed Lee by the river, the morning after his first gig at O'Malley's. I thought if Lee pleaded his case to Maggie, citing said kiss, she'd realize that she was still in love with him and call this stupid farce with Dane off."

Charlie shook his head in bewilderment, then turned toward me, shooting me a wicked glare. "Is that true?"

"I'm sorry I didn't tell you. It's just…"

"He didn't tell you that because if he did, he'd also have to tell you Dane made a pass at me and Vance threatened me within an inch of my life not to say anything." Sutton reached over, grabbed a bottle of wine, and took a huge gulp.

"Lord above, Sutton, you are so damn dramatic, he just… kind of threatened your livelihood. Anyway, Charlie, I'm sorry I didn't say anything. But, truth be told, that's not the whole of it."

"What?" Charlie and Sutton both bellowed in unison.

"I'm pretty sure Dane's—"

"What's going on?" Dane asked, waltzing into the kitchen in a three-piece suit, perfect dark-brown hair styled on top of his head. He leaned over the three of us, grabbing a scallop and popping it into his mouth. I could feel Sutton tense up as he got close to her.

"I just burned my hand. I'm fine." She hopped down and moved to the other side of the kitchen, letting Charlie bandage her hand.

"Where's the blushing bride?" I asked, plating the small cups of cornbread casserole and desperately trying to swing the mood in the kitchen back to cooking instead of the murderous rage plastered over Charlie's face.

"I haven't seen her. I did happen to run into Janelle, though. Damn, she is smoking hot. How did you nail that? Oh, that's right, the label bought her for you." He winked at Sutton before strolling out onto the veranda and down the back steps into our parents' yard.

"Hate his face!" Sutton hissed, as Charlie finished putting the burn solution on her hand.

"We all hate his face," I mumbled, turning the timer on the oven. I reached into Momma's fridge and pulled out one of the thirty-five bottles of white wine she had stored for the occasion. I handed it off to Charlie who opened it and poured three glasses, passing them to Sutton and me.

"So, what are we going to do, Lee? Are you going to tell my sister the truth?" Charlie ran his hands through his hair, mussing up the careful placement. "I can't believe that we're standing here, at her engagement party, having this conversation."

"We should wait, then," Sutton said, pushing off the counter. "Let's just try to get through this sham of a day and figure out how to tell her when it's over. Deal?"

"We've been through worse guys, we can do this," Charlie said, putting his glass in the middle of the three of us so we could clink them together. "I still don't forgive you for lying to my face, though, Lee."

"We might have been through worse," Sutton said, gulping down almost her whole glass in one sip, "but we might not recover from this one."

CHAPTER TWENTY-EIGHT

Magnolia

As I laid in the cool ceramic tub, trying to talk myself down from a panic attack, I heard a soft knock on the bathroom door. "Go away!" I yelled, figuring it was Lee. It had been months since he moved home, and it would be so poetic that he would find me back in the tub, crying yet again about marrying his brother.

Only this time, I was going through with it.

"Magnolia, it's Janelle. Why don't you go on and open up? Let's have a bit of girl talk before your big party."

I rolled my eyes, climbed out of the tub, and clicked open the bathroom door. Backing up, I lifted my long, emerald-green dress and perched myself on the bathroom counter. Janelle locked the door behind her, crossed the long, tiled-floor bathroom, and promptly dropped her panties, sitting on the toilet to pee.

"Oh, alright then," I said, turning my head the other way. "We're like that now, huh?"

"Girl, we're never going to be like that, but I had four Tito's before coming here because, in the interest of girl talk, I am nervous as hell about tonight." She wiped, flushed, and waltzed over to the sink to wash her hands.

"*You're* nervous? At *my* engagement party? Man, you are self-involved, huh?"

She let out a cackle and studied my face, crossing her arms. "Of course I'm nervous. My man is in *love* with you. I'm scared to death that he's going to drop some huge bomb tonight while everyone's toasting your engagement. He's not the type to wait for the nuptials and the 'speak now or forever hold your peace' shit. Especially when it concerns you."

I shook my head. "My God, Janelle. Let it go. I'm with Dane, and we're getting married. And you're on my goddamned payroll. Watch your mouth."

She tilted her head and played with the hem of her skirt. "He's in love with you, Magnolia. He has been his entire life. I've listened to the albums, heard the stories. I lay in his bed sometimes and stare at the picture of the two of you from a summer a million years ago when you were just friends, and he loved you then, too."

Janelle paused to collect her thoughts, perhaps holding back tears.

"I'm not stupid. Lee and I are together because of circumstance, not fate. But you and him, that's written in the stars. We all know it. Maybe not your fiancé, but the rest of us see it. Please, Magnolia, I have feelings for Lee. Don't be selfish and mess this up for all of us."

"Every single move I've made has been to keep things from getting screwed up again, Janelle."

She met my eyes, and for the first time, I saw how much pain she was in. But we were both in pain. All of us were, in one way or another.

"Lee is my friend. He always will be. But that's it. That's all there is to it." I bounced off the counter and flung open the bathroom door, stomping down the staircase of a house I hoped to own one day, toward a party I hoped to own today. I found my brother fussing over Sutton's wrapped hand in the breakfast nook, Lee sweating as he bounced around the kitchen, scrambling to put together plates of hors d'oeuvres. "What the hell happened?" I demanded, rushing over to Sutton.

"Easy, bridezilla. It was an accident," Sutton snarled.

I flinched. "I'm worried about you. God, can you please stop being like this? Can't anyone just be freaking happy for me?" I grabbed a half-empty bottle of white wine conveniently sitting on the counter, sipped straight out of the bottle, and shot them all a dirty look before marching toward the veranda to my hiding spot behind the azalea bush.

I sat there, stewing, gripping the bottle of wine like it could somehow cool down the heat rising in me. We all knew this was bullshit, but I had to go through with it. Too late to back out now, right? I glanced up at the big, whirling ceiling fan on the veranda, remembering how, as a kid, I'd come out here wishing for everything I had now.

And, for whatever reason, it still wasn't enough.

I wanted to marry Dane and get it over with. The second I was Magnolia Wilder, everything would be different. Maybe, once I signed the paperwork and

Dane and I got married, I could wiggle my way into a bigger share of the Trust and buy them all out, securing the fate of the bar on my own. And just like Eunice, I would live happily ever after on Jones Street in my big, southern townhome.

When he wanted to be, Dane could be a good man. He worked hard. He was easy on the eyes. Since we'd been engaged and planning the wedding, he'd been less aggressive, like he won some sort of contest. He was calmer, more collected. Aside from the upcoming trial, which always had him on edge, he had a sweet demeanor about him, even with his brother lurking on the sidelines, watching our every move.

That would be good enough for the rest of my life, right?

Dane found me on the terrace, sipping straight out of a bottle and staring up at the ceiling. "Hey, baby, what are you doing out here?" He leaned in and kissed me on the top of my head, and I rubbed his back as he sat next to me.

"Just a case of the nerves, is all. I'll be in shortly. How are you feeling?"

"I'm feeling good. Believe it or not, I'm a little nervous, too."

A quick laugh escaped me. "The unshakable Dane Wilder is afraid of a party? Color me shocked, y'all."

"It's not the party, Magnolia. It's you. It's us. It's Lee hovering around. You know, this isn't exactly the situation I was hoping for when we said our nuptials."

I studied his face. He looked tired and not quite himself. Something was eating him up inside. "You sure that's it, Dane?"

"I'm sure, darlin'. Let's go on in and socialize a bit before Momma comes looking for us."

We walked into the party, arm in arm. Before we hit the floor-to-ceiling French doors, Dane took the wine bottle out of my hands and took a long gulp. After we made our rounds, listened to a handful of toasts to our health and happiness, and everyone in Savannah surveyed my ring like it was the rock of Gibraltar, I took a break from socializing to check on Sutton.

She worked quietly, cleaning up the carnage that was the Wilder kitchen after working her ass off. She looked exhausted. It occurred to me that we were all tired, emotionally drained, and not like ourselves.

"Wanna sleep over tonight, like old times? You can bring some left over key lime pie, and I'll raid the bar for booze. We can have some good old fashioned girl talk. Does that sound good?"

Sutton didn't look up from the pans she was scrubbing. "No thanks, Magnolia. I just want to go home and go to bed."

I tried to hide my disappointment. "Well, maybe soon. I'm tired, too. Will I see you tomorrow at the menu planning meeting for the Historical Holiday Tour?"

Sutton slammed down the pot she was scrubbing into the hot, soapy water, then winced from her earlier wound. "God damn it, Magnolia. You're not my fucking boss. But, yes, princess, of course I'll be there to save your life and be there at your beck and call, just like I always am."

My head snapped back, and I fought down the tears and rage trying to bubble up inside of me. "I'm sorry, Sutton. If you don't want to do it, then don't do it."

"Maybe you should take your own advice." She grabbed her bags off the counter, leaving her mess behind.

She stopped in the doorway before pushing open the swinging door to the back entrance of the kitchen, keeping her back to me. "We're all just a little exhausted from having to take care of you all the time. When are you going to step up and be the friend that we all are to you?"

Later that night, after the party had cleared out and I had performed the part of the dutiful future wife, I staggered into the bar and let Kasey go from her shift. I turned on the radio, cranked up the volume, and got to work putting away the few bottles used that night while cleaning up the rest of the bar. It wasn't a huge task, since taking a look at the register and the credit card slips it was yet another quiet night at the bar.

I thought about shooting Sutton a message and apologizing, but I wasn't sure exactly *what* I would be apologizing for in the first place. She was clearly upset about something, and if she didn't want to talk to me about it, I couldn't force her.

I felt like the second Dane slipped the ring on my finger, my friendships started slipping away. Charlie didn't stop by as much as he usually did. Jordan and Doyle were distant unless it concerned either one of our businesses or the trolley tour. Sutton was clearly growing more distant by the minute.

And Lee and I only saw each other in passing, which was, of course, mostly of my doing. I thought if I kept him at arm's length, I could start to move on.

All of it was part of moving forward and becoming someone in a serious relationship—not to mention a business owner—but I hated feeling like I was joining one family but losing the one that had become my whole world. I'd already lost so much in the last twenty-eight years. I couldn't handle losing anyone else.

I lifted up my phone to text Sutton when the door to the bar flung open. "We're closed," I called out. I heard feet running through the bar, and I looked up, my heart racing. If I'd forgotten to lock the door, and if there was a break-in, they'd take what little I had.

"I'm so sorry, Magnolia," Sutton cried, running behind the bar and wrapping me up in a long, tear-soaked hug.

The two of us stood there, crying all over each other and holding on until my arms started to fall asleep.

When I finally pulled away and wiped the tears from her round, red face, I asked the question I'd been wanting to ask her for weeks. "What's really going on, Sutton? And please don't lie to me."

She sighed and looked nervously around the bar. "Let's get this place cleaned up and then we can talk, okay?"

Sutton helped me close down, and after flicking off the lights, we headed up to my apartment with a bottle of rum, mixers, and a blender. She got the floor situated with blankets and pillows, and I poured the pina colada concoction into an oversized vase. I grabbed a pack of comically large straws left over from a bachelorette party and a couple of bags of chips before meeting her in the living room.

We sipped and snacked quietly for a few minutes before I put my hand on her knee and met her eyes, pleading for her to tell me what was on her mind.

She let out a heavy sigh before spilling the story about Dane coming on to her. She explained how she was going to tell me everything until Vance showed up and threatened to have LaMonte fire her. I listened, stone-faced, my skin crawling with each new detail.

I suspected Dane was involved in our spat somehow, but I didn't want to admit it to myself. Hearing her say it out loud brought me to tears so fierce I could hardly catch my breath.

"I told Lee, the night of his first gig when I was in the green room crying all over him in just my bra," she started, a stark sadness lacing her voice. "We thought we'd try to come up with a plan to tell you, to gather up some more evidence, but I guess… I don't know Magnolia. I really don't know what to say other than I was terrified."

"I get it. I've done some stupid things so that I didn't lose what I have, too," I offered through wracked sobs.

Sutton nervously pulled at her bottom lip with her teeth. "That's not all of it, I'm afraid."

I pulled the blanket up to my neck, bracing for the bombshell Sutton was about to drop. The way her face turned white as a sheet told me this was going to be one of those moments where I'd better hold on tight.

"This land, this building, it's worth a lot," she started softly. "And I'm not sure if you know this, but it's also not protected by any sort of historical society. Or really protected by anything…"

Sutton got quiet for a moment, and I jerked my chin at her to go on, shaking under my blanket.

"I overheard at work that Dane was shopping the property around to some huge investment firm out of Atlanta. They're looking to tear down the building and put up one of those mixed-use high-rises—shops on the bottom, condos on top."

Being betrayed by my fiancé and having my future father-in-law threaten her was bad enough. But selling my bar, my family's only legacy and the land that it stood on for a high-rise?

A quiet, angry, "Wow," was all I could muster.

"So, I guess none of it really mattered, then. Not you raising money as fast as you can and Lee investing into the Trust. No matter what, Dane was always going to try and sell this place right out from underneath you."

"Wow," was all I could say again.

"I'm so sorry, Magnolia. This is all my fault."

"No, Sutton. It's not your fault, and don't ever let me hear you say that again."

She wiped her cheeks with the sleeve of her shirt. "Do you hate me?"

I shook my head. "No, I couldn't. Ever. You're my sister, Sutton. Nothing will ever come between us. I'm sorry some foolish man tried." We both murmured a faint, bittersweet laugh, and I leaned in to her, putting my head on her shoulder. "Just promise me you won't ever keep anything like that from me again," I said.

"Promise. What are you going to do?"

I shrugged. "I'm going to marry him. I need to get my claws into that Trust somehow, or I'll lose everything. Nothing about this situation changes. It's still a business deal."

Sutton shook her head and then took a huge guzzle of our drink. "Magnolia, you can't go through with this. He'll make you sign a pre-nup. It's just so awful to me you'd marry Dane and then lose your happiness in the midst of it all."

I leaned over and grabbed her hand. "The bar is my happiness. It's everything. I had a great romance once. That's enough for me."

Sutton started tearing up again.

"Oh my gosh, that just sounds so awful! I seriously can't get behind this. I mean, I will if I have to because I love you. But it's going to be so hard for me to watch, especially since that *great romance* is still in Savannah and is clearly still crazy about you after all these years."

Hearing her say what we all knew all this time made my stomach do a somersault.

"Wonder why Lee never told me the truth, either," I muttered.

"I think it's because he's still in love with you, and you're still in love with him, and he was just hoping and praying you'd figure that out on your own."

I almost opened my mouth to respond to Sutton when she yawned into a huge stretch and laid back on her pillow.

"If this is what you want, what you truly, genuinely want, I will stand by you every step of the way. Maybe once it's all said and done, there will be less drama. We're off to a good start. I haven't had to pull you out of any bushes recently."

My best friend's tired eyes rolled back in her head, and I realized how exhausted I was, too. I curled up next to her, and Pickle settled in between us, purring wildly. Before I knew it, my eyes were opening to the dawn of a brand new day.

And, I hoped, a brand new start for me and Sutton.

CHAPTER TWENTY-NINE

Lee

I'd just left another awkward, silent brunch with Janelle and was making my way over to Charlie's when my phone buzzed. A picture of Sutton wearing a crooked chef's hat and a goofy grin flashed across my screen.

"Hey, where are you? We need to talk." She sounded tired and like she was hurrying through the streets of Savannah on foot.

"I'm outside of Collins Quarter, heading toward Charlie's. What's up?"

"Can you meet me at Sixpence? I can be there in, like, ten minutes. I'm still in pajamas, though. Don't judge me."

"Have I ever?" I let out a quick laugh and made my way toward the pub. I bellied up to the bar, waiting for my pajama-clad friend to arrive.

She walked in looking like she had been up all night crying, but she slapped a wide-toothed grin on her face as soon as she saw me. As she got closer, I saw a semi-crazy glistening in her eyes.

Sutton was scheming, and it was written all over her face.

"Whatever crazy-ass shit you're up to, the answer is no," I said, as she sat down, pulling up the sleeves of her hooded sweatshirt to her elbows and rubbing her hands together excitedly.

"Shut up, you're going to want to hear this." She signaled for the bartender, who had seen her coming a mile away and dropped an already-poured hard cider in front of her. After a long sip, she took a deep, steadying breath. "She's still in love with you, you know."

I watched her suck down half of her drink, eyes darting around wildly, and I realized she was looking for anyone that knew Dane or my family. She didn't want anyone overhearing this.

"What did you just say?" I kept my voice low, but my heart was about to leap out of my chest. I heard her, of course, but I wanted her to say the words again.

I *needed* her to say the words again. To tell me what I had been waiting for so long to hear.

That Maggie still loved me.

"Magnolia's still in love with you. She referred to you as 'the greatest romance of her life.' Now, she did make it sound like it was final, but she also called her marriage to your brother a business deal again. You don't business-deal-marry someone if you're not still, after all this time, in love with someone else."

That wasn't exactly what I wanted to hear, but I pressed her on anyway. "I guess I don't follow."

She growled and rolled her eyes. "Listen to me. We have until February before this sham of a wedding happens. Dane's gone to trial, he left this morning. So, you have from now until early January to try and change Magnolia's mind. She wants to marry a Wilder so she can become a bigger part of the family Trust and save her bar. Why can't it be the Wilder she loves?"

I shrugged. This wasn't shaking out like I had hoped it would. "Sutton, I have a girlfriend. I mean, well, you know what I mean."

"Maybe if I get to the part where I tell you I spilled *all* of the beans last night, like every single bean in the pot, you'll get it through that thick head of yours that even after Magnolia found out the truth about Dane, she still wants to marry him." She was blinking feverishly and staring at me like this was good news.

"Sutton, if she heard all of that, which I mean I'd love you to elaborate on that part more instead of whatever this insanity is," I gestured wildly in between us, "and she still wants to marry Dane, what does that even mean?"

"That she still loves you!" she shrieked, giddily bouncing around in her seat.

I groaned and put my head in my hands. "Sutton, I love you, but I am not following a word you are saying right now."

She squealed again, an incoherent sound that made her neighbor on the stool to her left jump, and slapped a ten-dollar bill on the bar. "Don't you worry that unbelievably pretty little face of yours, Leland Wilder. This is all going to fall into place just like it should."

I sat at the bar for a few more minutes after she dashed out the door and tried to figure out what in the world she was trying to get at. I had no idea what she meant. And I wouldn't even know what to do about it if I did.

Or did I?

After spending the afternoon with Charlie, I ran a quick errand before I stopped by the bar to help Magnolia and Jordan finish setting up for the Historical Holiday Tour.

"I'm back here," Magnolia hollered from her office.

Jordan was nowhere in sight, but his signature was everywhere. He'd hung up strings of holly berries and strategically placed small Christmas trees and poinsettias all around the bar. Alongside the twinkle lights Maggie and I had already peppered around the place, the room now had a cozy, inviting vibe.

I found her sitting at her desk, flipping through a bridal magazine, dog earring pages and making notes.

My heart sank. After my conversation with Sutton, I almost believed I'd walk in and find her ripping up all the wedding-related bullshit she had littered our office with and calling the whole damn thing off.

"Hey," I said, leaning on the doorframe.

She looked up and offered me a half-smile, before going back to her wedding plans.

I crossed the office and sat across from her, observing her for a few moments. She had her hair, longer than when I had arrived in Savannah a few months before, in a half top knot on her head, and she had on minimal makeup, putting her sexy, kissable freckles on full display.

It took everything in my power not to jump over the desk, rip her out of her seat, throw her ass on the desk, and ravage her. "I thought I'd check in and see if you guys needed any help, with the decorations or whatever," I said instead.

She shook her head, not looking up from the glossy pages of Savannah Bridal. "You saw the bar when you walked through. Does it look like anything else needs to be done?"

I bit my lip, trying not to laugh. She certainly didn't sound like someone who was still in love with the man sitting in front of her. Her walls were up, and there was no knocking them down.

Not yet anyway.

"I just left Charlie's," I said, hopping up to fix a drink from our office stash. "He wants you to stop by later. He has some paperwork from Jordan about the trolley stops for the tour he needs you to look over. I guess they're making some changes to the itinerary, so they're having a little impromptu meeting."

She tossed the magazine on the desk, picked up her phone, and made an exasperated noise at whatever she was reading on the screen. "They're starting now. I'm going to go," she said, grabbing her purse. "Do you need to be there?"

"Nope, I already gave my input. I'll get the bar open. Take your time."

"Thanks, Lee. See you in a bit." She rushed out of the bar, and I hoped to God she didn't see my rental outside… or what was on top of it.

CHAPTER THIRTY

Magnolia

After what felt like a completely useless meeting, I left Charlie's and stopped in to Treylor Park to pick up an order of fried chicken and waffle tacos—Lee's favorite—to bring back to the bar as some sort of peace offering.

On my walk to Charlie's studio, my mind kept circling back to what Sutton had confessed. Each word felt like it had carved out a new wound. The closer I got to Charlie's, the more I wondered if I could really go through with this marriage. Every step I took felt heavier, like the weight of Sutton's revelation was pressing down on me, making me question everything.

But where I should have felt grief, a weight seemed to lift off my shoulders. I didn't have to pretend anymore. I didn't have to put on a show because what I had wanted, this arrangement with Dane, was becoming just that. A business deal.

It also opened up a wound I didn't know was festering. I was more hurt that everyone had lied to me and covered up Dane's dealings instead of telling me the truth.

Was that my fault? Were they protecting me because I wouldn't stop beating them down with a stick, insisting this is what I wanted with Dane?

Lee had been in this bar almost every day for months, holding this in. He knew about Dane going after Sutton. He knew about his father threatening her. He had to know about the business deal Dane was cooking up with investors to sell this place from underneath me, and he had held on to all of that for months without telling me. I felt hurt, but more than that, I was terrified.

The thing that scared me the most was that Lee didn't believe in our friendship enough to trust me with the truth.

How could I get us back to a place where he was the friend who could tell me anything, even if it hurt?

I pushed open the bar door, and there he was, sitting on the stool by the to-go window, guitar in hand, playing a soft, mellow tune. His fingers moved across the strings with such ease, the music flowing effortlessly, as if the world outside didn't exist. I hadn't realized how much I missed hearing him play so freely, how much I missed the way he got lost in the chords, his eyes closed, lost to everything except the music. For a moment, he looked so damn handsome, so *him*, it hurt to breathe. I had to remind myself that nothing was the same anymore. But still, the pull was there, undeniable and strong.

"Hey, I brought dinner," I said cheerily, dropping the bag on the bar and making my way around the back, dragging a stool behind me so I could join him.

"I'd know that smell a mile away. Thank you, doll."

"Not a problem. I have to say, that meeting was bullshit and felt a little like a setup. What are you up to?"

Lee raised an eyebrow, swallowing a bite of his taco. "Nothing. I'm serious. I was over there, and they said they had some changes to the trolley schedule and asked if you could stop by and talk it through with them. Don't shoot the messenger." He was clearly lying, but if we were going to be friends again, maybe I needed to prove to him that he could still talk to me about anything.

"So, how's Janelle? Are you guys doing okay?" I didn't really want to know the answer, but I was trying. And if it meant hearing about his love life, then so be it.

"She didn't tell you? She's back in Nashville for the holidays. Her family participates in these hugely festive things leading up to Christmas with her mom's sorority sisters, who are also weirdly her sorority sisters, however that works. They have all these brunches and shopping trips and cookie-baking parties that they go to."

I chewed my food and smirked. "Sounds fun. You didn't want to go?"

He motioned around the empty room. "I have a business to run, clearly. Besides, Momma would murder me if I wasn't around for my first Christmas back in Savannah."

"That's true. Besides, I'll need your help tomorrow night when the trolleys pull through. Kasey had to go out of town. I guess her cousin's brother's someone or another is having a baby? I don't know."

Lee smiled and pushed the chips and salsa toward me so I could grab some before he ate it all, like he was prone to do. "As you wish, boss."

I rolled my eyes.

"So, what are your plans for Christmas now that Dane's out of town?"

"Well, I thought Charlie and I were going to do our cookie baking, Santa waiting thing, which these days equates to getting drunk on spiked eggnog and passing out. But he said he might have plans with someone. You wouldn't happen to be kidnapping my only living relative on Christmas Eve, would you?"

Lee held up his hands, feigning innocence. "No, ma'am, I know better than to come between a twenty-eight-year-old Pruitt tradition. Besides, if Charlie had a choice to hang out with me or get beat up by you, I bet you he would choose the latter."

"Mmhmm, well. Who knows." Once again, I was feeling mighty suspicious at what was coming out of his mouth. "And Eunice, I assume, will be holding court after midnight mass as usual?"

"And she'll be up at the crack of dawn, baking, cooking, cleaning, and making the house look pristine for her Christmas Day open house, as if no one had ever lived there before."

"She's a trooper, that one. Hopefully, I can put an end to that craziness when I'm the Wilder matriarch." I could tell, without even looking at him, that what fell out of my mouth had the same effect on both of us. I could almost feel our hearts sinking in unison.

"Did you decide to put a tree up, at least?" Lee asked quietly when we had both recovered.

"No tree for me this year," I sighed, picking at my food. "Who would see it but me?"

"What's Pickle going to use as a recon station now? Surely, this is her favorite time of year to plan stealth attacks."

I worked my face to hide how upset I was. Christmas was always my favorite holiday, and it meant the world to me. Charlie and I would spend hours picking out the best tree we could afford, real of course, and we decorated it with the same painted shells my momma always put on her tree year after year.

Keeping our Christmas tradition going was one of the last things that connected Charlie and me to our old life on Tybee Island. To our parents. But we were older, both moving on. Maybe it was time to start something new on my own.

"Customer," I said, nodding toward the window. I cleaned up our plates, wiped the salsa off the bar, and made us another drink. After checking my phone, I settled back down, waiting for Lee to wrap up with the to-go orders and send everyone off to something, presumably, more fun.

Savannah was a huge tourist hot-spot in the summer and fall months, but around the holidays, we didn't see many folks around town that weren't local.

Not like O'Malley's saw many people anyway.

Since Lee was gracing the small, intimate stage at O'Malley's on a regular basis, business had picked up a bit, but not like I wanted.

Not like I *needed.*

I started to panic. I needed to plan this damn wedding, walk down the aisle, and somehow get my soon-to-be-husband to realize he shouldn't sell this place to the highest bidder and just hand it over to me.

With a shaky hand, I passed Lee his drink and got my stuff together. If he could handle the bar, maybe I could finish picking out my flowers and table settings. Two things Eunice wanted a decision made on by the first of the year. Once they were finally checked off the list, I could get her off my back.

Until we shopped for the dress, of course.

"I'm going to head upstairs for a while. Will you text me if you need help?"

He looked nervous and defeated. I knew he wanted to tell me something, but kept his mouth shut, as usual. Maybe buying him his favorite meal to try and butter him up wasn't going to work after all. There'd still be that unbreakable wall between us.

"I'm good, go ahead," he finally said, and I shot him a half-hearted smile before making my way up the back staircase.

The second I entered the apartment, I could tell something was different. The rooms were darkened, and a faint, shimmering light bounced off the walls. I heard the low hum of Pickle purring somewhere in the distance, and I called out for her. Usually, she met me by the door, ready to attack should it finally be the intruder she'd been waiting on for years. I followed the sound of her rumbling into the living room and sank onto the couch. I buried my face in my hands and let out a deep, raw sob.

A Christmas tree—a real, fresh off the lot balsam fir stood proudly in the corner of the room. I stood up to get a closer look and fought back another wave of tears when I realized the ornaments were all my momma's. I'd never seen anything so gorgeous in my entire life.

On top of the tree, resting ever so gently, was the sea-star covered with shells that crowned our family tree for my whole young life. I struggled to catch my breath.

Did Charlie do this? I briefly thought it could have been Dane, but Christmas was never his thing. And, truth be told, only one person knew how important this tree, these ornaments, were to me.

"Merry Christmas, Magnolia," Lee said, his voice catching slightly as he leaned on the doorframe, watching me take in what was in front of me. "You should always celebrate the holiday in the way you love. I hope you're not mad."

I shook my head and dabbed at my eyes a bit. "I'm not mad, Lee. These are joyful tears." I turned to look at him, fighting the urge to rush across the room and into his arms. "Thank you. It looks just like Momma's did."

"I hope so. Charlie drummed up an old picture from when y'all were kids so I could see what it looked like. It's not exact, but it's—"

"It's perfect. It's absolutely perfect," I interrupted.

A wide, toothy smile spread across his face and reached his eyes. It was the kind of smile I was used to seeing when we were together. The kind that only happened when he did something that made my heart melt.

When he made one of those grand gestures to prove how much he loved me.

"You should get back downstairs," I said, snapping us both out of the moment. "Wouldn't want to miss that one, random customer that could stop by."

"You got it, boss," he gruffed, scratching the back of his head and looking down at the floor. "See you later." He walked down the stairs, and Pickle hurled herself out of the tree and on to my lap.

"What are we going to do about him?"

She licked her lips and twirled twice before falling asleep on my thighs.

"Believe me, girl, I wish I could kiss him again. But we're just going to have to keep dreaming."

I sat in the quiet for a while, just watching the room move with the quiet twinkle of the lights. I wondered briefly what would make someone do something so extravagant, so out of this world? Why would someone do something so crazy for someone?

Love. Loyalty. Friendship.

And I knew, deep down, those were the reasons why I was doing the crazy, extraordinary thing that I was doing, too.

Later that night, I had Sutton on speakerphone while I flipped through bridal magazines, my stomach a circus of butterflies and nervous energy.

"Did you get the picture I sent of the tree?" I asked.

"I did. It really is beautiful," she sighed wistfully. "I hope you weren't an asshole and thanked him properly."

"Of course I did. I was very kind once I stopped sobbing." I added a sticky note to the top of the page I was perusing, scribbling a quick "maybe." "What do you think about dusty-rose for your maid of honor dress? Is that too springy? February's so hard because technically it's still winter, but it's the South, so it could be ninety degrees that day."

Sutton grumbled. "Throw me in a garbage bag. This whole thing is trash anyway."

"Sutton, stop. Besides, you know I would do that to you just to spite you, so don't test me."

"I'm bringing Ryan as a date, I think. I don't know. We've been running on the river together. He's kind of cute but like so, so goofy."

"Sounds like a match to me." I faked a laugh, trying not to get upset. On one hand, I was happy for Sutton. On the other hand, I wished things were simple for me like they were for her.

How nice it would have been to date Dane, figure out he was a jerk on my own, kick his ass to the curb, and free up my heart for the person who would treat it right.

Thinking like that could get me in trouble, though. I had to save the bar. There was no other way around it.

My throat tightened a bit, and I threw the magazine down on the coffee table.

I felt trapped.

"I'll be there in the morning. I got a super cute dress off Amazon that looks like a decorated tree. It has a star on one wrist with tinsel and ornaments up and down the sleeves. When I hold my hands above my head, I'm a goddamn balsam fir. It's magical."

"I can't wait to see." I could practically see my friend prancing around the bar, throwing her arms up like she was auditioning for *America's Next Top Tree.* The mental image was so ridiculous, I couldn't help but snort-laugh. "Thanks for helping out during the trolley stops. It really means a lot to me. I'm glad we're on better terms. I really don't know what I'd do without you or your questionable fashion choices."

I could hear her grinning on the other end of the line. "My hope is, by New Year's Eve, we'll all be exactly where we're supposed to be."

CHAPTER THIRTY-ONE

Magnolia

Lee was the first one to arrive on the morning of the Historical Holiday Trolley Tour. We quietly danced around each other, and I tried to keep my distance. After finding the Christmas tree in my apartment the night before, I didn't want to let on that my heart was calling out to him. But, the way he was acting, I was pretty sure he could hear it as loud as a siren.

I could feel the weight of his gaze following me around the bar as I hurried to ready the space. He was standing there, hands shoved in his pockets, trying to look casual but clearly brimming with anticipation. His eyes, still that intense blue, kept flicking over to me as if searching for any hint of how I felt.

He had this self-satisfied grin on his face from last night's big stunt, like he was waiting for me to confirm that it had worked, that it meant something. I could see the mix of hope and nervousness behind his smile, and it twisted my heart more than I'd care to admit.

I tossed a handful of beer koozies that looked like tiny, knitted ugly sweaters onto the bar. "Are you going to help me out today, Lee, or are you just going to stand there giving me googly eyes all day?"

Lee smirked, his eyes twinkling with amusement. "Well, I was trying to see if my googly eyes would get me out of manual labor, but it looks like you're not having any of it." He stepped closer, grabbing a box of festive cocktail napkins and giving me a mock salute. "Alright, boss. What's next on the to-do list?"

Charlie showed up next with bacon and biscuits, and Sutton, Jordan, and Doyle weren't too far behind. Soon, we were all assembled, and I felt a little more comfortable now that the gang was all together and Lee and I weren't alone with the swirling emotions that had me on edge.

We all got to work shaking together the premixed holiday-themed cocktails and laying out the small gingerbread cupcakes Sutton had baked. As we got the bar ready, every now and again, I would look up and catch Lee staring at me, smiling wildly and watching me work.

"That boy has it bad for you," Jordan said, leaning in to me as we lined up the small, plastic cups along the bar. Every ticket to the trolley tour came with a sample-sized glass of a signature drink and a small bite. It was up to the guests whether or not they wanted to stay longer and spend more money. With the Christmas music blaring, and the bar decorated like the North Pole, we had hoped that people would stay for a while.

"Well, it doesn't matter. I'm marrying his brother. You should know that. You're officiating it."

"As your internet-vested pastor, I have to advise y'all to have at least one more romp in the sheets so you know *exactly* what you'll be missing when you shack up with the less-favorable Wilder brother."

"That doesn't sound very pastoral of you, Jordan. Will you pass me that spiced sangria? I'm going to put that out, too."

"I'm just saying. Dane's out of town, Janelle's out of town, and the man bought you a Christmas tree. Oh, and soon enough, a whole bar." He raised an eyebrow, his smirk edging into full-on mischievous territory. "Maybe it wouldn't hurt to show a little… gratitude?"

I rolled my eyes. "Sounds like prostitution to me, pal."

"That's when it's a job. And honey, it would be leisure to have that man in the sheets. Trust me."

Doyle poked his head around the corner from the storage closet, pretending to be scandalized. "I heard that, Jordan! But he's not wrong, Magnolia."

"Don't ambush me, y'all. I need to get in a sales-like mind frame to make money tonight, and I am also working on a day buzz. So back off. Wait, before you back off, pass me that whiskey."

The first trolley stopped by right on time, and guests flooded in. Their trolley host shuffled them all inside, and while they sipped and snacked, they also heard the history of O'Malley's Pub and how my family emigrated from Ireland, landing in Savannah.

"This is Magnolia Pruitt." The host gestured toward me as I waved awkwardly behind the bar. "She's a fifth generation O'Malley and the current owner of the pub. The family has worked diligently to keep it in the O'Malley family tree, and they're one of the last old, great Savannah families."

I gave another flick of my hand to the crowd from behind the bar as the tour guide went on to talk about the Hibernia Society and how the group put together the very first St. Patrick's Day parade in Savannah.

"Stay as long as you want," he called out before heading out the door. "You can get on this trolley and go to the next stop or get on the next one coming by in a few minutes. They'll be comin' around all day."

Everyone filed out the door and back onto the trolley.

"It's okay, Maggie," Lee said, as the crowd dispersed. "It's early, and this thing runs all day and night. People will come back."

As the day dragged on, and we heard the same twenty Christmas songs on repeat, the entire group started to feel defeated. The buzzing energy from the morning slowly drained out of the room, like a balloon with a slow leak, as people came, took one look, and left. Quickly. Even Sutton, decked out in her ridiculous Christmas tree costume, looked like a sad, deflated version of herself—branches drooping and all.

"I have to make a few phone calls," I lied, rushing off to my office. "Someone come get me if anything exciting happens. Like we actually make a dollar today."

I shut the office door and dropped my head on the desk. The door between the green room and my office was slightly open, and I heard someone rummaging around on the other side.

Slinking out from behind my desk, I tiptoed across the office and quietly peeked through the gap in the door. Lee was in the green room getting his gear together, bending over as he rifled through his guitar case.

He pulled out the guitar he wanted and strummed a few notes, his fingers dancing effortlessly over the strings. I watched him move around the room, jeans hugging his body just right, the light gray t-shirt pulling across his muscular arms. The sight of him so at ease with his music made it hard to look away.

A flutter of nervous energy shot through me, and I was probably drooling a bit. Dane was handsome, but Lee was the total package. His eyes were broody and blue, and his body was perfect. Tight, lined muscles ran up and down his arms and the way he poured himself into his jeans made what was going on in *my* jeans do a little jig.

My heart hammered out of my chest at the thought of what was underneath his clothes. I knew. I remembered. One didn't quite forget something like that.

I leaned against the bookshelf behind me, only to hear a crack as a shelf gave way, sending picture frames and inventory logs tumbling to the floor.

"I'm going to play for a bit and see if that will make people stick around," Lee called out from the other side of the door. "You'd make a horrible spy, by the way."

A flush of warmth crept across my chest as I scrambled to pick up what had gotten knocked over, hoping he hadn't come through the door. As I bent over, my shirt rode up my back and my jeans dipped down below my hips. I heard a soft moan behind me, and my lady bits started up an old, familiar dance.

"Let me help you," he said, crouching down next to me. Our eyes locked for a moment, and the air in the room changed from embarrassing to electric. My gaze landed—and stayed—on his lips, and his on mine.

I coughed, fumbling to my feet with a handful of beer catalogs in my hands. "Can I help you set up?"

He shook his head and came up toward me so that the front of our bodies lined up, barely touching. He put the logs he had in his hand behind me, pressing me up against the cold metal of the desk. Our arms grazed, and my entire body shivered. He leaned in and his lips ran over my ear, and I let out a small, startled gasp that slowly melted into a moan. "Any requests, Maggie?"

I let my head fall back, exposing my neck as if offering it on a platter. The memory of his touch flooded back, and I could almost feel his tongue tracing the vulnerable skin, igniting a shiver that ran down my spine. It was like the past was messing with me, blurring the lines between then and now.

"I meant for songs," he laughed, pulling away from me.

My chest was heaving, and I was sure—more than sure—my eyes looked wild and glazed over with desire.

"Christmas songs, you know? 'Frosty the Snowman?' 'Up On The Rooftop?' 'All I Want For Christmas Is You' perhaps?"

"Frosty's fine," I stammered. I opened the door to my office and ushered him through it. "Just get out."

As he walked past me, he let out a soft, airy laugh. He stopped and locked eyes with me again. "You're awfully lucky your jeans aren't as tight as they look, baby. You would have definitely felt what's been hiding in my stocking ever since I saw you bending over if they were."

Guitar in hand, he took the stage and fiddled with the acoustics for a minute before starting his warm up. The next bus was due in fifteen minutes, so he rushed through it. I stood, dreamy-eyed, in the doorway of my office. He strummed the beginning notes of "Still Crazy After All These Years," and I slammed my office door.

Once I regained my composure and heard guests milling around in the bar, I decided there were enough bodies and buffers around to hide the fact that I had almost ripped my pants off in my office and let Lee bend me over my desk just moments prior.

"Why do you look like you're about to have a stroke?" Sutton asked, as I meandered toward her in a daze.

"No reason." I shrugged, heading behind the bar.

She followed behind me, whisper-shouting, "Did you two have a moment behind that closed door? I heard something crash. We all just kind of looked at each other and decided to let nature do its thing. You know?"

"Oh my God, stop. No. I did knock over my bookshelf, though. Because I was looking at Lee's ass. Like a creep."

Sutton giggled and poured us two eggnogs. She handed me one, and we cheers'd. "It's a nice ass, girl. I don't blame ya for one second."

"It's just like there's still something there. I know it, he knows it." I gestured wildly around the bar. "I think the entire city knows it. But it is what it is. I almost feel like he's trying to make me squirm to see what I'll do. I'm not taking his bait, though. We've been down this road before, and we all know how that ended."

Sutton scoffed. "Yeah, you were an idiot then, and you're an idiot now."

I shot her a scowl and pretended to busy myself with dirty dishes so that I didn't get distracted by Lee crooning on stage.

Sutton shrugged. "Well, you know what I always tell you. I will support you in whatever you do if it makes you happy. I will not support misery. But I will stand by you no matter what choices you make."

"Why do I feel like this has some sort of deeper meaning than me almost possibly hooking up with Lee?"

"Because you and I both know it does."

***

Lee's hunch that if he whipped out his guitar, people would stay was spot on because we had a packed bar all the way until I had to do last call and basically throw the crowd out. Once everyone left, our friends included, Lee and I got to cleaning. I turned on the stereo and tied on my apron, dragging the trash can behind me to toss in empties.

Lee followed behind, wiping up tables and collecting glasses in a plastic bussing bin. "I think it was a really great night, Maggie. Don't you?"

"I do, but I'm getting awfully nervous that people will only stick around if your handsome face is on stage crooning."

He laughed. "Oh, I'm handsome now?"

I rolled my eyes. "You are. We both know it. Don't distract me now. I'm trying to clean this mess up. I'm exhausted."

Before I could even register what was happening, he had me in his arms, holding me close and swaying to the low, country ballad blaring from the speakers. I didn't hesitate. I inched toward him, letting him rest his hand on my lower back.

"I know why you're with my brother," he said gruffly, bringing our joined hands to his chest. "It will be easy, and he'll never keep you on your toes or ever make you feel anything less than complacent. It's the safest path, and that's why you're picking him."

"Picking him?" I momentarily lost my balance and almost fell headfirst into a table. I took a step back, putting some distance between us. "I didn't realize this was now a meat market and I had a choice."

"Oh, you have a choice, alright. You've had one since I came home, and you know it."

"Speaking of that… How am I supposed to know you won't get up and leave again? This whole partnership is *insane*. You're here, but for how long? After the wedding? And what's going on with you and Janelle?" I was rambling, hard. But I was *big* mad. I threw my hands on my hips and stared him down. "You almost *kissed* me tonight, Lee. I know you were going to. I know when a Wilder

196

man wants my tongue in his mouth."

He winced and turned away from me.

"I need to play it safe, Lee. I can't let you get between Dane and me, no matter how much you try to tempt me. I *need* to get control of the Trust and keep this bar in my family, and there's only one way to do that. What you're doing isn't fair. To me, to Janelle, to your brother. Oh my God, imagine if we had an affair and your momma found out? Jesus…"

"You're playing it safe? Seriously? I see the way you look at me." He closed the space between us and put his hands on the bar, locking me in between his arms. "We both felt what happened between us tonight in that office. What happened just a few months ago, right there on top of that very ice chest? It's been happening little by little since I got back. You want me, I want you. So, why don't you call this charade off and stop playing it 'safe?'"

"I have to play it like this! I didn't let another man near me for almost *seven* years after you left. Dane is my first real relationship since then. Do you honestly think I could survive someone else leaving me? That's all anyone ever does is leave! My heart cannot take another person in my life dying or walking out or going to Nashville—"

"You told me to go! You broke my heart, Magnolia. You told me to leave you. I didn't walk out." He moved away from me, pacing the length of the bar, running his hands through his hair.

"But you would have. Someday. You would have woken up and realized I was holding you back from everything you ever wanted, and you would have resented me. And that, Lee, would have been worse than you dying or leaving or walking away. Staying with me because you felt like you had to would be the worst possible thing you could do to me." I choked back a sob caught in the depths of my throat. When I looked up, he had tears in his eyes, too.

Years of pain and heartache were threatening to unfurl. The grief I held inside for so long was bubbling up to the surface, and I couldn't keep any of it locked in anymore.

I did let him go. I *begged* him to leave. I'd never be able to live with myself if he stayed behind for me instead of going to Nashville and living out his dream. I'd spent almost every moment since then both full of regret and patting myself on the back for that decision.

The earthshattering ache of remembering that final conversation and all the things we said to each other came rushing to the front of my mind, and I winced. The beautiful reveries we shared alongside the harsh accusations, the guilt and the agony of it all consumed me, practically bringing me to my knees.

"I am sorry, Lee, but if we didn't break it off back then, you wouldn't have any of the beautiful things you have now. The Grammy, the money, the fame, none of it. You would have missed all that just to be stuck here with me."

His voice cracked as he glared at the floor, a mix of hurt and anger swirling in his eyes. "Stuck with you. Are you kidding me?"

"No, I'm not. Everyone knew out of the five of us, I was the one who was never gonna go anywhere, and I knew if I asked you to, you would have stayed."

He watched me for a moment, his eyes heavy with sadness, as if what I just said tore his world apart. "I would have stayed in a heartbeat."

"I know you would have, so I let you go."

"Magnolia…"

I threw my hands up. "And I'm letting you go again. I can't do this anymore. I'll call Dane and have him shred the paperwork and dissolve the partnership. You know you want to get back to Nashville and pick up where you left off. Janelle is miserable here anyway. I won't let you stay behind because you feel sorry for me."

He let out a long sigh followed by a sarcastic, annoyed laugh. "You think I feel sorry for you? That's why I'm doing this?"

I could barely look at him. The shame, fear, and confusion of the decisions I'd made over the last few years and months were swelling in my chest. "Yes," I whispered.

He crossed the bar in seconds and placed a hand on my shoulder, lifting my chin with the other until our eyes met. "You've got it all wrong, baby. I'm here because I believe in you. I've read the business plan. I've seen your vision for this place. It will be the best goddamn bar in Savannah, and I want to see it come alive. I want to help you. I want to be here for you, with you, while you do this." He pulled me against his chest and ran his hands through my hair. Cupping my face, he met my gaze again, pulling me close as I fought to look away. "I *do* want to pick up where I left off, you're right about that, but not where I left off in Nashville. That book has ended."

A tear slipped down my cheek.

"I don't think our story is quite finished yet," he whispered in a low, hoarse voice. "If I had to take a wild guess, we have a few more chapters left in us."

I let myself melt into his embrace letting quick, fat tears fall down my cheeks and onto his shirt.

He held me close for what felt like an eternity before he finally asked, "Do you really love him? Do you honestly think you have a forever with him?"

"It's… *different*, but I do care deeply for him. As far as forever, how can anyone know?"

"Oh, believe me, Maggie. When you want forever with someone, you know."

"What makes you say that? You've had relationships that have been tailor-made by your label. Nothing is real in your world."

"Because I've loved you from the second I laid eyes on you, and from that moment on, I've wanted forever with you. That's how I know."

CHAPTER THIRTY-TWO

Lee

The morning after the trolley crawl, Sutton and I met for coffee. After I had told Magnolia that I'd loved her my whole life and knew I wanted to spend the rest of my life with her, she pushed off my chest and bounded up the stairs to her apartment. I texted her when I got back to my place, letting her know that I'd finished cleaning and had locked up, but she left the message on read and didn't respond.

I couldn't stop replaying the look in her eyes before she walked away—conflicted, unreadable, but with something buried there that kept pulling me back to the memory like a magnet. Did I scare her off by saying too much? Did she feel even a sliver of what I'd been carrying around all these years? She was so close, right there in my arms, and for a fleeting second, it felt like maybe she wanted to stay. But the silence of her reply was deafening, leaving me caught between hope and the hollow ache of losing her all over again.

"You should do yourself a favor—do all of us a favor, really—and stop trying to screw this up." Sutton grabbed our coffees from the barista and took the seat next to me. "The tree thing was perfect. The declaration of undying love? A bit overkill, even for the resident songwriter."

"I'm not trying to screw anything up, Sutton. My feelings are legitimate. They always have been. She's the one that pushed me away, not the other way around. I've never stopped loving her for one second. She's in everything I do. All of my music, every song I write is our song." I fidgeted with the cup in my hands. "This was all your idea anyway."

Sutton took a sip of her coffee and leaned back in her seat, watching me closely. "She's right, though. If she asked you to stay, you wouldn't have the life you do, you know? And she'd always feel guilty about that."

I nodded. That part was undeniable. I'd been grateful for my success as a musician, but it came at the ultimate price.

Losing her wasn't worth any of it.

Moving to Nashville was me proving a point. To my family, to my friends, to everyone who thought I couldn't make a name for myself if it didn't have "Esquire" attached to the end of it. And it felt good. It felt really fucking good.

But not nearly as good as being near Magnolia or having her in my life.

"You don't think having some sort of sham wedding with my brother isn't going to make her feel guilty someday? How's it any different?"

Sutton smiled and leaned in to me, placing her hand on my arm. "I think she loved Dane in her own way. I can't speak on how she feels now that she knows the truth, but this is an orphan we're talking about here. She's lost everyone she's ever loved, including you. Dane is here, for the most part. There's always the promise he's coming back at any rate. He might be an asshole, but he's here, and he *wants* to be here. And, more importantly, she'll never leave Savannah. This is where she belongs."

"Even if it's all fake? If it's all for money?"

She sat back and picked at her scone. I could tell she was choosing her words carefully, and I sat on the edge of my seat. "It's not about the money, Lee. Have you ever talked to your momma about how she and Vance got together?"

"No, I haven't," I said and nodded for her to go on. My heart was drumming in my chest. Sutton knew something I didn't know, and it was likely the missing link to everything that's been happening since I left.

"It's none of my business, you know. But Eunice and Magnolia met for lunch around the time the agreements got drawn up for the bar. She didn't go into detail, but she let it slip that Cole and Eunice were once an item and that it ruined her friendship with Magnolia's momma, Diane. Apparently, Diane and Eunice were best friends."

I flung myself back in my seat and ran my hands over my face. So many things suddenly clicked into place. "And, let me guess, my grandfathers each had a hand in that?"

Sutton shrugged. "You know, she didn't confirm nor deny that, but I have a sneaky suspicion. The timeline makes sense. Eunice went to Boston for college while she was still dating Cole, and she met Vance somewhere in the city when he was at Harvard. They were engaged shortly after that."

She stuffed some scone in her mouth and chewed quickly before continuing. "And, according to the plaque on the wall of the Wilder Law Firm, your maternal grandfather became a partner alongside your paternal grandfather only a few weeks after Eunice and Vance announced their engagement. I saw the framed newspaper cutout announcing his promotion on the wall when I was catering a mediation there a few weeks ago. A quick Google search brought up your parents' engagement announcement around the same time."

"Are you a chef or a private detective?"

She chuckled. "Little bit of both."

"And you think this is why she's marrying Dane? Because it's a business deal, and if my momma could do it, Maggie can, too?"

Sutton leaned in toward me again and offered me a sympathetic smile. "I don't think so, Lee. I know so. Because I heard it straight from the horse's mouth."

***

After my workout and a few hours on the guitar with Ryan, I swung by to see Charlie. I considered stopping by the bar to talk to Maggie, but with everything she knew about my brother, the Trust, and all the other pieces of the puzzle, I knew I wasn't the one who could change her mind.

But maybe her brother could.

"All I'm saying is that she thinks she's alone in this world, and she's not. Do you think she feels she has your support?"

Charlie was still working on Maggie's mural little by little, but with all of his custom holiday orders, he had fallen behind. But there it was, almost finished, staring at me.

It was beautiful. Because *she* was beautiful.

"She has my support, Lee. Please don't come up in my studio and accuse me of not being a good brother. Magnolia and I are adults now, but we're still very close. That said, though, what decisions she makes, romantically or otherwise, are completely up to her."

"You'd really let her walk down the aisle toward a man that's aggressive toward her, controlling, manipulative, and not to mention probably cheating on her…"

Charlie stopped what he was doing and turned toward me. "Wait, what? That's a pretty lofty allegation there, my friend. Don't say something like that if you can't back it up."

I told Charlie about the shadows in his video calls with our family and how I had a gut feeling that Dane's proposal to Maggie wasn't all tied up in flowers and romance. He was up to something.

"Well, it could have been room service or housekeeping. I've known you my entire life, I wouldn't trust a hunch of yours." He was laughing, but I could tell I struck a nerve.

"I'll find out one way or another, you can believe that."

Charlie watched me with sad eyes for a few moments, working through something on his mind. "Lee, I love you, but when you and my sister broke up, you weren't here to see her heart shatter. You didn't hold her when she fell asleep at night screaming in agony. You didn't find her, shit-house drunk on the floor of your bathroom, clutching a picture of you and listening to your demo tape—she knew every song you wrote was about her. And it killed her."

He crossed the room quietly, pulling open his fridge and yanking out a couple of beers for us, and handed me one. Still keeping his eyes on the ground, he was no doubt remembering how his sister was in relentless, gnawing pain. Because of me. I looked up at my oldest friend's face, slightly more weathered now than it was when we first met—but he was still that fiery, freckled redhead kid—and I realized that my leaving must have hurt him, too.

Charlie took a deep, cleansing breath before going on. A faint smile began to play on his lips. "You weren't there when she started picking up the pieces, either. When she started coming out of her room, fixing herself up, strapping on a smile whether it was real or not. The first time I heard her laugh, like, really laugh, after you left, it was like music to my ears. I actually went into my room and I cried. And then, when we lost Uncle Cole, I saw bits of her chipping away again, but she was so strong at that point, it didn't break her completely."

He sprang up from his stool and crossed the room again, this time heading to the canvas shrouded with Magnolia's likeness. He studied it for a moment before turning to me with a weary look.

"Look, Lee, I trust my sister. She's stronger than both of us put together.

Whatever decision she makes, I'll stand by her. But if you're thinking that telling her about Dane possibly cheating, on top of all the other crap he's pulled, is going to change her mind, you should absolutely do it. Just don't expect it to have the effect you're hoping for."

I listened, nodding as his words sank in. He was right—Maggie was strong, no doubt about it, but she also deserved to know everything, even if it wouldn't change the outcome.

CHAPTER THIRTY-THREE

Magnolia

On Christmas Eve, our whole group had assembled for brunch in the bar. I was keeping the doors closed to patrons for twenty-four hours, and in between obligations of church and cookie swaps with his momma, Lee and I had plans to slap a fresh coat of paint on everything during the brief break.

"So, Dane's really not coming home for Christmas, huh? Did he at least send flowers?" Doyle was hovering over me as I whipped up pitchers of cinnamon-spiced Sangria.

"He did and a lovely vase from Tiffany's, which I promptly had to re-box and shelve before Pickle smashed it into a thousand pieces."

"Speaking of the devil herself, who's going to take Pickle when you move in with Dane?"

I shrugged, casting a sideways, confused glare at him. "Why wouldn't I take her?"

"Um, honey, the Drayton is strictly pet-free. And besides, Dane hates Pickle."

"Everyone hates Pickle," I countered, stealing a glance at Lee who we all knew loved her to death.

I hadn't given much thought to moving in with Dane with everything else going on. But with the wedding approaching, things like furniture and the fate of my possessed cat all hung in the air.

What I *had* thought about—more than I wanted to admit—was that night on the bar floor, Lee's voice shaking as he told me he'd loved me his whole life. It wasn't just his words; it was the way he looked at me, like nothing else in the world mattered but me and him and the space between us. I could still hear the catch in his breath, feel the weight of his hand on my wrist, steady and warm, like he was anchoring himself in the moment. Anchoring himself to *me*.

I should have said something—anything—other than running upstairs and pretending I hadn't felt my entire world tilt. But I did. And now, with Dane's ring on my finger and a million plans I couldn't unravel, I wasn't sure how to make it all feel right again.

"Well, I'm not taking her. My sister Tally's permanently moving in with me and Jordan. Don't tell him yet. He's going to murder the both of us. But she's got this insane poodle named Nancy Reagan who would shred Pickle up like lettuce… Actually, now that I think about it, that's a showdown I would love to see."

I giggled and handed Doyle two full pitchers and sent him on his way.

Sutton took his spot at the bar. "I didn't get you in the Secret Santa, but I wanted to give you this at any rate," she said, sliding the bowed box toward me.

"Oh! I got you something, too, but you're not my Secret Santa pick, either. It's just something small." I pulled out a gift bag from behind the bar, and we both dug into our gifts.

Because of my notoriously lazy wrapping job, her gift from me was revealed first. I'd gotten us matching Alex and Ani bracelets that said Sister on them. I dangled my wrist to show her mine.

"Bestie bracelets! We haven't had these since we were kids." She slipped hers on and leaned over the bar to give me a hug and a kiss on the cheek. "Finish opening yours," she said, nodding toward the gift.

I pulled off the rest of the shimmery wrapping paper to find a white box. Inside was a framed picture of all of us, taken selfie-style from our impromptu brunch the weekend Lee came home.

"I figured you could use an upgrade of the gang, including the newest editions to the Savannah Sweethearts." She smiled, peeking over to see her handiwork.

"I love it. Dane's missing, though."

Sutton grimaced and leaned back in her seat. "Sorry, I had a feeling you were going to say that. But I feel like Dane's been missing since you two got together, to be honest."

She had a point. Ever since we started dating and he decided to join his father's firm, he'd been spending less and less time with me and hardly ever spent time with our group at all. Not to mention, all of his alleged scheming and plotting probably took up a good chunk of his time.

I wondered, for the first time, what would happen to all of us when Dane and I got married. What would become of the brunches and the wine tastings, the sleepover parties with Sutton and me, and sometimes Charlie, that still lingered into our twenties?

Would we still go to Tybee Island together every Memorial Day weekend? What about the trips to watch Sutton run her marathons or to see one of Charlie's exhibits when his work got picked up in a different city?

Or what about just getting together because we had nothing better to do and we just wanted to be around each other?

If I was living life like a Wilder, I was going to have days packed so tight with charity work and socializing, I really wouldn't have time for much else, especially while running the bar, too.

Sutton slid off the barstool and joined our friends, all sitting around the table covered in poinsettias and cheer, smiling happily at one another and laughing at something my brother said. My heart ached.

Friendships, especially ones like ours, were always teetering on the edge, vulnerable to the seismic shifts that life threw our way. Weddings, babies, divorces—these milestones were supposed to be beautiful, but they often left scars. Not all relationships had the strength to weather those storms. As I reflected on everything I'd lost, it hit me—my friends were the ones I'd miss the most. The idea of losing them felt like a heavy weight in my chest, a reminder that even the best moments could change everything.

"Magnolia Louise Pruitt, get that sullen sulk off your face and try these gingerbread pancakes before your business partner here inhales them all!" Sutton was keeled over laughing as Lee shoveled three pancakes in his face at one time, choking and gagging.

As I sat down, everyone was in a roar over it. Lee met my eyes across the table, smiling proudly. He'd never had to worry about losing anything, not the bar, not our friends, not his family.

But for me, I had to risk it all just to survive.

CHAPTER THIRTY-FOUR

Lee

"So, have you told her yet?" Charlie lingered in the corner of the bar with me while our friends exchanged gifts and wrapped up the brunch. Everyone had somewhere to be.

Including me.

"Not yet, no. I'm waiting until everyone clears out. Will you be up there with her tonight? It's y'all's first Christmas without Cole and…"

Charlie nodded, patting my back. "Of course. Sutton made her a whole batch of fried chicken and chocolate chip cookies, and I ordered some side dishes from Treylor Park. I'll do a big spread and stay the night. She'll be fine, Lee. We have her, don't worry."

I watched Maggie move around the room, hugging our friends and passing out kisses on the cheek and cheers with her glass. She looked vibrant and happy, but I could tell something was eating at her. It was written all over her face.

And, as usual, I was the only one who noticed.

"I'm not doubting your ability to take care of your sister, Charlie. I'm just saying that—"

"That you love her and you want her to be happy, which is why you're doing what you're doing. I know, Lee."

What I was doing was not solely contingent on me, but when the offer presented itself, I took it as a sign and ran with it. It was almost like I was sitting on a mound of questions, and when I got the phone call after leaving Charlie's the day before, they'd all, somewhat, been answered.

"Will I see you after Christmas? I have to help Jordan and Doyle with a delivery for a big party tonight, so I have to run," Charlie said somewhat quietly.

"Yeah, man, you'll see me. I'll be by tomorrow. I have some gifts for you two and the cat."

"Of course you do," he chuckled. "Alright, brother, see you tomorrow. Merry Christmas, Lee."

"Merry Christmas, Charlie." I watched him glide through the bar and kiss his sister on the cheek. Jordan and Doyle waved over their shoulders before piling out the door, and Sutton followed behind with Charlie and Ryan in tow.

"Man, Ryan and Sutton, huh?" Maggie locked the door and slipped on her apron, starting work on cleaning up the brunch table.

"It's kind of weird, right? Like, they're a great fit, but they're not."

She smiled softly. "Same could be said of a lot of couples around here, I think."

I let out a puff of air and joined her at the table, clearing up dishes and putting the poinsettias back around the bar. Her comment opened the door to a bigger conversation, but I decided to let it ride on the wind.

That night, there were bigger fish to fry.

I watched her work, cleaning up the mess we'd made. She took such pride in everything she did, and from what I understood, that was the O'Malley in her. No matter what happened, the bar would come back to life. She just needed a little bit of a financial push to make it happen.

Magnolia didn't need me to make her dreams come true. Every success she was going to have was because of her. She was the hardest working person I'd ever met.

Soon, she'd be getting ready for New Year's Eve, and hopefully, she'd glide right into the New Year with a successful business.

We'd already hired a few more people so that our friends didn't have to pick up the grunt work and they could continue to enjoy the bar as guests. I'd called in a bookkeeper friend of Momma's to help out with the finances.

And with her soon-to-be husband due back any day now, she'd be just fine.

"Maggie, I gotta talk to you about something. Can we sit?"

"Sit? No way. I'm not getting all tangled up in another one of those 'pick me, choose me, love me' rom-com diatribes with you again, Lee. Charlie should be back in a few hours, and I want this place cleaned so I don't have to come downstairs at all tomorrow unless I need to fix myself a drink."

"Magnolia," I said her name sadly, yet sternly. "I really, really need to talk to you."

She could tell by the look on my face and the tone of my voice that something was wrong, and it wasn't another one of my speeches. Speeches which were epic, by the way, so I wasn't sure why she was throwing so much shade.

"Is everything okay? Is it your momma? Is it Dane?"

I took a seat at one of the tables, and she joined, sitting next to me, her eyes trained on me but nervously playing with the strings of her apron.

"Everyone's fine, Magnolia. It's just... I'm going to be heading back to Nashville. After the New Year."

Her eyes widened in disbelief, and she quickly shut them, blinking twice as if trying to erase the shock from her face. "I see," she said. "That's big news."

"Right, it surely is."

She slowly eased to her feet and started cleaning again. I followed behind her, tugging her arm ever so slightly, turning her toward me. "Don't you want to know why I'm leaving, Maggie?"

"Is it because I didn't stop my life to 'choose' you? Because if it is, I'm not interested," she snapped, ripping her arm back.

A laugh escaped me. "No, though, we both have to admit I did try to pack that charm on, huh?" A wave of sadness washed over me, a finality that I didn't realize I'd been waiting for had finally arrived. "I've been asked to open up for Marc Roberge on his solo tour. Ryan and I will both be going. We're the first act of three, so it's not a big deal, but it's a good gig."

Maggie nodded. She made her way to the long table, finally meeting my gaze at a safe distance. "I thought you weren't performing anymore, just writing."

I shrugged. "I mean, this will be a huge chunk of money, and our album is, like, a quarter of the way through. It will help me sell some more music and make some more money. In the end, this is a good idea for us, the Trust, the bar, you know?"

"Right. Well, will you come back for the wedding?"

I shook my head. "I was never coming to the wedding, Magnolia. In no world of mine would I ever stand witness to you marrying my brother. Which is the second half of this conversation."

She studied me from across the room. I could feel the knots forming in my stomach, and I knew I had to choose my words wisely here.

"Just be careful, Maggie. With your heart. With Dane. With my family. But mostly, with your soul and the very essence of, well, you."

"What's that supposed to mean?"

"It means that not everyone on this earth has your best interest in mind and not everyone cares about you enough to keep your feelings safe." I paused the slow crawl I was making toward her and scrubbed a hand over my face. "I know it took you a long time to patch your heart back together after I left, and I'd hate to see it get smashed into a million pieces again."

She slowly lowered herself onto the bench that lined the back wall of the bar, staring blankly at the table. Before I said more than I should, I made my way to the door. If I didn't walk away and put some space between us, she'd never have the freedom to figure out what I knew, and had known, on her own.

"For what it's worth, though, Magnolia Pruitt, breaking your heart was the worst thing I've ever done. And if I had the chance, I would spend the rest of my days gluing all of the pieces back together, even the ones I wasn't respon-sible for."

CHAPTER THIRTY-FIVE

Magnolia

"He did not say that! What the hell is that supposed to mean?" Sutton was hissing from the other end of the phone while I popped her famous fried chicken into the oven.

The moment Lee left, I bounded up the back staircase and dialed her number. We'd been rehashing everything that had transpired between Lee and me over the last few months, and when my brother showed up for our annual Christmas Eve tradition, I'd completely ignored him.

"Magnolia! The movie's starting," my brother called from the other room.

"Alright, well, I should get going. Thanks again for dinner. And for listening to my shit," I added.

"Anytime. Be careful not to overcook the chicken, that's my hard work there so don't mess it up because you, for some reason at almost thirty years old, have no idea how to use an oven, or any other appliance. And just because Lee's leaving—temporarily, mind you—doesn't mean everything is changing."

"Everything's already changed. It's going to change even more after I'm Mrs. Wilder."

"The wrong Mrs. Wilder, if we're in the interest of being honest," she quipped.

"We're not in the interest. Merry Christmas, babes. See you tomorrow."

I hung up the phone and padded into the living room, carting a plate full of cheese and crackers and a couple of glasses of wine. I handed the plate and a glass off to my brother and sat next to him on the couch.

Pickle jumped up on the table and helped herself to a piece of cheese, hissing at Charlie as he tried to bat her away. I rolled my eyes and turned the volume up on *Meet Me In St. Louis*.

"This really isn't a Christmas movie," my brother said, like he did every year.

"It was Momma's favorite, though. Judy Garland's 'Have Yourself A Merry Little Christmas' was her favorite song. Don't you remember?"

Charlie shrugged, the least sentimental of the two of us. I wondered briefly what it would be like not to have an emotional connection to every song, tradition, holiday, or person that crossed my path.

"I can't stay all night, like I normally would," Charlie announced when the movie ended and we were two bottles of wine in.

I couldn't let him know how upset I was, so I just nodded. "That's okay, who wants to have a sleepover with their baby sister anyway?"

"Me. I would. Always," he chuckled, gulping the rest of his wine. "I have to get up at 5:00 in the morning to drop something off to a client. It's a huge piece, so there's nowhere for them to hide it without it being found."

"That's okay. I'm exhausted anyway. I don't think I could wait up for Santa even if I thought he would really show," I laughed, stretching out my body as I stood up.

My brother got to his feet, stretching himself. He kissed me on the forehead and wrapped me in a hug. "You never know, Magnolia. If he was going to show up anywhere, it would be here. No one deserves it more."

After my brother left, I washed my face and climbed into bed, looking around the room I had lived in since I was a child. A part of me would miss this place, my home, but the other part of me knew that growing up and moving on meant leaving spaces and places that brought you the most comfort. Skirting almost thirty years old and still sleeping in the same room I had when I was twelve was a little silly and strange.

But it was my home.

It was the room my momma had slept in when she was a girl. The room she grew up in, where she dreamed of falling in love and starting a family. The room where her and Eunice, just like Sutton and me, had shared secrets and hopes for the future together. Where, at separate times, the four of us talked about boys, school, outfits.

It was the same four walls where we cried together, laughed, and fell in love. I looked up at the ceiling, the same ceiling my momma had stared at when she was on the verge of making big life leaps. I batted off the tears that started falling down my cheeks.

The last thing I had left of her was this room.

But it was time for me to let it go.

***

On Christmas morning, I woke up to the sound of music coming from the bar. I grunted, rolling on top of Pickle who leaped off the bed and hissed at me. I checked my phone, hazily wondering if I missed some impromptu meet up of our friends. But there were no messages.

I threw on a hoodie and slipped into a pair of slides, making my way down the back stairs. *Maybe I'd left the music on before I closed up the bar.*

In the dimly lit room, the soft strumming of a guitar and the soulful, familiar voice that I'd know anywhere wrapped around me. I followed the sound, my heart quickening as I reached the stage.

There, alone under a single spotlight, Lee sat on a stool, plucking out a melody, Santa hat sitting askew on his head. His voice was heavy with raw emotion as he huskily sang "Have Yourself a Merry Little Christmas," eyes locked on mine. I stood, frozen in place, watching him sing while tears danced down my cheeks.

After the song ended, Lee put his guitar down and hopped off the stage, making his way toward me. He stopped, jutting his chin out toward the back wall, a nervous shadow passing over his face.

I turned slowly, and behind me, covering up most of the space between the bar and the office, was a large portrait. I recognized the photo almost immediately as a candid shot Charlie had snapped with his camera while the two of us were having a picnic in Forsyth Park.

As I inched closer, I realized that it wasn't a photo at all, but a piece composed of tiny, delicate items coming together to make up the composition of my face. I rushed toward the canvas, inspecting the details.

Small photos of my family members, some dating back to when O'Malley's first opened, spread across the larger-than-life cheek in front of me. Pictures of our friends, shots of Savannah's architecture, places that I loved, all inched across the canvas, closing in the gaps of my forehead and lips. And, peppered gently across the entire masterpiece, were lyrics of the songs Lee had written about me, scrawled in Lee's handwriting.

"Did Charlie do this?" I rasped, thick tears clogged in my throat.

I couldn't stop staring. Every memory, everything that meant something to me, made up the details of my face. I finally let a sob escape when my eyes landed on a photo of my momma holding me when I was a baby, right here in this very barroom.

"I'd love to take credit for this one, but Charlie really put his heart and soul into this over the last few months," Lee breathed out, and I felt him closing the distance between us. "Merry Christmas, Magnolia."

Turning toward him, I wrapped my hands around his neck, pulling him in for a hug, fighting down the urge to kiss his cheek, not wanting to open up the invitation for anything further to transpire between us. "Thank you, Lee," I whispered in his ear. "It's beautiful."

"It's my absolute pleasure, Maggie. And yes, she is."

I broke our connection and turned to face the artwork again. A wide smile crossed my face, warmth filling my heart for the first time in a long time.

The detail and care that only my brother could pull off was so evident in this design. I imagined guests walking by and gazing intently at this, a conversation piece for sure, and the pride I would feel as they fawned over it.

Every time I passed by it, I would remember Lee, who gave me this amazing gift. Lee, who would be gone, living out his dreams again in Nashville. Grief hit me like a tidal wave.

I turned toward him again, staring at him through blurry, tear-glazed eyes. Of all the grand gestures, and all of the heartfelt moments we shared, this was the most genuine, beautiful moment of my life. And I didn't want the feeling to end.

"Will you dance with me, Lee?"

He let out a sigh, pulling my messy, sleep-stricken head toward his chest. Our hands entwined, and Lee lifted them to his lips, softly humming a familiar, yet distant tune.

We swayed across the worn, wooden floor for what felt like hours, the room filled with the echoes of our shared history, of the last few months where we battled to stay apart, when all we wanted to do was this, right here.

He pulled me closer, hands finding the familiar place on my back, fingers tenderly tracing the curves he knew so well. I rested my head gently against his shoulder, my hair softly grazing his neck as I lifted my gaze toward him. I let out a soft, content sigh.

"I remember that sound," he said, voice thick with longing. Carefully, his hand slipped beneath my shirt, and his thumb traced smooth, soothing circles on the small of my back. Searing, intense desire shot through me. "I remember how you'd say my name in the dark when it was just the two of us. I remember the way it felt to have our bodies pressed together, just like this. I remember the warmth of your laughter echoing in my ears, the way your eyes sparkled when you were lost in thought, listening to me play my guitar and sing to you. I remember those quiet moments, wrapped in blankets, sharing secrets under the stars. I remember everything."

We exchanged a glance that poured over us, full of dreams we once held and promises kept, of laughter shared and tears shed. A silent conversation played between us, brimming with everything we wanted to say over the last few months but could never quite find the words for. The bond we shared, a testament to a love that'd only grown deeper with time and never truly dissipated, was a living, breathing thing between us.

"It's almost time for you to go," I whispered, pulling him a little closer, not wanting to let him go.

"You're right, but a few more moments with you wouldn't kill me," he chuckled softly.

Our dance continued, every touch, every look, every subtle gesture, a love letter—our song—written in a language only the two of us could understand as we moved in the silence, swaying to a rhythm only we could hear.

When I was ready to pull away, and separate us for good and to return to our lives without each other, the door flew open.

"What the hell is going on?" Dane slammed the bar door behind him and crossed the room faster than either of us could react.

He yanked Lee off me and landed a punch square in his face. I stood there, stunned and trembling, as they hit the floor, breaking chairs and tables in their chaotic fight. Their shouts and cries filled the air as they swung at each other.

"Lee! Just go!" I finally yelled, grabbing Dane by the back of his shirt and using what little strength I had to push him up against the bar and away from his brother.

Lee and I stared at each other for a minute, and in an instant, I knew.

This was his last attempt. The one thing he had left in his arsenal to pull me away from Dane. And while my heart sang a different tune, at the end of the day, my mind was still made up, and nothing was ever going to change it.

"I'll be gone after New Year's Eve," Lee said, wiping at his bloody lip. "And that's it, Maggie. Then, I am done. I'll truly be a silent partner from here on out."

The bar door closed behind him, and Dane and I stood quietly, staring each other down with chests heaving and adrenaline rushing.

I broke the silence. "What are you doing here?"

Dane laughed and stomped through the bar to my office, practically kicking the door down. He completely bypassed the enormous work of art that now looked sad, almost lonely in the darkened barroom. I followed him and watched as he flung himself into my desk chair, his face stormy with rage, opening the bottom drawer and pulling out a bottle of bourbon.

"It's not even 10:00 in the morning, Dane," I said, taking the seat across from him.

"My trial ended earlier than I anticipated, so I thought I would surprise you. Turns out, I'm the one surprised," he replied, sliding a glass across the desk to me.

"Well, this sounds cliche, but it wasn't what it looked like," I offered, deciding to take a long pull of the thick, amber liquid, time of day be damned.

"It was exactly what it looked like, Magnolia. I can't say I'm surprised, though. Lee bounces back in town, and everything is different between all of us, especially with you and me. I knew it was only a matter of time before I caught you in his arms."

I let out a nervous laugh. "It's not like we had our pants down around our ankles, Dane."

"Again, it was only a matter of time."

I imagined that the cool, firm tone he was using came from several years of courtroom practice. "Your brother was my first real friend, and he was my friend for a long time before anything happened between us. He's been my friend, first and foremost, since he came back. What he is trying to do for me and the bar is out of nothing but that friendship. You can't take that kind of bond away from us. We've all loved having him home. Just like we've all missed you while you've been gone."

He looked thoughtfully down at the desk, silence enveloping us. Perhaps he believed me. Maybe my words had sufficiently stroked his ego, allowing us to sidestep the explosive confrontation that had been brewing.

Dane grabbed his glass and hurled it across the room with a force that made me shudder. The deafening crash shattered the silence, sending shards flying and making me leap from my seat, my heart pounding and my skin crawling with a mixture of fear and shock.

"I can't undo what happened between your brother and me, Dane." I stood up and walked out of the office to grab a push broom and dustpan. At the broom closet door, I paused, leaning against it as I struggled to regain my composure. I didn't want him to see how deeply he had unsettled me, how my insides were shaking. I steadied myself, forcing my hands to stop trembling.

I needed him to believe he hadn't gotten under my skin—that was exactly what he wanted, after all.

As I cleaned up his mess, Dane just sat at the desk with his head in his hands.

"Please look at me, Dane." I dropped the broken glass into the garbage can, fighting against myself not to turn on my heel and run out of that room as fast as I could. I had to stay. Walking away would be just as good as signing the paperwork and handing this place over to him on a silver platter. "Again, I can't erase what happened between your brother and me just as much as I can't erase anything else that's ever happened to me. It's all a cocktail that's made me who I am today, this girl, the one standing before you, that you love. You love me, right?"

"Well, it's a pretty shitty cocktail, Magnolia. I'm sick of feeling like you're being pulled in three different directions. First, I have to compete with your obsession with this bar, which, by the way, is a sinking ship. And if my brother didn't swoop in to save your ass, you'd probably be declaring bankruptcy by now. Then, I have to compete with everyone else in the friend group. You and Sutton are on the phone with each other twenty-four hours a day, seven days a week, if you're not attached at the hip. And then my brother comes back, and you two are slow dancing in the dark and giving each other 'fuck me' eyes across the bar every chance you get. I came over to spend Christmas with you and celebrate the end of my trial, and I find you in his arms."

He flew up and paced the room, his hands raking through his dark hair. "Him coming back here like he has something to prove to you just never sat right with me. I just don't get it." He locked eyes with me as he said, "Why come back for your own sloppy seconds?"

I recoiled, fighting to keep the tears from spilling over. His words hit me like a punch to the gut, not just for the insult, but because he still wouldn't answer when I asked if he loved me. I struggled to hold back the tears as they threatened to pour down my face. "I'm the one that told him to go. Everyone thinks Lee is the one that up and left me, that he chose his guitar over our relationship, but it was *me*. I did it. I broke up with him over ten years ago, and I'm the one that told him to go. I'm the reason he went to Nashville."

I dumped the rest of the broken glass in the trash, staring at the shards for a minute, choosing my words carefully.

"Your brother is my best friend. We've shared countless memories and have supported each other through thick and thin, but what happened between us is behind us now. I was young and in love for the first time in my life, but I was a kid then. Years and distance have changed all of that, and everything is different now. And despite it all, I'm with you. This is how it's supposed to be, Dane."

"What? But I thought he broke your heart and ran off and met some girl who…"

I watched the wheels in his head moving and churning.

"The album, *all* of the albums, they're about you!"

"Maybe you should have another drink, Dane. And a seat." I pushed the bottle toward him, and he plunked back down in the chair opposite mine. "I should have told you, and I'm sorry I didn't. But you have to understand how young we were and how we felt a lot of things for each other very slowly over time, but it was true and honest and innocent, like we both were."

At the time, I didn't know what the future held for any of us, but I did know that I was a part of a love story that was so unbelievable—even to me as I lived and breathed it—that I would wake up in the morning wondering if it was all real.

The thing about young love is that it needs space to grow, room to breathe, and, most importantly, roots to anchor it. Instead of nurturing what we had, I had uprooted it completely, allowing Lee the freedom to grow on his own. By tearing us from the ground we shared, I gave him the chance to flourish, even if it meant sacrificing our shared future for his singular dreams.

There were nights when I'd lie awake, replaying memories of laughter and stolen kisses, wondering if I'd made the right choice. My life felt emptier, and blossoming into adulthood without Lee by my side was no easy feat.

I continued on, "I knew I was never leaving Savannah, not in my life and not for anyone, and I knew if I didn't let your brother go, he would never go on his own. That's quite the sacrifice for an eighteen-year-old girl who felt like she had already lost everything."

I sipped on my drink and looked out the window behind Dane, wishing I could stop the memories from flooding back, but I couldn't. They were relentless.

I knew that years down the road, we'd all be better for it—after Lee and I healed, went our separate ways, and grew up a little. I imagined he'd come and go, and over time, we'd slowly rebuild our friendship, gradually peeling away the scab that had formed over what was once the two of us so tightly fused together. I didn't expect him to stay away or to write an album about me that would become wildly successful. I never imagined he would move on with his life, while I'd be stuck here, listening to the same song on repeat, reliving our love story over and over again.

Yet, alongside the sorrow, there was an overwhelming sense of pride. Whenever I thought about Lee out in Nashville, a small, warm smile would tug at my lips. Once it stopped hurting so much, every time I heard one of his songs on the radio, I'd marvel at his talent and feel a deep sense of joy. I was so honored to have been a part of his journey, knowing that I had a hand in him sharing his music with the world. It wasn't all regret and pain that filled my thoughts, but rather a bittersweet acknowledgment that maybe, just maybe, I did the right thing.

I wondered if he felt that way about me now that he was the one letting *me* go.

I turned back to Dane, shaking my head to dislodge the memories. "And then with you, I found myself learning to pick up the pieces and put myself back together so that I was whole again. I was something entirely new with you."

He sat back in his chair and eyed me, letting out a long sigh that sounded like it had been sitting in his body for his entire life. I didn't have to wonder what he was thinking, and I didn't have to wonder what was coming next. I just had to wait for it.

"Are you still in love with my brother? I deserve the truth. You've been leading the two of us on for most of our lives, and you need to make a choice. It's him or me. Right now. You have to let one of us go."

Dane, for once, was right. I did have to let one of them go. History was repeating itself, and even though I had fallen in love with Lee Wilder all over again, I knew I had to set him free to keep being who he was meant to be. A decade had passed since we said goodbye, but nothing had changed for me. My heart was still his, and it always would be. But I couldn't hold him back then, and I sure as hell couldn't do it now—even though I knew watching him walk away again would tear me apart.

Lee Wilder had *ruined* me in every way, and I'd never be the same. But that didn't change a thing.

"The choice has already been made, Dane. He's leaving on New Year's Day, and you and I will be married a month after that. But I need your word, right here and now, that the bar is safe. No paperwork, no prenup, no investors. We get married, and the bar stays in my family for good."

He moved around the desk and wrapped me in his arms. I breathed in his scent of expensive cologne and a long morning of travel. It was jarring, going from broken glasses to a warm embrace, but I fought down the shudder deep inside me.

"Are you sure? That will be enough to keep you happy?" he sighed.

"As sure as ever," I lied.

CHAPTER THIRTY-SIX

Lee

Dane and I sat at opposite ends of Momma's table for her annual New Year's Eve brunch, irritation hanging heavy between us. We shot each other daggers with every glance, silently communicating all the things we wanted to say out loud but didn't so that Momma—or worse, Daddy—wouldn't get involved. We aggressively passed plates back and forth, noisily clanging silverware and slamming down our glasses.

"What time does your flight leave tomorrow, Lee?" my father asked, ready to be rid of me.

"Two p.m. I'm packed and, believe me, beyond ready to get back to Nashville and start this tour."

My momma rolled her eyes and passed down a plate of black-eyed peas. "It's been so nice having you here these last few months. I hate seeing you go."

Dane scoffed, and I bit my tongue for a moment. "I know, Momma, but I'll be back. I'll soon own a business in town, so I'll need to check on it from time to time."

What I was saying between the lines was completely obvious to my brother, and he shifted uncomfortably in his seat.

Never one to be outdone, though, he started yammering on about the wedding. "She's chosen our first dance song, and we settled on the appetizers. I tried to coax her into letting Sutton work a bit, but since she'll be the maid of honor, that may be hard."

"Well, darlin', she's in the wedding party. Magnolia is going to need Sutton more than you need her cooking that day. I sorely regretted not having my best friend at my wedding."

My father shot her a look, and I realized that Momma, Daddy, and I were the only ones in the room who knew what she truly meant.

"I get it. I'm just worried that LaMonte will bring in some second-class caterer and that we will lose the appeal of having Sutton as our chef for the evening. Everyone is so accustomed to having her delight their palate."

I groaned and rolled my eyes from my side of the table, watching this absolute idiot shovel food into his face and not even realize how important it would be for Magnolia, the woman he was about to marry, to have her best friend be there for her on their wedding day and not cooking, like hired help.

Someone that was his friend once, too.

It just went to show how out of touch with reality my brother was and always would be. It killed me that this was the kind of bullshit Maggie was going to be subjected to for the rest of her life. But this is what she wanted. This is what she chose, even ten years ago when she told me to walk away.

"What's the first stop on the tour, Leland?" Momma asked, changing the subject.

"Atlanta, and then we move to South Carolina," I said, chewing my food and keeping my eyes on the table. If I looked up, I knew I would find my brother staring me down, jealous yet again that the conversation had moved on to me.

"They can't be paying you a lot," my father interjected. "You're the first act of four, which, for someone with a Grammy Award, that's kind of like singing Karaoke at O'Malley's for a living."

"I should be so lucky," I slipped.

"Oh *fuck* you, Lee! I won. I got the girl in the end. Please, just leave and move on," Dane said, standing up so fast my momma jumped and knocked her drink over. I moved just as quick as him, though, and before we knew it, we were tangled up and throwing punches over my momma's dining room table like we were teenagers.

***

"You're a moron. Seriously. That last black eye barely healed and now you have a fresh one. Some face to put forward for your last show at O'Malley's for who knows how long." Sutton was icing my eye, and Charlie kicked open the door to his work room in his studio with a couple of cold beers he had confiscated

226

from next door.

"I found some cold prosciutto, too. It's not a steak, but it will have to do," he said, handing it to Sutton and cracking open our drinks before handing them out.

"I cannot believe the two of you are going to sit around and watch Magnolia marry this animal. I know she's hot-headed, but you guys should step in. He's quick with his fists, who's to say he won't get so mad at her that he hits her one day."

Sutton and Charlie exchanged a look, and I jumped off my chair. "What aren't you telling me?"

Sutton sighed and opened the prosciutto package, popping some of the thin-sliced meat into her mouth. "Nothing, it's not… He threw a glass on Christmas morning after, well, you know… It just missed her head." She looked to Charlie for help, and he just cringed. My blood was boiling. Sutton went on. "Now listen! We're not happy it happened, either. We both had separate conversations with her about it. But there's not much we can do, her mind is made up."

Charlie nodded. "You know my sister, Lee. When she makes her mind up about something, that's it. It's done. And this is what she wants. Whatever we say about it now doesn't matter."

I paced the room, looking back and forth between the two of them. "I'm just not even going to show up tonight. Forget it."

"Lee, she's counting on you to play tonight. If you don't, people will leave." Charlie watched me wearily. "She's sold about 250 tickets for this exclusive event, and people are dying to see you, especially since the tour was announced."

"Well, maybe my brother can fix it for her since he's such a fucking hero," I spit before storming out of the studio.

Later that night, I sat on my bed in my hotel room, surrounded by the last pieces that were left of me to pack to take back to Nashville. I checked the clock before reaching for my phone, which was buzzing like crazy from the nightstand. I knew she was going to be pissed—beyond pissed—and I didn't want to deal with it.

She made her choice, and frankly, she needed to live with it at this point.

I couldn't save her or even try to take care of her anymore. I'd sent Ryan over to do a couple of covers and said my goodbyes to Sutton and Charlie. There was nothing left between me and Magnolia, and in a little over a month, she would be my sister-in-law. I'd given her all the help I was willing to.

I threw my phone into the drawer, slamming it shut, and closed my eyes.

I wasn't starting a new year living for Magnolia Pruitt. In fact, I wasn't spending another second on her ever again.

CHAPTER THIRTY-SEVEN

Magnolia

"Where the hell is he?" I paced restlessly in my office, then wandered into the green room and dramatically flopped down onto the couch.

Sutton opened the door to the bar, revealing a hunched-over Kasey, her ear pressed to the now-empty space. She jerked back, eyes wide with panic, and attempted to play it cool, though it was obvious she was spying.

Kasey took one look at me draped across the sofa and turned her attention to Sutton. "Is she okay? There's, like, a million people out there asking questions." She shut the door behind her and leaned back on the cool wood.

"Ryan's doing a great job. I don't see the problem." Sutton shrugged.

"I'm fine," I answered for myself, flinging an arm over my face. "I guess I just don't get it. He wants to buy the bar, then he wants to be a silent partner. He wants to do these gigs to make us money, then he doesn't show up. And where the hell is Dane?"

"He's not here yet, but I saved him a spot with Charlie and Eunice," Kasey answered quickly. "Should I just shut it all down? I really don't know what to do. The three new hires are freaking out. Magnolia, can you please come out and see everyone?"

I shot Sutton a desperate frown as a wave of sad realization washed over me. "It's over, isn't it?"

"It's been over, Magnolia. Go out and do what you need to do," she answered, topping off my bubbles.

I lifted myself off the couch and took a swig of my champagne, glaring at Kasey. "Just go out and train. You're going to be the manager of the bar soon, so please step up," I snapped.

She made an agitated noise and threw open the door, stomping out toward the front of the bar. Her voice was laced with anger as she addressed the new employees, who looked stressed and nervous about their first official shifts.

"Just let things be how they are, Magnolia," Sutton murmured, crossing the room to stand beside me. "If Lee isn't coming back, he's a silent partner. Just like y'all discussed. Isn't this what you wanted all along?"

I nodded. It was what *he* agreed on. But where did that leave me?

Maybe I always knew, deep down, that he'd go back to Nashville someday. Maybe I always knew that he'd just throw some money at me—an investment, he once called it—so he could go back to strumming his stupid guitar, just like he always wanted.

And I'd still be here, in Savannah, behind the bar and carrying on my family's legacy, just like *I* always wanted.

Nothing—and yet somehow everything—had changed.

I skulked out of my office but threw my shoulders back and slapped on a fake smile when Eunice caught my eye from across the room. A slight frown settled on her face, almost like she could read between the lines of my body language and knew something was wrong. Charlie pulled a chair out for me.

"I thought I'd see my son here tonight." Eunice planted a kiss on my cheek as I sank down in the chair next to her. My brother shot me a sympathetic smile and pulled out another chair for Sutton, who was following behind me to join us.

"I think he's on his way." I lifted my arm to check my watch. "He must have gotten caught up at the office with Vance."

"I meant Leland." Eunice gestured to the stage. "I thought I'd get to say goodbye."

"You and me both, Eunice," I retorted.

We made pleasant talk with one another and folks that had stopped by the table to say hello and to inquire on the whereabouts of Savannah's favorite country singer. Every time someone asked me how the wedding plans were going, I felt like I was going to throw up.

Sutton, not helping the situation as usual, kept topping off my champagne.

"Stop watching the door," Charlie finally said, an icy tone lacing his voice. "He's not coming."

"Who, exactly, isn't coming?" Sutton slurred, then hiccuped. "Looks like she's getting stood up by *both* Wilder men."

I rolled my eyes. Eunice politely excused herself, flitting over to hold court at the table full of Daughters of Savannah Civic Society. She looked over her shoulder, brow twisting with concern, and a worried expression settled on her face.

"You're an ass, Sutton," Charlie spat when Eunice was out of earshot. "She feels bad enough. It's written all over her face. Look at her. She looks positively bedraggled."

Great, Charlie was drunk, too.

Ryan finished serenading the room, and I took the opportunity to slide into my office to find some peace. I checked the clock, and it was rounding toward midnight and a new year.

The year I was going to become Mrs. Dane Wilder.

My stomach flipped in that familiar, nerve-wracking way, and my heart dropped.

What was I doing?

Was this going to be my life now? Perpetually torn between two worlds— one where I waited for Dane to emerge from his law office, only joining me for special occasions, or the other, where I'd always be watching, waiting, forever gazing at that door, hoping it was Lee that walked through it.

This was the reality of it all now, though. I had made my choice, and it was time to live with it, no matter how much my heart was shattering into a thousand tiny pieces.

"Five minutes until the countdown!" one of the new bartenders called out. "Y'all come up and get your glasses filled!"

I stepped out of my office and leaned against the doorframe, watching the bar erupt in excitement as the crowd gathered together to start the countdown. The buzz of anticipation, the eagerness in the room, only strengthened the weight I felt on my shoulders. Loneliness crept into my bones, and I felt a heavy sadness as I took in the scene.

But yet, as the clock ticked closer to midnight, a flicker of hope sparked within me. Despite the weight of my solitude, there was the promise of new beginnings and the chance for a fresh start in the coming year.

On the surface, I had everything I wanted. The bar was packed, and money was coming in. I toyed with the huge ring on my finger, remembering that I'd soon be marrying into a family that loved me. I had the greatest, most supportive friends in the world.

And that was enough for me to be happy, wasn't it?

The crowd began to swell, energy bubbling through the room. I felt a knot of anxiety tightening in my chest, a gripping, sudden panic where there was once a spark of belief that maybe I *did* have it all.

Charlie and Sutton sauntered toward me, holding each other up and smiling ear-to-ear, like one should be doing when the promise of new beginnings was on the horizon and you were surrounded by everyone you love.

That ball dropping and the finality of it all, that this year, full of laughter, love, tears, and reverie with someone I cared about so much was coming to an end. And it was over. For good this time.

And somehow, that single realization completely overshadowed any trace of faith I had in this new chapter.

"Will y'all excuse me for just a second? I forgot to feed the cat." I shot Sutton a look, silently begging her not to follow me, before bounding up the stairs to my apartment.

I collapsed to my knees in the kitchen, a raw sob escaping me as I tried to stifle the sound. Downstairs, the countdown to the New Year had begun, their voices brimming with anticipation and excitement, completely unaware of the breakdown unfolding above.

I could hear the optimism beaming through the floorboards, a promise of better days ahead, even if it lasted only sixty seconds as the ball made its slow descent toward midnight.

And there I was, alone, with those very same promises of better, brighter days ahead of me, too.

And yet, I'd never felt more trapped in the past.

After midnight, I could hear the quiet lull of the bar as it cleared out, and Sutton stumbled her way upstairs to say goodnight. I was on the couch with Pickle, watching the aftermath of New Year's Eve in Times Square. Litter, lingering couples, and smiling faces peppered the screen.

"Are you sure everything's okay?" She sat down on the loveseat across from me, pouting sympathetically.

"I'm sure. It would have been nice to kiss my fiancé happy New Year, though," I lied.

"He just walked in. Kasey's showing the newbies how to close the register, and there's a few of them cleaning up. I'm sure he'll make his way up here soon."

I nodded, playing with the hem of my dress.

Sutton sighed and stood on her long, lean legs. She reached forward and kissed me on the top of my head. "Happy New Year, Magnolia."

"Happy New Year, Sutton."

I nodded off on the couch at some point, watching the city workers in New York scramble to get the square back in one piece before the morning sun rose. I could feel the stillness of the bar below me, and I sat up to check the clock—2:00 a.m.

"I should go check on things down there, huh?" I scratched Pickle's head, and she purred loudly, scrunching herself up tighter in her little calico ball.

The smell of cigar smoke smacked me in the face as I made my way down the stairs. As I got closer, I could hear soft music and murmuring coming from the green room.

Slowly, I opened the door to the bar from the back hallway and slipped into the barroom. I tiptoed through the sea of empty cups, bottles, napkins, and stubbed out cigarette butts that littered the floor.

I thought Kasey had the new team cleaning up?

From the other side of the green room door, I heard her voice and that telltale shrill giggle of hers followed by a deep moan and a groggy response from a man.

So, instead of cleaning up, she was getting lucky in my green room. I thought about running back up the stairs and firing her in the morning, but my gut told me to kick in the door and call her out on her shit right then and there.

When I opened the door, the sound that came out of my mouth was almost guttural, animal like. I hurled myself forward and grabbed Kasey by the back of her head, flinging her away from the couch and onto the floor from the kneeling position I found her in.

Sitting on the couch, eyes slanted, still feigning pleasure with a half-lit cigar in between his fingers, Dane growled, and instead of apologizing or even acknowledging me, his eyes fell to Kasey.

"What the *fuck* is happening?" My voice was shrill and uncontrollable, and from her spot on the floor, Kasey laughed.

"What's it look like, sweetheart? I was giving Dane here a New Year's kiss," she toyed, scrambling to her feet when I lunged at her.

"Are you kidding me, Dane?" My breath picked up speed as I crossed my arms over my chest, a current of shock and disbelief threatening to knock me over where I stood.

"Oh, whatever, Magnolia. I'm only guilty of the very same thing you are, aren't I? Sleeping with someone else? At least Kasey's not your sister."

My mind was reeling. Every time Dane left town to go to trial, Kasey mysteriously disappeared. Whenever I couldn't find her, I couldn't find him, either.

This had been going on right under my nose for a long time, I suspected.

What a damn fool I was.

I flew into my office and opened the safe, making sure that Kasey had deposited the cash from the night into the drop box. If she was capable of putting my fiancé's penis in her mouth, she was capable of stealing from me.

Dane followed me in and closed the door, cigar still dangling between his fingers. He took a drag and slowly moved to the chair on the opposite side of my desk, his eyes trained on me the entire time.

I took a seat, too, and poured us both a drink, even though I could tell he was already beyond drunk. It didn't excuse his behavior, though. He couldn't have been drunk every time he slept with Kasey.

"Kasey? Really, Dane. Of all the people in Savannah…"

"She's been in love with me since we were kids, and we both know how that can keep you loyal, even if it's to the wrong person," he said, a cat-like grin spreading across his lips.

"Well, I think it's safe to say that we're calling this whole shin-dig off. I don't ever want to see you in this bar, or on my property, ever again."

His eyes were unfocused, and he was rocking slightly in his chair, but he guzzled down the entire pour of bourbon before him, an irritated scowl landing on his face. "Funny thing about that is, this so-called property of yours belongs to the Wilder Trust, love. And if you're not marrying into the family, well, I don't know how much stake you have left anymore."

I pulled back on my own drink so that he couldn't see me wince. "How?

I haven't even signed the paperwork yet."

"You didn't have to, Magnolia, because Cole already did." He watched me closely, waiting for me to react violently, to get good and mad so I started swinging, and I realized that he'd been doing that all along. Egging me on so that I threw the first punch, making it seem like self-defense when he finally knocked me senseless.

I balled my hands in my lap, willing my fists not to take on a life of their own and end up meeting his pearly white teeth. "He's dead, you idiot."

"Now, that can't be true Magnolia, his death certificate was never filed. And believe me, I checked since I'm the one who was supposed to file it with the state." Dane took another puff of his cigar, ashes falling to the floor. He let his head fall back, and he smiled up at the ceiling.

I trusted him with the death certificate, thinking he'd sort it out with the law firm like he said he would. He assured me everything was handled, and there was nothing else needed on my end. White hot, blinding rage was boiling inside me. He was trying to push my buttons and get me to lose it, but I wasn't about to give him the satisfaction.

"Are you still in love with my brother? I deserve the truth this time, not that bullshit monologue you spit out at Christmas," he scoffed.

"Well, I'll tell you what, Dane. I wish I never moved to Savannah, and then I wouldn't have met you or your idiot brother." His face darkened the second I said it, but I couldn't take it back now.

"You *are* still in love with Lee, aren't you, Magnolia? I can't say I'm surprised, honestly. I mean, hell, look at Kasey. She's pathetic enough to follow me around Georgia because of the pull I've had on her since middle school."

I took another sip of bourbon and slowly set the glass back on the desk, trying to hide how much my hands were shaking.

"Who I am or am not in love with, Dane, is no longer any of your concern. Though I will say, I wonder how much longer you would have gotten away with this. I mean, honestly, were you going to leave the room on our wedding night so Kasey could slob on your knob for a few minutes? What would your momma say?" My voice was dripping with sarcasm.

He laughed. "What do you care for? You never wanted me. You just wanted to be a part of my family so you could keep this piece of shit bar, no matter who got hurt along the way." He was tripping over his words, and it surprised me that tears formed in his eyes. "I've loved you for a real long time, Magnolia."

"That, Dane Wilder, is very hard to believe at the moment." Relief was slowly overshadowing the fear and anger that was engulfing me. "But you have to realize this is not how you show someone you love them, and this is not how I will spend the rest of my life. No matter the cost." I stood up, locking the door to the safe and pocketing the key, then walked around the desk flinging open the door to the bar. "Until I see some concrete proof otherwise, this bar is still mine and you're now trespassing. So, I suggest you, and that trollop of a girlfriend of yours, get the hell out before I call the cops."

"That's it, Magnolia?" Dane rose from his chair, wobbling as he tried to stand, reaching an arm out toward me. "After all these years? After everything you and I have been through?"

"No, there is one more thing." I stomped back through the office and hurled open the green room door. Kasey, now sitting on the couch, jumped up to her feet and took a few paces back to put some distance between us. "You—you dumb, backstabbing bitch—are fired."

When I reached the front door, after catapulting over the garbage strewn across the barroom, I stormed out of O'Malley's and bounded down the street as fast as my feet would take me.

I found my way to the river and onto an empty bench overlooking the dark brown water. Only then, when I was alone, aside from a few straggling celebrators dancing and hollering through the cobblestone streets, did I allow myself to truly cry.

They were not tears of betrayal. Nor were they tears of a broken heart. I cried for the woman who had, for the better part of her life, made choices and sacrifices not for herself, but for everyone else.

As selfish as I had felt over the last few months, nothing compared to how I had almost given up everything to keep the bar open. How I had dove, headfirst, into a relationship and engagement with someone just to gain control over my family's livelihood—their blood, sweat, and tears.

And, in the end, none of it mattered anyway. It was all for nothing.

I stood up, quickly gathering my hair into a top-knot. With a deep breath, I sprinted down the river walk, determined to get to where I knew I needed to be as quickly as my feet could take me.

If we were all going down and everything was in shambles, I decided I might as well go out in a blaze of glory.

Lee

I was tossing and turning in bed, restless all night. Something felt off, as if the air had shifted, and I could sense the winds of change sweeping in with the new year.

I'd talked to Janelle at midnight, and our conversation was dull and flat. I knew, just as she did, that we were over. I think we were both waiting until after the holiday celebrations had ended to call things quits.

Of course, I had kept my distance from O'Malley's and the New Year's Eve party. I was leaving on a 2:00 p.m. flight back to Nashville to start the first leg of the tour, and as much as I wanted to see Magnolia one last time, I couldn't bring myself to say goodbye.

Because I knew it would be permanent.

Before we both knew it, she would be my sister-in-law, and while the thought ate away at me—and, frankly, was the reason why I couldn't sleep—I knew in the end it was the right thing for everyone.

Wasn't it?

Understanding that she was going to marry Dane, knowing with all of my heart she would never truly be happy, felt like a punch to the gut. I couldn't shake this gnawing sense of helplessness. It was like watching a train wreck in slow motion, knowing exactly how bad it's going to be but being powerless to stop it. I hated that she was going through with this, that she was making this grave mistake. And even though I tried to convince myself it wasn't my place anymore to interfere, deep down, I felt like I should've done more. Something—anything—to change the outcome.

All night, I wrestled with the brutal waves of self-loathing that just wouldn't quit. I kept asking myself if I should've fought harder or if I'd somehow failed her. It was like a constant loop of regret and frustration, playing over and over in my mind. I knew she was unhappy and with someone who didn't deserve her, all the while just trying to do what she felt was the right thing to do. Every time I thought about it, the sting of knowing she was settling and that she could end up hurt felt like a raw, unhealed wound.

As I drifted in and out of a fitful sleep, a soft knock on my door woke me. I checked the clock—3:15 a.m.

I rolled over, figuring it was someone lost in the hotel, trying to get into the wrong room after too many celebratory drinks. But the knocking grew louder, more urgent, and my stomach dropped.

Something was wrong, and I could sense it with every fiber of my being.

I threw on a pair of jeans and stumbled over my half-packed bags and open guitar cases. *Another unfinished thing in my life,* I thought before cracking open the door slightly to see who was on the other side.

"What are you doing here?" I pushed the door open wider, struggling not to pull her into my arms. Something wasn't right, and it was written all over Magnolia's beautiful, freckled face.

She looked at her feet and then back up at me, sad eyes meeting mine. I watched her eyes trail over my chest, taking in every detail as if she was trying to memorize my body. Or maybe she was trying to remember. I knew I could recall every one of her curves, every freckle in places the sun never hit.

Her gaze was intense and full of longing, and I sensed she was struggling to keep her cool. She shifted back and forth on her toes nervously.

After letting out a long sigh, she took a small step back, putting some space between us. "I don't… I'm not really sure why I'm here. It's been a really, really long night. Long few months, actually. I don't know, I just think… I don't know what I'm doing here." She fumbled with her words, her sentences coming out in a jumbled mess.

"Maggie, are you alright? Is it Dane? What did he do now?" I couldn't stop myself. I had to reach out and touch her. I closed the space between us and rested my hand on her arm, gently tracing circles with my thumb. I felt a wave of goosebumps spread across her skin, and she shivered slightly. Her stormy gray eyes met mine, and a glimmer of something brighter surfaced, overshadowing the fear and panic I knew she was trying to bury down.

"See, the thing is," she started, moving her eyes from the spot where my hand rested on her skin to the waistband of my jeans. She bit her bottom lip. "See, you know how…"

Before I could even think to invite her in and pour her a drink so she could unload whatever was on her mind, her lips crashed into mine with a force that caught me off guard. Her fingers were already tangled in my hair, pulling me closer as if afraid I might slip away.

I didn't have time to think; a deep, carnal instinct took over. With a swift kick, I slammed the door shut and spun her around, my hands never losing their grip on her. Pressing her against the wall, I lifted her dress, my finger gliding over the soft curve of her stomach, toying with the sensitive skin. She arched into my touch, a low, throaty groan escaping her lips, sending a shiver down my spine.

In one fluid motion, she jumped up, wrapping her legs tightly around my waist, her hips grinding against me with a need that was impossible to ignore. Even through the thin fabric of her dress, I could feel her heat, her body pulsating with desire, urging me to explore every inch of her.

With a firm grip on her backside, I carried her—our mouths still locked together, our breaths coming in quick, desperate gasps—down the hall to the bedroom. In a swift, effortless move, I tossed her onto the bed, the weight of the moment heavy between us as I hovered over her, both of us knowing there was no turning back.

Her gray eyes met mine, wide and filled with something raw, almost desperate. Her wavy, golden-red hair, usually so neat, was tousled now, a few strands clinging to her flushed cheeks. There was a wildness in her look that sent a surge of need through me—an electric charge I couldn't control.

She licked her plump, pink lips, the tip of her tongue trailing slowly over them. The sight of it made my pulse race, my focus zeroing in on her and those lips I was dying to feel against every inch of me. I watched her throat move as she swallowed, her chest rising and falling with each shallow breath

"I'm sorry. I shouldn't be here," she murmured, sitting up to unbutton my jeans. She locked eyes with me as she pulled them down, and I tripped over myself trying to scramble out of them. She ran her fingers softly, gently, over my growing hard-on, and then looked up to meet my eyes. "But I want you," she whispered with a sultry edge. "I need you, Lee."

That was all I needed to hear. A loud, rumbling moan escaped me, and I leaned into her, kissing down her neck and chest.

I lifted the black and gold glittering dress up over her head, caressing her front. "Why are you dressed like a flapper?" I rasped, voice draped with desire.

She giggled as she ran her hands over my thighs, her voice an urgent quiver but still dripping with sarcasm. "New Years Eve, remember? The huge party you skipped out on, leaving me without a Grammy Award winning artist on my stage."

She scooted back on the bed, laying herself gently on my pillow. I tossed the bedazzled number on to the floor and ran my hands over her silky legs. "Let's not talk about that now," my voice was low, breathy.

A deep, aching need surged through me. The way she looked at me, like I was the only thing that could satisfy whatever hunger burned inside her, made me feel like I was going to lose it right then and there, without the satisfaction of even tasting her.

I opened her up to me, pushing my knee between her thighs. Hovering over her for a moment, I watched her face closely.

For the first time in months, she radiated happiness. She looked like she knew what she wanted, and she wanted it right then and there. And it looked like that thing that she wanted was me.

***

When we were finally spent, Maggie rested her head on my chest, our breaths syncing up in a soft, shared rhythm. The tension and urgency from before had melted away, leaving us in a deep, calming stillness. In that quiet moment, words didn't matter; our hearts did all the talking, the warmth of our bodies saying everything that needed to be said.

I had thought I loved her before, but this moment—this one moment that changed everything between us—hit me hard. I realized I never wanted to be without her, never wanted to leave her side again.

But I was heading back to Nashville.

"I'm sorry you have to leave today," she whispered, as if reading my thoughts as she ran her hands across my stomach.

There was no way I could walk away this time, not after this moment—not even if she still wanted me to go. But what could I do about the label? Could I really let Ryan down like that?

I released a resigned groan. "I'll call the tour director in the morning and see if we can cut the tour in half. It won't be long. But what about the wedding?"

She sat up on her elbows, staring at the ceiling. "Well, I don't think…"

Her phone buzzed on the nightstand, breaking the peaceful moment. We looked at each other solemnly; our little slice of paradise abruptly shattered.

Her eyes lit up with surprise, then fear, as she realized who was calling her in the middle of the night. "Charlie? What's wrong? It's four in the morning."

Maggie chewed on her bottom lip, her face dropping in shock as she listened to Charlie's erratic, incoherent screams from the other end of the line. "No, I'm not there!" she shrieked, hurtling off the bed and yanking her dress back on as fast as she could. I jumped up, too, but she was already out the door and down the hallway before I even had a chance to put on my shoes.

CHAPTER THIRTY-NINE

Magnolia

I hung up on Charlie and sprinted through the empty streets of pre-dawn Savannah, my heart pounding with every step. As I neared McDonough Street, I saw the black smoke rising and heard the wail of sirens in the distance. Lee was hot on my heels, shouting my name and trying to close the gap between us.

But it didn't matter now. Nothing did.

I rounded the corner and rushed at the police tape, desperately trying to push past it. I screamed and flailed, hitting at the officers who were trying to hold me back.

My life, my family's legacy, the last bit of history I had to tie me to my mother, to Uncle Cole, was on fire.

O'Malley's was going up in flames, burning fast and furious, down to the ground.

"What happened?" Lee shouted, finally catching up to me. His feet were a mess, bloodied and smeared with black grime from running after me in just a pair of jeans.

"We don't know yet," the officer holding me back said.

I ran my hands through my hair as I howled, watching the fire destroy everything I loved, every memory I had.

"Your brother's over there," he said to me, pointing in the direction of an ambulance housing my brother. He was wrapped in what looked like tin-foil, and his dark, soot-covered face was streaked with tears.

"Charlie," I cried, rushing toward him. "Charlie, please tell me what happened!"

He shook his head wearily and stood up, letting the shock-prevention wrap fall to the ground. Pickle, wide-eyed and terrified, spotted Lee. She leaped down, scrambled up Lee's leg, and settled into his arms.

"Magnolia, I'm so sorry," he said, wrapping me in his arms. I could feel him batting down sobs and trying to steady himself. He pulled back, studying my face, almost as if he was trying to figure out if I was real or a ghost that had materialized out of the flames. "Dane called me and said the bar was on fire, so I came as fast as I could. I called the fire department, but I got here before they did. I ran upstairs to see if you were there. I was calling out for you, but—God, Magnolia, I thought you were dead!"

"Where's my brother?" Lee spat angrily, handing Pickle over to me as he paced through the crowd.

"I don't know, Lee. I tried looking downstairs, but the smoke was too thick," Charlie said, tears pooling in his eyes as he pulled me into him again. "I found the cat in the staircase between the apartment and the bar. I thought you were dead, Magnolia. I thought I was alone. I thought you left me."

My brother started bawling and shaking, and Pickle purred wildly between us, trying to get us to calm down. We sat on the tailgate of the ambulance and quietly watched everything our family had worked so hard for turn to ashes in the night.

As the sky began to lighten, the fire department almost had the blaze somewhat under control but not quite. Eunice and Vance had shown up, but no one had seen or heard from Dane.

Eunice pulled me into her arms, kissed my tear-soaked face, and cried over and over again about how happy she was that I was alive.

But we were all on edge. No one could get into the building to make sure it was truly all clear, and no one could tell us yet how the fire had started. And more importantly, no one had seen Dane since I left him in my office.

And in my heart, I knew.

Dane had torched my entire life.

CHAPTER FORTY

Magnolia

I sat in the Wilders' living room, nursing a hot toddy, Pickle purring like a lawn mower in my lap. I was in shock and kept toying between bursting into tears and wanting to get up, walk out of the house, and head home to get some sleep.

But I had no home. Home was now a pile of soot on the corner block of McDonough Street, along with everything I had worked so hard for.

It had been hours since the fire started, and still, no one had seen Dane. The fire chief, holding court in the Wilders' dining room, told Eunice and Vance that it was a good sign his cell phone was still ringing and hadn't shut off. Apparently, the main system can go down if it gets too hot.

Charlie sat on the couch next to me, and as the hours dragged on, Doyle, Jordan, Sutton, and Ryan had all joined us at the Wilders'. No one knew what to say, except for Sutton, who was laying on the threats thick.

"I will find him, and I will stab him," Sutton proclaimed loudly, not caring whose house she was in. "I know his spoiled, frat boy ass had something to do with this."

Eunice shot her a sharp look from the dining room, and Sutton hurled one right back, urging her to say something. Sutton was in full attack mode, and we all knew not to mess with her.

Doyle shrugged. "Well, that couple—you know, the ones getting it on in the alley—they said they saw someone leave the bar but couldn't tell if it was a man or a woman, on account of being too busy, you know, boning in a dumpster."

Ryan cackled, and I rolled my eyes. "I left out of the front of the bar, so if someone left out the back, it wasn't me."

"Was it Kasey? They still haven't found her, either, last I heard," Charlie mumbled, keeping his eyes on the carpet below his feet.

"So, let me get this straight," Sutton paced the room. "Dane and Kasey have been a thing for how long? And we're just finding this out now because…"

"I knew," Lee said, lingering in the doorway, hands shoved in his pockets. He'd kept his distance from me most of the morning, but I could tell he was batting down every urge to crash across the room and pull me into his embrace. "I didn't have concrete proof, but I had an idea."

Sutton screeched and rushed over to Lee, pushing his chest. "You were going to let that asshole marry Magnolia?! Are you *kidding* me, Lee?"

"Not for nothing, but we were all going to let that asshole marry Magnolia," my brother noted.

Lee met my eyes across the room and offered a sympathetic, sad smile. Whether or not he was right, it didn't matter.

Nothing mattered. Not right now.

I was numb, deeply aware of the fact that almost everything I held close was now gone. Dane included. No matter what he was up to.

Sutton kept roaring and pacing, and Eunice, finally having enough, slammed her hands down on the dining room table.

"Sutton James, that is enough," she said, firm yet calm. "Why don't y'all head off and get some rest, and we'll call you if Magnolia or Charlie need anything? Magnolia, dear, please come in here. We have some questions."

I handed the cat off to Charlie, who was still as stiff as a statue, staring at the floor, and I doled out half-hearted hugs to my friends before ushering them out the door. I took a seat at the dining room table, and Lee joined, sulking down in the spot next to me.

Eddie Donovan, the chief of the Savannah Fire Department, sat at the table with weary, tired eyes. He took a long sip of his coffee and let out a heavy sigh.

"Now, please don't take offense, Ms. Pruitt," he began, choosing his words carefully. "Where were you tonight, after the New Year's celebration at O'Malley's?"

Lee and I both turned our heads slightly toward each other, and I shifted uncomfortably in my chair. "I was with Leland, sir. After the bar emptied, I went to his place to… talk."

Vance threw his hands up in the air and jumped out of his seat. "Well Jesus, Magnolia, of course Dane probably engulfed himself in flames if you were off with Lee doing Lord knows what!"

Eunice shook her head and placed a reassuring hand on her husband's arm, trying to calm him down.

"I know that you're not going to like what I'm about to say, Vance, but I'd left Dane in my office with Kasey after catching her giving him a blowjob in my bar." Hysteria was starting to set in, and I actually chuckled.

Eddie Donovan's face flushed as he nearly spat out his coffee, and Eunice let out a gasp so loud that Lee almost jumped out of his seat.

"Now, I'm nobody's fool, but I'd like to see the insurance policy y'all took out on the bar," I started, willing my voice not to shake. "I know Dane neglected to file my Uncle Cole's death certificate and forged his signature to sign the bar over to the Wilder Family Trust. Dane wasn't too happy to get caught last night, so if I had to guess, this wasn't any sort of accident. This might be smelling quite like arson."

I met Eunice's eyes across the table, and Eddie groaned, angrily typing up a text on his phone as he walked into the foyer.

"I'm sorry, Eunice," I whispered, "but I can't marry a man who would not only steal my business but burn it down to the ground for a quick buck. O'Malley's was my home. And the betrayal? The cheating? What kind of life was I about to have married to your son?"

Tears began to trickle down her cheeks, and I could see the heartbreak in her eyes—both for me and for her family. But I knew she was mostly heartbroken for her best friend, my momma, and the love of her life, my Uncle Cole.

And, if I had to guess, she was heartbroken that another Wilder man had swept in and ruined everything for another O'Malley like me.

CHAPTER FORTY-ONE

Lee

I dropped Magnolia and Pickle off at Sutton's apartment, staying for a while to order a few things on Amazon that I hoped would make her stay more comfortable.

Losing everything meant losing *everything*, and while I couldn't snap my fingers and fix Maggie's life the way I wanted to, I had to do something.

She'd turned down my parents' offer to let her stay at their house on Jones Street while she figured out her next move. I couldn't blame her, but when we were leaving and she was saying goodbye to my parents, it almost felt like she was saying goodbye forever.

"I think we're good now, Lee. You should probably go," Sutton said hours after I knew I had worn out my welcome. I'd missed my flight and checked out of the hotel, but I still couldn't bring myself to leave her side.

"I'll just say goodbye, then," I said, giving Sutton a half-assed smile. She was still fuming over what I'd said earlier, and rightfully so. I was an asshole—an asshole who thought, for sure, he was doing the right thing.

I knocked quietly on the spare bedroom in Sutton's apartment and opened the door slowly. Curled up in a ball, with Pickle sitting up protectively behind her, Magnolia was in a puddle of her own tears.

"I'm going to head out," I coughed, running my fingers through my hair.

She didn't look up; she didn't even move. She just sighed and said, "I never want to see you again for the rest of my life, Leland Wilder. You or anyone else in your family."

CHAPTER FORTY-TWO

Magnolia

A little over a month had passed since the fire, and while there was still no sign of Kasey or Dane, a few new clues had surfaced.

Turns out, the fire was started behind the bar, and alcohol was used as an accelerant. Though Kasey was smart enough to turn off the security cameras over the doorways, the business behind mine had theirs facing the alley and caught the two of them scurrying out the back.

Given the size of the building, it was hard to pinpoint the exact time the fire started, but either way, the fact that they hadn't shown their faces in Savannah in a month was telling.

Before his bank accounts were frozen and his credit cards were put on high alert, Dane had emptied out all of his accounts.

And all of the money in the Wilder Family Trust.

Some days, Sutton would walk with me to the charred remains of what used to be my home. She'd sit with me on the sidewalk as I held vigil to the ashes, mourning all the history that was erased the second the flames ate away the foundation.

On this particular day, she'd packed us a picnic lunch, and we sat on two camping chairs, passing a thermos filled with champagne back and forth.

It was, after all, my wedding day.

"You know, I figured Dane was a villain, but in the like, talk down to you in public and make you wear a ton of Lilly Pulitzer type of way. Not in the full-blown soap opera drama, literally ruin your entire life type of way," Sutton said, pulling greasy, paper-wrapped pieces of fried chicken from the picnic basket.

"I wish it didn't cost me the bar," I said sadly, watching her pull side dishes out of her bag. "But, at the end of the day, I suppose I dodged a bullet. He would have done it after the wedding, and what if I had been inside when it happened? Maybe that was the plan all along. Murder. Not just mayhem."

I studied Sutton for a moment as she nodded along, only half-listening. She rummaged through her oversized bag, pulling out a stack of plates.

"Why do you have so much food? I know I've been stress eating, and you've been stress frying, but this is absurd. Even for us."

She laughed, looking over her shoulder. "Don't hate me, okay?"

I turned around as Jordan, Doyle, and Charlie crossed the street, each carrying their own camping chair and picnic basket. Jordan even had arms full of flowers and a folded-up table on his shoulder.

"Sutton, I didn't want to make a big deal…"

"We're your wedding party, and we all took the day off work at any rate, so please, let us enjoy the break." She smiled, grabbing my hand and squeezing it. "And the good company."

My brother helped Jordan and Doyle set up, then popped open his chair in the spot next to me and kissed the top of my head. "How ya doing, baby sister?"

"Weird day, y'all, I won't lie. Where's Tally?" My question concerning Savannah's newest resident, who'd recently moved in with her brother and Jordan, was directed to Doyle, but for some reason, my own brother answered.

"She's still a little intimidated by all of this. She kept yammering about bad juju and the spiritual ramifications of holding a seance outside of a burned down bar."

Doyle laughed and rolled his eyes. "They've been spending time together, if you couldn't tell. My sister did ask me to give you this, though. It's a box of sage. You're supposed to light the ends of them, but… maybe it's not best to play with fire at the moment."

For the first time in what felt like forever, I let out a long, legitimate laugh. "Tell her thank you for me. And thanks for coming, y'all. Really, I appreciate it."

Sutton docked her phone into Jordan's portable speaker, choosing a fun and upbeat playlist, and we all sat back in our chairs, snacking away and toasting to a wedding that didn't happen, lined up on the sidewalk in front of my burned-out bar.

If someone had passed by O'Malley's at that moment, on their way to something better, of course, the scene would be the least weird thing they saw in

Savannah that day. But for us, it was just a typical afternoon—day drinking and a portable feast fit for a wedding party.

"Alright, I'll be the one to bring up the elephant in the ashy room," I said, standing up and leaning on the table to face my friends. "Has anyone talked to Lee?"

Everyone let out a collective groan, and my brother leaned over to rest his elbows on his knees, dropping his head in his hands. I knew that this time was different, and they wouldn't lie to me about this. I'd hoped.

"I talked to Ryan yesterday," Sutton spoke first, surprising me. "They're only doing a quarter of the tour they were supposed to. But, that said, he doesn't think he's coming back. Either of them."

I walked up to my friend and grabbed her hand, holding it in mine for a moment, mad at myself for—as usual—forgetting that this situation didn't just break my heart. It broke all of ours.

"He broke up with Janelle, though," Jordan said from the end of the line of chairs, fussing with a bottle of expensive champagne. He pulled out five delicate crystal flutes from his bag and filled up the glasses carefully. We all stared at him, the least likely to know about Lee's personal life out of all of us.

"What! Y'all really need to step up your Instagram game. These were a wedding gift, by the way. There's six, but, well, you know." He stood, passing out the glasses to us, and we all stood in a circle, holding our glasses in the middle, eyeing each other.

"I'm not giving a stupid speech," I said finally.

"I'll start," my brother declared, lifting his glass. "I'm sure there's something witty I could say about this being your phoenix moment. Rising from the ashes a different being—stronger, better, and all that." He shot a sad, sullen look to the hollowed-out bar behind me. His childhood, my childhood, rendered to dust.

We all raised our glasses, holding them together in a circle as he continued. "It's simple, and it's cliche, but it's true. Here's to new beginnings."

"And! To Magnolia Louise Pruitt, who never needed a man to live out her dreams. Just some strong drinks and even stronger friends," Sutton added.

"Might I add, good friends are great, but good food and a hell of a lot of laughs for the years to come are absolutely on our radar. Especially after this," Jordan piped up.

"To the Savannah Sweethearts. May we build our walls, but may we never, ever let them crumble again," Doyle finished, and I glanced around at the faces of my friends, old and new. My family, my strength, my everything.

"I love y'all. Thank you for never leaving me behind," I said, eyes filled with tears.

"So, what are you going to do now, Magnolia? You've got quite a lot of free time now that there's no social obligations on the radar," Doyle said, as we all refilled our glasses and took our seats, passing around the dishes of food. "Imagine having to go to bridge club in a few weeks. Speaking of… What are you doing about your honeymoon?"

I laughed and glanced at Sutton, giving her a playful wink. "Sutton and I are going. It's the one thing Dane didn't manage to return or cash in."

"Y'all are going to Ireland? Together? Lord above, I am so jealous," Doyle said, and Jordan nodded next to him excitedly.

"We sure are. I canceled all the romantic bed and breakfasts, though, and most of the sight-seeing. We're going on a full-blown pub tour, renting a car and staying in Airbnbs along the way. I'm really looking forward to it. Plus, I have a ton of research to do while I'm there."

My brother cocked his head to the side and smiled proudly. "And what kind of research would that be? I have a feeling I know, but I wanna hear it straight from the phoenix's mouth."

"Well, big brother, I'll be stopping in and out of Ireland's quaintest pubs and visiting the town where our family emigrated from." I looked around at the eager faces of my friends, and I knew, deep down inside, that even if I came home and told them I was going to become a stripper, they'd still support me.

"When we get home, I'll start looking for a new place to build O'Malley's again. From the ground up." I smiled. "And it will be all mine."

CHAPTER FORTY-THREE

Lee

Ryan and I were sitting in the greenroom of Ybor City Brewing in Tampa, sipping on some local brews and getting ready to open up for Ira Wolf, who was opening for Marc Roberge of O.A.R. Not exactly the country gig we were used to, but we took what we could get to get me the hell out of Savannah.

I was staring at my phone when Ryan threw a rogue drumstick at me.

"Don't call her, man. It's her wedding day. Or it was. Just leave it alone."

I shook my head. "I wasn't going to call her. I'm not that stupid."

"Don't text her, either. Just leave her be. She's probably surrounded by her brother and everyone. Sutton's probably there…"

"You miss her, huh? I get it, man. She's a great girl," I said, burying down a laugh.

"I miss her, I miss Savannah, I miss the whole group. I miss the food. This is so fucked up. Did your asshole brother have to—"

I held up my hand to stop him in his tracks. "Believe me, brother, I understand. Truly, I do."

In a little over a month, we'd gone to four cities, and nothing felt the same. Janelle and I had parted ways as soon as our plane landed in Tennessee, amicably, of course, considering none of it was real in the first place. Letting everything, and everyone, walk away was like ripping off a Band-Aid and exposing the wound to the open air.

It felt good at the time, but now every moment brought a sharp sting.

"Hopefully, she doesn't meet someone in Ireland, man. You know the kilts and those accents. I would be so screwed…"

"Kilts? That's Scotland, you idiot. Who's going to Ireland?"

He went white as a sheet, like he had a secret that he'd been keeping and let it slip. "Um, no one is."

I crossed the room and towered over him, glaring down with my guitar in my hand ready to swing if he didn't open his mouth.

He leaned back on the green room couch, holding his hands up defensively. "Sutton and Magnolia. They're going on Magnolia's honeymoon together."

I paced the room, running my hands through my hair, thinking about the two of them, in a foreign country, with my crazy ass brother and his even crazier girlfriend on the loose who knew where.

Ryan stood and walked over to the mirror, fluffing out his hair. "It's not some *Girls Gone Wild* thing, man. They're going to research the O'Malley family's hometown and visit all the pubs so Magnolia can really connect with where her family came from. And when she gets back, she's planning to rebuild. Sutton called it Magnolia's phoenix moment. She's a genius."

After the gig, Ryan went to explore Ybor City, and I went back to the hotel to sulk. I sat on the outdoor patio overlooking the Hillsborough River, alive with soft, pulling waves and the lights of the famous Riverwalk.

Something about the long, winding pathway made me homesick for my own river and the familiar path that ran along its edge.

I sank down in a poolside chair and called Charlie.

"Yeah, man. I'm dropping them off at the airport tomorrow," Charlie said after listening to me whine about being worried over the girls traveling overseas to potentially have the greatest time of their life and why was I being so selfish? "They'll be fine. Let them go have fun. My sister needs this. The only time she leaves Savannah is to watch Sutton run her races. She'll call me every day, and I'll text you," he promised.

"Alright," I sighed.

"I know you love my sister, Lee. We all know you do. She knows you do, too. But you have to give her space now. Don't pull your John Cusack in *Say Anything* shit. The last thing she needs is you holding a boombox over your head outside of her window, if you know what I mean."

"So don't buy her another bar," I laughed.

"No, don't. I have a feeling when she comes back, she won't want the same things as she did before."

"Yeah, brother. I'm kind of worried about that, too," I confessed.

CHAPTER FORTY-FOUR

Magnolia

After two long, amazing weeks in Ireland, Sutton and I arrived back on Georgia soil exhausted and full of amazing ideas.

The last thing that Savannah needed was another bar. But, after a wild, drunken trip in and out of small pubs in tiny, Irish towns, we knew what it did need.

"So, pub actually stands for Public House? That sounds… weird. I guess I don't understand what you mean," my brother said, staring at me from across his studio with bloodshot eyes.

"What's your issue? I'm the one with jet lag," I laughed, opening the pizza I'd grabbed from Vinnie's on my way over.

"Tally's like, really, really pregnant. And a little bit needy." He smiled, looking down at his feet quietly.

My head snapped back, letting out a howl. "So, is this, like, a thing now?"

"It's something. I don't know if it's a *thing*, thing. Shut up." He glanced away for a second, running a hand through his hair before looking back at me, a wide grin still playing on his lips. "Tell me more about what you mean by this Public House scene. Or what did you call it? A 'third place?'"

I told Charlie that our best moments were spent in the tiny pubs that felt more like a common room, or a living room, than an actual bar. There wasn't any pretense or loud music, it was just a place for the community to gather and talk and share some pints.

"A third place is like that cozy, tucked-away spot you can't help but be drawn to, even when you've got a million things to do. It's not work, it's not home, but something in between—the kind of place that wraps you in its warmth the second you step inside," I said, pausing to take a sip of my drink and glance at him.

He was scrolling through the four-million photos I had taken on my phone, barely looking up as I continued, my voice gaining a slight edge of excitement.

"Picture the low hum of conversations, the familiar clink of glasses, the easy smiles exchanged with strangers who somehow feel like old friends. It's where life slows down just enough for you to catch your breath, to savor the small moments—like sharing a cup of coffee or a laugh across the table. There's no pressure here, just a sense of belonging, like you've found a little corner of the world that's just for you."

I wanted it to feel like the heartbeat of the neighborhood, the backdrop to quiet moments that turned into memories, where love stories bloomed and friendships deepened. Some place where you met someone's eyes from across the room and realized that maybe, just maybe, something magical was about to happen.

In the city where our family had emigrated from, Galway, there was a pub that had a warm fireplace, books for trading that lined a wall, and more importantly, friends gathering every night. We'd spent most of our time at Butler's Pub meeting distant relatives and taking a thousand pictures of the place, writing down what was most important to us.

I couldn't wait to bring something so comforting and unique to Savannah.

The most important revelation on the trip, however, was the clarity I'd found. I felt the grip of O'Malley's, of Dane, of the things I thought I wanted gradually slipping away.

And more importantly, I felt like my last night with Lee, though necessary and beautiful, was our last night for a reason.

It had been time to move on, even though part of me still missed what Lee and I had, even if it had been brief. The comfort of the familiar, the warmth of our shared memories—it had been hard to let that go. But deep down, I had known that clinging to the past would only hold me back. I wanted to shine on my own, to discover who I was without being tied to anyone else. The desire to step into my own light, to build a life that was entirely mine, had grown stronger with each passing day. It hadn't been about forgetting Lee or erasing the moments we had shared—I would always carry that with me. It had been about finding out who I could become, and I needed to do that on my own terms.

And of course, Sutton had sweet talked her way into snagging Butler

Pub's famous cottage pie recipe, so that was a major win.

"Well, you look great. Happier, almost," Charlie said, as if he could hear my thoughts.

"I am happy, Charlie. My whole world, our history, might have burned to the ground. But look at what we still have. Look at what we'll *always* have."

He nodded and passed me back my phone, finally sitting down next to me to pull a gooey, cheesy slice of pizza from the box.

"So, what's next for Magnolia Pruitt?"

"Moving on. Rebuilding. And finally—for the first time in my life—figuring out who I am on my own."

CHAPTER FORTY-FIVE

Magnolia

St. Patrick's Day in Savannah had come and gone, and the city was sweltering on the brink of another summer. It had been almost a year since Lee had come back, and life as we knew it was shook to the core, finally having unraveled at the seams.

Though a part of me felt sorry for the loss of income during one of Savannah's biggest party months, I'd remained hopeful for better days ahead.

In the dead of night, Sutton and I had just left a long evening at Eunice Wilder's house. Sutton had catered the affair with her new catering company, Savannah's Sweethearts, and I was her bartender on call.

"That was a weird party," Sutton mused, ripping off her chef's coat as we walked down Jones Street. "Who throws a party to celebrate April Fools Day?"

I laughed, peering in the darkened windows of some of Savannah's booming businesses, now sleeping after a hard day of tourist placating. I paused in front of an old building, looking it up and down. "I think she was trying to give us business, Sutton," I laughed, shoving my face against the window, pointing to the for sale sign.

"This is the third one you've stopped at this week, Mags. It was an antique shop. It won't have a kitchen."

I shrugged, and we carried on down the street to her condo, my temporary home, linked arm in arm.

"You'll find it," she said, breaking the silence. "And it will be perfect."

Since we'd been back, every time I stopped when I saw a for sale sign in a window, I'd done extensive research on the building. But nothing felt right. Nothing gave me the vibes I wanted for my new bar.

Or if it did, my new business partner would just find something else to nitpick. Mostly trivial things, like not being zoned for liquor, or like tonight, that it didn't have a kitchen.

More often than not, she'd tell me she felt spirits inside, insisting that we couldn't run a successful business if we were too busy being haunted.

"Think his tour is done? Lee, I mean," I asked quietly, as we turned the corner to our street.

"Who else would we be talking about? Stop obsessing," she chuckled.

We crawled the stairs to Sutton's condo on historic Oglethorpe Ave. The place had Sutton written all over it—bright throw pillows that didn't match but somehow worked, oversized candles that smelled like heaven, cookbooks all over the place, and walls crammed with artsy prints she'd collected over the years. My things were scattered here and there—my favorite mug on the counter, my boots kicked off by the door, Pickle, glaring ominously at us from her perch on top of the kitchen cabinets—but all they felt out of place, like I didn't quite belong.

I was grateful, of course. Sutton had opened her home to me without a second thought, and I didn't take that lightly. But after living alone for so long, I missed having a space that was mine, a place where I could be still and sort through the chaos in my head. As much as I loved Sutton, her constant energy could feel like too much when all I wanted was to sit in silence and figure out what came next.

"What about something like this? I could buy the whole building, and most of these places have retail or restaurant space below?"

"Where are you going to get that money? Sorry, where are *we* going to get that money?"

I shrugged. "It might take some time, but it will happen someday."

I woke up the next morning and ran out for coffee and pastries. Sutton was off working a dry baby shower, which meant I had the day off. I'd planned on looking for a great space somewhere, possibly close to Charlie, but the vibe didn't feel right.

Munching on a danish and slowly walking through Chatham Square, I heard my name bellowed from behind me.

"Now wait up for me, darlin'. You know an old woman can't walk that fast."

"Good morning, Eunice," I said, kissing her cheek. "How are we today?"

As much as the sight of her still gave me somewhat of a panic attack, like her eldest son was going to come out of a bush and light me on fire—or worse, ask me to take him back—as time went on and we spent more time together, I felt some of that fog lifting.

"Just fine, just fine. Wanna take a bench with me? I'd like to chat with you about something."

I nodded and presented her a bag with a fresh pastry to see if she wanted a nosh while we talked.

"I just left B. Matthews, otherwise I would. But thank you. You really are so kind, even though I know my boys destroyed you."

A few months ago, that might have struck me like a hatchet to the heart, but today, I just shrugged and took a seat next to her, listening as I sipped on my coffee.

"Before Dane scooted off to who knows where with that trollop, Vance and I were talking with his realtor friend Joseph. You know that good ole' Christian boy who frequently hangs out at the titty bars?"

I spit my coffee into Eunice Wilder's lap.

"Did you just say titty? On a Sunday?"

"Now, it's a new era. If I learned anything from our whole ordeal, it's that when you try and keep things shoved into a mold where it doesn't belong, it combusts. So shit, fuck, titty, and then some, darlin'."

I stared at her with my jaw hitting my knees for a solid thirty seconds. I couldn't believe what my ears were hearing, and frankly, they were burning. "So, what about Joseph, frequenter of the less finer establishments here in town?" I finally asked.

"Well, as I said before Dane and what's her face absconded, Vance and I were fixin' to buy you two a house, just down the street from us on Jones." She kept her eyes trained in her lap, which was now covered in my coffee, and wouldn't meet my eye.

She knew what my reaction was going to be.

"You're not giving me anything," I said it quickly and sternly, and I meant every word. I wasn't taking anything from the Wilder family ever again.

"It was once a bed and breakfast. It's zoned for a liquor license *and* has a commercial kitchen. We thought, someday, you and Dane would restore it and that it could be your project—you know, when Dane eventually got you to loosen your grip on O'Malley's."

I nodded. "I'm glad to finally hear someone admit it."

"I didn't really know. Not until after everything came to light, at any rate. Vance and I were going through some of Dane's files. He had an investor from Atlanta looking at the space to build high-rise condos and commercial space below."

"Oh, I know," I laughed. "I appreciate you, Eunice, but I can't let you give me this property."

Her head snapped up. "Oh, sweetheart, no. I wouldn't dare insult you like that. You'd lease—to own—and you'd be responsible for all of the renovations."

She stood to go, bending down to give me a kiss on the cheek, and I smiled up at her. I knew I didn't have to give her an answer right then and there, and it warmed me to know that she was self-aware enough not to just hand me something.

Because I wasn't taking anything from anyone anymore.

"I don't know how I'd come up with the money for the restoration, though."

Eunice turned back around and smiled. "You've been named President of the Wilder Family Trust as of this morning. What's now back in there—securely— is yours. Vance filed Cole's death certificate and his will, which now makes you the sole owner of whatever is left of O'Malley's. The land it stands on, the insurance pay out, everything is yours now, and everything that Dane fraudulently signed with Cole's name is now null and void. You also have the personal shares leftover from Vance, myself, and, of course, from Lee. That money's yours, Magnolia. Whether you're a true Wilder or not, you're still a part of this family."

She tucked her purse under her arm and scooted through the square, not looking back at me once.

***

I crashed Sutton's baby shower, and when she saw me burst into the kitchen of a family I'd never seen before a day in my life, she threw a cookie sheet down on the marble countertop and growled at me.

"That look on your face. I don't like it, Magnolia. It's got Wilder drama written all over it, and I don't have time right now!"

"Girl, do you need help? Why don't you let me take over whatever this is," I quipped, gesturing to the pile of burned shards lingering on the counter.

She threw her arms up in the air and yelped. "I feel like I've lost my mojo! Ever since Ryan left Savannah and I left LaMonte's, it's like I have no one to impress!"

"Wait, you were trying to impress Ryan? Never mind. Let's save that. Sutton, you're one of the most talented chefs in the entire city. When you left LaMonte's, restaurants scrambled to try and get you to come on staff. Pass me that gouda. Honestly, you only need to impress yourself at this point. The rest of us know what's up."

She shrugged and leaned back on the sink. "Those are cookies, Magnolia. You're putting gouda on gluten-free cookies."

We both let out a series of wild cackles followed by long belly laughs. When I composed myself, I walked over and wrapped her in a hug.

"What did you need to tell me? Seriously, if Lee is back…" She sighed into my embrace.

"He's not. It's nothing. Let's get this situated and go grab a drink when you're done."

"Thanks for stopping by," she said quietly, fixing up a charcuterie plate as I made my way to the door. "Sometimes I forget what it's like to have you all to myself. I'm really thankful for your help."

"I hope so, girlfriend, because I'm going to be needing yours real soon."

Lee

The last leg of our mini-tour naturally—and of course, ironically—took us to Savannah.

I didn't tell anyone I was coming home, but Ryan let Sutton know, who told Jordan, who said something to Doyle, who fessed up to his sister, Tally, who of course had to tell Charlie, since the two of them had started officially dating.

A doozy, as usual.

If Magnolia knew, or my momma for that matter, I'd not received any screeching phone calls nor was I greeted at the airport by the police—or worse, Sutton—telling me to fuck off.

Charlie called when I was in the air and left a voicemail asking me to stop by the shop when I got into town and promised the place would be clear of anyone wanting to beat me upside the head with a blunt object. Which was good, I supposed.

We dropped our luggage off at the hotel, which felt weird to me once again. This was my home, and I was back to feeling like an outsider. But I guess that was what happened when you were away for long enough—it no longer belonged to you in the way it once did.

Kind of like the people living there.

"What's up, my man?" Charlie wrapped me in a huge hug and the normally quiet, sullen artist was all smiles and pep when I walked through the door.

"Man, she's done a number on you, huh? I can't wait to meet her," I said, looking around for some sign of the new girlfriend.

"She's gone back to her hometown with Doyle for her baby shower. Honestly, everyone thinks Magnolia and I are nuts, but Tally and Doyle give us a run for our money where siblings are concerned." A smile played on his lips. "How long are you in town for?"

My heart skipped a beat at the sound of her name, but I shrugged it off and pointed to the fridge silently asking for a beer. Charlie nodded. "We're leaving the day after tomorrow. Marc has a solo gig tonight for a charity, no openers, and then the show's tomorrow. You should come."

He winced, then let out a long, dramatic sigh.

"Charlie, come on, man, what is it?"

"Opening night at Magnolia's new place. It's a soft open, so just friends and family. And before you ask, no, you're probably not invited. And no, I was not under any obligation to tell you about it."

Months before, Charlie and I had talked about me giving my stake in the family's Trust to Magnolia. And as we talked over FaceTime, he let me know that not only did my momma give up hers, but my father did, too.

Charlie told me about the old bed and breakfast that my parents had bought for Magnolia and my brother for a wedding gift and how Maggie was leasing-to-own the property from my parents.

She'd not only built a bar on the first level, but had the second floor bedrooms for rent to guests, and the third and fourth levels she'd turn into an apartment for herself eventually.

The property was massive—of course, my parents thought that Maggie and Dane would one day fill it with children, living happily ever after.

At least one part of that was true.

"She's really happy, Lee. I think she finally figured out that she didn't need anyone's approval or help to make her dreams come true." Talking about his sister always made Charlie's eyes light up, but this time, there was something else beneath the surface. "Can I show you something?"

He led me to the back storage room, a space crammed with canvases, buckets of paint, and what I assumed was discarded trash—but for all I knew, it could've been his latest masterpiece.

Charlie crossed the room and yanked a tarp off a large framed piece leaning against the wall. I had to crouch and steady myself with my hands on my knees.

There it was, slightly burned around the edges but no less perfect—Magnolia's portrait.

My throat tightened with tears as I stammered, "How?"

Charlie patted my back as I stepped closer to the canvas. Some of the photos had melted at the edges, along with a few pieces of handwritten lyrics, but the damage only added a rugged, hardened edge. Kind of like that night did to all of us.

"The fire started in the back but didn't reach the barroom until it tore through the green room and office first. After I checked upstairs and found Pickle in the back hallway, I kicked open the door and grabbed it off the wall." He turned to meet my gaze, but his eyes were far off, lost in the memory of that horrible night. "I don't know if it was pure adrenaline or shock, but somehow I managed to get the cat and the portrait out. I guess I thought… if Maggie was gone, at least I'd have this left of her. She doesn't know I still have it. She never noticed it leaning against a truck in all the chaos, and Eddie Donovan called me when he left the scene, told me they'd stashed it at the firehouse for me. I picked it up the next day."

The trauma of that night—almost losing his sister and their family's legacy—was written all over Charlie's face. I struggled to catch my breath, my voice hitching as I whispered, "She's beautiful."

"She sure is," he replied, his own tears choking his words.

"You're giving this to her tomorrow night, I suppose?" I asked, finally managing to get out a full sentence without breaking down.

"I am," he replied, his eyes dropping to his feet. "And as much as I wish you could be there, it's probably best if you keep your distance."

"I will. I'll hide out in my hotel until the show and then I'll head back to Nashville and figure out what the hell I'm going to do with my life now."

Charlie led me back to the front of the studio, stopping to pull out another round of much-needed beers for us. "How's the album coming?"

"Just about done writing the songs and then we head to the studio to start recording. We've decided to call it *Wild Fire*. Of course, I had a lot of material from my short stint back home last year."

He pulled back on his beer and studied me for a minute. "Remember when we were kids, and you used to say that my sister was the kind of girl you'd write songs about? Do you think that's still true?"

Without thinking, I blurted out my answer, even though we both already knew what I was going to say. "Yes, I do. I loved her when we were kids, and I love her even now—more than ever, really. Even when we don't talk, she's there, in every corner of my heart. She's the deepest part of me, woven into my soul in a way that'll never change. She's always been my everything, and no matter what happens, she always will be."

"You should tell her that, then. No surprises, no pretenses, no guitar. Just tell her."

I rolled my eyes. "I thought you just told me to leave her alone. And besides, I'm not invited to the big party, remember?"

Charlie checked his watch, and a shit-eating grin slipped across his face. "You've got about ten minutes, but she's probably at O'Malley's. Whatever is left was just bulldozed to the ground today. She goes there to talk to our momma sometimes, especially when she's nervous."

I didn't even say goodbye to Charlie. I just flew out the door and ran through the streets of Savannah as fast as my feet could take me.

I had to see my girl.

CHAPTER FORTY-SEVEN

Magnolia

I promised myself the last time I'd come here that it would be the last time. But there I was again, standing in front of the empty space where my bar, my home, used to be.

I was never good at staying away from things that were long gone. Never good at ending chapters or at saying goodbye. And I was never, ever good at letting go.

But this really was the last time. I'd given the land to the city with the promise that they'd use the space to build a home for orphans. I'd set up a separate trust, aside from the pre-established Wilder Trust, called the O'Malley Project, which would help orphaned children with resources they might need as they grew into adulthood. Prom dresses, suits for interviews, pep talks before the big game. I wanted there to be a space in Savannah for these kids to go that felt like home, even if they didn't have one. Paying forward the support system that I was always so grateful for.

And I'd elected Eunice Wilder as chair of the board. If anyone could raise funds for displaced children or come up with ideas on how to best support them, it was Momma Wilder herself.

I opened my camping chair and pulled out my thermos of champagne, leaning over the threshold to my old apartment stairs, pouring a bit on the dirt. They'd break ground in a few weeks, but I wanted one last drink in the place I'd loved my whole life. The place where Uncle Cole lived and loved Eunice. Where my momma grew up and made memories with her best friend in the very same place I did with my own best friend. Where my parents met. Where I fell in love. Where I lost everything.

In life, there are never any guarantees that what we wish for, what we dream for, will ever work out the way we expect. But there's beauty in the journey, in the hope of it all. It just took me a long time to figure that out for myself.

One day, it felt like we woke up and were supposed to be adults, but deep down, we were still kids playing pretend. I once read that the mind of an adult isn't much more mature than a teenager's—we just have different bodies and bigger responsibilities. Maybe that's why older folks can still be playful and why our twenties and thirties feel so confusing. Deep down, we're still those sixteen-year-old kids, stumbling through life, trying to make sense of it all.

Maybe that was why Eunice and Uncle Cole always had that strange banter, like they were sharing some inside joke the rest of us couldn't quite catch. Why my momma, no matter how grown she got, still played in the sand like a kid, scooping up shells and laughing wild and free while the waves lapped at her feet. Maybe it was why Dane and Kasey could never really let each other go or why Charlie still found himself sketching out comics, just like he used to.

And maybe it was why, after all this time, I never could let go of my first great love.

I leaned back in my chair and sipped slowly on the bubbly, giggling as the fizz tickled my nose.

"I love that sound more than anything in the world," I heard from behind me.

I didn't have to turn around to know who it was. It was the voice I'd know anywhere. The one that used to drift through my radio, the one I used to let sing me to sleep. And now, even after more than twenty years since the day we met, just hearing it still made my heart race like it had no idea time had passed.

"What? Did you hear that I was actually, for the first time in my life, doing something for myself so you decided to show up and ruin it?" I said coolly.

I could hear him snickering behind me. He strolled up to the empty space before us, hands in his pockets with his back to me, surveying the blank area before him.

"I'm so sorry," he whispered, still not turning to face me.

"It is what it is, Leland," I sighed. "It was just a building, I have the memories tucked away in my heart, and I'll pass them on, and my kids will pass them on, and their kids will, and on it goes."

I could feel myself tearing up, and my walls tearing down. Just being near him felt safe but vulnerable. Like I could finally say the things in my heart, because my heart was standing in front of me.

He turned around to face me, and there were tears in his eyes, too. "Loving you has always made me so sad. Like something I can't put my finger on, you know? It's bittersweet, I guess. Loving you my whole life has been the best—and the worst—thing I've ever done." He rocked a little bit on his heels and drew in a long breath when he was done speaking.

I studied him for a second and knew exactly what he meant.

He stopped right in front of me, kneeling down and resting his hands on my knees. Normally, I would've pulled away—after everything that had gone down, this kind of closeness wasn't something I wanted to let happen. But in that moment, neither of us moved. Maybe we needed it, both of us hanging on by a thread, standing at the edge of letting each other go.

"It's been bittersweet—the best and worst thing all wrapped up together—but it's been the *only* thing that's ever felt right. Since the day I met you, this scrappy, frizzy-haired, freckle-faced redhead yelling at me in the middle of the street, I've wanted nothing more than to love you for the rest of my life. And I promised I would. And I have. No one, not once, has ever come close to making me feel the way I do about you."

"Lee..."

"Please, let me talk."

I grinned, handing him my thermos. "First of all, I suppose I don't mind you being here if you're going to keep buttering me up, but what *are* you doing here?"

He took a long swig, still wrapped up in the intensity of telling me what was on his heart. "I have a gig tomorrow night. I wasn't going to stop by but..."

I raised an eyebrow. "My brother have something to do with this visit?"

He sat down on the sidewalk, pulling his legs up to his chest and wrapping his arms around his knees. "He has this knack for sensing when people want to go and be quiet. When they want to run and hide. And when all that running and hiding just won't work anymore, he knows to tell them they should race across the city and tell the person they love that they let them go once, and they don't ever want to let them go again."

I nodded, clearing my throat nervously. "And did you say what you intended to say?"

He shook his head. "I couldn't, even if I had a million years ahead of me, tell you what I really need to say."

"I get it," I shrugged. "And while it fills my heart so much, believe me… I just don't know if it can be part of the plan right now. I've spent so many months trying to make things work for me. To become someone that doesn't need anyone else to save her. I don't need Prince Charming."

He smiled, dipping his head a bit, and his pool-blue eyes glistened with tears and laughter. "Girl, when I tell you this, I mean every word of it. No one, not one person you've come across in your life, ever thought that you needed to be saved. I think we always knew that, in the end, the princess would save herself."

"I'm *not* a princess," I said firmly.

"God damn it, Magnolia. Can't you just read between the lines? You're right. You're not a princess. You're a badass bitch that has pushed every shitty thing that's come down the road right out of her way, and you've become the best version of yourself while doing so. And you'll never stop becoming the person you were always supposed to be. But you still are, and always will be, the kind of girl someone writes songs about. There's no doubt about that at all. Whether you like it or not."

Since they'd been on the road, Ryan and Lee had shared the first single from their new album, titled "I Will Wait." The track told the story of two people who had been in love their whole lives but never could quite get it together. Right person, wrong time. It was a promise from the singer that, no matter how long it took, he would be waiting whenever the girl he loved was ready to love him back.

What was different about this album, though, was Lee and Ryan performed it themselves instead of selling it off track by track. It was the first record that they'd performed under their new band name, Wilder Days.

It was a beautiful song, and Sutton and I had heard it for the first time when we were prepping for an event a few months ago. When I heard his songs come over the radio, I wanted to fall to my knees and pick up my phone, but at the end of the day, it had to be something that came naturally. I had to be ready. I had to be willing.

And today, I wasn't.

Recognition washed across his face, and he knew I wasn't ready to surrender to him.

"I appreciate you coming here today. I appreciate everything you've done for me," I said sadly.

"I know you do. I'll be waiting here, Maggie. I'll wait for you forever. As long as it takes."

"You'll be the first to know." I smiled.

***

"This is like a Lifetime movie that just doesn't quit," Sutton said, dancing around as she washed dishes in our new, massive kitchen. She would use this as a base for Savannah's Sweethearts, while also cooking a delicate, but delicious menu for Maggie O'Malley's.

We had just finished our soft launch, and we knocked it out of the park. I had two investors who had flown in from Charlotte almost falling off their barstools, salivating at the business opportunity, the drinks, and, of course, Sutton's cooking. They'd promised to send over the paperwork in the morning, and I was biting my lip raw, anxious over what was about to unfold for Sutton and me.

But the subject of Lee's pop-in at the graveyard of our past was the biggest drama, and excitement, of the night—or so I thought.

Charlie walked into the old antique kitchen, carrying the remainder of dirty glasses and plates. "Okay, sorry, can you repeat the entire conversation again? What did he say? Also, we had a couple check into room A on the second floor. So, if Lee shows up tonight, maybe keep it quiet?"

Sutton and I rolled our eyes in unison.

"The entire building is sound-proof. Not because of me, but do you think I want to hear *them*," I scoffed.

"True. So, Lee has his gig tonight, and we're just not going? Sounds rude, but okay," my brother said.

Sutton whipped her head around. "Honestly, Charles Abner, you have your *own* drama with Tally. If your sister doesn't want to talk, you can't force her arm. If we're not going to this show, which we've received front row *and* backstage passes to, we're just not going to go. We shall respect that."

"I just really like O.A.R.," my brother mumbled, plunking the dishes in the sink.

"Right. Because that's what's important right now, Charlie," Sutton said, chucking her washing gloves and sponge at him. She turned toward me. "So, he really said he would wait for you?"

I nodded, pushing stoppers into bottles of wine. "He sure did. He said as long as it takes. I can only assume he and Janelle are history?"

Charlie nodded and helped me move the leftover bottles into the industrial fridge. With my insurance money from the bar fire, we'd gutted the place and turned it into exactly what we wanted. A true public house and inn. With all the extra, modern trimmings.

"You can't lead him on forever," he said, and Sutton and I nearly snapped our necks as we turned to glare at him.

"In all the time you've known me, I've never been the type to lead someone on," I growled, snatching the bottle of wine from his hands and shoving it, maybe a little too neatly, into the perfectly organized fridge. "Except, you know, that one time I almost married someone to save my bar."

"So, is it lyrics or the truth? And how do we find out? Stay tuned to the next episode of Savannah Sweethearts! Truly, someone call Hallmark," Sutton laughed, putting the rest of the dishes into the vintage cabinets.

"Well, it's my decision, right? And besides, I don't know how a relationship, especially with Lee, would even pan out. After everything that happened, what could we possibly have to say to each other?"

Sutton laughed as she shoved a set of pans into the storage under the sink. She turned to me, crossing her arms and leaning on the sink. "Probably, as I've said before, a lot of things that were left unsaid."

"Alright, enough drama, and if we're not going to the concert, I have something to announce," Charlie said, and Sutton and I turned slowly his way.

"Charlie, if this is another one of your stupid hijinks with Tally and her damn seances, count me out," Sutton said, throwing her hands up.

My brother stifled a chuckle and turned toward me, grabbing me by the shoulders and scooting me around the bar. "That was one time, Sutton! We both just really like spooky stuff."

Charlie kept guiding me until we reached the front of the inn where guests would check in for their stay. The foyer was straight out of another time, oozing with history and charm. The ceiling stretched high, with crown molding that whispered of old-school craftsmanship. In the center, a massive chandelier sparkled with crystals, throwing a warm, golden light across the shiny hardwood floors. Dark wood paneling lined the walls, broken up by tall, arched windows draped in heavy velvet curtains that looked like they'd seen a century of guests come and go.

To the left of the entrance, a grand staircase wound its way up, the banister carved with care, practically begging you to see what was upstairs. Antique furniture, like a plush settee Eunice had found at an estate sale and a big mahogany hall table, added to the cozy yet grand feel of the place. The air smelled faintly of polished wood and a hint of lavender, making you feel right at home in this elegant, yet welcoming space where every corner held a piece of the past.

Charlie turned my body toward the check-in desk, and a piece of my past was staring straight down at me. The piece Charlie had created and Lee had commissioned seemed to gaze directly at me, a playful smile on her lips. She looked a bit rough around the edges—didn't we all in those days?—but it was still so stunning it nearly brought me to my knees.

"How?" I murmured, and Charlie explained how he not only tried to save me the night of the fire, but also managed to rescue the portrait and Pickle in one heroic sweep. I couldn't hold back the sob that shook through me as I clung to my brother with Sutton beside us, also fighting back tears. The three of us stood there, tears glistening in our eyes, as we looked up at the artwork. In that moment, the past and future of O'Malley's finally came together as one.

CHAPTER FORTY-EIGHT

Lee

Ryan and I finished our opening act and sat on the outside patio of Moon River Brewing, sipping some beers and debating the rest of the tour. This was our last stop, and we had to decide whether or not to sign up for the second leg or drop off and have another opening act take our place.

"I love it here," Ryan said, taking a swig of his beer. "The food's good, the people are nice, all this shit is haunted. Did you know *this* bar is haunted? Like for real. One of the *most* haunted. Plus, Sutton texted me today when she knew I was back and wanted me to stop by."

I snickered into my drink, trying to cover my mouth. "Right. I'm sure you miss her."

"I do, man. Sutton is a great woman. She's smart, successful, and she's funny as shit. And what am I? An asshole backup singer-slash-songwriter that is the first of three acts in a small show. We're not going anywhere, bro. Years ago, maybe, but now? We're fluff. We're the band people pee to while they're waiting on something better."

He wasn't wrong. While I'd worked so hard to keep myself relevant in Nashville, the last year ruined everything for me, and by proxy, Ryan. I was lucky that he even stuck around with his talent. And now we were starting over. A new band and a new career path, but no place to call home.

But at the end of the day, there were some things left to tie us together. A city, and we were sitting in it. Guitars, and we knew how to use them. And women, who we loved.

"We gave up our apartments, so where the hell would we stay?"

Ryan chewed on his barbecue chicken nachos thoughtfully. "Hopefully, if it all pans out, with our girls. But for now, well, we'll figure it out."

CHAPTER FORTY-NINE

Magnolia

Sutton and I were sitting in the kitchen of Maggie's eating the leftover Eggs Benedict she'd made for the bed and breakfast guests. They'd all gone on their way to explore a beautiful day in Savannah, and our stomachs were growling.

But our pockets, and more importantly, our hearts were full.

"The bar opens in an hour, and I still can't find Pickle," I said, eyes darting around the kitchen suspiciously. The way the house was laid out, she had free rein if I wasn't careful about closing her in somewhere. And she knew it, taking full advantage of torturing patrons and guests of the inn.

Sutton looked around warily. "When I brought breakfast to room B this morning, I heard hissing and yelling, so, maybe check there? She's the devil."

It had been a few weeks since Lee had resurfaced. Charlie was busy holed up in the penthouse with Jordan and Doyle after Tally had her baby, which left him pretty tied up. Meanwhile, Ryan and Lee seemed to be making a habit of stopping by Maggie O'Malley's for drinks, hanging out with me and Sutton whenever they got the chance.

I still hadn't made up my mind about Lee. For once, I wanted things to be on my own terms. I was finally in a good place, and I wasn't sure if tossing a relationship into the mix was the smartest move. But then again, every time I caught a glimpse of him—those curls peeking out from under his hat, the way he'd smile at me from across the bar—it made it hard to think straight.

Right on cue, Sutton had done what she'd done almost every day for the past few weeks. "I'm going to start dinner early so I can go hang out with Ryan. You'll just need to heat it up, so, yeah… Is that okay with you?"

I grabbed her hand and squeezed it across the high-top. "Of course it is. Where y'all heading tonight?"

She clapped excitedly and jumped up to start her prep work. "Alley Cat Lounge! I haven't been. Have you? It's super swanky. I think, ugh, I don't know, we might become official soon."

"I'm really happy for you, Sutton." I cleared our dishes and lined them up in the dishwasher. "Seriously, you deserve this more than anyone."

She turned to me with sad eyes and put a flour-covered hand on my shoulder. "You know, Mags, you deserve happiness, too."

Later that afternoon, I stopped by Eunice's to drop off some cottage pie for her and Vance. She'd called in the order just as I was checking on some guests, and when I told her I had a packed house, she didn't care. She insisted.

I opened the door to the Wilder house, now just a few blocks from my own, and was immediately hit with the familiar scents of my childhood. The rich, earthy aroma of aged wood, the fresh roses that always seemed to be replaced like clockwork, and the faint trace of cigar smoke curling its way out from Vance's office. It was like stepping back in time, every detail pulling me into the past.

It was like a hug that wrapped around my shoulders and in an instant made me feel comfortable. But just as quick, I felt the hairs on my arms raise. As much as I adored this house, I hated it, too.

I'd loved two men that grew up in this house once, and it hurt me to no end just being in the same rooms they'd once walked through.

And it hurt to remember the feelings I'd had for both of them.

"In here, darlin'. I'm just powdering my face," Eunice called from the small washroom on the first floor. I kicked the swinging door to the kitchen open with my foot and dropped my packages on the counter.

On instinct, I opened up the wine fridge, pulled out a pinot noir from Jordan's shop, and poured two glasses.

"Oh good, sugar, thanks for getting us set up," Eunice said, as I finished plating the two cottage pies for her and Vance. "These are for you and me, though. Sit down, doll. I need to talk to you. And what better way than over some home-cooked Irish food and delicious wine?"

"Eunice, I can't…"

"Nonsense. You can. I phoned ahead to Sutton, and she called in your reinforcements. Have a seat."

I sat down at the breakfast nook and turned to look over the courtyard, a sprawling space I'd spent my childhood running around with Lee and Dane, getting covered in dirt, dust, and laughter. I let out a sigh, pushing back those memories.

Eunice sat across from me and dug into her lunch, munching away on her cottage pie and carefully taking sips of her perfectly paired wine. I didn't touch my food. I knew what was coming.

"So, my private investigator found Dane," she finally said, taking the bottle out of the chiller and refilling both of our glasses. "It turns out that because Cole's death certificate wasn't filed on time, he's actually been living in the Keys under Cole's name. When Vance finally filed the paperwork, it triggered alarms throughout the country. *And,* ironically enough, Dane had bought a bar on Islamorada—that's where they found him."

I couldn't help but laugh. I laughed so hard I sounded borderline hysterical. The thought of Dane rolling up the tailored sleeves of his white, custom-made button-down shirts and actually working made me cackle like a hyena. And however impolite it was to laugh so loud, and so crass, at the table I shared with his momma, I didn't care.

"And I assume Kasey is with him?"

"Mrs. Magnolia Wilder is with him as well, yes. Did this not come up on your background check when you took out lines of credit for the inn?"

"It didn't. But I can't say I'm surprised." I shook my head in disbelief. "Well, Eunice, you must be relieved. I mean, that Dane has been found."

"Relieved? Sure. Letting him rot in a jail cell in the Keys? Absolutely. I haven't told Vance yet. I'll wait a few days."

I feigned shock and threw a hand over my chest. "Well, bless your heart, Eunice Wilder. I never thought you had it in you."

"I've had this and much, much more Magnolia. Ever since your momma's house, your bar, burned down, I've been a different woman. I no longer live for the Wilder name. I'm living for myself. Which, I've noticed, is what you're doing, too, even with my youngest back in town?"

I placed my hands on the table around what was supposed to be Vance's lunch. "We are not talking about this, Eunice."

"Do you love my son, Magnolia? Do you love Leland?"

I sighed and looked back out over the courtyard. "Yes, Eunice. I do. I've loved Lee my entire life. He was my first best friend. He went out on a limb for me, invested in the bar, and believed in me when I couldn't believe in myself." I chewed on my lip, replaying those memories like a highlight reel in my mind. "You know, a few weeks ago, he actually showed up at the ashen, burned down graveyard of where I once lived, and he did this great, stupid Lee speech about how he would love me and wait for me no matter what. But I just don't know. I just… I just don't know."

She chewed a bit and joined me in looking out over the courtyard, watching a small bird bounce in between her azalea bushes. "You know, I understand what you're saying. I loved Cole for a long time, too. But you know who else I've loved for a long time?" Eunice turned and looked at me, placing a hand over mine. "You. I've loved *you* a long time, and I just want what's best for you. Despite what you might think, or how strong your pride is, what may be best for you is Lee."

I shook my head and pulled back my hand, using my fork to push around food on my plate. "I don't know, Eunice. I really don't know if I'm ready for that again. I have everything I've ever wanted."

"Listen," she said, leaning in closer, calm but assertive. "You and Lee have something special—a love that doesn't come around often. Don't make the same mistake I did." She paused, searching my eyes. I willed my face to stay even and flat.

"When Cole and I were younger, boy, did we have one hell of a love story. We fought, and there was drama of course, but we had some real good times. He could make me laugh like no one else. I always felt like I could be my real, true self around him, and he wouldn't judge or care—he would just love me more." She sighed, her face falling as she succumbed to the memories. "But I walked away from it. I told myself it was for the right reasons—security, stability, a comfortable life. And I got all of those things. On paper, I have everything I ever wanted, too. But deep down, there's always been this ache, this feeling that I missed out on something irreplaceable. Because the truth is, love like that doesn't just make you happy—it makes you feel alive."

Her words hung heavy between us, and I felt the weight of her regrets. Would they become my regrets, too?

"I care about you so much," she said, her voice softening. "I love you like a daughter, Magnolia, and I don't want you to look back years from now and feel the same emptiness I do sometimes."

I looked down at my hands, twisting a napkin around my finger. The silence between us seemed to stretch on forever, thick with things unsaid, until she finally spoke again.

"You will have it all, and you are well on your way. Your business is blooming, and *you* did that—all on your own. But that can't be the only thing you have in this life. The life I chose gave me everything I thought I wanted, too, but it also took something away—something I can never get back. You have a chance to do things differently, to grab on to that love with both hands and never let go. Don't let fear or practicality talk you out of it. This kind of love… it's worth everything."

It was my turn to reach over and grab her hand. I rubbed my thumb across her knuckles and smiled sadly at her. "I'm so sorry, Eunice. I didn't know… any of that. About you, or Cole, or the emptiness you feel. I don't know what to say."

"You can say, darlin', that you'll give it a chance."

CHAPTER FIFTY

Lee

I was almost finished settling into Charlie's studio apartment after help-ing him move into the townhouse he was sharing with Tally and her baby girl, Libby. Sutton was on speakerphone as I unpacked and somehow had roped me in to planning some weird, southern tradition called a baby passing, where, like the phrase, you passed around the baby to new people in his or her life shortly after they joined the world.

"I mean, we really don't *know* Tally, so a baby shower would be weird. Plus, it's not Charlie's. But now it is? I don't know. Can you find some soft, sooth-ing songs to sing?"

"Sure can, doll. Ryan probably can, too," I laughed.

"I might be dating him, but he's not Leland Wilder. See you Sunday. Thanks, babe!"

I hung up and almost immediately there was a knock at the door. I shoved a box out of the way, clicked open the lock, and flung the door open, which let out a huge, ancient creak. Definitely needed some WD-40.

Magnolia stood in the hallway with her hair, now longer and curlier, stuck to her face and neck with sweat from the humid, Savannah day.

"Hey, is everything okay?" I reached out to grab her, but she pushed past me and dropped her purse on my counter top, looking around what was once her brother's place.

"So, you're staying? And you're renting Charlie's place?"

"Subleasing for now, yes. Is everything okay?" I asked again, as I watched her fling open the fridge, finding a couple of beers and yanking them out. She popped off the top and handed one to me, cheersing as we clinked the bottles together.

"They found Dane. In the Keys. He's been using my uncle's identity and got nabbed now that the death certificate and will have been filed. Apparently the 'life insurance' money was just a cash payout from Dane that he pushed through some shady associate of your dad's. Almost as if, I don't know, he and Kasey had been planning this all along. Anyway, I thought you should know."

I watched her drink the entirety of her beer in one long gulp, then turn to scour the cabinets for something stronger.

"Check the box by the window," I said. "There's bourbon in there."

"Thanks." She found the box, opened up the bottle, and took a long, hard pull before passing it to me. "You'll need it."

"Maggie, are you—"

"Shut up, Lee. Listen to me." She stretched out an arm so I wouldn't move closer toward her. "I love you. And you're staying in Savannah, right?"

I swallowed, trying to hide just how elated I was to finally hear her say those words again. "You love me?"

"Hush it, you idiot. Yes, I love you. You know it, I know it, your momma knows it, your brother knew it. Anyway, are you sure you're staying here? For good?"

"I've thought about it, but..."

"Are you staying here, Lee? In Savannah, Georgia? Or will you leave again? Or want to leave again, I should say? Answer the question."

I put both bottles down on the counter and crossed the small kitchen toward her, putting my hands on her shoulders. "No, Maggie, I'm not leaving. This is my home, and I intend on staying. Is that okay with you?"

She sighed and pushed me off her before crossing the room and flinging open the door. "It's fine by me. You and I have a date tonight, by the way, 7:30. And don't be late. Pick me up at my place. No Pickle petting beforehand, either! See you then."

I nodded and watched her fly out the door, slamming it behind her, my heart pounding in my chest. She was gone in a flash, her words still hanging in the air, but I couldn't help the grin spreading across my face.

She actually wanted me to stay. After all this time, after everything, she finally wanted me here. For the first time since I'd come back, I felt like I had a real reason to stay—and that reason was happy about it.

CHAPTER FIFTY-ONE

Magnolia

Sutton and I had just finished training our newest employee, Doyle's sister, Tally. We'd agreed to let her work here and there, when she was needed, so she could find her footing here in Savannah.

"I can't believe you trust Charlie with your baby," Sutton mused, wiping off the tops of wine bottles before re-topping them and passing them to Tally to line up in the fridge.

"He's a great daddy, are y'all kidding me? He's a good man. Works hard. Seems it runs in the family," she said, her eyes smiling as she shot me a look across the room.

Tally hadn't been around long enough to realize my mood swings and frantic pacing around the inn's kitchen weren't because of her or my brother watching the baby. I had thirty minutes until Lee showed up for our date, and I was only half ready.

I'd just gotten off the phone with Eunice, who let me know that Dane was back on Georgia soil, and between wanting to march straight to the police station to ring his neck and my nerves over this date, I was an absolute, adrenaline-charged train wreck.

"Where are y'all going tonight anyway? And is that how you're wearing your hair?" Sutton was leaning over the kitchen island, eyeing me up and down, and Tally turned to stare right alongside her.

"An old, familiar haunt of ours." I ran my hands through my hair. "Will y'all quit looking at me like that? Jesus. Ever since I stopped those keratin treatments my hair just does whatever it wants to do I guess." I sighed, and Sutton poured three glasses of wine from the bottle she'd been closing up, and we all took seats on the barstools lining the island.

"You know I used to be a hairdresser, right? I could help you, if you wanted me to," Tally mentioned, her attention on my frizzy, washed-up seaweed head.

"I feel like that's the fifteenth job you've listed off," Sutton laughed. She hopped up and pulled some leftover charcuterie out of the fridge, setting it in the middle of the table. "Eat, Magnolia. We know your track record on a boozy, empty stomach. Never good."

"I could create some beach waves if one of y'all had some hairspray and a flat iron. It would take probably five minutes." Tally jumped up and ran her hands through my fuzzy, sticky red hair. I sighed, throwing my head in my hands.

"Do you remember when Little Orphan Annie had her makeover after getting to Daddy Warbucks's mansion? Slap a little bow on the side of your head, and that's exactly how you look," Sutton said, cackling so hard she almost choked on an olive.

"Shut up," I hissed, tears in the corners of my eyes from laughing.

"Are you going to call Lee 'Daddy' tonight?" Sutton was on a roll, and if I wasn't howling and bent over cracking up with her, I would have slapped her.

"Please, Tally, help my hair. And bring that hot tool down here so I can beat my best friend with it when you're done."

Once Tally finished fussing over my frizzy mess, Sutton ran up to my portion of the house and grabbed a top and a tight pair of jeans. We all crowded in the small, downstairs powder room to see the final result of the night's efforts.

"Lee might be calling *you* 'Daddy' tonight, you look that good," Sutton snorted, as I pulled down my shirt, surveying myself in the long, antique mirror Eunice had pulled from an estate sale for me.

"Would you shut up with the daddy stuff, please? My behind does kind of look good, though," I noted, spinning around and almost knocking the drinks out of Tally and Sutton's hands.

"If I wasn't an absolute basket case myself, I'd think y'all were as nutty as a squirrel turd," Tally giggled, shrugging as she exited the bathroom.

"Did she just call us crazy?" Sutton and I both asked in unison, falling over each other laughing.

"Seriously, she ain't wrong," Sutton said, holding my hand in hers. "You're going to be fine tonight. I know you're nervous about another new beginning, but this one isn't quite so new. It's just a new chapter of an old, familiar story."

I shrugged and let out a long, cleansing breath. "I don't want another chapter in our old story. I want something different this time. That old book was so painful and exhausting. Maybe we won't have a book. Maybe we'll have a song. You know, our song? I'd always asked him to write something just for us, back when we were dating, so it fits."

Sutton nodded, and Tally yelled from the front foyer that Lee had arrived. As we made our way to the front, I laughed quietly to myself that still, after all these years, the sight of Lee standing in my sitting room, hands in his pockets, looking around aimlessly and in awe of the inn, made my stomach flip-flop like a teenager again.

When he turned to look at me, his eyes drank in every detail, and he bit his lip, his gaze washing over me like a tidal wave. Across the room, Sutton fanned herself dramatically, while Tally rolled her eyes and pulled her toward the Public House area of the inn.

"You look beautiful, Maggie. You really do. And this place, wow," he said, gesturing to me and the lobby surrounding us.

"Wait until you see the rest of it." I couldn't help but smile, a big ear-to-ear grin that I meant with every fiber of my being. I could hardly believe he was here and that this was real.

"I can tell you, without a doubt, I am truly looking forward to that," he said, his cheeks flushing red and his eyes filling with desire.

"Let's get on out of here before we're undressing in my lobby and scaring all my guests," I said, grabbing my purse from behind the check-in counter. "We have some very special reservations tonight."

We walked down the wide, sprawling steps, and I turned to marvel at my new home. Through a dimly lit window, I could see the pub in full swing, people talking, clinking glasses together, and moving about inside.

In a corner, under an antique standing lamp, a woman sat typing on her laptop, looking up to observe her fellow patrons in the bar.

"Who's that?" Lee slipped his hand in mine, and we both stood watching her for a moment from the bottom staircase.

"Her name's Claire. She got in last week from St. Augustine, Florida. I guess she's from the area. She's working on a romance novel."

"Maybe we'll give her something to write about tonight," he said, pulling me toward him and planting a kiss on my cheek. "Where are we going anyway?"

"Back to where it all began. But this time, we're going to write a different story. Or song, or something. It all sounded really good when I was shoved in the bathroom with the girls."

He chuckled. "Wherever it is, Maggie, I'll just be happy to spend the night with my girl by my side after all this time."

We kept our hands intertwined as we walked the sleepy streets of Savannah. We stopped in front of the Mercer house where, from the window, the caretaker of the estate, Sarah, waved at me.

"All the years I've walked by this house, and I've never seen someone inside this place. It's still a museum, right?"

Sarah opened the front door, and it let out a howl, as if it hadn't been opened since one of Jim's Christmas parties decades ago. "Come on in, y'all. We're all set up for you."

"In? We're going inside? Legally? Shit," Lee said nervously, lifting his arm up and fighting the urge to run his fingers through his curls, opting to not disturb them in the humidity.

We walked through the small courtyard in front of the Mercer house, and I leaned in to give Sarah a hug. She extended her hand to Lee, and he looked around her to catch a glimpse inside the house.

Sarah let out a small laugh. "It's nice to finally meet you, Leland. Your momma is a great friend of mine. As is Ms. Pruitt, here. You'll get to look around, but this is a museum, after all, so be mindful of that. Not like the last time y'all were here."

Her eyes were playful as she shot me a wink and extended her arm for us to walk into the black-and-white tiled foyer. A look of recognition poured over Lee's face, and he smiled. I could tell he was remembering the night we'd broken into the sprawling home and how it set us on a course to where we were today.

"Poetic, Magnolia. Meeting at the start," he whispered, as we followed Sarah through the hallway, looking into the rooms we once ran blindly through during the night so long ago when we were just kids.

My heart pulsed with memories, and it almost felt like yesterday when we stood in this same, long hallway, our hearts beating erratically, but for different reasons. Back when things were simple. But I think, deep down, we knew then what we knew now.

That we were made for each other and nothing could stop that.

I squeezed his hand a few times, and he pumped mine back, and we locked eyes for a second, only breaking our gaze when Sarah opened the back door to the courtyard.

"I assume you two are very familiar with this old door here," she laughed, and we both nodded in apprehensive agreement. "The courtyard's all yours. Oh! I have something for you two. I'll be out in a minute. Go get settled in."

The courtyard was aglow with a canopy of twinkling lights, casting a soft, magical shimmer over everything. What was once a multilevel space with a pool now sprawled out as a single, flat expanse, enveloped in lush, cascading greenery. The old pool area had been transformed into a serene oasis with vines draping gracefully from the trellises and potted plants adding vibrant splashes of color.

In the center of the courtyard, a small, intimate table had been set up, adorned with flickering candles that danced in the gentle breeze. The table, draped in a delicate white linen cloth, was flanked by two plush chairs. Soft, ambient music floated through the air, blending with the subtle scents of blooming flowers and fresh greenery, creating an atmosphere of cozy elegance and romance.

"How the hell did you pull this off? This is incredible, Magnolia," Lee said, hopping down the staircase excitedly.

"You think I pulled this off? You better send your momma a thank you bouquet tomorrow," I laughed, watching his eyes twinkle under the lights and the stars.

He pulled out a chair for me, and I sat down. The carriage house door opened, and Doyle appeared with a bottle of champagne, donning a full-blown tuxedo and a shit-eating grin.

"Lovebirds," he cooed, shooting me a wink. Sarah sneaked up from behind us and gently placed two crystal glasses on the table in front of us.

"The estate's prized Baccarat's. Magnolia, please don't hurl one at his head, or worse, trip and knock over the table. I've seen you in action. I know these things are possible," Sarah said, and we all erupted in laughter.

"Dinner's on its way out," Doyle chirped, a formal tone lacing his voice. "Savannah's best chef is sadly tied up with her new beau, but we've brought in some excellent dishes from a few different local places. I think you'll be pleased."

Lee let out a cackle at Doyle's over-exaggerated performance, and I joined him. It felt good to laugh, to let the bubbles of the champagne hit me in the nose, to let go of everything that had been winding me so tight.

Ever since I'd talked to Eunice and learned that Dane and Kasey were behind bars, that the rest of the money was being moved around to its rightful place—mostly my bank account—I felt a freedom like I'd not felt in a long time.

Or ever in my life, if I was being honest with myself.

Everything I had was mine, and mine alone. The Inn & Public House was received with rave reviews. People loved the atmosphere, Sutton's food, the accommodations, and the service. Sutton and I had worked so hard, and we both reminded each other, regularly, of just how lucky and strong we were.

And now, I was sitting across from a man that I'd loved my entire life, who loved me back, and we were starting on a journey unlike one we've ever been on before. A real journey, just the two of us, and the friends and family that were genuine, loving, and truly happy for us.

We enjoyed our small plates from several local, Savannah-based chefs, and bottles on bottles of wine from Jordan and Doyle's shop. When we finished dessert, Doyle turned up the stereo from the second floor of the carriage house, letting the music pump softly throughout the courtyard.

"Dance with me," I said huskily, a deep sense of happiness and relaxation washing over me. I pushed my chair away from the table and reached my hand out to take his.

"For the rest of my life, if you'll let me," Lee said, his eyes sparkling with a soft, dreamy look, showing just how happy and content he was.

We moved for a few beats, the grass tickling my ankles, and I leaned back to look at his face. For the first time in the almost-twenty years Lee had been in my life, I never felt more comfortable or confident than I did in that moment.

"I'll let you," I said, moving my face slowly toward his.

"What? What do you mean? Wait, are you saying…"

"I'll let you dance with me for the rest of my life, you idiot."

Lee let out a laugh, letting his head fall back, but keeping our arms locked together. "Are you serious, Magnolia? You mean it? This is it?"

I smiled and nodded my head. "I mean it, Lee. It's always been you. It will always be you. All you have to do is ask."

He dipped his head toward mine, his voice low and gruff in my ear, sending chills down my spine. "Magnolia Louise Pruitt, will you be my girl?"

"I've never had a choice, Lee. I've been your girl from the start."

EPILOGUE

Magnolia

"The trees are up, the tables are ready, the staff is working so you don't have to, *and* I left the mimosa-making to you because—in the interest of full disclosure—I'm really nervous I'll make them too strong because frankly I am scared Momma is going to kill us today."

I rolled my eyes, flicking on my mascara and fluffing out my now shoulder-length, natural curls. "How do I look?"

Lee crossed the room and wrapped his arms around my waist, dipping his forehead down to meet mine. "Like a goddess, as usual. How could you ever doubt yourself? You're still the most beautiful girl in the world, Maggie. You always will be."

I put my hands on his chest and pushed him away playfully. "Get changed, please. Everyone will be here shortly. And you're not mucking up our first Christmas brunch at the inn by wearing sweats and drooling over me."

"Fair enough," he laughed, kissing my cheek quickly. After all these years, and everything we'd been through, every sweet touch still set fire to my blood and made my soul sing out. All the heartbreak, the tears, and the ongoing legal drama with his brother had done nothing but solidify us closer together. Today would be the day the last piece snapped neatly into our wild-ass puzzle.

I sat on the edge of the bed and reached quietly underneath, pulling out a box. After knowing each other most of our lives, it was hard to surprise Lee, but I think I knocked it out of the park with this one.

I placed a hand over the small, wrapped gift, marveling at the glistening ring on my left hand. Lee had proposed to me a few weeks after our "last first date" at the Mercer house, and I still looked down in shock every now and again at how gorgeous, and modest, the ring was.

Apparently, he'd worked with a jeweler at Levy's to create the low sitting, quadruple diamond band, coming in at over two karats. He said every diamond was a phase in our lives. The beginning when we were kids, the middle when we fell in love, a stone for the time we were apart but our hearts still called to each other, and the last stone for our future and what was to come.

And something major was coming today.

When we were ready, we made our way down the long, wide staircase from our two-floor home above the Inn and Pub, holding hands and giggling as we made our way to our friends.

Everyone we loved gathered around the table. Eunice and Vance, Charlie and Tally, Sutton and Ryan, Jordan and Doyle, and the last two seats were left for us.

When we walked into the sprawling dining room, everyone stood, and we passed out kisses and hugs to our guests. When I reached Doyle, he leaned in and whispered in my ear. "Will you let me know? I don't want to be caught off guard," he said, and I nodded quickly.

"The trees look beautiful," I said to Lee, as we took our seats at the head of the table.

"All real, by the way. Only the best for my girl." He put my hand in his and brought it to his mouth, kissing the top and rubbing his thumb across my ring, smiling widely, knowing.

Sutton and I had worked tirelessly putting together the menu for our Christmas Eve brunch. Charlie shoveled some French-toast bake onto his plate and passed the dish to me. "Do you still want me to come by tonight? We have a sitter right now, but Tally could stay home with Libby if you needed me."

I put my arm around my brother's shoulders, my eyes filling with tears. "No, Charlie, I'll be fine. It's probably time we started making new traditions anyway. I love you for asking, though. I love you for everything."

"I love you, too, baby sister. Though, you have been crying a lot. Is everything okay?"

I nodded, using my napkin to dab at my eyes. "Everything's fine. Perfect even. It's just Christmas, you know? Lots of emotions this time of year. I wish Momma, Daddy, Uncle Cole... I just wish they were here."

"Me too," he said, passing the next platter my way, full of Sutton's famous biscuits and gravy. Southern Living had just done a huge write up about our business, and the dish was at the top of their list of things to try when guests checked in.

The bookings had been pouring in ever since.

"Baby, you forgot the mimosas," Lee said brightly, leaning in, and I glanced around the table to make sure everyone had finished their meals.

"Doyle, could you help Lee and me with the drinks, please? Can't believe I forgot the mimosas, silly me," I cackled, shooting crazy eyes at him from my end of the long table.

He hopped up, kissed Jordan on the cheek, and the three of us scurried into the kitchen. I busted into the mudroom off the veranda and slammed the door behind me.

"Stop making so much damned noise, Maggie. They're going to think we've gotten into it again!" Lee whispered, knocking into the coat rack and toppling it over.

"Shut up, Lee! Doyle, please help me," I cried, jumping up and down, trying to get my zipper up.

"Holy shit on a shingle, girl! This dress is fire," Doyle said, zipping me up.

When I found the dress at the bridal shop, I just knew it was the one. Slipping into it, I couldn't help but fall in love with how it seemed to glow with this soft, almost magical light. The ivory fabric shimmered with a kind of quiet elegance, and the short sleeves draped over my shoulders like they were made just for me. Beneath the delicate lace overlay, the silk lining felt so smooth and luxurious against my skin that I never wanted to take it off.

The dress hugged my body in all the right places—especially all of Lee's favorite places—showing off my chest in a way that felt natural but so flattering. As I moved, the slight train at the back trailed behind me with just the right amount of drama. The tiny, glistening beads woven into the lace caught the light perfectly, and I felt like I was wrapped in a soft whisper of romance. Honestly, I'd never felt more beautiful in my entire life.

And I couldn't wait until Lee saw me walking toward him in this dress.

After assessing the dress situation, I quickly pinned my curls up, letting some tendrils fall around my face, and reached under the sink for the rest of the things I needed.

I handed two small boxes to Doyle, dabbed on some makeup, and turned to my friend, trying not to cry. "How do I look?"

Doyle put his hands on my shoulders and eyed me up and down. "Like a woman who is confident, kind, and gorgeous. Like someone who deserves this day more than anything."

"Nice words, but I still feel like I'm going to puke. Okay, get him out of here. Don't forget the drinks. Or the music. Love you, bye!"

I shooed him out of the room and took another long look at myself. This was the moment that I'd longed for, waited for, for almost twenty years. It wasn't the day that I'd envisioned, and it wasn't perfectly planned, and it wasn't how it, in theory, was supposed to go. But there I was, standing in that dress, and it felt right in a way that nothing else ever had.

And, like I'd told my brother, it was time for new traditions.

I made my way through the kitchen, hearing the soft music pumping through the dining room. I lifted my dress and took a long inhale, jumping back as the kitchen door flew open.

"I *knew* it," my brother hissed, scanning me up and down. "You've been acting like a loon, more than usual, for days. Why didn't you tell me?"

"It's a surprise," I said, holding my hand to my chest, trying to keep my heart from leaping out and splatting against the wall. "Do you think everyone knows?"

"No, they don't have a clue. Sutton's complaining because she's thirsty and was promised mimosas, though, and Lee and Doyle are just standing by the tree whispering. You probably have a good three minutes before there's a mutiny. Think that's enough time for a grand entrance?"

"I was just gonna kinda kick in the door there and pray for the best. What are you thinking?"

"We rush up the back staircase, and you let me walk you down the stairs, and down the aisle, to your groom. It would be my honor, Magnolia."

My brother rushed toward me and wrapped his arms around me. We both shook as we tried to stifle down the sobs inside of us. While planning the wedding, which took all of ten minutes in between early-morning romps in the sheets, I never thought about asking my brother to escort me down the aisle.

We stood at the top of the stairs, lined with portraits of our family, some we didn't even know. Next to us was a framed picture of Charlie and me with our momma and daddy, and we stood for a minute to look at it before starting down the winding staircase.

"You look beautiful," my brother said quietly. "They'd be really proud of you, you know? Uncle Cole, too. He'd be through the roof at what you've done here."

We reached the bottom of the steps and into full view of the table of our loved ones, and heads spun to look at us, catching the movement out of the corner of their eyes. Everyone gasped in unison, and Eunice stood up, covering her mouth and, what I'd assumed and hoped, were tears of joy.

"Please stand for the bride," Doyle yelled, improvising, his head darting around in confusion since I was supposed to appear from the kitchen door behind him.

As we passed the table of our family and friends, I noticed there wasn't a dry eye. When I reached Lee, I met Vance's eyes from across the room, and he nodded his head toward me, and for the first time in a long time, I saw the Wilder patriarch smile.

I joined Lee by the Christmas tree, and he shook my brother's hand before wrapping him in a hug, both of them whacking each other on the back.

"I don't think I need to tell you to take care of her," Charlie said quietly. "But the offer to kick your ass if I see fit still stands, brother."

"I'd never let either of you down, Charlie. Not a chance. Though, I would like to see you try and handle a fight," Lee retorted, and they both laughed.

Lee turned to me and smiled, bending down to whisper in my ear. "I thought you'd run away on me. I was getting a little nervous."

"I'm your girl, Leland Wilder, and I intend on making that official today."

Once we said, "I do," and Doyle rushed out to his car to pick up the cake, which Sutton heavily criticized, we danced the day away with our family and friends. After dessert, when everyone had gone their separate ways to celebrate Christmas Eve, Lee and I, as husband and wife, made our way upstairs to our home.

When I opened the door to our living quarters, Pickle flew out from inside the tree and crawled up Lee's entire body like a howler monkey, resting on his shoulders.

"Do you think she knows I'm her step-dad now?"

"No, I think she's got some weird, decades-long, deranged love for you. I can commiserate." I took a deep breath, the dress tightening around me as I exhaled. "Hey, help me out of this dress. It's getting a little claustrophobic."

When our friends and family had gathered at the Wilders' for Thanksgiving, Lee and I decided that day, on the walk home, that we'd surprise them with a wedding. I ran out the following Monday to secure a dress, I just didn't think that I'd be so swollen when I finally got around to wearing the damn thing.

"I have a present for you," Lee said once we were in our pajamas, munching on cookies, and watching *Meet Me In St. Louis* with Pickle purring away between us.

"I thought we agreed on no presents, just the rings," I said, trying to keep my voice even.

"It's nothing big. Well, it's kind of big," he said, jumping up and darting across the room. He plucked a gift from under the tree and handed the small, wrapped present to me. "Open it up," he said, jerking his chin toward it.

"It better not be a bar," I laughed, as I unwrapped the package. Inside was a blank CD case with no writing, no cover. Confused, I asked, "What is this?"

He coughed nervously and took the case from me, popping the disk into the CD player we only kept around for him to listen to his demos on. He pressed play and sat back next to me, on the opposite side now that Pickle had stretched out and taken up the entirety of one side of the couch.

The song was slow and obviously professionally recorded with the entire band. The bass, guitar, and piano notes floated through our place, coming from the speakers Lee had set up all over the house. After a few bars, his voice came over the speakers, clear and steady as he sang a song about a love he's had his whole life and how the happiest moment of his life was when he heard her say, "I do."

As the song went on, he sang about the storms they'd weathered through, but how they were each other's anchor no matter what. How he'd hoped that he was the kind of man that would make her daddy proud, how he couldn't wait to see their children, and how he hoped they looked just like her. How her momma was watching over them with love, and how he hoped that they'd have a love eternal, just like her parents.

I hugged my knees to my chest and let the tears fall, the music wrapping around me like a comforting embrace. It was during the last chorus that it finally clicked.

"What's the name of the song, Lee?"

"It's just a working title, but Ryan and I are thinking of calling it 'Our Song.'"

I laughed through the tears. "You finally wrote our song."

"I didn't write it, we did. All these years. Though, to be fair, most of my songs are about you." He leaned in, kissed the top of my head, and then gently lifted my chin so our eyes met. He kissed away my tears, then sat back with a smile. "I couldn't help but notice there's a gift under the tree from you to me, Mrs. Wilder."

I nodded, using the sleeve of my sweatshirt to mop up my face, which was soaked with emotion. "You can open it, if you want. My gift is a little better than yours, though, so don't get jealous."

He scoffed as he reached under the tree. "I write you songs, Magnolia. What could be better than that?" He unwrapped the present and flipped open the top off the box, staring at the gift inside for a few moments before looking at me in complete shock.

"You might write me songs, Leland Wilder, but I'm baking you a baby."

THE END

ACKNOWLEDGMENTS

First, to you, the reader holding this book—thank you for giving these characters, this story, and me, a chance. Whether you laughed, cried, or threw the book across the room at Magnolia (it's okay, I'd do it too), I hope you loved every moment. There's a nine-year-old girl inside of me with a fresh set of pens and a new notebook who is hopping up and down, more excited than she has ever been, to see this land in your hand, so thank you, again, from both of us.

Without the love and support of my family, there is no way I could have made it this far. And, because I am Irish, Italian and a native Bostonian, there are far too many people to name–but know that I love you all and I am so grateful for all of you.

Declan and Everly, my two beautiful children, you are my life's greatest work. I am so amazed at the people you are becoming, and I hope that, by seeing Mama fulfill her dreams (even if it took a while), you will know that you can do anything. Because you can, and I know you will. Mama loves you both so much, and I hope you always remember that you both are the greatest story of my life.

James, thank you for listening to me cry about not knowing how to use TikTok, or build a website, or pick a pen name, or any of the other 9 million things I have stressed about over the course of this relentless journey. Thank you for building me my own O'Malley's, and making merch, and just generally being one of my biggest fans even though I refused to let you read the book until it was done-done. But, most of all, thank you for giving me my happily ever after. This life with you and the kids, and the cats, and the dogs, and all the craziness and shenanigans is everything I have ever wanted. I love you and everything we have built together.

To my dad, Eddie, for sharing every single social media post I have ever made about the book or my author journey–your relentless support of me has not gone unnoticed. You have always been my number 1 fan, and I will always be Daddy's Little Girl.

To Bob, my siblings Ryan and Taylor, all of my crazy aunts, uncles, cousins, besties, neighbors and the entire town of South Boston (it often feels like) who have been cheering me on from the sidelines, thank you. I love you all.

Megan, my lifelong best friend and the Sutton to my Magnolia–there would not be a book without you. You have read every version of this, sometimes more than once, and you have picked me up off the ground time and time again when I felt like I wanted to give up (whether writing or not). This book has been published because you love me enough to refuse to let me give up on myself, and for that, I thank you a million times over.

To Anita, for being subjected to literally everything I have ever put pen to even if it was insane, and for pushing me to keep going and believing in me since the first full-length novel I stayed up writing for weeks on end–though the miles between us are great, the love never fades. I have always been so glad to have you by my side on this walk of life.

Pat Flaherty, there is no world in which I would publish my first book and not thank you for taking a look at a nine-year-old girl and believing in her and her writing so much that she never, ever gave up on that dream. There are certain people in this world that leave a mark on other's souls, and you have been one of those people for me. You were a wonderful teacher, and in my adult life, I am so grateful we have kept in touch and you have watched me grow from a shy, quiet 3rd grader to the published author you believed I could become.

To my SUPREME team of editors: Sara Coombe & Whitney Morsillo - this book would be a HOT mess if it weren't for either of you. Sara–the world's biggest thank you for dealing with me and all of my insane notes, texts, requests for advice and just generally being so kind and patient with me throughout the editing process. I am so glad you plopped into my life (see what I did there!?). Whitney Morsillo–your fine-tooth comb editing skills are amazing, as is your kindness, as I burdened you with all of my questions and woes. I can't wait to work with both of you again.

Alissa DeGregorio, you are an unbelievable artist, and someone I have come to completely adore. Thank you for the time and love you poured into this cover. You brought Lee and Magnolia to life! And Pickle, of course, can't forget about her. I am so proud to show off this cover, and I am so glad we connected.

To Syvlie T., Emily V., Stephanie B. and Quincy Y. - I am so grateful for all the advice and love you have shown me throughout this process, and for being the ones I trusted to read blurbs, chapters, to answer crazy questions and even give me advice on font placement over legs (is this aesthetically pleasing? LOL). I adore my friendship with each of you.

And lastly, to my Mom and Nonie, who nurtured my love for reading and storytelling so deeply that I had no choice but to write my own—I thank you. Words can't fully capture the sadness I feel knowing neither of you are here to read this story, though I have a feeling you'd both say it wasn't spicy enough (ha!). I love you and miss you more than I can say. I can feel you up there, alongside everyone we've lost far too soon, cheering me on. I keep moving forward because I know that's exactly what you'd want me to do.

So onward we go, to the next chapter.

Xo,

KH

ABOUT THE AUTHOR

Kelly Hennelly is a writer who loves to craft stories filled with heart, humor, and just a dash of chaos. With a passion for creating relatable characters, Kelly takes readers on unforgettable journeys of love, laughter, and the messy, beautiful moments that make life worth living. When not writing, she can be found spending time with her husband and kids, wrangling two cats and two dogs, traveling, and laying on the beach, always looking for the next story to tell.

Kelly's books are a mix of heartfelt romance and playful humor, with characters you'll fall for and a plot that will keep you hooked. *Our Song* is her debut novel, where childhood sweethearts reunite and discover that the past isn't quite as far behind as they thought.

To learn more about Kelly's upcoming books and musings, follow along on Facebook, Goodreads, Instagram, TikTok or visit authorkellyhennelly.com.